FORTUNE HOUSE

FORTUNE HOUSE

Kirsty Scott

WINDSOR
PARAGON

First published 2009
by Hodder & Stoughton
This Large Print edition published 2010
by BBC Audiobooks Ltd
by arrangement with
Hodder & Stoughton

Hardcover ISBN: 978 1 408 46064 1
Softcover   ISBN: 978 1 408 46065 8

British Library Cataloguing in Publication Data available

Printed and bound in Great Britain by
CPI Antony Rowe, Chippenham and Eastbourne

In memory of my beloved Dad.
With much love and gratitude

ACKNOWLEDGEMENTS

A huge thank-you, as ever, to my wonderful agents, Annette Green and David Smith, for their unfailing support. And to Sara Kinsella, my brilliant editor at Hodder, for her expertise and encouragement. A heartfelt thank-you to Carolyn Mays for sowing the seed that started the story, and Isobel Akenhead, Emma Knight and Tara Gladden.

To Fiona Gibson, for keeping me sane and laughing during the writing process.

Many thanks too to Susan Philliben, Claire McMillan, Plum Stirling, Sandra Lewis, Sue Parsons, Lorraine Ferguson, Gillian Bowditch and Sherry Arpaio for friendship, support and encouragement during a testing year.

To Mum, Niall, Rosey and Dave, thanks, as ever. And to Homer, Christina and Keir, thank you, and all my love.

PROLOGUE

SUNDAY, 8 JULY 1979

The best grass could always be found at the base of the fence-post. Deborah tucked her dress between her knees as she bent down, and plucked a thick green blade, placing it carefully between her two thumbs and putting it to her lips.

She blew as hard as she could but the only sound that emerged was a discordant squeak.

'No.' Fiona bent beside her. 'You've got to stretch it really tight. Like this.' She placed her own piece of grass to her lips and made it sing, a pure and painful note.

Behind them, Vonnie was scything at the undergrowth with her stick, and talking to herself, which she liked to do. Vonnie didn't need to practise blowing grass because she could do it already, almost as well as Euan. And she could whistle, which Dad said she shouldn't be able to do at the age of five. It wasn't just ordinary whistling, when you shape your mouth into a little kiss, but the real kind, fingers between her teeth, like a farmer calling a dog to heel.

'Try again.' Fiona handed Deborah another piece of grass and watched her carefully.

The second note was as feeble as the first and Fiona rolled her eyes in exasperation. 'Hopeless,' she said, giving a deliberate and grown-up sigh.

Deborah dropped the grass and glanced again

past the fence-post and down the track. There was still no sign of Euan. Go and have a quick look, Mum had said, because she knew that he sometimes stopped at the bridge and threw things into the river and forgot what the time was.

A hazy shimmer rose from the tarmac. The Firth of Forth was only a few miles away and Deborah wished she was there, by the sea. She could feel the dampness behind her knees where her skin was pressed together. Sometimes in the winter it was so cold that ice would form on the inside of the window panes in her bedroom. But last night she had lain in bed without even a sheet and felt like she couldn't breathe, so heavy the warmth all around her. It had been hot for two weeks now. An exceptional summer, Dad had said.

Vonnie had stopped scything and appeared at her side, still in her wellies, even though Mum had told her to change out of them before the Fletchers came, and they were here already, drinking pink wine from the good glasses and watching the salad wilt while they all waited for Euan to get back.

'Look.' Vonnie held out her hand. Her nails were thick with dirt and in the middle of her palm lay a half-dead cricket.

'Lovely,' said Fiona, who had climbed on to the gate and balanced herself on top, hooking her long legs over either side. She had come with them reluctantly to the bottom of the driveway. Everything they did now was pronounced either 'boring' or 'dumb,' even playing in the den they had made in the rhododendron bushes, and it had been Fiona's idea to make it in the first place. She had taken instead to fussing about her hair and what she was wearing, behaviour that had coincided with her being just about to turn eleven. Deborah didn't want to turn eleven if this is what it did to you.

Vonnie was still examining her cricket. 'I'm going to keep it,' she said, matter-of-factly.

'Mum won't let you,' said Fiona.

'She won't,' echoed Deborah.

Vonnie was always trying to make pets out of creatures she found in the garden. Beetles and worms, and once a fledgling that she found in the hedge. Mum had put her foot down when she found the bird wrapped in a doll's yellow crocheted cardigan in a shoebox in the sitting room.

'You should put it back,' said Fiona, and for once Vonnie obeyed her, placing the cricket on the verge. When it didn't move, she picked up her stick and gave it a little poke.

'Off you go.'

The cricket stayed where it was.

'I think you killed it,' said Fiona.

'I did not!'

Deborah sighed and got to her feet. 'We'd best get back,' she said, and made her way gingerly over the spars of the cattle grid and on to the drive.

Fiona jumped down off the gate, landing in a ballet pose. 'Killed it,' she said, and skipped out of the way of Vonnie's swinging stick.

They could hear laughter as they approached the house. Deborah's feet were hot. She would quite like to have gone inside and taken her shoes and socks off in the hall where the black and white tiles would be lovely and cool. They came through the side gate into the back garden. The grown-ups were seated around the fancy white table that Dad had dragged under the cedar tree, and they all looked round when the girls appeared.

'No sign?' said Mum.

Deborah shook her head.

Mum put down her glass of wine and gave a gentle tut. 'Well, I think we should just start, and if there's nothing left for Euan then that's his lookout. I'm sorry about this. Girls, hands. Darling, could you help me with the plates?'

Dad got to his feet and followed Mum into the house. By the time Deborah had washed her hands in the downstairs loo and supervised Vonnie, who never used soap, and sometimes not even water, everyone was round the table. It was a very fancy lunch. Poached salmon and a salad with orange slices and radishes from the vegetable plot, and new boiled potatoes with parsley sprinkled on top. Deborah finished first and sat back. There was ice cream for after and she wished everyone would hurry up. The grown-ups were taking the longest. They would have a bite to eat then sit back and hold their wine glasses without actually drinking from them, and talk.

Mrs Fletcher talked the most. She wore a bracelet that jangled every time she moved her arm, and she moved it quite a lot, reaching over to touch Mum or Dad on the elbow or shoulder as she spoke, or swat away a bluebottle or a wasp. Mum didn't wear jewellery, just her watch with the brown leather strap and her wedding ring. Deborah watched her mother across the table. She was playing with the stem of her wine glass with slim, brown fingers. She just had to look at the sun and she went brown, Dad always said. Dad was calling her Caroline, which he did in front of visitors. He was always relaxed when the Fletchers came round. Mr Fletcher was his best friend and they liked to slap each other on the back a lot, especially when they were laughing.

The ice cream was brought out, and devoured, along with the berries that Mum had crushed to make a sort of sauce. Vonnie asked if Euan was going to get a big row, which made all the adults laugh, and Mum said, yes, a *very* big one.

And then the phone rang deep in the house, and Mum excused herself, pressing her napkin against her lips and rising from the table.

In years to come the sounds would merge: the shrill nasal tone of the telephone and then the noise that followed. There must have been a gap; a silence while the other person was talking. Deborah knew that, but she could never remember that there had been. Just the ringing of the phone and then the other noise that took them all by surprise, a cry so raw and so sudden that everybody jumped. Dad was on his feet and the Fletchers too and they didn't even notice that they had knocked over a glass of wine in their hurry to get inside.

The noise didn't stop. It was Dad's name that Mum was shouting. David. David. David. David. Over and over again until it didn't sound like words at all, just an endless call. And then somebody said, 'God.'

Deborah sat stock-still watching the opened door. Nobody came back through.

'It's okay,' said Fiona. She was older and she had to say that. But it was a terrible noise that had come from the house, and Deborah knew that it wasn't okay. She found Vonnie's knee and squeezed. Vonnie was swinging her legs because her feet didn't touch the ground.

They waited, straining to hear, and then an engine roared into life, fading in the frantic spit of gravel from a car on the driveway. A few moments later, Mrs Fletcher appeared in the doorway. She was walking slowly and her eyes were wide as if she were terribly surprised.

'Is everything okay?' said Fiona.

The wine, what was left of it, dripped through the fancy white metal and on to Deborah's socks, her new white socks from Woolworths. Three pairs to a packet, with a bow on the cuff.

A wasp settled on the wasted plates.

'Please can I leave the table?' said Vonnie.

CHAPTER ONE

MONDAY, 21 DECEMBER 2009

The smell from below the dressing table was becoming unbearable. Caroline shifted her foot and nudged the small panting form wedged at the back.

'Out!'

Hector staggered to his feet and slunk past her, mouth open and eyes bulging. He really was the ugliest dog you would ever see, an overweight Border terrier, pushing seventeen with a baleful gaze and an awful odour, as if he were rotting from the inside. He shouldn't be upstairs at all, but Min was always spoiling him and must have carried him up and then forgotten about him.

Caroline watched as he tottered stiffly across the Navajo rug and out on to the upstairs landing. At least he didn't attach himself to your leg at every opportunity like Riley, the Jack Russell. Min had refused to have Riley seen to, arguing that it was a natural urge. But then, her mother-in-law was a great one for indulging natural urges, thought Caroline, even at the age of eighty-eight.

She looked back at the mirror. The eyeshadow she had just applied had settled into the lines of her skin like paint on cracked pottery. She rubbed at it and noticed the charcoal still on her fingers from her sketching, as dark as a bruise. She picked up her lipstick. It was almost done, the stub of the coral tip curving to a sharp point at one side. You could tell a lot about a woman by the shape of her

1

lipstick; she remembered that from a Sunday supplement. A one-sided curve like hers meant she was creative, outgoing and fell in love easily. None of which was really true, apart from being creative. She sketched it neatly across her lips and pressed them together.

She went easy on the powder, remembering the chalky kiss of old aunts and gave her hair a final brush. Her jewellery was strung on a varnished wooden mug tree. It was the art club Christmas supper, so something dramatic would be in order. She picked off a silver lariat with a piece of amber the size of a small egg and slipped it over her head. The stone settled, cold and heavy, over her breastbone.

Hector had stopped at the top of the stairs and could go no further. Caroline bent and scooped him up, holding her breath as she carried him down and plopped him on to the parquet in the wide, oval hall. The tree was unlit, so she bent beneath the branches and flicked on the switch at the skirting. It was a much bigger tree than normal, a Norwegian spruce, a good seven feet tall, but the hall was big enough to take it, and with everyone coming this year she had wanted something special. The girls would doubtless complain that she had topped it, as she did every year, with the *Blue Peter* fairy they had made out of a small plastic doll and one of David's good cotton hankies; a fairy so aged now that she listed at the top of the branches like a tiny drunk, one eye half shut, her extravagant tinsel fringing frayed and dull.

The whine of the hoover faded away and Hanna, the cleaner, appeared at the dining room

2

door.

'Caroline, do you want me to make up the children's beds now? It's no problem.'

'Would you mind?' said Caroline. 'I suppose some of them might be bringing sleeping bags, but that would be lovely. Thank you.'

Hanna nodded and smiled. 'Busy house tomorrow.'

'Yes,' said Caroline. It would be the first time in years that they had all been under the same roof. Three daughters, two sons-in-law and five grandchildren. And, of course, there was less space to work with, now that she and David didn't share.

'Busy is good.' Hanna pulled the hoover across the hall towards the stairs with the cord bunched in her hand like a lasso.

'It is,' said Caroline.

'You look nice,' added Hanna. 'I like your necklace.'

Caroline put her hand to her throat. 'Thank you.' She smiled after her. Such a lovely girl. A little too thin, perhaps, but then she was always on the go, holding down three cleaning jobs and an ironing business. Caroline had liked her straight off when they had first met. She had been looking for a replacement for Miss Maxwell, who clicked her false teeth in and out and smelled of Mr Sheen, even if you met her in the street, and who had only retired when her knees gave out. A colleague of David's had recommended Hanna. Just a sweetheart, she had said. Caroline had been worried that Hanna would not want to come this far out of the city, but it didn't seem to be an issue for her, and now she got the train down from Edinburgh twice a week, and Caroline picked her up at the station. It was Hanna's sister who had first come to Scotland from Lodz. Hanna had followed a year later with her little boy. She must have been only about twenty-one when she had Marek, the same age that Caroline had been when she first became a mother. Sometimes she brought Marek when she came to clean, but not often enough for Caroline. He was a beautiful child, small for his age, with Hanna's fair colouring and serious grey eyes. Caroline sat with him at the piano as Hanna worked and helped him pick out simple tunes.

'He's musical,' she told Hanna, who had grinned with delight, and said maybe it was because she was always singing to him. Caroline had smiled and understood. When she was Hanna's age she had sung to a small boy too.

Hector had made it as far as the drawing room door, but didn't seem to realise it was slightly ajar and was standing staring at it, as if his glassy concentration alone might get him through three inches of panelled oak. Caroline nudged him in the right direction with her pointed patent toe and he scuttled round the edge.

Min was in the high-backed chair by the window, engrossed in the crossword, the paper held at arm's length so she could see, a slim Silver Cross pen suspended and trembling slightly in her other hand. There had been a day when she could finish the puzzle in fifteen or twenty minutes, but now she left out great chunks and took offence if Caroline tried to help with a word or two.

She glanced up as Caroline came in and laid the paper on her knee. She had been wearing the same trousers for more than a week, a grey hound's-

4

tooth check that didn't show the stains Caroline felt sure must be there.

'Let's have a look,' Min said brusquely, and Caroline twirled before her. 'Very elegant.'

Caroline bent forward to kiss the downy, proffered cheek and caught the scent of brandy and something slightly stale.

'I'm going to give Hanna a run up to Edinburgh in about fifteen minutes, before I head on to the restaurant. Do you want anything before I leave?' She glanced down at the large crystal tumbler at Min's elbow, empty save for a sliver of ice cube.

'Can you stick one of my programmes on for me?'

Caroline retrieved the remote from the large ceramic bowl on the coffee table, and tried not to smile. 'One of my programmes' meant *America's Next Top Model*, which was Min's current obsession. David despaired of his mother's viewing habits. 'She's a highly educated woman,' he complained. 'It's unedifying.'

But Caroline had laughed at him and thought what harm could a little light relief do in a life such as Min's, shrunk by old age to little more than the house and the passenger seat of the car.

She found an episode on ITV2 and placed the remote on the table by Min's elbow.

'And what's happening about these two?' Min inclined her head to the window where the gardeners, Boyd and Charlie, were still working on the marquee on the back lawn under the harsh glare of the floodlights they had strung up on the old cedar.

'Charlie said they should have it all in place tonight bar the heaters. They won't be much

5

longer, I'm sure.'

'You really are absolutely barking bloody mad to be doing this outdoors,' said Min, and not for the first time. 'The frost will come and everyone will be frozen half to death.'

Caroline sighed. She could see Min's argument but the frost hadn't come and if the weather continued the way it was, they might not even need the heaters. Charlie had said he had never known anything like it. There was still work for them to do in the garden, besides erecting the marquee which would hold the hundred or so people now coming to David's retirement party.

Caroline glanced at her watch. He had only a few hours left of his last day, unless he went for drinks with the reporters, which he thought he might have to do. He had insisted he didn't want any fuss. No need to miss your night out, he had said. I don't mind. Which, after forty-odd years of marriage, she knew to mean, I don't care.

'You get him to yourself now, Caroline,' their friends had said when they learned of his leaving. 'What are you going to do with him?' Caroline had not responded. As a woman married to a man of words, she had learned over the years that sometimes you didn't have to say anything at all. Sometimes all you needed to do was smile and they would fill in the answer they expected to hear.

Min was still looking out of the window. 'You'll need to have a word with the fat one about his arse,' she said suddenly.

'Pardon?'

'That one. His arse. It's always hanging out the back of his trousers.'

Caroline burst out laughing. 'And I wondered

6

why this was your favourite chair.'

'Eh?'

'Have you been eyeing up the gardeners, Min?'

'Certainly not! But I take exception to having his rear end thrust in my face all day.'

'So to speak.' Caroline perched herself on the arm of Min's chair and looked out of the window. It was hard to tell in the dark just what Boyd might be exposing, but his trousers were certainly low-slung. 'We could just close the curtains.'

'There's no call for it,' said Min. 'I can see the line, you know. Right down to his—'

'Min!'

'Well, I can.' Min picked up the remote and pointed it at the TV. The volume rose to a deafening pitch. 'There's no call for it,' she said again, raising her own voice. 'You can't have some bare-arsed boy running about the garden with the girls coming home, now can you?'

*   *   *

'Slow news day, what can I say?' The night editor gave an apologetic shrug.

David leaned forward and studied the mock-up laid out before him on the desk. It didn't look any better than it had at the 10.30 a.m. conference nor the one at 5 p.m. No exclusives, no compelling human-interest stories, not even a decent political line, and here they were five months away from a vote on independence. He shifted a polystyrene cup of cold coffee out of the way and perched on the edge of the desk.

'There's absolutely no chance of the parly boys turning up anything on the Cooper memo tonight,

7

is there?' Rumours had been circulating since yesterday of an internal Downing Street document hinting at government unease with the trend of the latest Scottish polls, which had moved enough in the last few weeks to make an almost certain 'no' start to look a little more like 'maybe'.

The night editor shook his head. 'Doubt it, this time of night. They've been trying all day and everyone's schtum.'

'And we're sure about this frogspawn?' David tapped the large close-up of a clump of eggs clustering at the edge of a small pond. It was a good shot, well framed and artistic, but it was frogspawn. 'It's not going to turn out to be a stunt like the pike that wasn't in St Mary's Loch?'

The picture editor laughed. 'It's the earliest yet in the Botanic Gardens. They had the whole press call. Horticulturalists, climatologists. Everyone was there. We're all doomed, apparently.'

'I'm not hugely keen.' David pursed his lips. 'It looks like someone's thrown up. Anything else?'

The picture editor slid another contact sheet across the table.

'Are you kidding?' David looked up at her and the picture editor shook her head, trying not to smile.

David looked back at the print. 'So you're telling me these are my options. Premature frogspawn or the First Minister in a Santa hat. Thanks. Great fucking swansong, guys.'

He laughed and they joined in and he felt a little of the tension go out of the room. They were all on edge, his deputies, unsettled by his leaving, impatient for him to be gone.

'Amphibians it is then.' He raised himself off the

8

desk. 'Good stuff. Thanks.'

They stood slowly, watching him, and he waved his hand at them. He'd already said he wanted a normal Monday, whatever that might bring, and it hadn't brought much. But he'd worked under too many editors who had opted for the grand exit; the speech on the floor of the newsroom, so cringingly self-indulgent or caustically bitter that you had to curl up your toes in your shoes just to stand the sound of it. He had agreed, however, to the party, which had been Caroline's idea, and, if nothing else, helped mask the fact that he had not chosen to retire—which was the company line—but had been leaned on to leave.

'Go on. Go and get that poor fucking excuse for a paper on the streets.'

They trooped out, the picture editor closing the door gently behind her with one hand. He knew they pitied him. A fresh eye, the men had said when he was called upstairs to the room with thick carpeting and good artwork on the walls. New editorial and executive leadership. It's a time of change.

In truth, he had seen it coming. Newspapers, as most people knew them, were dying. Newsrooms were being merged and consolidated; the workforce retrained for twenty-four-hour coverage. Online was all. It had happened to so many before him and would happen to those who followed on.

But he wasn't ready to go and he could have stayed and seen it through, the biggest political choice Scotland had ever faced. To stay part of a union that had held for more than 300 years, or to go it alone as a small independent European

9

nation. He wasn't a dinosaur. He still had the hunger and he had the experience to guide the paper through the next few momentous months: a good grounding in straight news with this very paper, three years in London with *The Times*, then Cape Town when the older children were young, then five years in Westminster and then back here, political editor then columnist then editor. It had been a strange appointment for the time, when all other editors were young and unproven. The media supplements had loved it. Doyen, they'd called him, the hack's hack, a man of substance in an industry of ego and impermanence. He'd kept all the cuttings.

He spun his seat round and looked out through the window. He could just make out the sharp upper line of Salisbury Crags in the dark. He wondered where the kestrel was; the female that hovered possessively above the rocks every day as if the city of Edinburgh were hers.

The office was reflected back at him in the dark glass. It was almost empty, just some papers and books and the caricature of him by the paper's previous cartoonist that he had not wanted to take from the wall. If you closed your eyes it was actually a good likeness. Grey hair, a little longer than it should be, curling at the nape of his neck. Nose a little more beaked than his, eyes a laughing, stony grey. The cufflinks were magnificent. He was known for his; collected them. But the cartoonist had made them enormous, almost Herculean, one shaped like an inkwell, the other the Scottish flag.

His mobile rattled suddenly on the desk and he snatched it up, willing it to be something important: a story change, a tip-off, anything that would require his attention. It was Charlie, one of the gardeners. He must have been in his van because David could hear the noise of the engine and the radio playing low in the background, and Charlie was talking a little too loudly, the way people do with hands-free.

'I'm really sorry to bother you at work, but Mrs Haldane had left before we did and we needed to let you know to keep the marquee clear for the time being. It's secured, but I'm going to bring down some extra pegging, just in case the wind picks up again. It might not be tomorrow, though, if that's okay.'

'Of course,' said David. 'That's fine. Thanks for letting me know.' He liked Charlie. He had known him since he was a boy, and he had grown into a good man. He was a former soldier who had seen action in Iraq and Afghanistan, and talked with the measured, honest tone of someone who had seen more than mere words could ever convey.

'Well, I better let you get on,' said Charlie. 'Red-letter day, eh?'

'Yes,' said David. 'It is that. Thank you.'

He placed the phone back on the table and looked again at the cartoon on the wall, then stood and lifted it down and laid it on his desk. His secretary would clear it all out tomorrow morning and have it delivered to the house, the remnants of his tenure folded in bubble wrap and stacked in some recycled cardboard boxes. He had the book, of course, a history of devolution commissioned by one of the smaller Edinburgh publishing houses, and there had already been some approaches about writing columns and the like, but this was still a dismissal and it hurt more than he had been

11

able to tell anyone, however cushioned it might be by the fat cheque and the fine words.

The reporters had urged him to come down to the pub when he was done and he had said he might. But he had left it too late now. Most of them would be gone, leaving only those with nothing better to do or nowhere they wanted to be.

He picked up his coat and slung it across his arm and opened the door. The newsroom stretched before him, a confusion of desks and piles of paper and long neglected plants; business blending into features, then sports, the arts desk and at the furthest end, news, the point where it had all started for him.

He moved along the back wall, and down towards the nearest door. The late reporter was engrossed in something on her desk, one hand rooting in a bag of crisps. The subs were fixated by their screens, fingers flashing as they cut and pasted, teased and fitted words and images into column inches. Someone must have spotted him because a little burst of applause rippled across the room, awkward and half-hearted. He raised his hand but kept his eyes to the front because they were stinging now and if he looked round it would be his Margaret Thatcher moment, the wet blink of tears that would come to define his going. Somewhere over near the newsdesk a phone started to ring and the clapping faded as quickly as it had started. He stepped out into the hall.

*   *   *

Charlie eased the van out of the steady flow of traffic and stopped on a single yellow line beside a

12

charity shop with a large lopsided reindeer in the window. On the other side of the street, the queue for the pub was already a good way up the street. Yellow light spilled from the door, which was wedged open and framed by two black-suited bouncers and the kind of short gilded rope you were more likely to see at a Hollywood premiere. Four girls in Santa hats and tinsel scarves were singing lustily at the edge of the pavement, clutching each other in tipsy hysterics.

Boyd hesitated as he reached for the door handle. 'Quick pint?'

Charlie shook his head.

'You sure?'

'Yeah.' Charlie leaned back in the driver's seat and gave a deep stretch. He was still stiff from the five-a-side last night and it had all been for nothing because they had lost 4–1 to the council boys. He was getting too old for such capers. At forty-two, everything hurt a little more, took a little longer to snap back into shape.

But then Annie had been up about 2 a.m. and Gail had elbowed him sleepily to deal with her. Annie had played with his hair as he had carried her back through, stumbling over the wash basket in the hall and the mob of soft toys that crowded the floor of her room. It was getting to be a bit of a habit, these late night visitations, and he wanted to be cross. But the grip of small arms round his neck, the warm weight of her in her pyjamas dissolved his anger; such an odd mix of love and rage that only a child can stir.

'Just one?' persisted Boyd.

'Nah, mate, you're on your own.' Charlie nodded towards the queue. 'Just you and Santa's little helpers.'

Boyd cracked a smile and Charlie grinned back sheepishly. What Boyd needed wasn't a drunken lass with her roots showing under a brim of fake fur, but a good woman. For all his bluster, he'd been a bit of a lost soul since his wife had left him. Not that she'd been a good woman. Charlie had always found her sharp and brittle, the kind of person who thought badly of you from the start just to save time later on. There had been no one of any substance since and that was two years ago, although Charlie knew Boyd had a bit of a thing for the Haldanes' cleaner. She was a looker, a Polish girl, and nice enough from the few brief conversations he'd had with her over the past few weeks, but she had a wee lad and Boyd could barely look after himself, let alone a ready-made family. He was young yet, though. Just thirty-four, so plenty time to find the right girl.

'Okay,' sighed Boyd. He levered himself out of the passenger seat. 'See ya.'

'I'll phone you tomorrow, mate. Okay?'

Boyd nodded and swung the door shut, crossing the road with his hands plunged deep in his pockets. Charlie watched him join the queue a little way back from the Santa girls, saw him give one of them the once-over. He smiled to himself and rubbed his eyes. A pint wouldn't have gone amiss, but his head was buzzing with everything that needed to be done before Christmas Day. New pictures to the website designer tonight or tomorrow at the latest, quotes for two new jobs, and the final adjustments on the Haldanes' marquee. Field and lawn fixtures was a new angle for the business, but a necessary one in these

14

recessionary times. It was good money: £1,500 for one decent-sized marquee with roof and wall lining and coconut matting on the floor; wood would set you back an extra £500. It all fitted nicely with the garden work, which hadn't tailed off yet this winter with the weather being so queer. Across at the pub, the doormen had let the Santa girls in. Boyd was still at the back of the queue. Charlie raised his hand in a final farewell, pulled the handbrake off and swung the van back out into the roadway.

*   *   *

Gail was asleep, sprawled across the sofa, her swollen belly rising and falling with every slow breath. He put the car keys down as gently as he could on the table and watched her. Her chin was low and doubled, almost touching her chest and her feet were propped on the sofa's wooden arm. She hated that her ankles were puffy; hated the extra weight she was carrying. He had told her that he didn't care, a small lie, because he did. He wasn't one of these men who found his wife more attractive in pregnancy, revelling in swelling breasts and belly. He liked the old Gail, curvy with great legs, and an arse that could get him hard just with the thought of it.

Her eyes flickered open. 'Hey,' she said sleepily and reached up to wipe the corner of her mouth.

'Hey.' He bent and kissed the top of her head and put his hand instinctively on her belly.

'What time is it?' She swung her legs gingerly off the sofa and sat up.

'Just before ten,' said Charlie.

She smiled at him and yawned. 'You hungry?'

15

He shook his head. 'I got a fish supper with Boydie on the way back.'

She patted his tummy as she stood up. 'You'll be as big as me, babe.' She yawned again. 'I'm done in. Do you mind if I go up?'

'No. I won't be long.' He took her place on the sofa and found it still warm from her.

'Do you want a beer?'

'Would you mind?'

She disappeared into the kitchen and came back with a bottle of Becks, opened and cold.

'Thanks, love. Did Annie go down all right?'

She nodded. 'Are you remembering you need to go to Argos tomorrow? I swear it's the last bloody Flora's Castle in Edinburgh and if we don't get it . . .'

'I'll get it.' He took a slug from his drink. 'Hey.' She had turned again for the door.

'What?'

'Come here.' He put his drink down on the floor.

She shot him a warning glance. 'There'll be none of that.'

'No.' He laughed. 'Just come here.'

She moved back over to him and bent awkwardly and he caught her head in both hands and kissed her deeply. She tasted of raspberry tea. 'Night, love,' he said against her mouth.

'Night, babe.' She stood up and trailed her hand through his hair as she lurched off.

He lay back against the sofa and exhaled. The new baby was coming, but not tonight; what was left of it was his. He heard Gail move into the bedroom, the blinds go down and the en-suite door squeak open. Oil. Another thing for tomorrow's

16

list. His head felt heavy. He picked up the TV remote and switched it on; anything. Sport, a chat show, the news, even. Background noise. He closed his eyes and let the exhaustion take him.

*   *   *

Sometimes he was so still that she thought he had stopped breathing. Hanna leaned forward and peered at the bed. Marek's eyes were still open, but his thumb had fallen from his mouth. He must have sensed her movement because his eyes slid sleepily towards her.

'Shhh,' she whispered, and carried on singing, an old Polish lullaby, the words so familiar to her they came without thought.

His eyes were closing now. Hanna sat back in the chair, humming, watching the day go out of him; her little man in his pirate pyjamas.

When he was finally asleep she went into the sitting room and dug her cigarettes from her bag. She had bought a new Zara top with some of her Christmas bonus from the Haldanes and had laid it out on the back of the sofa. It was black, a bodice cut with sheer sleeves. She lifted the hem and felt the soft drape of the fabric. They were nice people, the Haldanes, and such a glorious house. One day she would have a home like Fortune House with so much space and light. Mrs Haldane was one of these women who cleaned before you got there, so there was never really that much for her to do. Not like the Robertsons in Polmont. So much dirt: scum and hairs in the shower and bath, the crusted remains of food on the kitchen counters and table. She wondered if Mrs Robertson knew of the magazines under Mr Robertson's side of the bed, the ones Hanna suspected he left for her to find, different almost every week, opened and spread out so she would see when she knelt to dust. Filthy pig.

It did bother her sometimes to think what she did for a living. On grey days, in a house so dirty it made her stomach turn. I have an education, she would think, stooped over to scour out a bath. Few people ever asked if there was more to her. They just assumed she had come from nothing. Which was not the truth. They had a good life in Lodz, her and her twin sister Dyta, good; but much too ordinary. When they were teenagers, they would lie in Dyta's bed and talk about where they would live. America. Milan. London. An apartment for the two of them, fresh flowers every day and lovers at the door. Everything changed when she fell pregnant. He had been in her class, Marek's father, studying for a business degree as she had been. He had asked her out and she had gone, even though he was more a party boy than she normally went for. They drank too much, to fill the silences between them, and she remembered laughing and dancing and then being back in his lodging room. It was over very quickly and she had cried afterwards because she had not wanted it. He kept apologising, sullenly, until she wanted to scream at him. Sorry. Sorry. Sorry. Sorry.

She told him that she was pregnant, only out of courtesy, after she had been to the doctor and had felt the surge of relief when she saw the fear in his face. He transferred not long after to Warsaw and was nothing but a bad memory when Marek entered the world. She had not wanted a baby,

18

until the moment, within seconds of his birth, when Marek looked at her with his bewildered eyes and she felt her heart go out of her. She finished her degree, thanks to her mother, Mamo, and Dyta, but a lesser one than she had wanted. It didn't matter. She had Marek and he was everything. She got a job in an accountant's office; small-scale, and tried not to think too far ahead.

It was Dyta who first suggested Edinburgh. A friend of hers had come and done well. Good friends and good money. Dyta followed her the next year and phoned every week with a fresh plea for Hanna to join her. It's beautiful and safe, she said, with lots of green spaces and big enough that you wouldn't feel trapped, but not so big that you would feel intimidated or hopelessly lost.

So many people were going then and Lodz seemed hollowed out all of a sudden. The zloty was seven to the pound at the time and the wages Hanna was getting were a pittance compared even to Dyta's tips from an evening's waitressing on George Street. So she promised Mamo it would not be for ever and booked the flights.

She had grand plans where she would use her degree, and she still had them, but she needed to make money and the cleaning jobs came easy and paid well. In recent months, however, people had started to drift home in ever greater numbers. The Polish economy was stronger; pay and conditions were improving. Every time she talked to Mamo, she would know of another daughter or son who had returned, but Hanna wasn't ready to leave. Not yet.

A small gust of air blew in from the window and Hanna walked over and pushed it open, perching

19

herself on the seat underneath. If she leaned to the left she could just see across the dark blur of the Meadows to the lights of Lauriston Place. Someone had flirted with her today: Boyd, the gardener from the Haldanes, the one with the eager smile and the knowing eyes. She had not dated much since she had moved over to Scotland. Men tended to panic when they learned about Marek, worried she was looking for an instant father for her son. But Boyd knew she had a little boy and he still seemed interested. Maybe she would wear her nice new top next time she was down, as unsuitable as it was for cleaning.

She lit her cigarette and blew the smoke out into the mild night like a coil of frozen breath and sang again but for no one but herself.

*　　　*　　　*

Min awoke with a start. The man on the television was laughing, his head flung back and his mouth wide in scornful derision. She sat up. Hector was whining and the fire had gone out. Where was everybody? She raised herself unsteadily and made her way to the door. Her neck hurt.

'Hello?' The hall was lit by a small Tiffany lamp on a desk by the stairs and the fierce white lights of the Christmas tree.

'Hello?'

Hector had staggered towards the front door and was whining again. Min followed him. What time was it? Where had they gone?

She opened the door and felt the wind, warm and strong on her face, saw the giant white structure flapping at the far end of the garden.

Panic rose in her chest. Where was this? Where was everyone? They hadn't told her where they were going. She wouldn't know where to look. She moved out on to the broad stone-flagged step.

'Hello!'

Somewhere inside a door slammed. Hector disappeared beneath a shifting bush. The wind caught her voice and her fear and carried it out into the blackness.

CHAPTER TWO

'Sorry, sorry, sorry, sorry, sorry!' Fiona burst through the door and dumped her bags and coat in a jumbled heap of wet wool and good leather on the floor by the hallstand.

Birgit was standing by the stairs. Her jacket was on and zipped to the neck and her Radley bag was strapped firmly across her chest. Her mouth was set in a petulant line.

'Things kept popping up as I was trying to get out the door. And there was just the longest queue on Clerkenwell Road. It took for ever to get through the lights. Did you get my text?' Fiona bent and grabbed her purse from her handbag and fished around for a handful of notes, pulling out more than she ought to. Guilt money. 'You'll probably need to grab a taxi. It's chucking it down out there. Are you going to be okay?'

'I don't know,' said Birgit curtly, taking the money and stuffing it without counting in her coat pocket. 'The class starts already.'

Fiona flashed a flat smile. And maybe it's not

21

hugely convenient for my au pair to bugger off to night school when I've got so much to do before tomorrow. 'Well, you better run,' she said as cheerfully as she could.

Birgit nodded and moved past her towards the door. She smelled of perfume. Not the Bobbi Brown eau de cologne that Fiona had bought her for her birthday, but something much less subtle.

'Ben is sleeping. Jamie is in his room and Daisy has had supper and bath. She has a little more of the eczema on the back of her knees. I have put the cream on,' said Birgit, sliding her feet into her short black boots that were lying by the front door. 'And I have hung Allan's good shirts in the utility.' Her tone changed to one of reverence, as if she'd laundered the Turin shroud.

'Thanks.' Fiona nodded distractedly. She had picked up the mail and was rifling through it. Bill, bill, junk, White Company catalogue and two Christmas cards. Two? It was four days to go until Christmas Day; there should be a fat pile arriving every day by now. If things didn't pick up they would be well down on last year's tally. She knew it was daft to keep count but she always did. Sometimes even at other people's houses, totting up quickly in her head when they weren't looking. Mantelpieces and window frames and those curious card wheels you get from mail order catalogues.

She heard the door open and half turned, her eyes still on the letters in her hand. 'Have a good class,' she shouted. 'And sorry. Again.' The door shut emphatically on Birgit's muttered, incomprehensible reply.

Daisy was in the kitchen on one of the high

stools by the breakfast bar, a pair of scissors in her hand, the *Guardian* lying in tatters on the countertop. Her brow was furrowed. 'I'm trying to make a people chain.' She held up a tangle of slashed newsprint. 'How do you make a people chain?'

'Gosh, I can't remember.' Fiona lifted the scissors from her hand and bent to kiss Daisy's head. Her hair was still damp from the bath, sharply combed by Birgit into long, wet, separated streaks. She smelled clean and faintly antiseptic.

'Birgit showed me how, but I've forgot,' said Daisy. 'I want to join them at the bum.' She sniggered, and Fiona shot her a warning glance.

'It's not I've forgot, it's I've *forgotten*,' corrected Fiona. She moved across to the wine rack and slid out a bottle of burgundy, her fingers lingering on the beaten silver of the rack handles. She adored her kitchen. It was a walnut Smallbone of Devizes, with a giant centre island and cabinets that looked as though they were floating above the floor. An utter indulgence, but she so loved to cook and Allan had agreed that it would be an investment if they ever decided to sell.

She was sorry she wouldn't be doing Christmas dinner this year. She had planned on a goose and had pre-ordered one from a supplier in Oxfordshire before Mum had called in November with the unexpected news that Dad was retiring and they wanted everyone home to Fortune House for a retirement party. Taking the time off wasn't really the problem because the practice pretty much ground to a halt until 4 January, or D-Day, when the phone would be ringing off the hook with wives looking for a divorce. And it was almost always wives. Driven to despair by the extra workload and the forced intimacy of the holiday season. A flash of tinsel and the scales fell from their eyes. Sometimes it was the discovery of an affair, sometimes the deepening mire of a financial mess, but most often it was the simple realisation that when everything was unwrapped there was no love left, just a mortgage and children and a sex life too miserable for words.

They would always try to articulate, and for £350 an hour she would listen closely, keeping her face composed as the details tumbled out. Of course, since the Solicitors Family Law Association code of practice had come into play, the emphasis was on compromise, so a lot of the more sordid details never made it to court. Although there was one television presenter that Fiona couldn't look at in quite the same way since learning from his now ex-wife that he insisted his dick be addressed as Eric the Red; but only when tumescent.

She had felt she couldn't really argue with her mum, however. It was four years since they'd been in Scotland for Christmas and two since she'd seen Deborah and the kids; three since she'd last seen Vonnie, and that was only a fleeting dinner when Vonnie had been in London for a conference, which she had actually bunked off to go shopping. So it would be turkey cooked to a gagging dryness with all the old traditional staples served on the Portmeirion dishes, with one cracker each from Jenners. Mum didn't do change, and she didn't really like help in the kitchen, so the best Fiona might get to do was sprinkle hundreds and thousands on the trifle.

She found the corkscrew and twisted it deftly

24

into the top of the bottle. 'Birgit said you've got your itchies back.' She raised an eyebrow at Daisy. 'I hope you've not been scratching?'

'I don't like the cream,' said Daisy. 'It smells like sick.'

'It doesn't smell like sick. It doesn't smell of anything. It's fragrance-free.' Fiona pulled out the cork and poured herself a large measure of wine. She should have let it breathe, but it had been a bitch of a day trying to get everything finished up before she had to leave and she needed it right now.

'Can I have some wine?' Daisy slipped momentarily off her seat to retrieve a fallen piece of paper from the floor.

Fiona smiled and found a sherry glass and tipped in a small amount, then raised her own to Daisy.

'Chin chin.'

'Chin chin,' said Daisy with a big grin. She took a little sip and screwed up her face. 'What's chin chin?'

'It's like saying cheers.' Fiona leaned back against the counter.

'Cheers!' said Daisy.

'Bottoms up!' said Fiona, laughing.

'Bums up!'

'No, not bums. Bottoms. Anyway, Grampa says *slàinte*. You'll need to practise that. *Slàinte.*'

'Slaaanj.' Daisy pronounced the old Gaelic toast perfectly, even with her estuary English. Fiona smiled. Dad would be impressed. But then he adored her Daisy; her sunny, smart, uncomplicated girl.

Fiona took another sip. 'Where's Jamie?'

Sometimes it was almost easy to forget she had an older child. Her first. The baby with the shock of dark hair and captivating lopsided smile who had lengthened like a shadow into a twelve-year-old with sloping shoulders and downcast eyes.

Maybe it was typical for his age, but he seemed to have sunk more into himself these last few months, if that was possible. He'd started senior school in the autumn, but while his friends from primary had settled fine, he seemed to be taking an age to find his feet. And if he was like this now, what in God's name would he be like as a teenager? She'd thought it might just be hormonal and had had a horribly stilted chat with him about the whole body hair, falling testicle issue a few weeks back. She could have asked Allan to do it, but that didn't seem right, even though he had always been good with Jamie, a damn sight better than his real dad, whose contact now was limited to the odd phone call and three-yearly visits when he flew in first class from Chicago and took him out to dinner to talk loudly at him. Such an arse.

'Jamie's in his room,' said Daisy brightly. She was his greatest fan and saw nothing beyond the fact that she adored him.

'Well, you need to be in yours. I've got a hundred presents to wrap. Go on, off to bed.'

'A hundred!' Daisy's eyes widened.

'Thereabouts,' said Fiona. 'Now go. Scoot.'

It wasn't until later, when the wrapping was done, that she tapped on Jamie's door. He was sitting against his bed with a book spread across his legs. He'd come down briefly for something to eat but she had been seeing to Ben who had been woken by his nappy rash. Jamie had disappeared

26

upstairs again the moment he had finished.

His room was surprisingly tidy, the floor clear of everything except his trainers and a discarded sweatshirt. His warlock figurines were set out neatly on his desk, an army of grotesques that Fiona loathed. She wished he would grow out of them. She didn't want him turning into the kind of 'Dungeons and Dragons' geek she had come across at university with a spittle-laden laugh and desperate, clammy hands. On his bedside table he kept the tank that held his stick insect. He had called her the Stig, after *Top Gear*, even though she was female. Fiona didn't care much for the stick insect. She wasn't freaked by it, but there was something about a creature that existed only to conceal itself that unsettled her. The walls were bare apart from a poster of the Solar System that had come free in the *Sunday Times* and a height chart in the shape of a giraffe he had had since he was a toddler and seemed reluctant to take down, even though he must have been about nine the last time they had marked it.

'You should get some sleep, Jamie. We've got a lot to get done tomorrow before the flight. Okay?'

He nodded at her and for a second she thought about asking him again if everything was okay. She didn't, because every time she had recently, he'd said, 'Yes, fine,' like he was talking to a teacher.

She leaned her head against the door jamb. 'Are you looking forward to going to Gran's?' It would be pretty dull for him—his other cousins were both girls and, together with Daisy, were liable to be cliquey.

He nodded again, but said nothing.

'Well, night, darling,' said Fiona.

27

'Night, Mum.' He offered her a wan smile.

She was in bed by 11.30 p.m. She left the light on in the en-suite and the door slightly ajar so Allan could see where he was going without having to turn the top light on. She'd assumed she would be asleep before he got back; she had counted on it, but at 11.50 p.m. she heard his key in the lock. She willed him to stay downstairs for a nightcap, to watch the late news. But after a few minutes she heard his footsteps on the stairs and then he was in the room.

She heard him piss, wash and gargle in the loo and then saw him emerge through half-shut eyes. The bed dipped as he got in and rolled towards her. She shut her eyes tight and steadied her breathing.

The hand landed on her hip and slid down and she felt her stomach sink. She jerked slightly, and murmured, hoping it would put him off, but she felt her nightie being lifted as he pressed himself into her.

Fuck.

His hand was on her breast now, searching for the nipple. She used to like that. She used to turn towards him, willing and aroused.

He was whispering, but she didn't want to hear. She wanted to scream at him, but she didn't; gave a little grunt instead, which he took for assent.

She felt him part her legs and go into her, and gritted her teeth. Tomorrow, she thought, poised to head for the bathroom when he was done and wash him off her, in Scotland, she wouldn't have to do this. Two whole weeks when she wouldn't have to do this.

28

The letters were so tiny, really. Small and not so very dark. But the words were huge: **freak bent job wanker**. Jamie couldn't get them out of his mind, even though he had deleted them long ago. And there would be a fresh lot soon. Maybe even tonight. He looked across the room at his mobile phone on top of the bookcase by the door. The woman on the phone had said he could try leaving it lying about downstairs, see if his mum or Allan got nosy and picked it up, if he couldn't bring himself to tell. But he knew his mum would go ape and call the school, or her law firm, or the police or something and it could only get worse. So much worse.

He looked down at his book. The note that Daisy had pushed under his door was still in his hand. 'Night night jamie boy love your sister Daisy Anne Flemming.' She always spelled it like lemming. She was only seven but she seemed to understand and she knew enough not to knock and not to pry. Not like his mum who barged straight in with her disappointed eyes and her endless questions.

He stood up and walked across the room. He could leave the phone here when he was up at Fortune House. Say he forgot it. He looked down at the screen. It was off. Definitely off. As blank as a sleeping eye. Dead. Off. He covered it with his book, just in case.

*   *   *

Deborah held her wrists under the cold tap,

29

waiting for the blood to cool and take the fire from her face, neck and chest. She looked up into the mirror. It wasn't a ladylike blush, a faint colouring high on the cheekbones. It was a full-on reddening, crimson and angry as if she were about to spontaneously combust. So unfair and far too soon. If it had just been the hot flushes she might have twigged earlier, but there was the nausea and the bone-numbing fatigue she sometimes felt, and then her gums had bled when she hadn't even been brushing her teeth and she had panicked. Two of the mums at Katie's school had recently been diagnosed with cancer: one ovarian, one breast. One of them, all she'd had was a stomach-ache that wouldn't shift and a week later she was given six months to live. Deborah had wept for her and her soon-to-be-motherless girls, and a little for herself and her fears.

It had almost been a relief when the doctor had said perimenopause. It's unusual in a woman your age, he added, but not unheard of. She was only thirty-eight, not even the eldest in the family, but already shrivelling up inside like a barren old hag.

She turned off the tap and dried her hands and arms on the hand towel. It was a mistake to have put such a large mirror over the sink. She caught sight of her belly, the curve of flesh extruding over the top of her high-leg pants. She had always been apple-shaped, even as a child. But after two children her tummy could pooch out like a full-blown pregnancy if she breathed out all the way. Just last year, buying a moisturiser in Debenhams in a gathered skirt, a make-up girl had asked her when she was due. Too mortified to correct her, she had made up a date. Except the girl wouldn't

30

let it drop. 'You're big for four months,' she had said, turning to her colleague. 'Isn't she big for four months?'

Deborah took a last look in the mirror. So she looked pregnant, but would never be again. She breathed back in and slipped her nightie over her head.

Doug was propped up in bed behind a large hardback spy novel. He loved his spy novels although anyone less like a secret agent you would be hard pressed to find. For a start, he had riotously wavy hair and you never got curly spies, and while he did work for the government, it was in agriculture and fisheries and not as a covert operative. And he wore pyjamas: top and bottom and fastened all the way.

'You've been an age.' He smiled at her over the top of his book. 'Are you coming to bed?'

'In a minute.' Deborah pulled the hairbrush through her hair and tipped a dollop of hand cream into her palms, rubbing it in vigorously, up as far as her elbows. She squeezed past the end of the bed to feel the radiator. It was cool to the touch but the room was too warm, so she parted the curtains and opened the window on to its first notch. The garden was dark, illuminated only as far as the front flowerbed by the weak yellow wash of light from the porch. Elsa had said she'd be back 'after midnight', which could mean anything. Deborah sighed. She wanted her elder to be rested and in good form for the family tomorrow, but she'd barely spent an evening in the house since the term had finished, and the zippy little car that waited, engine idling impatiently, beyond the beech hedge most evenings was driven by Matt, the

31

boy of the moment. Although he wasn't really a boy at all, and Deborah had seen the look in his eyes as Elsa had sauntered down the path: hungry and expectant.

She stepped back for an instant, knocking her ankle on the bedpost. There was no space in their room. Just enough for the bed, a fitted wardrobe and one chest of drawers, which was given over to Doug for all his belts and ties and sensible navy socks. It meant Deborah had to keep her smalls in a roll-away plastic tray under one of the wardrobe racks, which meant Doug sometimes got more than he bargained for if he switched on the light as she was bending over to get a bra and pants.

Now, if they had their extension she could have a dressing room, and there would be more space downstairs. But the quotes they'd got last month had been so much more than they had been expecting and there was no way they could do it unless Doug made Grade Eight. As with everything else in the civil service, however, it was taking an age for his application to go through. Deborah glanced over at him. He was starting to look sleepy, his eyes a little unfocused as he followed the words on the page. Nothing riled Doug. Not the fact that he might not get the promotion, not the fact that she was old before her time, not the fact that Elsa wasn't home yet and she'd caught Katie typing 'bare butt' into Google on the downstairs computer.

She took a last look out of the window. The clouds were clearing and above the glow of the city she saw the distant blinking lights of a plane on final approach to Edinburgh Airport. Behind it, and fainter still, another set of lights.

'I really wish we weren't so near the flight path,' she said, twitching the curtain shut.

'Oh God, not this again.' Doug closed his book and dropped it on to the floor. 'What horrid affliction are we going to catch this month from a frozen lump of crap that falls from a 737?'

Deborah climbed across him and into the bed. 'It's not like I made it up. It was in the *Mail*, that woman in Windsor whose son got Nile River virus and they'd never been overseas. Ever. Plane droppings was the only plausible explanation.'

'Plane droppings?'

'You know what I mean.' Deborah settled herself against him. 'Just because it sounds implausible—'

'Doesn't mean it's not going to happen!' Doug clutched her arm in pretend dread. 'Actually that might explain my sore tummy. It's probably Nile River virus. Or ebola.' He rubbed his lower gut. 'Feels more like ebola.'

'You've got a sore tummy?'

'Just a bit. Lower gut.'

'I hope that fish wasn't off.' Deborah twisted to switch off the light. 'Do you think the fish was off?' That's all she needed. The entire family struck down with diarrhoea and vomiting just in time for Dad's big do.

Doug leaned across and kissed her in the dark. 'Fish was fine,' he said, with a smile in his voice. 'Night night.'

'It didn't taste quite as fresh as I'd thought. It might have been off. Do you think it was off?'

'It was fine,' said Doug pointedly. 'The sky will not fall. Love you. Night.'

'Love you too.' Deborah settled back against the

33

pillows. She knew she wouldn't sleep until she heard Elsa safely home. She glanced over at Doug in the new dark. He was facing away from her, his breathing slow and steady. She reached out a hand and laid it on the covers above his warm form and he grunted gently. She worried too much, she knew that, but of all the things she had cause to fret about, the love of Douglas Warrender had never been one of them. She patted the covers absently and hoped he was right about the fish. He was right about most things, was Doug, although he was wrong about the sky. Deborah knew that more than anyone. Sometimes it did fall.

*   *   *

'So.' Matt placed a cluster of drinks on the table and plonked himself down on the stool opposite Elsa. 'Have you told your mum and dad yet?'

Elsa shot him a look. 'No.' She reached for one of the ciders and swallowed a mouthful. It was her third and, blessedly, starting to take effect.

'They might notice, you know,' said Matt. 'That you've jacked it all in.'

'I haven't,' said Elsa. 'And I'm not jacking it in. Just taking time out.'

'You told them about the exam, though?'

Elsa pulled a face. 'Yes, but can we not talk about this tonight?'

Matt smiled. 'Wait till they're pissed at Hogmanay and dump it on them then.'

'They don't get pissed,' said Elsa. 'Dad'll probably be okay, but Mum will throw a complete fucking wobbly.' She sighed. It was all right for Matt. He was done and dusted; he graduated in

34

the summer and was now taking a year to figure out what he wanted to do, which he could afford because his mother was something big in party planning, and obscenely wealthy. But Elsa had found her first term so utterly intense, and everyone else seemed to be coping with it. And then she'd failed jurisprudence, which was kind of crucial for a lawyer. But if she'd done the kind of studying she needed to, she'd have had no life at all. Absolutely none.

Matt's mobile jangled suddenly on the tabletop and he glanced at the incoming text. 'That's the others. They're going on to Jongleurs. Wanna move after this?'

Elsa nodded. 'I'm just going out for a fag. You coming?'

Matt shook his head. 'Bog,' he said.

Elsa picked up her cider and made her way alone through the throng until she reached the door and joined the little group of smokers clustered around the entrance to the pub, sheltering from the thin smirr of rain under the eaves. She was trying to stop, or at least that is what she had told her mum and dad to avoid the lectures and the pained expressions. Edinburgh's famous Lawnmarket was busy. A long queue of clubbers snaked along the pavement from the entrance to Blues, and, a little way further up the road, an elderly drunk pirouetted off the kerb and jigged his way across the road. Elsa could hear his singing in the distance, faint and warbled. She stamped her feet, feeling suddenly chilled. It wasn't exactly cold, so she hadn't slipped on her coat to come out, but she was only wearing a long-sleeved T-shirt.

Matt appeared after a few minutes and slipped his hand into her back jeans pocket for the cigarettes, his fingers lingering on her buttock.

'You ready to go?'

She nodded and offered him her lighter and watched the flame illuminate his features.

He took a deep drag then leaned forward to kiss her. She tasted the smoke and the warm sourness of beer. He snaked his arm around her waist and pulled her in and she felt her cider splash down the leg of her jeans.

'Matt.' She started to laugh and tried to right herself, but he held her tight and steady and kept his mouth on hers. She felt a flash of embarrassment because people would be watching. But she adored him. And it was him who had put the idea of Quito in her head. A month at a project for street kids, then two travelling. He was already signed up and there were still spaces. And it was hard to argue with him when he looked at you through the dirty blond hair that flopped over his eyes.

'Matt,' she said again. He sank his mouth on to her neck and she felt the hard pinch of his teeth. She pressed into him and closed her eyes.

*   *   *

Vonnie laid her head back against the seat and watched the three elderly women at the table on the other side of the lounge car. They had followed her through from the sleeper carriages just as the train had pulled out of Euston and had seated themselves noisily near the bar, like hens settling in a coop. After much fuss and deliberation, and flirting with the young barman, they ordered cherry brandy all round.

It had made Vonnie smile. The only other person she'd ever known order a cherry brandy was her grandmother, Min. It had always seemed such a frivolous drink for someone so fierce. Min liked her brandy with a dash of lemonade, which, even as a child, Vonnie knew meant the tiniest of splashes. Sometimes the rich ruby colour would stain her lips, and even her teeth until she reminded Vonnie of the men she had seen in *National Geographic*, the ones who chewed on betel nut until it looked as though their gums were bleeding.

Vonnie reached forward for her own double vodka and sipped it. The only other person to emerge from the sleeping compartments was a man in his early forties, with a face that Min might have compared to a skelped arse: bright red and shiny, and a suit he had obviously worn for days, bagged around the knees and crotch. He had given Vonnie a cheesily hopeful smile that she had not returned.

The man sat down two rows in front of her but positioned himself so that he was in her line of sight. When his phone rang, and it had rung maybe three times since they left London, it played the theme tune from *Hawaii Five-O*. She thought about phoning Mike and talking dirty, just to make a point, but it was only 4 p.m. in Vancouver and he would be working and a little taken aback.

The women had finished their brandy and had moved on to gin and bitter lemon. Vonnie wondered if they were sisters. There was some physical resemblance between them, but that

37

might just have been their age and mode of dress.

The loudest, a large woman with thin, blonded hair, had shrugged off her cardigan to reveal a polyester sleeveless top which bared her arms and their pendulous 'bingo-wings'. Vonnie watched in fascination as the woman gestured to her companions as she talked, and the flesh between her shoulder and elbow swung and trembled. Not that she blamed her for taking off a layer. It was so warm; had been ever since she arrived. Everyone was saying how un-Christmassy it made them feel. Even the old university friend with whom she had broken her journey in London had been obsessing about the temperature. She'd dragged Vonnie out to the small patch of garden behind her Crouch End semi to point out a still flowering summer clematis, clinging stubbornly to the stump of a dead apple tree. 'A clematis in December!' she had said accusingly, as if Vonnie herself had forced it to bloom. 'It's not right.'

Even if they weren't related, the women knew each other well, the conversation slipping easily between them.

'Do you get the radio on the train?' said the largest, to no one in particular. 'I like the radio, me.'

'Don't know,' said her friend. 'You maybe do.'

'First thing in the morning. Radio.'

'Aye.'

'News though. Can't be doing with music in the morning. News.'

The third put down her drink and gazed out of the window. 'Mostly bad, though, isn't it? News.'

'Bad. Aye. That's the news for you.'

'Is this Peterborough yet?' asked the smallest of

the three.

'Peterborough? We're no' even in Watford, hen. Peterborough!' All three laughed and then fell quiet.

'I like toast,' said the largest finally, nodding to herself. 'Toast in the mornings. Radio. Then toast.'

Vonnie turned and looked out of the window to hide her smile and caught the glint of her new earrings. She felt the familiar rush of sick pleasure. They were gold and shaped like small olive branches and had cost £350, added to the credit card that was not yet maxed out. Her friend had egged her on, but she hadn't needed much persuading. A present to herself after she'd bought the cufflinks for Dad. Anyway, Dad was always extra generous at Christmas, and probably more so this year, what with her coming home, and the golden handshake he was bound to be getting. 'How are you for cash?' he would ask, when Mum was out of the way; and Vonnie wouldn't need to reply. Some to be getting on with, and then the fat book of American Express traveller's cheques to take back with her. Dad would see her right. He always did. This year, in particular, she was counting on it.

An hour passed, and eventually the elderly women raised themselves from their table and smiled at her before following each other, a little unsteadily, out of the lounge car. Vonnie glanced across at Hawaii Five-O. He had fallen asleep against the window with his mouth open and his phone had gone quiet. The bar was shut but she had the half-bottle of vodka from Duty Free in her case. She scooped up the paper she hadn't read and the dregs of her drink and headed for the cabin.

She slept fitfully, even though she had forked out extra for a single-berth cabin. She woke when the train pulled into Carlisle and then again when it stopped at Carstairs Junction for the Glasgow section to be decoupled and set on the track to the west. She had raised the blind and seen the giant structure of the state hospital on the hill, with its spotlights and razor wire, and had shuddered at memories of a breakout and an axe killing and blood on the road on the TV news.

She must have slept for only half an hour more but her dreams were unkind: betel nuts and shiny earrings and madmen with red staining their teeth.

The steward woke her just before 7 a.m. with a small metal pot of weak tea and two bourbon biscuits wrapped in plastic. She sat on the edge of her bunk and watched out of the window as the train slipped into the great grey city. Between Haymarket Station and Waverley it slid into a long tunnel, emerging suddenly at the foot of the castle rock. Vonnie felt a rush of excitement. The trees in the gardens danced in the easterly gale, illuminated by the orange of the Princes Street lights. The Christmas decorations were up, and high on the top of the Balmoral Hotel someone had fixed a giant, sparkling star.

She rummaged in her bag and found the vodka again, tipped a measure into her mouth and, smiling, raised the bottle to the city. A toast to celebrate her arrival. And one more little sip. For old times' sake, and just for the hell of it.

CHAPTER THREE

'It's just been an utter nightmare since they put these tram lines in.' Caroline eased the gearstick into neutral and sat back, tapping her fingers against the wheel. It wasn't even 8 a.m. but already the traffic on the North Bridge had ground to a halt, a long queue of cars and buses stretching over the rise towards the Royal Mile.

The sun was up, illuminating the tops of the high grey buildings. Vonnie watched the Christmas lights draped around the porch of the Carlton Hotel blink frantically on and off. She was pleased to be here but she would have been better pleased to be moving.

'It can be up to forty minutes at rush hour to clear this lot,' said Caroline. She turned and reached out a hand and touched Vonnie's cheek. 'It's lovely to see you. And I do like your hair that way. You look tired, though.'

'I didn't sleep much last night.'

'No, you look *tired*.' Caroline shifted into gear and the car crawled forward a few feet. 'Are you taking care of yourself?'

Which is, thought Vonnie, Mum-speak for, 'You look crap; how much are you drinking?'

She changed the subject. 'When are Fiona and Debs arriving?'

The traffic had started moving again and Caroline's eyes were back on the road. 'Deborah's picking up a couple of things for me in town this morning and they'll all be down for lunch. Fiona's flight gets in about teatime.' She paused as the

41

traffic slowed to another stop, and pulled on the handbrake. 'Did you not get a chance to see her when you were in London?'

'I didn't really have time. I only got about a day and a half as it was.'

'That's a pity,' said Caroline. 'You could all have come up together.'

'Mmm,' said Vonnie. She leaned back against the seat and stretched.

'And how's Michael?'

'He's fine.'

'It's a real shame he couldn't come over with you.'

Vonnie felt the first prickle of irritation. You look tired. It's a pity you didn't see Fiona. It's a shame you didn't bring Mike. What next?

'He's got his thesis due in February, Mum. He couldn't take the time.'

'Well, maybe next year,' said Caroline. 'Does he know what he's going to do when he gets his PhD?'

'He's had a couple of offers already. From his department, and McGill University in Quebec, and University College, London.'

'So you might be moving back?' Caroline glanced quickly across at her, and Vonnie almost laughed out loud. Less than twenty minutes and she had managed to find her trigger.

'I don't know. Probably not.' She sighed. The last five years had been so beautifully uncomplicated, no pressure on them to make any decisions. But then Mike had to go and finish the course he had spent almost a decade studying and all of a sudden nothing was for certain. She loved Vancouver; everything about their life there, but mostly the fact that it was easy. And she was enjoying her course. She'd even become something of a minor celebrity after the anthrax outbreak at Chilliwack last year. Channel 9 had been looking for a soil scientist to interview and the department had put her up because she was way more photogenic than many of her colleagues, for whom the word boffin might have been crafted. She'd been asked back since to do a semi-regular science spot for kids, which was kind of fun.

'It would be lovely if you moved back,' said Caroline, and must have realised that she had touched a raw nerve because she added, 'Work going okay?' a little more brightly than she ought to.

'Yeah, it's great,' said Vonnie. 'They don't pay me enough, though.'

They both fell quiet. The traffic had eased and they were now zipping down Newington Road towards the south. Vonnie stared out of the window and found herself counting Christmas trees in windows, the way she had done as a girl. She got to seventeen before Caroline spoke again.

'I'll need to warn you about Min.'

Vonnie burst out laughing. 'It's a bit late, Mum. You should have warned me about her when I was four.'

Caroline frowned. 'Vonnie, that's not funny. She had a bit of an episode.'

'An episode? Is she okay?'

'She's fine. She got a little disorientated last night when we were out, a bit confused.'

'She didn't wander off or anything, did she? Has she done it before?'

'No, no, no. She was pretty upset when we got home but she seems to have forgotten about it

43

today. I think she lost Hector in the garden, and she couldn't find him, from what I can gather.'

'Is he still going?' said Vonnie. 'Jesus, he really is the Dog That Wouldn't Die. Is she okay, though?'

'She's fine,' repeated Caroline. 'It's only to be expected at eighty-eight. She's had a couple of these episodes. Just minor. The doctor said they might be mini strokes. He's not sure, but you need to go easy on her.'

'Go easy on her?'

'You know what I mean,' said Caroline. 'Don't wind her up.'

'Mum, she winds herself up,' said Vonnie. 'Have you given her a pep talk yet about terrorising her great-grandkids?'

'Vonnie.'

'Didn't Dad tell me that she taught Deb's Katie to say, "Fuck this for a game of soldiers"?'

'Vonnie!' Caroline tried and failed to sound cross.

'Okay, okay.' Vonnie laughed. 'I'll go easy on her.' She shook her head. 'Anyway, how's Dad? How did his last week go?'

'It was good. Your father had a nice time. He had lunch with the Deputy First Minister.'

Whoopee, thought Vonnie. The Deputy First Minister.

'Is he all right about it all?'

'About lunch with the Deputy First Minister?'

'No. About leaving.'

'He's fine,' said Caroline unconvincingly. 'He's had a good run and he's really done a marvellous job. And he's got his book to do and he's been talking to the *New Statesman* about a column, so that's all good.'

44

Vonnie shifted round as far as the seat-belt would allow and tucked one leg under her. 'But it's kind of weird they let him go with the vote coming up, isn't it?'

'They didn't let him go, Vonnie. He's retiring.'

'But he wanted to stay, didn't he? Come on, Dad lives for elections, he's the original political whore. Why couldn't he have gone in the summer once it was over?'

She saw her mum's fingers blanch white on the wheel and felt a stab of irritation. She couldn't abide the middle-class gloss that Caroline applied to situations. Lunch with the Deputy First Minister. As if that might compensate for a career ended too soon. And at such a time, too. Vonnie felt very removed from the vote and all the fuss that surrounded it, even though it had filtered through to the Canadian media. But for her dad, this must be as big as it was ever likely to get.

Caroline didn't add anything so Vonnie said, 'Well, either way it's their loss,' and turned back round to stare out of the window again. They had reached the eastern edge of the city and her first view of the Firth of Forth. It was only since she'd left home that this view excited her. Before, it always meant something was over: a cinema trip, a date, a holiday away. The firth was grey and choppy, where the estuary widened like a roaring mouth out into the sea, and the converging waters pushed up ranks of small, sturdy waves. White horses, her dad used to call them; if you caught one, you could ride it all the way to Norway.

'Have you decided how you're going to vote?' She glanced back over at Caroline who shook her head.

'I honestly don't know yet.'

They were going against the flow of traffic now, probably Christmas shoppers heading for Fort Kinnaird. The large white mass of the Cockenzie Power Station with its towering twin chimneys hove into view on the water's edge.

'Do you think they will, though?'

'Will what?'

'Split,' said Vonnie. 'Scotland and the rest of the UK. Go their separate ways.'

There was another pause. 'I think it's possible,' said Caroline.

They stopped briefly in Fortune itself while Caroline ran into the butcher's to pick up a ham joint. Vonnie stayed in the car and took the opportunity to run her fingers through her hair and brush on a quick dab of bronzer, in case her dad thought she looked tired too. She felt like a child again, sitting in the passenger seat, waiting for her mum. The town had changed little over the years. There was a supermarket now and one or two charity shops on the High Street, but beyond that it could have been preserved in aspic. A dog was tied up outside the chemist's. It was small and squat and wearing a checked coat. It glanced balefully at Vonnie through the glass.

'Can you hold this?' said Caroline breathlessly, sliding back into the driver's seat.

Vonnie settled the ham in its greaseproof packaging on her knee. A small piece of mince was attached to the outer paper, pink and raw and edged with fat. Vonnie lowered the window and flicked it out.

They took the eastern fork out of the town and followed a tractor for several miles along roads

46

that Vonnie knew she could travel in her sleep. The long swing to the left by the little row of cottages, over the bridge, and past the farm and the old kennels, now a fabulous L-shaped conversion with two giant SUVs parked outside and an extravagant treehouse hammered into the old yew. And then the small copse of conifers that hid their gate.

The house sat on the smallest of rises, a pimple really, but high enough to be remarkable in these flat lands. With the exception of Berwick Law and the hill at Traprain, you had to go north before the land really started to climb. Here, Vonnie liked to think, was where the country calmed itself, settling into gentle folds before it dipped into England.

Vonnie felt herself stiffen with anticipation as Caroline swung the car over the cattle grid and into the trees. She caught her first glance of the house, grey stone glinting through green.

'There!' She shouted like a child. The trees broke midway up the drive and the house came fully into view. It had been built as a manse and was a solid rather than elegant building, early Victorian and four-square, with tall sash windows and an ornate winter garden built on to the left-hand side, a curious indulgence for the ministers who had lived there long before them. Vonnie and her sisters had tried for years to persuade their parents to replace the structure with a proper conservatory, one that would be wind- and water-tight and could be used year round, but they had always baulked at the cost. So it stayed as it was: smelling of compost and mildewed cloth, its windows yellowed with age, the low sills edged with geraniums and tomato plants in various pots and stages of decay. At the front of the house, three broad stone steps led up to the storm doors, which tended to be kept shut unless guests were coming. They were open today, pinned back with an ornate boot scraper and one of Min's old curling stones.

Vonnie had never appreciated how lovely the house was when she was growing up. It was just home, the high-ceilinged rooms too cold in winter, the kitchen with its mismatched units and giant range cooker too hot in the summer. If she closed her eyes she could walk through it even now and know where she was: how far from the drawing room to the kitchen, the dip in the floorboards in the middle of the hall, the door jamb by the dining room with all their heights marked in fading pencil, the step on the stairs that creaked, the familiar feel of a brass door handle, the smoothness of the banister, the smell of polish and old wood.

In spring and summer she had practically lived in the garden with its herbaceous borders and old summerhouse and the two big lawns where you could play tennis if the grass was cut and you'd cleared away the dogs' mess, and could find a racquet. And the large clump of rhododendrons at the garden's furthest edge where they had made a den, the one that David was in the process of turning into a hide, or so Caroline had said.

The church the house had served was a little way further along the road. It had long since been hollowed out and redeveloped as a home, now with Austrian blinds bunched like falling knickers in the windows and a child's bright plastic swing set where the car park used to be.

When she came to understand such things, it

seemed a little ironic to Vonnie that a family of atheists and agnostics should pick a manse for a home. It had originally been bought by Great-Grampa Haldane in 1920 for the princely sum of £925. Grampa Haldane was born a year after they moved into the house, and was, according to Min, the apple of his father's eye. It was never in any doubt that the house would become his when his parents passed on. When he then died, unexpectedly and in his favourite chair at the age of sixty-three, Min was left on her own to rattle around the empty rooms. Not long afterwards, Min told David that she was gifting the house to him and Caroline and moving in with her friend Rena. She was away for almost fifteen years, until Rena, too, passed away, and David persuaded Min to move back. They had developed a granny flat of sorts at the back, on Min's instruction. It was an extension of what had been the coal bunker and outhouse; small, but with its own door and en-suite.

Vonnie couldn't really remember moving in, but the extra space had allowed each of them their own rooms, something which Fiona, in her more melodramatic teenage moments, said had saved her life. Vonnie had got the smallest room. It was at the back of the house overlooking the garden with just enough space for a bed, a desk and a single-width wardrobe. It was hers, though, and she loved it, and it made up for all the hand-me-down clothes that came after, which, by the time Vonnie got them, were almost rubbed through at the knees, and the waistbands stretched and slackened by Deborah's tummy. Vonnie would be back in the room tonight—they were always put in their old

49

rooms when they were home—and she could lie as she used to, conjuring up faces and other shapes in the pattern of the curtains; falling asleep to the medley of old, familiar sounds.

Caroline shifted into a lower gear for the last pull up the drive. All across the big front lawn were dark little mounds of earth.

'God, look at the molehills.'

'They're the bane of your dad's life,' said Caroline. 'He's always conjuring up new schemes with Charlie to get rid of them.'

'Charlie?'

'The gardener,' said Caroline. 'Charlie Mackinlay. From Gifford. Do you remember him? He was at the same school as you all. Older than you.'

'Vaguely,' said Vonnie. 'Was he in Fiona's class?'

'Between Fiona and Euan,' said Caroline. 'He was in the army but he got out a few years back and set up this gardening business. Actually I don't think you can call them gardeners. Landscape architects. Your dad's got various projects on the go with them. Oh, and we've got hens now.'

'Hens? Really?'

'Two French Marans and a Silkie,' said Caroline. 'The eggs are lovely. Except Pinky's off her laying.'

'Pinky?'

'She's the Silkie.' Caroline laughed. 'They do this sometimes. They're quite highly strung. You're supposed to dunk them in cold water to snap them out of it, but I can't bring myself to.'

'Highly strung hens. That's a new one,' said Vonnie. 'Where do you keep them?'

'Down near the vegetable patch. In their eglu.

That's what you call it. It's meant to be secure, but Charlie's had to put up an enclosure, because we think the fox was about. They're adorable. You should go and have a look at them once you've settled in.'

The car swung round the eastern corner of the house and on to the hard paving by the back door. Vonnie caught sight of the marquee dominating the back lawn.

'Jesus, it's a bloody royal garden party. How many people are coming to this thing?'

'I think about a hundred,' said Caroline, as if she didn't know exactly.

'God, Mum, I had no idea it was this big. How are you going to cook for that lot?'

'I'm not,' said Caroline. 'We've got a caterer in. It's Frances Fletcher actually.'

'Frances Fletcher is a caterer?'

Caroline cut the engine and tugged sharply at the handbrake. 'She started it after Bob died. She's been very successful. She does a lot of society parties and the like. Gallery openings, you know.'

'Good for her,' said Vonnie.

David must have heard the car or been waiting because he had opened the back door even before Vonnie had managed to extract her two cases from the boot.

'Vonnie!'

He held out his arms and she ran into them, folding herself into his crushing hug. He smelled of merino wool and shaving foam and the toast he must have just eaten. He looked older, his hair a little whiter than it had been last year, the bags under his eyes more pronounced. Vonnie felt as though she could cry. She said, 'Dad,' instead, saw

51

Caroline disappear behind them into the house, a small dog rush out.

David kept hold of her and bent his head on to her hair. 'How's my Vonnie?' he said and she heard the delight in his voice. 'How's my best girl?'

*　　　*　　　*

Even with the engine running and the radio on, it was obvious to Katie that Mum and Elsa weren't talking to each other. When they did speak, it was in the hissing voices that people used when they didn't want you to listen.

'I cannot believe this,' Mum said, and not for the first time. Mum liked to repeat herself when she was cross, although you never really knew who she was speaking to.

'Do you know how many germs there are in a human mouth?' She turned and looked at Elsa who had her eyes shut and her head on the back of the seat. 'You'll probably need a tetanus shot. Well, my girl, you're wearing a polo neck or a scarf for the duration. Disgusting. That's what it is.'

Katie stared out of the window and tried to pretend that she hadn't noticed what they were talking about. Up until the age of nine, she had thought you could get pregnant by sitting on a bus seat immediately after a man. She'd spent a lot of time strap-hanging on the way home from school until her best friend set her straight. The man's *thing*, she had told Katie over a shared bag of salt and vinegar Chipstix, has to go into yours. *Into* yours. All the way. Swear to God!

She had checked with Elsa, who confirmed that that was indeed the case, but told her not to tell their mum, although Katie thought that was silly because she must know already because Dad must have put his thing in her twice for Mum to have her and Elsa. Katie had vowed she was never going to do it. She would live in the woods with Sandy the cat until he died. And then she'd get another.

But if she knew now about the process, she had wondered exactly how it happened. More importantly, did the man peck at you and bite you like the ducks in Inverleith Park? It was Min who had started it all. She was Katie's great-granny and almost a hundred or something. She was called Min because she'd had a little sister who couldn't say her real name—which was Marilyn—when they were growing up. Great-Granny Min was too much for anyone to say and nobody ever did. She was quite fun, as much as a really old person could be, but she could also be very rude. Despite that, Katie's mum sometimes took her on days out with them, like the day at the duckpond. Mum had gone back to the car because she wasn't sure she had locked it, and while she was away, Min had pointed to a flurry in the water and had said the males often got violent 'when they're copulating', which was, said Min when Katie asked, duck-speak for mating. Katie knew that meant having sex. Sometimes, Min had added, the female ducks even got 'drowned in the frenzy'. Katie had tried to look up copulating when she got home, but she didn't know how to spell it and whether it started with a 'c' or a 'k'.

But now she knew it happened with humans too. She had seen the mark on Elsa's neck, like a brand-new bruise and had heard the shouting downstairs and then Mum yelling about a love bite

53

and 'how disgusting was that?' And they were still rowing about it now in the car on the way to Granny's.

'Disgusting,' said Mum again and Elsa snorted. She had been quite snorty in general since she went to university. She had on a long top with a big belt round her hips, and a little scarf tied round her neck, which Katie thought looked quite nice, but it kept slipping and Katie could see the edge of the mark. It looked sore and she winced again on Elsa's behalf.

Dad had taken his hand off the wheel and put it on Mum's knee and patted her, the way you did with a dog that was too excited. Katie was desperate for a dog.

'It's not funny, Doug,' Mum said. 'What are Mum and Dad going to say? Or Fiona? Oh, she's going to love this, is Fiona. Can't you just see it?'

They had all stopped fighting by the time they got to Granny's. Katie was pleased the journey was over because the roads on the last bit made her feel sick and Dad always made her sing because he said it helped. Although it didn't help that he sang too.

She loved Gran and Grampa's house. When she was really small she thought it was as big as a castle, and it was filled with all sorts of fancy things: grandfather clocks and old sewing machines, ornaments in glass cabinets, and interesting biscuits.

They rumbled over the cattle grid and up the driveway. Katie took off her seat-belt even before Dad had stopped. Gran was there and Grampa, and Min, and Aunt Vonnie, too, from Canada. There were lots of hugs and Mum shrieked at Aunt

54

Vonnie that she was bald, which was pretty rude, Katie thought, and not true because she wasn't. She had very nice hair, short and a little bit wavy.

Katie stared at her shyly, thinking she was beautiful. She wondered if Aunt Vonnie had Done It and got bitten in the process. For all that she was not nearly as big as Mum, she looked like she might have bitten back.

*   *   *

The only good thing about budget airlines, thought Fiona, was the fact that you didn't have to worry about the flight attendants.

She watched the frowning girl in the shapeless yellow blouse prepare for the pre-flight checks, assembling the safety cards and lifejacket with sluggish, almost mechanical movements. Allan, she suspected, would have barely given her a second glance, even though she was top-heavy, and he usually liked big-breasted girls. His only other option would have been a pale, skinny steward who didn't look a day over seventeen, with spiky dark hair and a small hole in the side of his nose where a stud ought to be.

She never used to mind that Allan loved women. It had been part of the attraction, initially: that he had been so flirtatious but had wanted her. She had heard about him long before she met him. 'He's incorrigible,' friends would say, with a false indignation that belied their obvious pleasure at his attentions. He was still in the City then, a fund manager at Lehman Brothers before they went to the wall. She'd seen him once at a party and thought he looked like Denis Leary, but with nicer teeth. They'd met finally at a late summer barbecue. It was a Friday night and Fiona had come straight from work and found herself the only suit in a sea of slip dresses and shorts.

'Didn't get the dress code?' he had said with a smile, taking her jacket and handing her a glass of Pimm's as if the party were his, which it wasn't.

So she had kicked off her pumps in front of him and unhooked the top buttons of her white silk blouse and said, 'Is that better?' and he said, 'Much.' She slept with him that night, something of which she was not proud, but he had called her the next day and the one after that. He still flirted with other women, but she never cared because he was hers and she had never been the possessive type. Over time she grew so practised in anticipating his ogling that she could enter a room and spot the woman or women who would catch his eye almost before he did. He knew it, too, and sometimes he would whisper, 'What do you think of her?' and Fiona would play along because it was harmless and even sexy. Sometimes they would make up a game when they were out, would sit in a café window and say, 'Blowjob for the next person to pass from the right,' and collapse in hysterics when it was a little old man with a dog in a coat.

He was highly sexed, but she was a match for him. She liked the power it gave her, and with a drink in her she could be talked into pretty much anything. Even after Daisy was born, they continued much the same as before. But then came Ben. It wasn't that he was a difficult baby, colicky or wakeful, but Fiona felt exhausted by the sheer physical onslaught of his needs. Small hands at your flesh, the life sucked from you. Allan had long since left the financial sector and was running the restaurant. He would come in after midnight and expect her to be awake, and, worse, willing. She came to resent his undiminished sex drive, eventually even his touch. If they did it at all, she needed a couple of drinks and for it to be over as quickly as possible. They fell into a pattern. She would hold off until he got so restless that she felt she had to give in, or until he was due to go away on a trip and she felt obliged to. She never climaxed. He started masturbating, openly, on the other side of the bed.

It was a problem, she knew that, but one she couldn't face confronting. It would mean a counsellor and revelations that she couldn't imagine articulating. How she suspected that he had sometimes gone elsewhere, and had surprised herself because she didn't want to know. How he once held her head at his crotch in a way that he had not done before, and had called her 'slut', a word he had never used.

Sometimes when she was with clients, they would describe something that she recognised, an instinctive revulsion at someone's touch, and she wanted to shout out, 'I know. I know what you mean.' And just recently, she had found herself imagining another life: one without him. A life of peace and clean sheets, a life where she might never have to have sex again.

The dumpy girl was making her way up the plane. She stopped at the row in front and smiled half-heartedly at Daisy and Jamie, pulling Daisy's seat back into the upright position with a pudgy freckled arm. She glanced down to make sure Ben's child belt was fastened, but failed to respond

57

to the greedy smile he gave her. Even if Allan had been here, Fiona doubted this girl would come back to haunt her any time soon.

At the far end of the cabin, the girl's spiky-haired colleague was holding the intercom sideways against his mouth.

'Ladies and gentlemen, as we make our final checks could you please ensure that all mobile phones and laptops are switched off and hand baggage safely stowed under the seat in front of you or in the overhead compartments.'

Fiona bent past Ben and pulled her bag out from under the seat and rummaged around until she found her phone, pressing the button until the screen faded. Then she lifted out the other mobile that had been lying beside it, leaned forward and held it over the seat in front of her.

'Jamie, before I forget, you left this in your room this morning. Stick it in your backpack, honey. I thought you'd want it in case you needed to call your friends or something.'

Jamie reached up without looking back and took the phone from her hand.

*   *   *

In the corner of the drawing room, on the saggy end of the big chintz sofa, Deborah kicked off her shoes and tucked her feet up under her, careful not to spill any of the lovely Bordeaux Vonnie had just poured into her glass. It was her second refill and her head felt a little hot, but then the fire had been lit, 'to take the chill off the room', Caroline had said, even though it must have been 12 degrees outside. As a child, Deborah had not liked this

58

room. It was the only one in the house where you had to sit up straight because visitors had come. And she had hated the Wally Dugs, the two small porcelain canines that sat each side of the fireplace, white and ghostly with black staring eyes. She looked at them now. They seemed smaller than she remembered and utterly harmless, their lacquered coats shining with the glow of the flames.

It was lovely to be home. She still thought of it as that. Even though she was grown, a wife and a mother, with a house of her own. As a teenager, Fiona had been desperate to leave Fortune House, keen for school to end and her real life to begin. But Deborah had never felt that way. Each time she stepped back through the door, she felt her spirits lift, as the old grey stone closed protectively around her.

And it was a wonderful house for children. Their own was too small, virtually identical to all the others in the street, and with a garden that the neighbours could see into. Here, you could play hide and seek and not be found, or run yelling around the grounds with no one to hear you or mind that you did.

Everyone was being charming to each other, the way families are at the start of a visit when they haven't seen each other for a while and wine is involved. Caroline and Fiona were squashed on to the small two-seater by the bay window with Elsa perched on one arm, a glass of wine rather expertly balanced in one slender hand. All Deborah's anger and anxiety about Elsa's love bite had gone. No one had mentioned it and Elsa had been trying really hard since they had arrived. Even Fiona had commented, shortly after she'd arrived, on how engaging Elsa was and how gorgeous she had turned out, although Deborah thought she had detected the slightest hint of surprise in Fiona's voice that her sister had managed to produce such a beauty.

Fiona herself was as glamorous as ever. She was wearing one of these lovely little crossover jersey dresses in peacock blue, the kind that Deborah never bought for fear of resembling a badly wrapped parcel. And the heels she had slipped off a while ago and that were now lying on the Afghan rug, one upright, one sideways, like dancing feet, were gorgeous little concoctions in suede and sequins. Fiona had inherited Caroline's feet—a neat size five and a half—while Deborah had got David's and was an eight by the time she was fourteen. Fiona used to tease her that you could float down the Clyde in one of her gym shoes and had made loud barge noises when she sat at the bottom of the stairs to tie her laces for school.

Fiona's Allan was coming up later. He was exactly the kind of man that Deborah thought Fiona would have married; the kind who didn't wear pyjamas, or if he did, certainly didn't fasten them all the way. He always made Deborah blush; said she was the sister he ought to have married, if only he'd met her first. Everyone laughed when he said it, in an 'Oh, Allan' kind of way, but it made her uncomfortable because it was so absurd and everyone would know that it was. She was plain and sensible, the absolute antithesis of what she imagined his ideal woman to be.

He owned a rather toney restaurant in Dulwich, which had done well, in spite of the credit crunch.

There had been a small feature in the *Telegraph* last year when his restaurant had won an award. Doug had been so generous about it, insisting they email Fiona to say they had seen it. He never seemed threatened by Allan, or anyone who had done well for themselves. And he never seemed bothered that David made such a fuss of Allan when he saw him. But then David liked successful men and he liked Allan. Deborah had always hoped that he liked Doug. He'd certainly never said anything to the contrary.

Katie was down on the floor with Daisy, stroking Hector and sniggering every time he farted, which was quite often. Katie would shout, 'Gas attack!' and they would pull their tops over their noses and wave their hands frantically in the air.

Daisy idolised Katie, Deborah could tell, and was pleased. She was a sweet girl, her niece, quite precocious intellectually, but without any trace of petulance or arrogance. There was only two years' difference between them, but Katie, at nine, was significantly bigger. She wasn't fat, but she liked her food and she had inherited Deborah's frame, so no one was ever going to call her petite. Daisy was petite; smaller than average for a seven-year-old with long brown hair and wide hazel eyes. Behind her glasses, she had a pretty, elfin face. It was the school that had picked up on her shortsightedness, not Fiona, something that Deborah knew had vexed her older sister, because her prescription was quite strong by all accounts. The glasses she was wearing today were rather stylish, mini Sarah Palin affairs with pale metal frames.

Riley had been banished to the kitchen after

attaching himself to Doug's leg and humping enthusiastically. He seemed to like Doug, or rather Doug's leg, which Doug, laughing, had said he would take as a sign that Riley wasn't the full shilling, given all the better shaped legs about the place. Min had taken offence and had gone a little frosty until he had asked her about Riley's parentage and she forgave him and was still chattering away, boring him with details of canine bloodlines. Deborah had noticed him, at least once, gently right the glass in Min's hand as it tipped to the side and some of her brandy sloshed out. Min didn't do wine outside dinner. It was never strong enough.

Jamie, meanwhile, was on his own in the high-winged chair to the left of the fire, with a glass of Coke he didn't seem to have touched, watching everyone else with a slightly blank expression. He was such a solemn boy, with Fiona's dark hair and heavy-lidded eyes. Deborah had noticed that he had recoiled a little at her hug when they had arrived from the airport in their hire car. But then he was at that horribly awkward stage where everything is growing and changing and nothing much makes sense. Deborah had wondered how Fiona was handling it because Fiona had never seemed to have had an awkward stage in her life.

Ben was still up and cruising round the sofas, his nappy hanging low and heavy, like a damp sleeping bag. He was wearing natty little tartan trousers in soft, brushed flannel, and Daisy was in a Fair Isle cardigan and a little purple kilt. Deborah wondered if it had been deliberate, if Fiona meant always to put her children in something Scottish when she ventured home, because she did. The way the royals liked to, fetching up in kilts and tweed whenever they crossed the border.

She talked about Scotland differently, too. In that vaguely patronising way that some exiles do, offering tempered plaudits as one might praise the work of small children or artists who couldn't see. It's really *awfully* good.

Down on the rug, Hector had grown tired of the petting and had staggered to his feet to leave the room. The girls had watched him go, still giggling at his last outbreak of wind.

'Why is he called Hector?' asked Daisy, standing up and taking a noisy sip from the lemonade David had insisted they must all be allowed, even though it would spell trouble for bedtime and he wouldn't have to deal with it.

Min broke off from lecturing Doug and leaned forward. 'Hector was the son of Priam and Hecuba,' she said tartly. 'He was terribly brave and very honest. A trusted friend. He killed Menelaeus, you know.'

The girls didn't know and they looked confused, as well they might, thought Deborah, trying to reconcile a flatulent Border terrier with a Greek hero.

'Eric Bana played him in *Troy*,' piped up Elsa.

'Eric Bana,' said Vonnie. 'Yum.'

'Not Brad Pitt?' Deborah grinned at her. 'Achilles not your type?'

'God, no. Give me dark and smouldering over blond and petulant any day,' said Vonnie, grinning back.

'Isn't your Mike blond?' asked Fiona.

'Maybe.' Vonnie laughed again.

'I have no idea what you're talking about,' said

63

Min, which Deborah knew was a lie because Min had seen *Troy* at least twice and was probably more celebrity-aware than anyone else in the room.

'And why is the other one called Riley?' demanded Daisy.

'Because he has the life of Riley.' Caroline eased herself off the sofa. 'I think this would be a good time for you lot to have supper and then you can watch a DVD while the grown-ups have dinner. Come on, kids. Kitchen.'

'What's the life of Riley?' asked Katie.

'Ask your Aunt Vonnie.' Fiona laughed.

'Enough,' said Caroline. 'Come on. Supper.'

'What is for supper?' asked Daisy.

'Pasta,' said Caroline.

'What kind of pasta?' demanded Daisy, which, as the child of a restaurateur, thought Deborah, was a reasonable enough question.

'Pasta pasta,' said Caroline. 'Come on, bring your drinks.'

Deborah half lifted herself from the sofa, aware that no one else was offering to help. 'Do you want a hand, Mum?'

'Would you mind, love,' said Caroline. 'If only to help me spoon some vegetables into this lot.'

'I'm allergic to peas,' said Daisy. 'They give me chives.'

'It's hives,' said Fiona over her shoulder. 'And no you're not.' She gave a tinkly laugh and held out her glass for David to refill. 'And runner beans don't bring you out in a rash either. Now off through with your gran and I don't want to hear that there's been any nonsense.'

And the one way to guarantee that, thought Deborah, putting down her wine with a sigh and following the small brood through the door, would be to come through and supervise what was going on yourself.

*　　　*　　　*

'I thought the whole point of devolution was that it would kill nationalism stone dead.' Fiona half stood to help herself to another spoonful of floury potatoes from the large Portmeirion serving dish in the middle of the table. 'Wasn't that what George Robertson predicted when the parliament first started?'

'Who's George Robertson again?' asked Vonnie.

'Former Shadow Scottish Secretary,' said David. 'He went on to be Defence Secretary when Labour got in in '97, and then Nato Secretary General after that.'

'That was always an odd appointment,' interrupted Min. 'Funny man. Right-wing factionalist. Didn't look good in a tank. Not like Thatcher. Very small mouth.'

Caroline smiled. Min loved her politics, almost more than David, and she was in her element tonight, when the talk had been of little else. Ordinarily Caroline would have minded; she had grown tired of the endless debate on independence which seemed to consume every broadcast bulletin and newspaper column inch. But tonight was different because they were all here: her girls and their children. They could have talked about Amy Winehouse or Armageddon and she would still have enjoyed the sound of their voices.

'The SNP realised that devolution was a

65

stepping stone, independence by stealth, if you like,' said David. 'Give them a taste of autonomy and the natural response will be to want more in increments.'

'Mission creep?' said Vonnie, her mouth now full of grilled aubergine.

'Well, if you think about it,' said Deborah. 'We always had separate judicial and education systems and we just added to it. Abolition of student tuition fees, free care for the elderly, better deal for teachers, ban on fox hunting—'

'The world and his wife have banned fox hunting,' said Fiona dismissively. 'Jesus, I think even Belarus has just done it.'

Deborah ignored her. 'Freezing of council tax, higher spend on the NHS, no new nuclear plants, higher renewables targets, abolition of prescription charges, smaller class sizes—'

'Yes.' Fiona raised her fork like a judge's gavel. 'But you're being subsidised for it all. It's something like £2,000 per head that the English subsidise the Scots.'

'That is simply not true!' said Deborah. 'An absolute myth.' Her cheeks were very flushed. 'And you're English now, are you?'

'I'm British,' said Fiona. 'So are you, and this is the biggest bloody mistake that's ever been made. Honestly, it's a joke! I just think it would be a disaster.' Fiona laid her cutlery on her plate. 'Have any of you even thought about what this will mean? It's not some romantic ideal. It's a permanent split. It's division. No more United Kingdom. No more Great Britain. Just Scotland, on its own; trying to manage on its own. I tell you, everyone in England is watching this with utter bemusement, and a fair few saying let them go for it, see how they get on.'

'We could manage fine on our own,' said Deborah. 'Maybe even better.'

'Yeah, like you did at the start of the credit crunch,' snapped Fiona. 'Oh, no, that's right, the Scottish banks came crying to Westminster for a bail-out. Not Holyrood. Westminster.'

'That's not fair,' said Deborah testily. 'Holyrood was not in a position to help.'

Fiona gave a little dismissive shrug. 'I know there's the whole argument about the push for nationhood worldwide, but we're attached, for God's sake,' she said. 'There's shared land as well as shared history. And yet we're just sleepwalking into it. And the legal side of it. Don't even get me started. Nightmare. Utter nightmare. And as I understand it the SNP haven't even spelled out how they intend to do it, if the vote's a yes. They just say they would start the negotiations with Westminster afterwards for some kind of independence settlement. So, in essence, they're asking you to vote for something you don't fully understand. Isn't that right, Dad?'

'You could put it like that,' said David.

'Or you could say that's a load of utter bollocks.' Min rapped her knuckles on the edge of the table and they all turned to look at her.

'We all understand it fine,' said Min. 'We are not sleepwalking into anything. We have had generations to consider this. The union is dead. We're ready to be on our own. No point in perpetuating something that's patently not working.'

'Well, that's your view,' said Fiona. 'But it's not everybody's.'

67

'Only a fool would think it wouldn't work,' snapped Min.

'Thanks,' said Fiona sniffily. 'But I think you'll find it's the fools that win out in May.'

'Mum, where do you stand?' Vonnie must have realised things were getting a little fraught.

'On the side of the weary.' Caroline laughed.

'Elsa?' said Vonnie.

Elsa shrugged her shoulders. 'I'm not really sure. But I think, if you look at some of the Scandinavian countries and at Ireland, they've all done okay, so there's no reason why Scotland shouldn't stand on its own two feet.' She glanced over at Deborah and Doug.

'What I don't get'—Fiona lifted her fork again—'is defence. How are you going to work that? What happens if there's a nuclear strike? What do you do then? Are you going to have some kind of Dad's Army of old plodders to deal with the fallout?'

David raised his hand with a grin. 'That would be me, then.'

Deborah gave a loud snort. 'The Scottish regiments have been the backbone of the British army for generations. You're the ones who should be worried about that. What will you do when you don't have the Black Watch to do your dirty work for you any more?'

'Weren't the Black Watch disbanded?' said Fiona sweetly.

'Subsumed,' said David. 'Into the Royal Regiment of Scotland. You should speak to Charlie about that. He was KOSB.'

'Eh?' said Vonnie.

'King's Own Scottish Borderers.'

'Charlie the gardener?'

'Yes, Charlie the gardener.'

'I can remember when he was in short trousers,' said Deborah.

'Anyway.' Fiona wasn't going to let the subject be changed that easily. 'How are you going to pay for it all?' She raised a hand before Deborah could respond. 'And don't say oil, because it's running out.'

'Like my drink,' said Min. She tapped the table again. 'Refill, please.'

It was Doug who rose to top her up, and, Caroline suspected, to take the heat off Deborah, so flushed now that her cheeks looked hot to the touch.

'What are the latest polls?' Doug asked David.

'System Three for the *Herald* on Tuesday was forty-two against independence, thirty-six for.'

'Wow,' said Vonnie.

'Although, weren't the *Telegraph* figures last week more like fifty against and thirty for?' added Doug.

'They were,' said David.

'Where does the *Scotsman* stand on this?' asked Vonnie.

'Pro,' said David.

'I thought you were against it?' Doug looked puzzled.

There was a slight pause. 'I'm not the editor,' said David.

There was an awkward silence. David's face was impassive.

'It is unusual, though, Dad,' said Deborah, 'to have an editor whose views are the polar opposite to the paper's editorial line, isn't it?'

David looked directly at her. 'As I said, I'm not the editor.'

Caroline went to open her mouth and remonstrate, but Vonnie pre-empted her, grabbing a fork and tapping it insistently against her glass.

'And on that note,' she said pointedly. 'We've been very remiss about toasts tonight.' She smiled at her dad and Caroline saw his face soften. Only Vonnie could get away with it, she thought. Anyone else and he would have retreated further into his funk. And he was in a funk, not matter what he was telling himself.

Vonnie rose to her feet, a little unsteadily. Caroline had meant to watch how much Vonnie drank. Of the three girls she had been the most willing to experiment, sick on cider when she was fifteen, and brought home in a police car two years later for ordering a round of vodkas in a Haddington pub the day of her Highers results.

'So.' Vonnie cleared her throat and raised her glass. 'Dad. Newsman *extraordinaire*. To the end of one great era; and the start of something better. We are all so proud of you and excited for you.'

It was perfectly pitched. David smiled and raised his glass back to her, and everyone else got to their feet, rising in a scrape of chairs, all except Min, who sat where she was, clattering her spoon noisily off her crystal flute, as if she were topping an egg.

'*Slàinte*,' said David, still seated.

'*Slàinte*,' said Fiona, Deborah and Vonnie.

'Cheers,' said Doug.

'Down the hatch,' said Min.

Caroline sat back down, her glass suspended in front of her. She could see David's image through the curve of crystal, faint and distorted. He was

70

speaking.

'And to all of you. For making this occasion, this holiday very special indeed.'

'Pud!' said Vonnie when everyone took their seats.

Caroline stood up again to start gathering the dishes. 'Do you think Jamie will want any?' she asked Fiona. He had been invited to join Elsa with the adults, but had managed only about ten minutes before he looked so pained that Fiona told him to go off and watch TV with the girls.

Fiona shook her head. 'He'll be fine. If he's starving he can have a bite to eat before bed.'

'Talking of bites,' said Min, lifting her glass and pointing it towards Elsa. 'That's a corker on your neck, young lady.'

Caroline heard Deborah's horrified gasp, saw Elsa reach instinctively for her throat and the pretty little polka dot scarf she had been wearing.

'Min!' said David.

'Min!'

'What?' Min looked reproachfully round the table.

'Min. Enough,' said Caroline.

'Enough what?' said Min. 'I'm just saying that's quite a bite on her neck. Or what do you call it these days? A hickey, is it?'

'Min!'

In the fuss that followed, one glass of wine was upended on to the tablecloth and a fork landed on the floor. Elsa blushed bright crimson, Deborah got to her feet, and David, clearly trying not to laugh, told Min to apologise. She did, but by the look on her face she wasn't sorry at all and had rather enjoyed the whole episode.

71

Caroline excused herself and carried the plates through to the kitchen, still shaking her head. It was warm from the range, and she pushed open the sash window by the sink. The tractors must have been out because the air smelled of newly shifted soil, rich and loamy.

Daisy and Katie had clearly tired of the TV, because she could hear them clatter into the hall from the small sitting room; such familiar noises, bumps and yells, shouts and giggling.

She opened the cupboard to the left of the window and stood on her tiptoes to reach the high shelf and the small plastic basket. The pain had started with the soup; that familiar dull ache just below her sternum. She lifted out the small box, opened it and removed the foil insert then squeezed one of the small pills into a cup and held it under the tap, watching the tablet fizz to nothing. She tipped it with a practised hand into her mouth. The children's voices were getting fainter as someone herded them upstairs. She could hear Deborah's voice, still indignant, remonstrating with someone on the other side of the door.

Caroline smiled. Such lovely, familiar chaos. She put her hand to her mouth, felt the tears start to come, hot and insistent. She could not stop them. She heard someone come into the kitchen; prayed that it wasn't David.

'Do you want a hand with dessert, Mum?' It was Vonnie. She had an armful of side plates which she laid on the table.

Caroline kept her face to the window and shook her head, unable to speak.

'Mum. Are you okay?' Vonnie was at her side,

looking round into her face. 'Oh, my God, Mum. What's up? Are you upset about what Min said? It's just Min. Okay, it was a doozy, but it's just Min. Elsa will be fine, although I'm not so sure about Debs. She's mortified.'

Caroline shook her head. 'No. No, it's not that.'

'What? What is it?' Vonnie put her arm round Caroline's shoulder and Caroline turned and clung on to her in a desperate hug.

'Mum!'

'It's just lovely to have you all here,' said Caroline. 'It's really, really lovely. You have no idea.'

*   *   *

Jamie stood in the centre of the dead boy's room, looking at the bed. Although it probably wasn't his bed, because, while it obviously wasn't new, it didn't look that old. He leaned forward and touched the duvet. It was a navy striped one with a matching pillowcase. He knew it had been his Uncle Euan's room without anyone telling him, because it looked as if no one had been in it for a very long time, and it would make sense to them to put him in the boy's room because he was the only one.

Besides the bed, there was a white wardrobe that looked like it might have come from Ikea, and a wooden chair that appeared to be very old and not very steady, and a high bookshelf with a carved wooden duck providing the support for the books at one end. Jamie reached for the duck and lifted it down, catching the falling books with his free hand. The carving was rough and unpolished but quite a good likeness. He had seen another one similar in one of the display cabinets in the big room downstairs. He turned the carving over, but found no initials. He placed it back where it had been and pulled out one of the books. It was *Swallows and Amazons*. His mum had tried to get him to read it a couple of years ago but he hadn't liked the look of it. He opened the cover. On the fly-leaf had been pasted an ornate certificate with gilded edges and fancy black writing.

Euan Haldane. For General Excellence. Fortune Primary School, June 1976.

He closed the book and turned it over in his hands. It can't have been a favourite because the pages weren't curled and separated but close and straight, almost as though it had never been read. Maybe Euan hadn't liked the look of it either.

He put it back up with the others and wandered over to the window. In daytime it would look over the back garden and the big tent David was having put up for his party. His mum had said Euan used to string a wire from his room to one of the trees and fly things down it to scare her and Deborah and Vonnie, like the owl that David stuffed after it flew into the summerhouse window and died. Jamie didn't think he'd get away with that at home. If he and Daisy made too much noise on the trampoline when they were in the garden, his mum said they had to be quiet or she would get an ASBO and how embarrassing would that be for a lawyer?

He thought of the boy he had seen downstairs in the photo on the top of the piano. He had a funny haircut and he wasn't smiling, but he looked a bit like David. There was another one, too, of Euan

74

when he was small and in a thick jumper, holding a little girl's hand. That was probably his mum because she came next, and when he died it made her the oldest.

He was thirteen when he was knocked down, his mum had said. He had been on his bike and in those days they didn't wear helmets. She always made him and Daisy wear a helmet and had just bought him one of these ones like the Germans wore in the war, the ones that come right down over your ears and look pretty cool.

He sat on the edge of the window and wondered how bad it had hurt. He had broken his arm when he was nine when he fell off the climbing frame in Battersea Park and the pain was so bad that he had been sick, so sore he couldn't imagine it ever going away. Had Euan lain in the road, hurting? Had he been awake after? Did he know he was going to die or did it happen immediately? His mum said it was a lorry. Jamie closed his eyes and tried to imagine the moment of impact. There must have been blood. If blood comes out of your ears then it's really bad, so it must have come out of his ears. Jamie had once seen a crow die right in front of him. There had been a fight with a buzzard and the crow came down through the trees just when he was getting near home and had flopped about on the road edge, eyes wide and staring, body jerking as if it were fighting to stay alive. He had watched it until it had stopped moving and the eyes had gone still and staring. It was the most terrible thing he had ever seen.

The curtains were still open and he tugged them shut to get changed. He kept his T-shirt on, but slipped out of his jeans and pants, leaving them where they fell on the floor, and pulled on his pyjama bottoms. There was still giggling and the odd shriek coming from the girls' room, even though Deborah had been up a couple of times to tell them to be quiet. He smiled to himself. Daisy always went a bit funny when she was with Katie, trying to be really grown-up. But she had still waited for him outside the loo and given him a quick hug before she went to bed, making sure no one could see.

He switched off the light by the door and made his way cautiously to the bed. It wouldn't be Euan's. They wouldn't have kept it all this time. He lay down and pulled the duvet up. It smelled of washing powder, but not the kind that his mum used.

It had almost destroyed David and Caroline when Euan had died, his mum had once said. Jamie wondered what would happen if he died. Sometimes he thought his mum might not mind so much, what with Daisy and Ben and her job. He couldn't imagine her being destroyed. There wasn't anything so bad in the world that it could destroy his mum.

CHAPTER FOUR

WEDNESDAY, 23 DECEMBER

It started as a faint V shape far away near the sea's edge, then the noise reached him, the familiar honking call carried on a weak wind, and now they were almost overhead, circling above the lower field.

David leaned his elbows on the wooden shelf and trained his binoculars on the geese as they came out of the lightening sky. For all their grace in the air, the landing was clumsily exuberant, a noisy free-for-all. They settled into the stubble, maybe fifty of them or more, where they almost disappeared against the browny-grey of close-cropped wheat.

His eyes fixed on one, a young male, dainty, almost, in the way he picked across the vegetation, much smaller than the greylag or the barnacle. David reached down with one hand and found his coffee cup and took a quick sip. It was instant and faintly bitter, but he hadn't wanted to set the coffee machine going because the longer he was in the kitchen, the more chance someone else would get up. It was quiet when he had emerged from his room, but the house seemed different: full and expectant. There were at least eleven variously sized pairs of shoes and boots discarded by the front door; small cardigans and jackets hung lopsidedly over the backs of chairs; a large, expensive-looking handbag—most likely Fiona's—was propped on the hall table, smelling of rich leather and extruding sheafs of papers. He suspected she didn't really need to bring work up with her, but it made her look busy and important.

He had switched on the radio instinctively when he woke to listen to the news. On a normal weekday a car would arrive just after 8 a.m. with all the papers, a fat stack of newsprint for him to read on the way in. He would glance through, ripping at will if something was of interest, chatting with the driver, checking his BlackBerry for messages. He

77

glanced down at his watch. He would be halfway to Edinburgh by now and well up to speed on what the day might bring. He tried to remind himself that there had been many days at work when he had wished he was here, hidden by leaves with nothing to face but the sky.

The young male had stopped his strutting and squatted low on to the field. David swept the binoculars back up into the sky to search for another skein.

'Good morning.'

It was Vonnie, her hair tufted from sleep and sticking up above her left ear. She had picked up his old Barbour jacket from the pegs at the back door and hung it round her shoulders.

'You know this isn't a very good hide,' she said, sitting down close to him on the bench. 'Because I can see you from the back door.' She slung her arm around him. 'So what have you got there?'

He smiled and lifted the binoculars from his neck and placed them over her head.

'Pinkfeet,' he said. 'They've just come in.'

'And they'd probably be called that because they have pink feet,' said Vonnie with a smile. She peered out into the field. 'They're all sitting down, though.'

'They have pink on their beaks as well. Actually, up, look.' He swivelled the binoculars for her. 'There're more, just coming in.'

He sat back as Vonnie watched the geese approach, tracking the birds across the sky.

'See the way they fly,' said David. 'It's an incredible set-up. They put the older and stronger ones at the front and rear, and the young ones in the middle. I don't know if you can see from here

78

but each bird flies slightly higher than the one in front. It's more efficient, cuts down wind resistance.'

'They all look the same size,' said Vonnie.

'They will be, roughly. But it's harder to fly out front, because you don't have a slipstream, you get tired, so they swap after a while. There! The one at the front.'

'It's veered off,' said Vonnie.

'Watch the back ones,' said David. 'Is one of them coming up front?'

'Yeah,' said Vonnie. 'That's really neat. I didn't know that.'

David smiled at the faint twang in her accent. 'You're getting more Canadian by the day.'

'And you are such a twitcher.' Vonnie kept the binoculars trained on the sky. 'They're not stopping, though. Where are they headed?'

'Another field, maybe. Or further down. Maybe as far as the Solway.'

'Is it Iceland they're from?' asked Vonnie.

'Possibly. Or Spitzbergen. Greenland, maybe.'

'But they winter here,' said Vonnie.

'If you can call this winter,' said David.

Vonnie slipped the binoculars back over her head and looked around.

'I can't believe you pinched our den,' she said.

'You weren't exactly using it,' said David. 'And it's not finished.' He pointed to the largest of the rhododendron bushes that made up the little copse. 'Charlie and Boyd are going to put some cladding against that, mostly to keep out the wind but also for cover.' They had already widened a gap in the smaller of the two bushes, trimming back branches to make an almost rectangular viewing hole. There was a bench and a broad, slanted wooden shelf in oak, chosen because it should weather well.

Vonnie giggled. 'I probably shouldn't be telling you this but we used to have a pee pit over there, when we couldn't be bothered going in to the loo. Well, Fiona and I did. Deborah didn't use it. Of course.'

'You are a foul creature,' said David.

'I do love this, though,' said Vonnie, looking about. 'You should have a Keep Out sign up.'

'No need. Your mum's never been one for birdwatching,' said David. 'It involves sitting still.'

'What about Min?' said Vonnie, grinning.

'She'd bring a blunderbuss,' said David. 'She thinks anything winged is after her Virginia creeper.'

'What else do you get?' Vonnie looked back out over the field.

'There was a fieldfare here last week,' said David. 'They're pretty rare.'

'We saw a sea eagle on Vancouver Island last Easter,' said Vonnie. 'At least Mike was sure it was. It was huge; right above the cliffs.'

'Do you remember when we saw one on Mull?' David smiled at her and Vonnie frowned. 'You were pretty small.'

'Vaguely,' said Vonnie slowly. 'I think I do, yes.'

He knew she was being kind; she would have been too young to remember, only three or four at most. It was Euan who had spotted it with the binoculars he had got for his birthday that year, a brand-new set of Canon ones in a stiff black leather case. He had scratched his initials clumsily into the lid that holiday and David had been cross

80

at the mess he had made and they had not spoken until the eagle lifted off from the headland the day they all went rock fishing.

'Can I have some of your coffee?' Vonnie was peering into his cup.

'Go ahead. It's pretty dire, though.'

Vonnie took a sip and pulled a face. 'That was quite a debate last night,' she said. 'I didn't realise Fiona felt so strongly about it all, the whole independence thing.'

'Well, she has good reason to be concerned,' said David. 'It's an absolutely monumental decision. And pretty much irreversible.'

Vonnie handed him back the mug and got to her feet, bending over to kiss the top of his head. 'And this is pretty much undrinkable. I'll go and make us some real stuff.'

David watched her make her way back up the lawn to the house. She had a loose, long-limbed stride, almost like a boy, but the face was far too pretty for anyone to get confused. He smiled after her. Vonnie was one of the few people who knew how to be around him, knew what to say and what not to, when to stay and when to go.

He lifted the binoculars again but the sky was empty. It looked like it might be a lovely day; the clouds had eased out over the estuary to a thick grey line on the horizon and the sun had cleared the trees by the driveway's edge and was shining low and full on the house.

Vonnie was back within ten minutes, with two cups of fresh coffee, but also the news that almost everyone else was up, and Hector had been sick in the hall and breakfast was on the go.

81

Elsa wiped the steam from the bathroom mirror and bent close to the glass to study the mark on her neck. If anything, it was darker than it had been the previous day, a deep bluish red, about the size of a 10p piece. She could have died when Min had pointed it out last night. She pressed her fingers on it and watched it blanch. Not even make-up would help much yet. She should have bitten Matt back, and he could have seen how his mum would have handled it. Although, if what Matt said was true, she'd have been so pissed she wouldn't have noticed. Elsa had met his mother only once, and briefly. She was up in Edinburgh for a friend's funeral and stopped by his flat. Elsa remembered a handsome woman, slim as a reed, but with a cold laugh and a reluctant handshake. It had been unsettling, Elsa remembered, the way she looked at Matt; almost greedily. But then he was her only son, and his dad was an utter bastard, or so he always said.

She sat on the edge of the bath to comb out her hair. There was no extractor fan and even though she had pushed open the window, the room was still filled with steam. It was a good-sized bathroom and the bath was huge, but Mum had reminded her that the plumbing was so dodgy it would take almost an hour to fill, and the water would have run cold before the end. So it was showers only. There was a large heated towel rail, a wicker bin lined with a plastic bag and a small stool tucked under the sink. On the back of the door was a big brass hook for hanging your robe and, below it, a small framed print: 'Please remember, don't forget, never leave the bathroom wet.' Elsa had loved the poem when she was little, and the cartoon that went with it, of a small girl with saucer-sized eyes. The printing and the picture were very faded now, but you could still make out the words, so familiar to her that she could recite them without thinking. Opposite the sink was a small, glass-fronted medicine cabinet. Elsa had already had a little peek, but it was filled only with aspirin and ear plugs, a half-empty bag of cotton wool balls, nail clippers and various tubes of ointment.

Matt had texted just as she was heading for a shower and asked how it was going.

Like being in Hollyoaks—not

Elsa had texted back. Which was a little bit mean, because last night had been fun, up until Min's outburst. Everyone had treated her like an adult, and David had filled up her wine glass as much as anyone's. And they'd given her a room of her own this time, even if it was tiny and right at the back of the upstairs and was the one her gran used to do her paintings. The walls were covered with them. Sketches and watercolours and some of her oil paintings. They were good, but not that good. The kind of thing you might buy on a holiday to remind you of a place you liked, but not something that would cost thousands, or even hundreds, thought Elsa. Although what did she know?

She'd forgotten what it was like to stay; it must have been more than five years since she'd slept over. The creaks and groans of floorboards, the odd plumbing noises from the radiators, the sweep of yellow light across the ceiling at night when a car passed by on the road, which wasn't often.

She was almost done when there was a soft knock at the door.

'Just a minute.' She stood up and wrapped her towel tight under her armpits and opened the door. It was Fiona. She was wrapped in a shortie robe and her feet were bare, with a rich red polish on her toes.

'I didn't mean to rush you.' She smiled. 'I wasn't sure if there was anyone in or not.'

'It's fine.' Elsa smiled back. She saw Fiona's eyes slip momentarily down and then up and she instinctively pulled the towel a little tighter. It was funny how some women gave you that look, a quick once-over, like a dog sizing up a rival. Girls at college did it, and sometimes they didn't even seem to notice that they had. She couldn't imagine why Fiona did it. She was lovely; really stylish and attractive, much prettier than Deborah, even though she was two years older. Her mum had always told her that Fiona was the pretty one, which she was, but the bossy one, too. Although her mum could do bossy, as well. God, couldn't she half.

Elsa stood back to let Fiona in. 'I hope there's hot water left,' she said. 'It was getting a little cool.'

Fiona rolled her eyes. 'Good old Scottish plumbing,' she said.

In the bedroom, Elsa slipped on a polo neck and her jeans and twisted her hair, still wet, into a messy top-knot. As she passed the bathroom door, she heard Fiona singing over the noise of the shower. It was loud and tuneless and so unlike her perfect auntie that Elsa started to giggle.

The kitchen was crowded with adults and children and steamy from an array of pots and frying pans bubbling and spitting on the range. The smell of bacon made Elsa feel a little sick. Jamie, Katie and Daisy were down at one end of the table, slurping over cereal bowls, like a pack of small dogs. Ben was in a little portable high chair that had been screwed to the table, carefully picking at the raisins that had been scattered on his tray like bird food. Deborah and Vonnie were over at the sink piling mugs and cutlery into the dishwasher and Doug was hovering by the cooker with Caroline, who was holding a large plate and a spatula. David was behind a newspaper.

Elsa grabbed herself a banana from the fruit bowl on the dresser, and perched on the edge of the chair nearest the door. Doug passed by with a plate of sausage and egg and bent to kiss the top of her head.

'Morning, toots.'

'Morning, Dad.'

At the sound of Elsa's voice, Deborah turned. 'You'll need to have more than that,' she said. 'How about some bacon and egg?'

'I'm fine.'

'An egg at least?'

Elsa shook her head.

'And you'll need to dry your hair before you go out. You'll catch your death.'

'Yes, Mum,' said Elsa. She saw Vonnie wink at her from over near the window and smiled back at her. She liked Vonnie.

'Where's Min?' asked Katie, rising from her bowl with a milky ring around her mouth.

'Having a lie-in,' said Caroline, with a hint of raised eyebrow. 'She was very tired after our dinner last night and old ladies need their sleep.'

Daisy pushed her bowl into the centre of the table and sat back with her hands pressed together like a little old man.

'Do you want some toast, Daisy?' asked Caroline.

Daisy shook her head. 'Elvis died on the toilet from constipation,' she said.

Elsa burst out laughing.

'Daisy! Where did you hear that?' said Caroline.

'Katie told me,' said Daisy. 'What's constipation?'

'Katie!' said Deborah.

'What?' Katie looked indignant. 'This girl told me at Brownies. She said her dad said it's not good not to go to the loo. She said Elvis didn't go to the loo and he died on the toilet from constipation.'

'What's constipation? repeated Daisy.

'It's when you can't do a poo,' said Elsa.

'Why can't you do a poo?' said Daisy.

'If you don't eat enough fruit and vegetables,' said Doug. 'Have a banana.'

Elsa giggled and saw that David had put down his paper and was smiling. She felt good for her dad; normally he wasn't that good at cracking jokes and he was always a little strange with his father-in-law. She watched David look around the table. He hadn't said much to her since they'd all got there, apart from asking her how her course was going and then she got the feeling that he didn't really listen to her reply. Which was just as well, because she had lied and said, 'Fine.' She wondered what he would think of her taking time

86

off. She guessed he wouldn't approve, but maybe since he'd retired he'd feel differently.

Caroline sat down with some sharply sliced toast. 'Can I change the subject and ask what you're all planning to get up to today?' She raised her hand. 'I can't join you because I've got too much to sort out for my do.'

Almost, thought Elsa, as if it were her very own party. She glanced quickly at David but he was back behind his paper.

'How about the Bass Rock?' said Vonnie. 'We could go and see the gannets.'

'They don't run trips in the winter,' said Caroline, scraping butter from the large rectangular pat in the butter dish.

Elsa watched her. Butter at Caroline's was never the spreadable kind, always hard and cold and unyielding.

'Well, does anyone have any Christmas shopping to do?' said Vonnie. 'We could go into Edinburgh. Or Fortune.'

'Ice cream!' shouted Katie, who was always the first to think of food, and remembered that Fortune had one of the best ice-cream shops in the whole of East Lothian.

'I tell you what.' David had put down his paper again. 'It's a decent day. Why don't we go to the beach? We can have a walk, Vonnie can see her gannets from there and then we can stop in Fortune on the way back for a cone. How does that sound?'

'Yeah!' Daisy and Katie screamed their approval from the messy end of the table and the adults shrugged and nodded in turn, probably because they couldn't think of anything better.

87

Elsa took the last bite of banana and dropped the limp skin on to the tabletop. A day at the beach with all the family. It didn't sound good. In fact, she had been right when she had texted Matt. Like being in *Hollyoaks*—not.

*   *   *

'I got a sore winkle.'

The small boy stopped in front of Hanna and fished down the front of his trousers, hopping gently from one foot to another.

'Really?' She tried not to laugh. 'Have you?'

The boy looked up and nodded. He had two small rivulets of snot stretching from each nostril on to his upper lip. He was a sturdy boy, probably big for his age, which she guessed to be about three. Someone had zipped him into a padded jacket that was too small and made his arms stick out unnaturally, like a little mini bouncer. Not bonny, she thought, and immediately chided herself for thinking so. To someone he was perfect.

'Look, see. Sore.' He had given up on trying to find his penis and had pulled down his trousers instead.

Hanna turned her head away just as a man with a black beanie hat came running over.

'Hey! You. That's enough. Not nice. God, I'm really sorry.' He tugged the boy's trousers back up, swinging him high in the air as he did so. Hanna called it aeroplanes when she did that with Marek.

'But I've got a sore winkle,' said the boy plaintively.

'He's got a sore winkle,' said Hanna, with a warm smile.

'Apparently so.' The man smiled back, looking relieved. He nudged the boy in the direction of the climbing frame. 'Go on, monster, go and have a climb.'

The boy waddled off and the man looked back at Hanna.

'I'm really sorry. That'll be my son, flashing the mothers in the playpark.'

Hanna shrugged. 'It's fine. It's kids.' She grinned. 'Now if it was one of the dads . . .'

The man burst out laughing and reached up self-consciously to pull off his hat. He was nice-looking, maybe late thirties, thinning on top but with kind eyes and a square, masculine chin. He had a wedding ring, too. Thick and solid, the lovely pale sheen of good gold.

Dyta had got a little drunk last night and called her picky when she wouldn't go on to a club with Dyta, her boyfriend and another man. It had been one of these nights when you worry that nothing will come right, even though you knew that one day it would. She looked at the man with the wedding ring and smiled again, kindly. One day she would meet someone who would be nice-looking and lovely, too, but he wouldn't look at anyone the way this man was looking at her now, because Hanna would be all that he could ever want.

The man turned and looked around the playpark. 'Is one of these yours?'

She nodded and pointed to Marek, bent on to his haunches near the flying fox, watching the bigger children swoop along the line of wire with their heads thrown back in abandon.

'This little one.'

The man nodded and stood awkwardly, looking

at her, then out over the park. At the far side of the playpark, over by the roundabout, Hanna saw a woman with two small girls watching her. It was the same look she had got at the first playgroup she had joined: defensive, a little suspicious.

She stood up. 'Nice to meet you,' she said to the man. 'I need to get my boy home now before he decides he's big enough for this flying thing.' She laughed and the man nodded again, realising he was being dismissed.

Marek was still bent close to the ground. She stooped down beside him.

'Hey, *kochana.* You ready to go?'

He turned to look at her, his face brightening with a spontaneous smile. He shook his head.

'Okay,' said Hanna. 'But I thought we could stop at the coffee shop for hot chocolate? Yes?'

Marek nodded and jumped to his feet, grabbing hold of her hand as he did so. She folded her fingers around his as they walked to the park exit. Sometimes she never wanted to let go. This tiny boy, who wasn't meant to be here, whom she hadn't wanted. Just one night with a man who meant nothing, and all the agonies that followed.

She looked down at him. He was chatting away to himself, a mix of Polish and English and nonsense. His hand was still clutched tight in hers, soft and warm. She felt the tears come into her eyes, still stunned, four years on, that something so beautiful could have come from something so wrong.

*   *   *

The stick swung in a short high arc and landed on

90

the water. Riley shot forward, legs kicking high like a small horse. The waves would only have been knee-high to Katie, but they washed almost completely over the dog. He grabbed hold of the stick and raced back on to the sand, dropping it at Katie's feet with frantic precision.

Katie bent and picked up the stick again. She was getting a little bored of the game, but Grampa had asked her to keep an eye on Riley 'to stop him rolling in faeces'. Katie didn't know what faeces was, but it didn't sound good. She hurled the stick back into the air. At least the stick-throwing stopped Riley doing that horrible grabbing thing with your leg, which Elsa said was him trying to have sex with it.

Anyway, Daisy had wanted to play hide and seek in the dunes and Katie hated hide and seek, especially the bit where the person is so close to finding you that you can hear their raggedy breathing and even if it's someone you know, the thought of them reaching you is so scary you want to be sick. And she didn't want just to sit and do nothing like Elsa who was perched high on the dunes, looking bored and texting like crazy. Although Katie did wish she had her own phone. Half her class had them already, but Mum said you had to be at least twelve because they fried your brain if you got one before then.

Dad had tried to get her to help dig the sand holes that he and Grampa were working on, but she'd got bored of that too. They were still at it and they'd been here for ages already. Grampa had taken his shoes and socks off and had rolled up his trouser legs, revealing white spindly calves with hair on that Katie didn't like to look at. He had some suede shoes on that had got stained when a wave came in and he'd jumped about and sworn. Dad had been sensible and worn his wellies but his face had gone all red with the digging. Katie wondered if they'd noticed that all the children had left, apart from Jamie, who was standing a little way back from them with his arms folded, watching in silence.

She was the closest in age to Jamie and on other visits to Gran and Grampa's they'd always ended up playing together. There was the time they'd found black spiky caterpillars on the road outside Gran's house and Jamie had called them all Hairy Fellow, which Katie had found hysterically funny for reasons that she now couldn't remember. And the slugs they'd tracked down and piled into a tin pail for Grampa, and next morning they had turned into a big horrid mush, which was gross and a bit cruel, but amazing all the same how they had kind of dissolved into each other. But she hadn't seen Jamie for ages and he was different now, and kind of weird. He didn't say much, just watched everyone from under his fringe, which was greasy and so long you couldn't always see his eyes.

Mum and Aunt Fiona had gone to the rocks at the far end of the beach. Aunt Fiona was sitting with her knees pulled up against her as if she were cold. Mum was kind of draped over the rocks looking like the Little Mermaid, but a lot bigger, and with clothes on.

Aunt Vonnie was closer, standing at the edge of the water watching birds with Grampa's binoculars. There was an island a little way off the beach with a white lighthouse and a gap in the middle. Katie felt a nudge at her feet. Riley was back, wet and quivering and staring intently at the newly retrieved stick. Katie ignored him and walked down to where Aunt Vonnie stood. She turned as Katie approached her and lifted the binoculars from around her neck.

'Do you want a look?'

Katie shook her head. Grampa always tried to get her to look at birds through them in the garden and they made her go cross-eyed.

'Can you go to that island?' she asked instead, pointing out to the rise of rocks just offshore.

'It's not really an island,' said Aunt Vonnie.

'But it's got a lighthouse,' said Katie.

'There are sharp rocks just a little further out, so they need to warn the boats.'

'Can you not go out at all?'

'Only if you're a lighthouse keeper,' said Aunt Vonnie. 'Would you like to be a lighthouse keeper?'

Katie shook her head. 'It would be worse than being a princess trapped in a tower. And you'd have to have a beard. They always have beards.'

Aunt Vonnie laughed. 'Not a good look for a girl.'

Katie laughed with her and looked down at Aunt Vonnie's feet. She had taken her shoes and socks off and her toenails were painted a purply black and she had a silver ring on her biggest toe. Katie generally didn't like feet, but Aunt Vonnie's looked nice.

Riley, distressed that his stick-throwing signals were being ignored, had started to whine.

'I think you drew the short straw,' said Aunt Vonnie, laughing. She bent down and grabbed the stick and hurled it into the sea way down the beach towards the rocks where Mum and Aunt Fiona were sitting, then turned and grabbed Katie's hand. 'Now, run!'

They galloped along the shore, past the men and their holes and Elsa texting in the dunes until Katie felt as though her insides were going to burst.

'There,' said Aunt Vonnie when she finally stopped a good distance away from anyone else. 'Someone else's problem.' They stood catching their breath and watched Riley emerge from the sea and search about wildly. He must have figured that Mum and Aunt Fiona were the best bet, because he set off for the rocks, a small white and brown flash along the sand and then he scrambled up beside them and they heard the faint wail as he dropped the stick and shook himself.

Aunt Vonnie laughed again and flopped down on to the sand; not the wettest kind nearest the water, but the soft, white sand that was further up. She grabbed two large handfuls and let it fall through her fingers.

'I used to eat sand when I was your age,' she said.

'Why?'

'Because I thought it would taste like sugar.'

'Does it?' Katie pressed her hands flat on the surface.

'Have you never tried it?'

Katie shook her head. Mum made her wash her hands if she'd even touched sand. She'd have a fit if she caught her eating it.

'You should try.'

Katie grinned and lifted a pinch of sand, glancing across at Mum on the rocks before she

94

tipped it into her mouth. It was gritty and crunchy and tasted a bit like salt and fish at the same time. She made a face.

'Not like sugar, is it?'

Katie spat it out. 'No.'

Aunt Vonnie laughed. 'What shall we do now?'

Katie shrugged. She didn't really mind. She was having fun anyway.

'Sand angels.' Aunt Vonnie threw herself back and Katie copied her, stretching out her arms and legs and windmilling them through the sand. She felt the grains go into her hair and up the sleeves of her fleece. Mum would probably say later that she had brought the beach home with her. She started to giggle. It was a kind of kid thing to do, but it felt grown-up with Aunt Vonnie doing it alongside her.

*   *   *

Fiona shifted Ben on her knees and brushed the spray of droplets from the leg of her jeans.

'I'm absolutely soaked. Bloody dog. Whose idea was it to bring it anyway?'

'I don't know,' said Deborah. 'I think he just got in one of the cars.' She edged her foot towards the stick and nudged it off the rocks and into the water. Riley stood and watched it disconsolately, knowing that he was out of his depth.

'Daw!' shouted Ben, gesturing towards Riley with a mittened hand.

'Go on, poochie, do us all a favour and jump,' whispered Fiona. She glanced at her watch. They'd only been here for just over an hour and judging by David's face when they arrived and found they had

95

the beach to themselves, they could be here all afternoon. She sighed; it was all too depressingly familiar. Countless family trips to this stretch of yellow sand. Interminable hours spent watching gulls or gannets circling pointlessly on rocky outcrops. Trailing after Caroline as she looked for sea coal or driftwood to sketch. Falling out with Vonnie and Deborah who never seemed to hate it as much as she did.

'This is tedious.' She turned to Deborah and pulled a face.

'The kids are enjoying it,' said Deborah.

Fiona followed her line of sight and burst out laughing. The two men were bent double now, scraping at their sand holes as if their lives depended on it.

'What are they like?' said Fiona, still laughing.

'They're trying to see who's got the biggest hole,' said Deborah, giggling.

' 'Twas ever thus,' said Fiona.

'If he's sensible, Doug'll let Dad win,' said Deborah. She paused. 'They do know the tide's going out, don't they? Because I think Doug's built a moat round his.'

Fiona smiled. Deborah could be so wound up; it was nice to see her more relaxed. She felt suddenly guilty for having had such a go at her last night. She watched her sister stare across at the men. Deborah's chin was down and doubled. She was definitely heavier than the last time Fiona had seen her, but then she'd really never lost the puppy fat that she had piled on when she was about eleven. Each pregnancy had added a little more. She must be at least a size 16 by now, and it looked like Katie in particular was following in her footsteps.

96

She was already a little barrel and always on the lookout for food. Elsa was an aberration, curvy but slim, with a curtain of shiny caramel-coloured hair and a belly so flat that even her low-slung teenage stance couldn't push it out further than the buckle of her wide leather belt.

Fiona knew Allan would notice the change in his niece. The last time they had seen Elsa she was practically still a child, her hair had needed a good wash and she favoured those baggy smocked tops that everyone was wearing. Fiona had felt her heart sink when they'd arrived yesterday afternoon and this gorgeous creature with boobs and a bum and insolent eyes had unfolded herself from a couch in the drawing room.

'Dad seems okay, don't you think?' said Deborah suddenly. Ben had wriggled away from Fiona, and Deborah reached out her hands to him. He scuttled across to her and she settled him on to her lap.

'About retiring?' Fiona shifted her position and looked at her sister, glad to be distracted from her train of thought. 'Actually I thought he seemed a bit tense. He almost bit Doug's head off last night, remember?'

'I suppose,' said Deborah. 'But I expected him to be really subdued. It must be hard.'

'Do you think he was fired?' asked Fiona. 'Allan said it sounded like he was, but I didn't want to ask.'

'No, I don't think so,' said Deborah. 'But I don't think he was ready to go, either. Anyway, they don't really fire editors, do they? They just nudge them out of the way.'

'Then why are they having this party?' asked

Fiona. 'If he wasn't really ready to go.'

Deborah shrugged. 'Well, you've got to mark it in some way, haven't you? It would look a bit odd if they didn't.'

'I suppose,' said Fiona. 'And he's still going to be writing. He always said he missed that.'

Deborah nodded and gave a little sigh. 'I think Mum's a bit stressed about it all, though.' She turned to face Fiona. 'Did you know she has an ulcer?'

'Are you serious?'

Debs nodded. 'I caught her taking some Zantac or suchlike in the summer. She said it's nothing to worry about.'

'God.' Fiona pursed her lips. 'Actually, you know, I was at this seminar last year and there was this paper on Japanese women and how they're getting sick because their husbands are retiring. It's practically an epidemic out there, apparently, stuff like strokes and mental illness. It's called Retired Husband Syndrome. They literally worry themselves ill at the thought of him being home with them all the time. Some have even committed suicide.'

'Really?' said Deborah.

Ben was tiring of her lap now and anxious to be crawling off towards the sea. Deborah sat him down beside her on the rock but kept a tight hand on his padded jacket.

Fiona nodded. 'The divorce rates are going through the roof.' She gave a little laugh. 'They call the husbands *sodaigomi*. Oversized garbage.'

Deborah smiled, her eyes still fixed on a digging Doug. 'That's a bit harsh.'

'Oh, I don't know,' said Fiona. She'd thought

98

much worse of Allan at times.

'They sleep in separate rooms as well,' added Deborah.

'I know,' said Fiona. 'And the house is big enough. Actually, that must be quite nice. The whole Doris Day, Rock Hudson thing.'

Deborah glanced across at her. 'I can't sleep unless Doug's right there.'

'Really?' Fiona laughed. 'I can't sleep if Allan is.'

'Does he snore?'

'No,' said Fiona. 'He doesn't snore.' She looked back towards the men. The digging had stopped and they were standing back admiring their handiwork. Fiona saw David turn to look for the children and give his trademark whistle. She levered herself to her feet and held out her hands for Ben. 'They're done,' she said. 'Shall we go and tell them how clever they've been?'

*   *   *

The blue Fiat Punto crunched across the gravel and drew to a tidy stop side-on to the back door. Caroline watched from the scullery window as Frances Fletcher eased herself from the driver's seat, but not before she had glanced in the rearview mirror and put a quick hand to her hair. Caroline smiled to herself, wiped her hands on the green chequered tea towel and went to open the door.

'Caroline, hello!'

Caroline bent forward for a kiss that wouldn't land and caught the whiff of a subtle, citrusy scent. Frances moved past her and into the hallway,

99

placing her handbag and the large leather folder she had been carrying on the hall table. She looked around, slipping off her long sable-coloured cardigan coat and draping it over the nearest chair. 'I thought it would be chaos here today. Where is everybody?'

'At the beach,' said Caroline. 'It's such a decent day and the children wanted to go.'

Frances smiled apologetically. 'And you're stuck here waiting for me.'

'It's fine,' said Caroline. She gestured towards the kitchen. 'Let's go and get a coffee before the hordes return.'

Frances picked up her folder, gave her hair another unnecessary pat, and followed her. In the kitchen, Frances laid out the folder on the table, pulling sheafs of papers from the pocket inside. Caroline filled the kettle from the deep Belfast sink and watched her.

She had always been an attractive woman, Frances, tall and slim, but with curves that she had taken to showing off in clingy wrap tops since Bob had died. Today she was wearing a deep turquoise version with a little camisole stretched across her cleavage underneath. They had known each other such a long time, and as much as she liked her, Caroline never felt completely at ease in her company. Perhaps because they had met through Bob and David. They had socialised a lot before the children, and then not so much afterwards, although the Fletchers had been at the house the day of Euan's accident. It was Bob that Caroline remembered most from that day, his kindness, his gentle, devastated eyes.

Frances looked up and smiled and Caroline

100

clicked the kettle on and sat down, very aware, all of a sudden, of her mossy-coloured cardigan with the missing buttons.

'So,' said Frances. 'I checked about the marinated tiger prawn skewers and that should be fine, although . . .' She shuffled her sheets of paper and pulled one out. 'I think the black pudding with baby plum tomatoes might work better instead.' She pushed the paper across to Caroline. 'It's roughly the same price and I think it would sit better with the tuna carpaccio and the roasted capsicums.'

'How much?'

'Just over £2 per head.'

'David does like black pudding,' said Caroline.

Frances took that as assent and reached across for the paper. 'Great, so maybe forty of the black puddings. You don't want to do more than that because not everyone is partial.' She picked up her hand-held computer and tapped the screen with the little stick. 'Now, for dessert, Valvona say it would be difficult to source fresh enough raspberries this time of year, so I wondered about swapping them for blueberries? We're still getting some lovely supplies from Poland, as good as we had in the summer.'

Caroline nodded. 'Blueberries are fine.' She didn't feel in a position to argue. Frances knew what she was talking about. Which had been something of a surprise. She had started the business out of necessity after Bob had keeled over on the fifteenth green in a game he was losing and was dead before he hit the ground. Frances had always been a good supper party hostess, but none of their friends had truly expected her to make a go of it, mostly because it was such a departure from what she had done before, which was occupational therapy. But she'd had a couple of commissions and then David had run a piece on the 'New Domestics' in the Saturday supplement and had got a feature writer to interview Frances. She'd got a Bute House supper party on the back of that and she was off. Now she had a staff of eight and a little van she used to deliver her food.

The kettle clicked off noisily and Caroline stood to make the coffee.

'Can I have a look at the marquee?' asked Frances. 'I see it's up now. Just to get a sense of where the serving tables should go, and the like.'

'Of course. If you hang on a minute we can take our coffee out with us.'

They were part way across the lawn, when the first car crunched up the drive. It was Doug and Deborah's people carrier and the rear door opened to disgorge a tumble of children and one very wet dog.

'Granny, Riley rolled in something really bad!' Katie burst forward and caught hold of Caroline's cardigan, breathless with importance. 'I'd been throwing sticks because Grampa said to and then he ran off when I was playing with Aunt Vonnie and nobody could find him and then Grampa did and he'd been in something pooey, and he's sooo stinky!'

'Oh dear.' Caroline turned as Riley shot past, heading for the back door, which was mercifully closed. 'Sweetie, can you make sure he doesn't get inside? He'll be looking for Min.'

Katie nodded and rushed off, tailed by Daisy, both still holding their noses.

102

'We are going to have to fumigate the car,' said Deborah. 'Hello there.' She beamed at Frances and bent forward to give her a warm kiss on each cheek. 'Do you remember Doug?'

'Of course.'

'I better not shake hands,' said Doug. 'I've been sitting holding him in the seat well.'

'What did he roll in?' asked Caroline.

'I think it might have been a dead seal,' said Doug. 'Is there a hose round the back? I'll get as much of it off as I can.'

'Thanks, Doug, there's one by the garage.' Caroline smiled. 'Where are the others?'

'Just behind us,' said Deborah. 'In fact, here they are . . .'

Caroline turned to see Fiona's hire car slip out of the trees. It came to a slow stop beside Deborah's and David emerged along with Vonnie. David was looking harassed. He crossed the short expanse of grass as stiffly as if it were a parade ground.

'Frances.' He kissed her warmly on the cheek, and then turned to Caroline.

'Did you hear about Riley?'

'Doug's just going to wash him.'

'Bloody dog,' said David. He smiled again at Frances. 'So, are we all set for Tuesday?'

'I think so. Just a few last-minute adjustments. Black pudding instead of tiger prawns.'

'Do I get a tasting session beforehand?' David smiled again.

'No.' Frances laughed. 'You're just going to have to wait.'

'Well, I better let you get on.' He nodded towards the back green where Doug had tied Riley

103

to one of the washing poles and was about to get to work with a sponge and a bucket of soapy water. 'I think my son-in-law could do with a hand.'

*   *   *

From the scullery window Min watched David walk away from the two women. She had been on her way out to supervise Riley's bath, which was turning into a bit of a circus, but had stopped to get one of the old towels she used for drying the dogs. It was Caroline who had caught her attention, standing ramrod straight, trying to look relaxed and failing miserably. Min had watched her daughter-in-law's hands curled tightly around the red mug she was holding, and sighed. Such a rigid girl, but not always so. She had curled her hands around David's like that the first time she ever came to the house. They had always been touching. Sometimes just a brush of fingers through his hair, a hand on the shoulder, subconsciously intimate. And now she held herself so far from him, stiff and remote.

Not like Rena, her dearest friend. Even the hand on the blanket of the hospice bed, plastic-braceleted and translucent, gripping hers with fading warmth as if they might be able to meld life through skin.

Min felt the catch in her throat. It had been such a surprise after losing David's father to have such love again. She knew that others had wondered what form of love it was. She herself did not know, only that it was as meaningful and heartfelt as anything she had shared with her husband. Rena had no family. She was an only child and had

104

stayed single, the description she preferred to 'never married'. It wasn't as if she had not had offers. Several, in fact, from men who would go on to wed someone else, but, doubtless, wonder over the years what might have been had Rena said 'yes'. She was a beautiful woman, tall and direct, with a ready, rasping laugh.

She had never been frightened of anything, Rena, until the cancer came. Blood in her vomit, dark as coffee grounds. They scheduled an endoscopy and braced for the worst, which, indeed, it was. And so terribly quick. Less than a year from diagnosis to her death. Min had watched her diminish; her frame shrink, her eyes blacken, as they do when the life is going from you. Such a precious time together when all the banalities are stripped away, and every touch and word has place and worth.

She glanced back out of the window at her daughter-in-law. She adored Caroline, had wondered often if there was something she ought to have said. But she felt it best not to interfere. No one outside it could understand the workings of a marriage, and to lose a child as they had done could freeze the warmest of hearts.

Frances was in full flow, hands twirling in the air as she described something to Caroline. Min didn't much like Frances. Mostly because she was a smart woman, but chose, often, not to show it. When they reached the marquee, Frances stood back and made a sweeping movement with her hand to let Caroline go in first.

'Silly bitch,' muttered Min.

'Pardon?' It was Doug, looking for the towel she had promised to fetch.

'The dog,' said Min curtly. 'Silly bitch.'

'I thought Riley was a he.' Doug looked confused.

'Not always.' Min handed him the towel. 'He swings both ways.'

CHAPTER FIVE

'I'm just saying, I don't think "crump" is a word.' Fiona bent over the Scrabble board and peered pointedly at the letters.

'It is.' Katie looked confused. 'It means to fall over.'

'That would be "crumple",' said Fiona. 'Do you have an "l" and an "e"? Because if you do you would have "crumple".' She sat back, took a sip of her wine and gave a tight little smile.

And if you had a heart, thought Deborah, you would let it go because she's only nine and trying really hard here, okay? It was the second time Fiona had questioned one of Katie's words. The last one had been 'tootsie' of which Katie had been inordinately proud until Fiona pointed out that it was a nickname and names weren't allowed. She'd even questioned Deborah's 'geo', arguing that it was a prefix. Deborah had felt utterly stupid because she hadn't spotted, as Fiona had, of course, that she could have rearranged it and had 'ego'.

Katie was still nodding her head. 'It is a word,' she said. 'Crump.' She reached defiantly into the small green cloth bag for more letters and set them out on her stand.

106

'We should really get a dictionary.' Fiona twisted round in her chair. 'Dad, have you got an *Oxford English* in your study? We've got another word query.'

David lowered his newspaper, but before he could answer, Deborah leaned forward and laid her hand on Fiona's arm.

'Fiona, let it go. Really.'

Fiona looked back at her coolly, her brow ever so slightly furrowed. Her cheeks were still flushed from the beach, but subtly so. She looked like the women in deodorant ads who wander about Scandinavian shores in pale grey cashmere finding interesting pebbles and looking sleek and lovely, even though they must have been whipped by a force six, salt-laden gale. Deborah had already looked in the mirror in the hall when they got back from the beach and found the Old Man of the Sea staring back. Ruddy cheeks and nose, and short, starchy hair.

'But—'

'Really,' repeated Deborah. 'Leave it.' She knew her voice was rising but she couldn't help it. This was so typically Fiona. Fine one moment, lovely, even, like she'd been at the beach, warm and confiding and fun, and then wham, down came the frost.

Fiona raised her hands. 'Okay, okay, I just think it's better that they know what's right and what's not.'

'My children know the difference between right and wrong,' snapped Deborah. 'It's just a word game. For heaven's sake.'

'God, Debs, don't get so het up.' Fiona folded her arms and raised her eyebrows at Katie, who had forgotten her pique and, along with Daisy and Jamie, was now sitting watching with vicious anticipation like the little old ladies who hog the ringside at wrestling matches. 'Your mummy is getting very cross,' Fiona added.

Katie nodded enthusiastically.

Deborah pushed back her chair. 'Fine. Let's just stop it here before it gets any more "het up", okay?'

'Debs. Come on. Sit down.' Fiona reached for her arm but Deborah pulled it away. Fiona gave another little laugh. 'Your mum and I used to fight all the time when we were growing up. Things could get pretty nasty over Monopoly, I can tell you.' She lowered her voice to a whisper. 'Your mummy used to go in a huff then too because she never got Park Lane.'

Deborah shook her head and motioned to Katie. 'Bed,' she said. 'If you want to leave the pieces on the board and we can play tomorrow, fine, but it's getting late. It's a good time to stop.' She was lying. She had no intention of playing Scrabble or anything else for the remainder of the holiday. She'd forgotten just how ruthless her elder sister could be. It wasn't just the winning that mattered to Fiona: it was the utter annihilation of her opponent. And anyway, who manages to get 'aegis' and 'flummox' in their first two turns?

If anyone else in the room had noticed their little spat they weren't showing any signs of it. David had finished with the paper and had found a Steve Martin film to watch. It was a new television, flatscreen and rather out of place in the drawing room with its staid seating and good clocks and burnished dark wood furniture. Her parents had hardly changed the layout. The biggest sofa, with its faded leaf pattern, was square on to the fireplace, as it had always been. The matching two-seater with the chunk of wood missing from one leg—where Euan had gouged it with his penknife in a mood one day—was at right angles, and David's favourite wing chair, re-covered in pale green velvet, was on the opposite side with another two-seater that had been Min's and was stuffed with horsehair. It wasn't the sort of sofa you could slump into, but, curiously, was the one that visitors always seemed to favour, even though it was the kind of seat that made you perch. The coffee table was still on the astrakhan rug, which must by now have indentations so deep they would never come out. It was a huge piece of furniture, with broad squat wooden legs that reminded Deborah when she was younger of a griffon's feet. She used to be able to get underneath it when they had been playing hide and seek. She smiled, trying to imagine herself doing that now, her bum upending it and sending everything on to the floor, magazines, papers and the curious ceramic bowl that held all the TV and DVD remotes.

Katie had not quite made it out of the door, but had stopped by the sofa and was watching the film.

'Hey. Upstairs.' Deborah chased her out into the hall and stood at the bottom of the stairs as she scampered up. 'Toilet and teeth!' she shouted after her. 'I'll be up in a minute to smell your breath.'

She paused for a moment by the Christmas tree, a tall Norwegian spruce by the edge of the stairs. There were a few presents underneath, but nothing exciting, gifts for the girl who came to clean and her son, whom Caroline seemed to dote on; a bottle of wine that had been handed in for David.

The door to the kitchen was shut but the smell coming from it was warm and deeply alcoholic. She found Elsa and Vonnie over by the range, stirring something in a large copper pan, like two tipsy witches. It was their own version of mulled wine, they said. Judging by the bottles crowding the tabletop, they had simply emptied the drinks cupboard into a pot and added some cinnamon.

She took the mug they offered her and another for Doug, gave Elsa a warning glance that she pretended not to see, and walked carefully upstairs, settling the drinks on the floor outside the bathroom as she saw to Katie's teeth.

Doug was in the bedroom shrugging on his shirt, his hair still damp from the shower he had just taken. It was one of the smaller rooms in the house, but Deborah's favourite, because it had been hers. It still had the same curtains, floor-length grey brocade affairs with an intricate swirling pattern that made your eyes go funny if you stared at them long enough. The bed was new, though. She had only had a single, but that had been replaced with a small double, white-painted and simple. It was directly above the kitchen with a warm patch on the floor over by the window where the heat of the range seeped through. It had been repainted in recent years, a lovely duck-egg blue with a matching lightshade.

'You're missing all the drama.' Deborah handed him a mug of wine and sat on the end of the bed.

'Hmm?' said Doug. He set his mug down on the doily on the dresser and looked across at her as though he'd only just realised she was there.

'I said you're missing all the drama. I've had my first fight with Fiona. Honestly, she can be such a cow sometimes. You know what she's like.' She looked at her watch. 'Actually that's pretty good going. More than a day. Normally we're at it after just a couple of hours. Oh, and Vonnie is getting your daughter drunk on this mulled wine.'

'Which one?'

'Which one? Doug! Elsa.'

He nodded but didn't laugh.

'What's up with you?' She took a sip of her wine.

He frowned as if he himself wasn't quite sure.

'Doug?'

'I've got a bit of a swelling.'

'What?' Deborah felt her fingers tighten around her mug.

'A swelling, in one of my balls.' He reached down and touched his hand to his groin.

'Doug.' She felt the coldness flood through her.

'No, it's okay, don't panic. It could be anything, really.' He had finished most of the buttons, but his hands seemed to want to keep moving and he buttoned the top one, too.

'When?' said Deborah. 'When did you notice? Just now? In the shower?'

'I thought I felt it a couple of days ago but I left it in case it was just a gland, or something. Remember I had that tummy thing, the soreness. I thought it might be from that. It's still there, though.'

'Are you sure?' She found herself reaching out a hand. 'Do you want me to . . . ?'

'No, it's okay.' He shook his head. 'Well.' He hesitated. 'Okay.'

He undid his belt buckle and zip and his

trousers pooled around his ankles in a crumpled heap. He was wearing blue pants—Y-fronts edged in white, faded slightly from the wash. He pulled them down.

'Here.' He touched his right testicle.

Deborah leaned back. It was hard to say just by looking but the left side of his scrotum did look a little bigger.

'I don't know,' she said.

He took her hand and placed it awkwardly on to the testicle. Deborah felt her cheeks colour instinctively. It was so strange to be handling him like this without so much as a drink in her. She didn't often give him oral sex, to be honest she didn't particularly enjoy it, but sometimes when she was really tipsy it felt okay. The very first time she had done it, it had taken him by surprise. It was after an unexpectedly drunken night watching a film, a comedy that had made them roar with laughter. She had finished almost the whole bottle of wine. And then, in a mad moment, she reached across and unzipped his trousers and had seen the look of utter abandon on his face and had felt, for the first time in her life, the sense of sexual power.

He moved her hand around and then over to the left side. There was a difference; almost imperceptible, but there, a thickening under the skin. She pulled back quickly, wanting to cry at the look on his face, the sight of his sensible socks poking above the crumpled legs of his trousers.

'Oh, Doug.'

'It'll be fine.' He pulled up his pants and bent to reach for his trousers. 'We shouldn't panic. It's probably glandular. It's normally younger men, you know . . .' He tailed off.

Deborah stood and grabbed him in a hug. 'It'll be fine,' she parroted, not sure what else to say, sick with fear. 'You'll call the doctor to get it checked. It'll be nothing.'

He nodded his head in agreement and she found herself over at the little sink in the corner of the room and washing her hands. She had loved the sink. She felt it lent her room such an air of sophistication and Fiona didn't have one even though her bedroom was more than twice the size. Fiona had told her she'd only got that room because she was smelly and needed to wash—she had tapped her hand to her armpit—'under there'. Her parents had even got her a mirror for over it from a saleroom. It was an old one with a curving top like a rising stage curtain. Some of the gilt was coming off and in the corner were the remains of an old sticker that she had pressed on as a teenager. She looked up into the glass and saw that she had gone white.

This wasn't happening. Her head was buzzing. Testicular cancer. It's the easiest to treat, isn't it? If that's what it was. It would be. What else would mean swelling like that? Oh, God. Lance Armstrong had it, didn't he? And he did the Tour de France and was cured and now he was going out with Kate Hudson or someone like that. But even if it was and they treated it and it went away, it could come back and maybe somewhere else. Thirty-eight and a widow. The girls. She saw herself clutching them, numb, in a front pew. A sob rose in her throat.

She turned quickly. Doug had taken her place on the end of the bed and was slipping his feet into his indoor shoes.

113

'Maybe you should call NHS 24? You could get it looked at tonight.'

He shook his head. 'No. I'll call tomorrow. One night is not going to make any difference. I've got Bupa, remember, through work. I should get seen quite quickly.'

She walked over and sat down beside him. 'It'll be fine,' she said again.

He put his arms round her and squeezed. 'I'm sure it will.'

She dug in the pocket of her cardigan, found a balled-up tissue and dabbed at her nose.

'There's no need to say anything,' he added.

'No.'

'Not until we know. One way or the other.'

She nodded again.

He stood up and cleared his throat. 'So what's everyone up to down there?'

Deborah swallowed. 'The younger ones are getting into bed, Elsa's having happy hour and Dad's watching a Steve Martin film.'

'Which one?'

'The one where the guy is some kind of scientist,' said Deborah. '*The Man With Two Brains*, I think.'

'Not the Man with One Ball?' Doug gave a flat laugh.

'Doug, don't joke.' She reached over and put her hand on his arm. 'Honestly, it wouldn't matter . . . to me . . .' She saw the look in his eyes then as she said it and realised it was such a stupid thing to have said because to him it would matter very much indeed.

*　　　*　　　*

114

'What?' Gail put down her book and tried to look innocent. The duvet bunched around her like a rising wave.

'Caught.' Charlie smiled. 'Someone has been having a snoop about, haven't they?'

She was such a kid at Christmas, always asking him what he'd got her, prodding anything if he left it under the tree, rooting in cupboards and drawers for clues. He'd been careful this year. In the locked file he kept in the loft for the proceeds of cash jobs was a small padded box that opened and shut with a satisfying snap. They'd had hardly any money when Annie was born; a small silver necklace was all he could afford for a baby gift. Gail still wore it every day. But now with the baby coming so close to Christmas and the business really taking off, he'd splurged. Her heart's desire: diamond ear studs from a jeweller's on George Street so hushed that when you went in you felt like you were walking through a church.

The shop girls had been lovely, though. He'd been upfront about how much he could spend and they'd fussed over him, bringing trays of baubles, asking about Gail's hair and eye colour, what she liked to wear. He'd enjoyed the attention. Women generally liked him, not so much the looks, although they weren't bad. He had a good build, especially in his chest and arms, although the tummy had gone a bit to pot since he'd come out of the army. His smile was the killer though. 'You'll break hearts with that grin,' his granny used to tell him, and so it had been, until he met the curvy brunette with soft eyes and a dirty laugh in the World's End pub. She was with the bank at the

115

time and had just been in one of the adverts where they all dance around and sing. She showed him her moves, self-conscious and laughing, in a tight green top and low-slung jeans, and that was that.

'I have no idea what you're on about,' said Gail. She made a pretend prissy face and picked up her book.

'The drawer in the study was left open,' said Charlie. 'And you know the deal.' He lifted his T-shirt over his head.

'What deal is that?'

'Forfeit.' He crawled across the covers and she squealed and hid herself underneath.

'You know the deal,' he said again.

'There is no deal.' Her voice was muffled.

He pulled the covers down. 'That's a blow job at the very least.'

'Crap!' She aimed a slap at him.

'Go on.' He was grinning at her now.

'No.'

'Go on. For your beloved.'

'No!'

'Please?'

She narrowed her eyes at him. 'A hand job. But that's pushing it.'

'Technically I think you'll find it's pulling it,' said Charlie, as Gail dissolved in a fit of giggles.

'Hand job.' She laughed. 'Push it or pull it, take it or leave it. That's your lot.'

He lay back on the bed beside her and reached for her breast, swollen and veined beneath the sheer material of her camisole. It felt hard. She unzipped his jeans and slipped her hand inside, still shaking her head.

He came quickly as a courtesy, and was

116

showered and asleep within half an hour.

*   *   *

'Babe.'

The elbow got him in the shoulder.

'Eh? Hmm?' Charlie raised his head off the pillow. Through the darkness, at the edge of the door, rimmed faintly in orange from the night-light in the hall, he could make out a small figure.

'Babe,' murmured Gail again, more insistently.

Charlie swung his legs out of bed with a sigh.

'Daddy.' It was more of a statement than an exclamation. He reached down. She was still warm from her own bed, the white-painted Princess one that had made her scream with excitement when he had assembled it.

'Not good, Annie.' He reached blindly for the door. 'Bedtime. Daddy's tired.'

'Daddy's tired,' said Annie matter-of-factly.

'Yes, he is and you should be, too.'

'I need a wee?' She phrased it like a question.

'Do you?' It was often an excuse, but he couldn't take the risk. He carried her through to the bathroom, blinking at the sharpness of the light as he switched it on. He deposited her on the toilet and sat on the edge of the bath yawning deeply. The floor was cold. Her small, soft legs swung back and forwards as she gripped the seat. She smiled at him.

'Nothing?'

She nodded in the exaggerated way that toddlers do and made a concentrating face. He wanted to laugh. There was no sound from the depths of the loo.

117

'All done?'

She nodded again and reached out her arms to him. He lifted her off and stood behind her at the sink, holding her small dimpled hands under the water to wash.

She still had her own night-light, a hypnotically whirling lamp that sent a succession of zoo animals spinning around in a steady, ceaseless circle. It would have kept Charlie awake, if not induced vertigo, but Annie seemed soothed by it. She clambered under her covers and he lay down beside her.

'Just two minutes, baby.'

She cuddled into him. She'd always been a good sleeper, even as a newborn, but she was obviously unsettled by Gail's pregnancy. They'd told her she was going to have a baby brother or sister and she liked to talk to Gail's tummy, but she'd been waking up for a good few weeks now, probably looking for reassurance.

Charlie closed his eyes, too. A small chubby finger landed on his upper arm and started tracing his tattoo.

He turned his head and looked at her. 'You've not to get one of these when you're grown-up,' he said softly. 'Okay?'

She smiled. She loved his tattoo; called it Daddy's Drawing. It was the regimental badge, with the motto underneath. *Nisi Dominus Frustra*—'Without the Lord, everything is in vain'. He'd worn a lot of cut-off tops after he'd got it done because the girls did love a serving soldier.

And he couldn't imagine another life, until Gail. He'd had girlfriends, of course, two of them long-term, but he'd never considered marriage, let

118

alone kids. The lads called him Greybeard because he was so much older and wiser compared to them. They had been as surprised as he was, the squaddies, when he told them he was getting married; even more shocked when they heard he was leaving.

Gail was a good bit younger: thirty-two to his forty-two, and she'd thrown in everything for him, the bank and the dancing, and had come first to Akrotiri and then, after a spell back in the UK, to Osnabrück. It was there, while he was on leave, that she had got pregnant with Annie. She only found out when he was back in Afghanistan. He learned in an email. 'Hey, Daddy,' she'd written in the very first line, and he'd sat and stared at it for a while, a swelling feeling in his chest. Then he stood and punched the air in pleasure. It changed things, though, as he had known it might.

Six weeks later they lost a lad he knew well near Lashkar Gah. They'd been on patrol just outside the town; had just had a brew and a fag and had moved off again across land so pitted with irrigation ditches it was like a rollercoaster. And then the bullets had started spitting into the dust and they all dropped and then he heard it. 'Man down! Man down!' He heard himself shout for the medic, but he couldn't get closer. The boy lay behind him, a good thirty yards. And the worst of it all was to lie and hear the gurgling because it had hit him in the neck. And who knows what he was trying to say. Someone's name maybe. Or maybe nothing; just primal fear. A scream that wouldn't come because his windpipe was gone.

Charlie had been asked to write a tribute for the official press release, the one that started: 'It is

119

with profound sadness that the Ministry of Defence must confirm . . .'

They liked input from the unit, not just the press office who could be talking out of their arses for all they knew of the lad. The boy had two small kids back in Berwick, a boy and a girl; he'd shown Charlie the pictures, proud as punch, not that he saw them much, what with the soldiering and the fact he had split from their mum.

Charlie knew then that he had to leave. He didn't want to be that smiling face on the MoD website. They liked to use your wedding photo, too, because you looked so happy in it. They always cut the bride out of it, out of respect for a new widow, but you could sometimes see her hand on an arm, nails painted fancy. Holding on.

He turned his head. Annie's hand was still on his tattoo but she was asleep, her mouth slightly parted. He blew her a silent kiss and raised himself off the bed, stumbling back down the hall from the soft, contented breaths of the smaller of his two girls to the loud, contented snoring of the larger.

CHAPTER SIX

THURSDAY, 24 DECEMBER

'I thought cheese footballs had been outlawed by the EU.' Fiona turned the carton over in her hands to study the small print.

'I love those!' Vonnie put down a mug of coffee in front of Fiona. 'Why on earth would they be outlawed?'

'Because they're not cheese,' said Fiona. 'They're . . .' She found the list of ingredients: 'Partially reconstituted vegetable fat.'

Vonnie leaned over and stuck her hand into the tub and brought out a handful. 'Technically it says *cheesy* footballs,' she said. 'So I don't think you could get them under the Trade Descriptions Act.'

'It's not Christmas without cheese footballs,' said Deborah. She was over by the sink rinsing through the plates the children had used at breakfast and staring blankly into the garden.

It was so Deborah, thought Fiona, to create busy, unnecessary work, when there was a dishwasher at her elbow.

'And Twiglets,' said Vonnie. 'Gotta have Twiglets. Stick that on your list.'

'I will not,' said Fiona. She picked up the coffee Vonnie had made her. Dark granules floated in a swirl on the top. 'Is this instant?' she asked.

Vonnie nodded. 'Why?'

'I don't drink instant.' Fiona stood up to look for the cafetière.

'We're out of the good stuff' said Vonnie. 'It's this or tea.'

'Tea, then,' said Fiona.

She switched the kettle back on and returned to the table and the list she had been making. She had offered to help with the food preparation while everyone else was away, if only to try to inject a little excitement into the menu. So she had scribbled down olives—pimento, and streaky bacon to wrap around dates, and fresh figs if she could find them and get them into the basket before Caroline demurred. Deborah, Doug and Vonnie were going into Edinburgh, David was

121

already away and the children had opted to stay at the house. Allan would be arriving late afternoon and would need to be picked up from the airport.

Deborah had finished the dishes and turned back towards the table, drying her hands on a tea towel. She looked tired. 'That's Mum back,' she said.

'Where's she been?' asked Vonnie.

'Gone to pick up the cleaner,' said Fiona.

'Pick up the cleaner? Where from?'

'The station,' said Deborah. 'She gets the train down from Edinburgh.'

'What happened to Miss Maxwell?' asked Vonnie.

'I think she died,' said Fiona.

'She didn't die,' said Deborah. 'She retired.'

'She must be about 106, then,' said Vonnie.

'She was always about 106,' said Fiona.

'Remember she used to do that thing with her teeth,' said Vonnie. 'She was lovely, though. Really kind. She used to bring us Easter eggs.'

'Hanna's lovely too,' said Deborah. 'She's Polish and she's got a little boy.'

The door had opened and Min came in.

'Who's got a little boy?' she asked.

'Hanna,' said Deborah. 'The cleaning lady.'

Fiona noticed that Deborah had raised her voice ever so slightly and saw her tug the edges of Min's dressing gown together and tighten the belt as she leaned in to give her a quick kiss and a hug.

'Do you want a cup of tea, Min?' Deborah asked.

'Please.' Min dropped her newspaper smartly on to the tabletop. She had made an effort at pinning her hair back but several long strands hung down about her ears.

In the hallway Fiona heard the murmur of voices, among them a child's voice: shy and unfamiliar. 'Does Hanna bring him with her?' she asked. 'The boy?'

Deborah nodded. 'Mum likes her to. He's a wee cutie, wait till you see him. She's teaching him piano.'

Min gave a loud sniff and picked up the tea Deborah had just placed in front of her. 'You know why she likes him,' she said, and blew vigorously into her mug.

The girls turned to look at her.

'Why?' asked Vonnie.

'She thinks he's Euan,' said Min.

The kitchen door opened before any of them could react. Caroline appeared first followed by a slim blonde girl, with short, cropped hair and a warm, slightly shy, smile. She was holding the hand of a small boy with a runny nose, who in turn was clutching the leg of a soft and rather stained plush dinosaur.

'Hello, everyone.' Caroline was beaming. 'This is Hanna. Hanna, you know Deborah and Min, and these are Vonnie and Fiona, my other two.'

Hanna nodded at them all.

'And this young man . . .' Caroline put her hands on the boy's shoulders and bent her head almost until it was touching his. 'This is my Marek.'

Fiona noticed the quick furrowing of Hanna's brow. It was gone in an instant and her smile returned.

'Well, I better get started,' Hanna said. She ruffled her fingers through Marek's hair then moved across to the sink and the cupboard underneath that held the dusters and polish and cleaning sprays.

'So.' Caroline bent before Marek and started to zip him out of his padded coat. 'What are we going to do while Mummy's busy?'

Marek looked at her shyly, the smallest of smiles curving his lips.

'Shall we play the piano?' said Caroline.

Marek nodded and Caroline stood and took his hand. 'You need to come and listen to this,' she said to them all. 'He's an absolute whizz, aren't you, love? A little star.' She led him out of the door without waiting to see if anyone would follow.

*   *   *

It was bliss to be out of the house. Vonnie had got Doug and Deborah to drop her at the western end of Princes Street and had walked its entire length then up the North Bridge and down on to the Royal Mile without having to speak a word to anyone. It was as busy as a Saturday afternoon, but Vonnie didn't mind the crowds. She ducked into a little knitwear shop and bought a cashmere beanie hat in periwinkle blue, which the assistant wrapped in crisp tissue and folded in a smart little paper bag with ribbons on the handle. Vonnie had told herself that she might give it to Fiona instead of the scarf she had brought from Vancouver, but she knew she would keep it, even though it wasn't cold enough to wear it. David had been true to his word and she had a thick wad of cash in her purse— more, even, than she had expected—and the promise of extra to go home with. She had told him she was a little short this year and he had nodded and asked no questions.

The rain had stopped and she walked on down towards Holyrood Palace and the parliament building. She had never been inside the parliament, so she joined the small queue of tourists and the curious waiting to go through the security scan. It was much nicer inside than out, but Vonnie found the ceiling with its profusion of angled beams too oppressive, like a lowering frown or a heavy sky.

She sat in the coffee shop, savouring a large cappuccino with an extra shot and some home-baked shortbread with the parliament crest stamped into the top. A TV crew had set up outside beside the small square pond. The reporter wore a red coat and her hair kept blowing across her face. She looked very serious, but then everyone who discussed the upcoming vote did. Behind her, a crisp bag skidded across the water like a small paper boat. Vonnie smiled. She knew they'd run out of money towards the end of the build but they should have gone for something that looked like a real reflecting pool, and not what amounted to an oversized fishpond. Especially if the vote was 'yes' and this became a proper parliament and not what Billy Connolly had called a 'wee pretendy' one.

It had been fascinating to see how polarised everyone in the family had been the night before last. Vonnie felt utterly ambivalent about it all. It would make no difference to her because she suspected she would never come back to the UK to live anyway.

She drained her coffee and wandered briefly around the gift shop, which was rather too twee for her taste. It was still dry outside, so she walked towards the Grassmarket where she came across a fossil shop and bought a geode for Jamie with a small hammer with which to crack it open. She felt quite sorry for Jamie. He always seemed out of place. She'd noticed that David seemed to ignore him completely; not deliberately, but almost as if he didn't see him. She hadn't seen them talk once since they had all arrived.

A small Christmas market had been set up in the centre of the street and she made her way over to the stalls. The clouds were clearing in the stiff wind, giving the odd flash of sunlight on the old stone of the buildings. The Grassmarket had been one of her favoured haunts when she started university. She'd danced drunkenly down the road in the wee small hours, arms linked with friends, and she'd lost her virginity just round the corner in Lady Lawson Street in a flat with high ceilings and a Blondie poster on the wall. Her first sexual experience with a boy whose surname she struggled to recall. He'd had a nice arse, though; she remembered that much.

She bought a cup of Glühwein and sipped it as she made her way down King's Stables Road and into Princes Street Gardens. She headed for the station, past the bandstand, where a team of black-shirted roadies was assembling the extra stages that would be needed for the Hogmanay party.

She reached the floral clock by the steps to the bottom of the Mound. It was the oldest one in the world; Vonnie remembered that from school trips. Someone had thrown a Starbucks cup in among the dwarf shrubs that made up its face. A deep booming rumble sounded behind her and she gave a little jump. The one o'clock gun, of course. There was a train back to Fortune at 1.30 p.m., or she could head up to George Street and have a mooch about. She opted for the shops.

In Space NK she tested out some lipsticks, dodging the black-clad assistants and their Pansticked smiles, then had a quick browse through Waterstones, but the queue for the till was too long and she couldn't be bothered waiting to buy the *Even More Dangerous Book for Boys* that she had picked up as an extra for Jamie. It was a shame because it seemed like the kind of book he ought to be reading.

The window of Hamilton & Inches was decked out like a glorious festive bazaar, rich swathes of luminous ruby-coloured silk dotted with shiny baubles: rings with no price tag; broad golden bangles; and the kind of watch that Fiona wore, with a busy face, and a rash of diamonds.

She walked on to Whistles and trailed her hands through the racks of silk and wool, but saw nothing that took her fancy. It was a different matter in Cruise. She hadn't been looking for anything in particular, but the boots jumped out at her. They were Nicole Farhi, soft grey suede and over-the-knee with a small heel and a rounded toe. She told herself she would just try them on, but they fitted so well and she suited them with her long, skinny legs. She could wear them with a skirt or over her jeans, the assistant was quick to point out. And then a woman emerged from the changing room with something tailored and black draped over her arm, and made such a fuss about how good they looked on Vonnie that it was a done deal.

Vonnie asked for them to be wrapped without

the box, and the assistant took her time folding them individually into acid-free tissue as if they were priceless relics being laid away for safe-keeping. Then she slipped them into a sleek black bag and propped them on the countertop.

Vonnie dug her credit card from her purse and handed it over. The shop was busy, but big enough not to look crushed. She chatted with the girl while they waited for the transaction to go through. She would finish work today, said the girl, but would be back in first thing on Boxing Day for the sale. She must have seen Vonnie's expression change, because she laughed and reassured her that the boots would not be reduced. They were new season, winter into spring. Not long in.

The girl glanced down at the machine, stubbornly silent on the desk. 'It takes ages,' she said kindly.

Vonnie flashed a quick smile but could feel the tightening in the muscles at the back of her neck. It should be okay. She couldn't be at her limit on this one, could she?

A few more seconds passed and then the machine gave a shrill, indignant beep and the girl glanced down again. 'Oh,' she said.

'Is it not working?' Vonnie tried not to panic.

The girl pulled the card from the device. 'I just need to call through for authorisation,' she said blithely. She went to move away from the desk.

Vonnie knew that wasn't good. If there was credit available, the card would work. It must have been the earrings she got in London, or the cufflinks. And there were people behind her now, shuffling their feet at the delay.

The girl sensed her hesitation. 'Unless you want

128

to use another card?'

She didn't have another card, at least not one that would work. She calculated quickly in her head. She would have just enough of the cash from David to cover the cost, but it would leave her almost skint. She ought to walk away, to say, 'I'm so sorry, I must have over-indulged,' and given a little nonchalant laugh. She looked at the black bag on the countertop.

'I tell you what, I think I'll pay cash.'

'If you're sure,' said the girl and handed the card back over.

Vonnie tucked it into the furthest reaches of her purse, and counted out the notes: £225 in tens and twenties, four £1 coins and two 50p pieces. She felt sick.

The till drawer shot open and the girl put in the cash, ripped off a receipt and handed her the bag. Vonnie hung it off her shoulder, wished the girl a very merry Christmas and walked out with as big a smile as she could muster.

Her mood darkened on the walk to the train. She hated being short, hated it especially at this time of year. It wasn't as if she had a taste for really high-end designer stuff all the time. She mixed and matched. The jeans she was wearing were as cheap as chips.

She could feel the bag bouncing on her shoulder; a black millstone. She shouldn't have bought them. Why did she always do this? She owed so much already on her cards that it would take her years to pay it back, unless she got some amazing job with a stellar salary, which wasn't likely in her line of work. She glanced at her watch. It was twenty minutes or so until the next train and she didn't fancy hanging around the station, so she ducked back into Jenners and watched the fish in the Crème de la Mer concession as she tried out the various lotions and potions on the back of her hand.

She moved over to the Molton Brown stand. The soaps and shower gels were arranged in neat rows. She loved Molton Brown toiletries. One bottle could last for weeks. And it wasn't as if she'd brought any with her. She'd had to use what was in the bathroom at Fortune House, a generic pine gel that lathered poorly and smelled like floor cleaner. She lifted down a bottle of naran ji. It was on offer, £11 instead of the usual £14. She walked to the till, already fishing for her purse and the two £20 notes that it still held. What the hell. It was Christmas. And as Min always used to say, 'In for a penny, in for a pound.'

*   *   *

Deborah watched the small girl with the misaligned bunches chew distractedly on the leg of the doll she had lifted from the toy box. Like everyone else in the waiting room for the emergency surgery she seemed to have a bad cold, and every so often she removed the doll's limb from her mouth and gave a deep, wet, hacking cough. Deborah pursed her lips. Her girls had learned very early on to cover their mouths when they coughed, and also to stay well away from the box of playthings in the doctor's surgery. The girl's mother, a whey-faced blonde, who looked barely out of her teens, was crouched over in a chair near the door, biting her nails and leafing through an

130

old edition of *Now!* with some minor celebrity on the cover, giggly and knickerless, an emphatic black cross masking her genitals as she slid from the back seat of a shiny car.

Doug had been gone for about five minutes. They had managed to get him an appointment at the emergency surgery just after 1 p.m. and they had waited only fifteen minutes or so until his name was called. They had already decided that he would go in on his own because there would be an exam and the last thing he needed was her bursting into tears, which she felt she might do at any moment. She'd been awake most of the night, lying next to him in the dark, listening to his steady, somnolent breaths, wondering how he could sleep. What if it had spread? What if he needed chemo? Maybe it isn't, maybe it's just a cyst, a swollen gland. But how long had it been there? Did he check himself? She'd always given herself a regular breast exam and had had a rather awkward talk with Elsa about doing the same just last year, but she had never thought to ask Doug if he checked himself regularly. She'd gone on David's computer last night, under the guise of looking for carol concerts, and had read as much as she could. It did seem to be a younger man's disease, but not exclusively. And then there was that young snooker player who had died; such a lovely smile and a pretty, adoring wife and a brand-new baby, and all of it for nought.

She swallowed and studied the clock, which was ringed rather inexpertly with a fat loop of purple tinsel, wanting to be anywhere but here.

The Tannoy crackled suddenly into life and the small girl with the bad cough was summoned. She dropped the doll on the floor and followed her mother through the double doors. Deborah opened her bag and rummaged around for her Christmas list. Just Daisy's present to get and a couple more things for the girls, and the bag of stocking fillers to pick up from the house.

She looked up just as Doug emerged into the hallway. In his right hand he was holding a white card and her heart gave a lurch. It must be something, otherwise why would he get a card? He paused only long enough for her to cross the room and fall into step beside him. She didn't say anything; just looked up at him.

'I've got an appointment at the Western General on the 28th,' he said. He glanced down at the card. 'Mr Swann. He's a consultant.'

'That's good. That's soon. So, is it . . . ?'

They had passed through the doors and Deborah was vaguely aware of the mild blast of wind on her face.

'They'll probably need to do a biopsy and have a proper look.'

'But he could feel it. The swelling?'

'Yup,' said Doug, 'he could feel it. He took some bloods as well.'

'Can they not take you tomorrow?'

'Deborah, it's Christmas Day.'

'Of course it is.'

'It's just four days away,' he said. 'It's pretty quick considering. I thought it might be a couple of weeks before I could get in to see anyone.'

They had reached the car and he unlocked it and they settled into their seats.

'It doesn't mean he's worried about it, does it?' She turned to look at him. 'The fact they're seeing you so quickly?'

'No.' He put his head back against the seat. 'It's private health insurance. He seemed quite okay about the whole thing. The biopsy will tell us if it's cancerous, and if it is, they can do what's called an orchiectomy, which is removal of the testicle. You can be out in a day.'

'So he thinks it is cancerous?' She felt her hands tighten around the seat-belt.

'No,' said Doug patiently. 'He's just giving me all the possibilities.'

'So it still might not be.'

'It still might not be.'

'Okay.' Deborah took a deep breath. 'Okay.'

She faced out the front again. It had started to rain, heavy intermittent drops falling fatly on the windscreen.

'I love you,' she said suddenly.

'I love you too.' Doug started the engine and switched on the wipers. 'Now, let's go and get this Trainspotter Barbie or whatever it is that you want to get Daisy.'

Deborah gave a laugh, a great gulping sob. 'Transformer Barbie.'

'What on earth does she turn into?'

She fastened her seat-belt and wiped her eyes. 'Some kind of rocket, I think. I'm not sure.'

'Half woman, half gadget. Now that's a Christmas present.'

His hands were on the wheel, but the handbrake was still on and he didn't seem able to move. She reached over and lifted his hands off and took them in hers, gripping tightly. He was still smiling at his own joke but his palms were as warm and clammy with nerves as they had been on the night they had met.

*   *   *

Hanna kept her foot pressed on to the pedal at the base of the large silver bin and pulled as hard as she could at the liner. It shifted towards her slowly, stuffed full as it was and wedged almost solidly into the sides. She twisted the handles tighter and kept heaving until the bag eased out. She tied the handles deftly and propped it against the kitchen door, then took out a fresh black liner, shook it open and folded it in and over the sides. Caroline didn't expect her to do this, but she had finished everywhere else and it was a good half-hour until she would have to leave for the train.

She'd hardly seen Marek since they'd got there. Caroline's two granddaughters had adopted him, although in the last hour they seemed to have grown tired of playing families and he was now out in the garden with Jamie, the older boy, who was patiently kicking a football to him. Hanna glanced out of the window. Marek's cheeks were flushed with exertion, and his nose was runny, but he was having such a nice time. Jamie seemed a gentle soul. Caroline was at the edge of the lawn, occasionally clapping her hands together when Marek got anywhere near the makeshift goal: two empty flower pots upended on the grass. Hanna watched her. It was lovely Caroline was so nice to Marek, so interested in him, but sometimes it was a little too much. She'd already seen the present under the tree in the hall with his name on the elaborate tag, a huge box that would be difficult to carry home and would dwarf the other presents she

134

had bought for him herself.

And he had a grandmother who missed him terribly, and kept his picture by the bed in a small gilt frame so she could kiss it every night before sleep. Mamo would be here at Easter and would be staying for a whole week, something that delighted Hanna, but Dyta, not so much. Dyta had rolled her eyes when Mamo had called to say she had booked her flights. 'You'll need to find your rosary and give up smoking,' Dyta had said. 'And no men.' Although the last bit only applied to her. She had been seeing the same guy for two weeks now, a record for her. Hanna tried not to hear them in the next-door room, the soft mumbled groans of pleasure. She hadn't thought she would miss sex that much, but she did. Sometimes, in the shower, she would look down at her body, still so firm and lovely, and have a little cry that it was unknown and untouched by anyone but her.

Despite Dyta's fuss, Hanna knew she was secretly pleased that Mamo was coming. They had always had a tempestuous relationship, lots of rows and anger and then huge hugs and remonstrations of love to make up. Hanna, on the other hand, was the good girl, the girl who had made only one huge mistake, but it had brought Marek, so, in Mamo's eyes, not so much of a mistake after all.

She crossed over to the sink and rinsed her hands under the taps. She couldn't hear the tumble drier, so the towels must be finished and ready to be folded and hung back on the bathroom rails.

The utility room was halfway down the short corridor to the back door. Hanna lifted the black bag to carry it out to the wheelie bin, but as she passed the utility room door she saw a figure

135

standing by the washer. It was Caroline's mother-in-law. The dressing gown she had been wearing earlier was gone and she was in just a slip, but the straps hadn't been fixed over her shoulders, so it hung low around her waist, exposing her breasts and belly. Hanna felt a cold little slap of shock. She had never seen an old woman's body before, the breasts little more than pendulous flaps of skin, all sense of weight and roundness, all sense of sexuality gone. Hanna's free hand went involuntarily to her mouth; she laid down the bin bag.

Min stared at her. She looked irritated. 'I can't find my coat,' she said.

Hanna found herself nodding. She stepped into the utility room.

'I can't find my coat,' repeated Min. 'Who are you?'

'Hanna. I . . . I help Caroline.' She moved towards the older woman, looking around for something to cover her with. What if the children came in? There was a pile of freshly folded clothes on a chair by the window and Hanna pulled a sweatshirt from the top. It looked like it might be Jamie's, black with a dragon curving red across the middle. She hung it around Min's shoulders and guided her to the seat, pushing the clothes to the floor with her knee. 'You have a sit down and I'll get Caroline.'

'I can't find my fucking coat!' said Min belligerently.

'Caroline will know where it is,' said Hanna soothingly. 'I'll go get her.' She turned and ran for the hall, panic buzzing in her chest. There had been an old woman in their apartment block in

136

Lodz and Dyta had found her going to the toilet on the stair, mumbling to herself and crying as she did so. They had giggled over it that night and Mamo had grown fiercely angry and told them to feel pity and feel shame.

Caroline was still in the garden, standing now in the makeshift goal. Hanna called out to her. She was breathless and smiling when she reached her. 'Is it time for you to go?'

Hanna shook her head. 'It's your mother-in-law.'

Caroline's face changed in an instant. 'Is she okay? What?'

'She's all right,' said Hanna, 'but I think she's a little . . .' She struggled for the right word. 'A little upset. She's looking for her coat but she's not got dressed properly.' She pointed towards the utility room. 'She's in here. I found a top for her. She's looking for her coat and I didn't know where it was.'

Caroline was already past her and running. Hanna followed and saw her stop at the utility room door.

'Min? Oh, Min.'

Min was still on the seat and Caroline bent before her.

'I can't find my coat,' said Min. She was twisting her fingers agitatedly and Caroline reached for her hands and held them steady. 'It's my good coat. I can't find it.'

'Your coat is in the hall,' said Caroline firmly. 'We'll go and get it but first we'll get dressed. Okay?' She lifted the sweatshirt from around Min's shoulders and started shrugging it on to her arms.

'What's it doing in the hall?' said Min.

'It's on a peg, Min. It's always on the peg in the hall.'

'A peg,' said Min.

Caroline raised the old woman to her feet and leaned forward to lift up the straps of her slip and zip the sweatshirt closed. It was too big on her diminished frame, the staring red dragon so incongruous against her white, veined skin.

Min looked up and saw Hanna at the door. She pointed at her. 'She took my coat!'

Caroline shook her head. 'No, Min, no one took your coat. It's in the hall. We'll go and get it now. Okay?'

Min was still pointing. 'She took my coat! Thieving bitch. Thieving fucking bitch.'

Hanna saw the tears well in Caroline's eyes.

'I'm sorry,' she said, guiding Min to the door. 'She doesn't mean it. I'm so sorry.'

Hanna found herself nodding, almost frantically. 'Will I call someone?'

Caroline shook her head. 'I'll just get her back to her room. We'll be fine, won't we, Min? We'll be fine. We'll get your coat.' She stretched out a hand as she passed and gripped Hanna's arm. 'I'm so sorry,' she mouthed again. 'I'm so, so sorry.'

*   *   *

Caroline settled Min on to the couch in her little living room. She slumped back against the cushions and closed her eyes. She was still wearing her coat. Caroline had reached for it as they had crossed the hall and Min had clutched it like a comfort blanket, wrapping herself tightly in its thick woollen folds. She seemed to relax when she had it on and all the fight had gone out of her. Caroline bent down and felt her forehead. She was cool and a little clammy despite her several layers. She muttered at the touch.

Caroline went into the bedroom and lifted the comforter from the bed's end, trying not to notice the piles of clothes on the floor and the faint stale smell of urine and old cologne. She had never asked Hanna to clean in here, and did it herself once a week. But with everyone here and the party to plan, she had not got round to it this week.

The dogs had been asleep in their beds but had wakened when they had come in. Hector had settled himself at Min's feet, but Riley was running around in circles. He grabbed hold of the end of the comforter as Caroline carried it back through and worried it.

'Off!' She gave the blanket a vigorous shake and he whirled round with it, like a small ornament, growling fiercely. He was still attached to it when she laid it around Min, pulling it up only as far as her waist in case she overheated. She had fallen asleep, her mouth hanging open.

Caroline sat down on the arm of the chair opposite. The room was tiny. It had been an outhouse previously, and the original plans for the granny flat had included a bed-sitting room, but Min was adamant she wanted two distinct spaces, mostly because of her beloved books, hundreds of them squeezed into the bookcases that lined three of the four walls. A lifetime of literature and learning. She had been a classics teacher, one of the few working mothers of her generation, and a good one, Caroline imagined, if a little strict. David said she had a belt that she dipped in whisky

139

to give it extra sting.

The only gaps in the bookcases were filled by photographs. Min with David as a small boy. Min with her beloved Rena. And with David's father. Caroline remembered a jolly man, thin and wiry, with a whiskery kiss and a penchant for single malt and unfiltered cigarettes—which was probably what did for him well before his time.

Caroline looked at the woman in the silver frames. She was attractive with a glorious head of auburn hair and a broad, confident smile. She had been skip for the Scottish women's curling team and had lobbied, unsuccessfully, to be allowed to take part in the first world curling championships in 1959. She had always said that the Canadian who won hadn't been a patch on her girls. Actually, she said he'd been a useless bloody arse.

Most of the photographs were of Min with Rena. They were old friends and Min had moved in with her a year or so after David's father had passed away when she had decided Fortune House was too big for her to manage alone. They had taught together at a school in Glasgow, Rena's birthplace. Min had introduced Rena to curling, and the two of them made a formidable pair in the Eastern League. She was older than Min, already white-haired when Caroline met her, and great fun. She had been such a support when Euan was killed, strong and capable when no one else had the heart for it. She did what needed to be done. Made sure food was available, even though no one was eating, kept visitors at bay, and the girls with a semblance of routine, taking them out for walks and swimming. She had done all the laundry too, but Caroline had noticed, even in her blackest grief, that Rena left the sheets on Euan's bed, didn't even straighten and smooth them, so they were just as they had been on the morning he had slipped from them and out of their lives.

Caroline bent to look closer at one of the prints. Min and Rena were sitting on a garden seat, both with one hand raised to shield their eyes from the sun. But their other hands were lying on the wooden slats and close enough to be touching. It wasn't until years after Min had moved to be with Rena that Caroline had begun to wonder if they had been more than friends. They had always been affectionate with each other, a kiss on the cheek at every parting and hello, arms linked when they walked. There was nothing more specific Caroline could point to, and David certainly seemed not to notice, but she had just got a sense that their relationship had changed; shifted to another level. Or maybe it was noticing that her relationship was changing that made her think it.

Min had never said anything, and when Caroline had once hinted at it to David, he had looked at her as if she were mad, burst out laughing and told her not to say anything to Min because she might quite like to be a lesbian and it would give her ideas. Caroline knew he must have thought about it, though, when Rena died from stomach cancer and Min was utterly bereft, more so, Caroline remembered, than when she had lost David's father.

Caroline looked back at the supine figure on the couch and felt the rush of anxiety. She should probably call the doctor again, but Min would be so cross, and last time she had taken a turn she had been fine after a long sleep, with little recollection

141

of what she had done or said. Was it just age? Little flashes of memory loss? Or was it small strokes, as the GP had wondered? She would have to apologise profusely to Hanna, who would understand—she was sure of that. Fiona could run Hanna and Marek into town to catch the train because she would have to stay here in case Min had a relapse. She felt a prickle of indignation. She had so much to do and David had just assumed he could take off for hours.

She stood up and picked up Min's phone. He should know what had just happened. It rang six times and then went to voicemail, as she had expected it would. She was waiting for the long high beep that would give her the signal to start talking when Riley hopped down from the couch. She felt him at her feet, then the scrabble of small legs on her ankle. She tried to shake him off but his claws dug deep into her trousers. She hated when he did this. He invariably left a small stain, and was still moving when dislodged.

She heard the tone and started to talk and as she did so she caught sight of herself in the mirror above the fireplace, pale, harassed and shaking slightly with the rhythmic motion of a small humping dog, Min supine on the couch behind her. She felt the hysterical laugh bubble up instinctively inside her. It was so absurd. Christmas Eve. I have a dog masturbating on my leg, a mother-in-law who doesn't know which end is up, a house full of offspring, and a husband who has gone awol. She switched off the phone before she had even started to speak. She waited until the giggles had subsided, and Riley had dislodged himself, to phone the surgery.

'Do you want a pink puffle or a purple one?'

'Pink!' Daisy clapped her hands excitedly and peered over Jamie's shoulder. He manoeuvred the mouse and the small circular creature on the screen turned bright pink.

'What do you want to call it?'

'Pooey!' Daisy giggled.

'You can't do rude words,' said Jamie. 'You get reported.'

'Constipation!' said Daisy.

'Daisy.'

Daisy thought for a moment. 'Pig,' she said.

'Pig?' Jamie turned round to look at her. 'You sure? Pig the pink puffle?'

Daisy nodded. 'Mmm. Pig.'

'Okay,' said Jamie. He typed in Daisy's chosen name. 'Pig.'

Daisy squeezed in beside him. 'Can I make another one?'

'No,' said Jamie. 'You've been on for ages. My shot now.'

'Aw,' wailed Daisy.

'Remember Mum said no fuss or neither of us would get to use it. It's Gran's computer.'

Daisy emitted a small snort.

'Why don't you go and wrap my Christmas present,' said Jamie.

Daisy's face lit up and she jumped off the seat. 'I wrapped it already. There's sheep on the paper.'

'Sheep?' said Jamie.

'Christmas sheep,' said Daisy. 'But it's a surprise.' She wandered over to the door, turning

143

just as she got to it. 'Do you like baseball caps with fire on them?'

Jamie tried not to laugh. So that was what he was getting. For a second he thought of saying 'no', but she would have panicked and it would have been mean. 'Yeah, they're pretty cool,' he said, and basked in her delighted grin.

The computer that Caroline said they were allowed to use was ancient; big and solid-looking. It dominated the desk in the room Caroline called the den. Compared to his own computer at home, this one felt like the size of a washing machine. Jamie knew David had a laptop in his study, but he would have been terrified to use it even if David had said he could—which Jamie was pretty sure he wouldn't.

At least the connection was quick. He had heard Caroline tell Vonnie that they had 'broad band'. She had said it like two separate words, the way old people sometimes say motor car.

He logged out of Club Penguin and went to YouTube where he idled away fifteen minutes watching the videos. He liked the river-dancing chimps best. Daisy had got upset when he showed it to her, saying it was cruel to make monkeys dance like that and she hadn't believed him when he said it was just made up and if you looked closely you could see their legs looked different from their bodies; and anyway no one could train chimps to dance like that.

Caroline was shouting from the kitchen that lunch was ready. He was famished, which was probably from all that running about with the cleaner's little boy. He was quite an okay kid, but it had got a little wearing after a while, especially when Caroline had disappeared off. Marek had said he was hungry and Jamie had taken him into the kitchen and given him juice and a KitKat which he had got all over his face and hands. Jamie hadn't been sure what to do so he had given him a tea towel to wipe it off but that just seemed to spread it around even more. He had been quite relieved when his mum had come to say she was running Marek and Hanna back into Fortune to get the train.

He went to switch off the computer then paused. He hadn't intended checking his email, but he could do it quickly now. If there was anything bad he didn't have to look at it. There had only ever been one from them; they always texted instead.

He logged quickly into Hotmail, his breath quickening when he saw the little gold envelope that meant you had mail. His eyes slid quickly down the list, two junk and one from his friend, Edmund, just a what's up. The pinching knot in his stomach dissolved. Just Edmund. Nothing else there. He cleared the screen and stood up, feeling suddenly lighter. Maybe later he could switch on his phone and there would be nothing there, either. Maybe nothing would happen this holiday. Maybe they had forgotten about him. Maybe it was over.

*   *   *

'Anytime this century, pal.' Fiona edged the hire car right to the bumper of the Nissan Micra that was a good twenty yards behind the queue of traffic crawling towards the car park exit at a snail's pace. 'Arse!'

145

Allan stretched across and laid his hand on her knee. 'Fun with the family?' he said.

'It's not that,' said Fiona. 'It's this prick. Come on, arsehole. Move it!' She shook her head exaggeratedly, hoping the driver was looking in his rear-view mirror. She had detoured through the town, and the boot was filled with food shopping from Waitrose. If she took any longer, the vine leaves would have gone limp and Caroline would have resorted to cheese and pineapple on a stick for tonight's Christmas Eve nibbles.

'And a merry Christmas to you,' said Allan with a smirk. 'You've got your Scottish accent back. You're rolling your "r"s.'

He lifted his hand away and stretched. He had emerged from Arrivals looking surprisingly unruffled while everyone else in the terminal building was milling around like ants whose nest has been disturbed. He had given her a vigorous and wet kiss on the mouth and had said his customary 'darling', which sounded more perfunctory than heartfelt. Alongside his case he was carrying a large glossy Ronit Zilkha bag, which probably meant he had bought her Christmas present on the way to the airport, although if it was the new silk-collared evening coat she might forgive him the afterthought.

'And how is everybody?'

'Fine.' Fiona kept the car as close as possible to the Micra. 'I've hardly seen Daisy. You know what she's like when she gets with her cousins. Apparently she said the funniest thing the other day. Everyone was down at breakfast and out she comes with, "Elvis died from constipation." I swear! From constipation! Debs told me. And

Jamie's . . . just Jamie. And Ben's been a wee charmer. Mum seems a little on edge, although Min's been acting up, so that might be it. You should probably know that. She's had a couple of funny turns. They had to get the doctor in to her today. Mum's put us in my old room, but there's no en-suite, I'm afraid. Dad's fine, actually he's a bit tetchy about the job thing, so best not to bring it up unless he does. Debs is as uptight as ever and Vonnie's okay. She's always okay. So, yeah, fine really. The usual.'

There was no comeback from the passenger seat. Fiona glanced across as she pulled the car to a stop at the exit barrier. Allan was already asleep, his head lolling against the tightened seat-belt. She shoved her ticket into the machine and overtook the Micra in the bus lane with an angry rev of the engine.

Allan didn't wake until they rumbled over the cattle grid at the foot of the drive. The house was ablaze with lights, almost every window a brilliant yellow square. None of the curtains appeared to be shut. Fiona felt a little of the tension go out of her neck and a flutter of excitement. She used to love Christmas Eve, more so even than Christmas Day which was never quite what you expected. This was the night when anything was possible: the perfect present, a thick fall of snow, sweets and crisps and lemonade with no one to say stop, enough. And the house did look lovely. She could see the fairy lights on the tree through the hall window, sharp and white.

Fiona parked beside Deborah's people carrier and carried the shopping round to the back door. She could hear music. It sounded like Tom Jones.

Allan went in in front of her and was rewarded by a whoop from Deborah and an unsteady hug. They pushed into the kitchen which was full of children. Daisy threw herself at her dad, and Jamie turned and grinned at him, too old for an embrace. Allan reached down and rubbed his head and he leaned into it like a petted dog. Ben appeared from below the table, holding on to a spike of breadstick and beamed as Allan lifted him into his arms.

'Hey, little chap,' said Allan. 'Kiss for Dad.'

Ben pressed his face into Allan's, leaving a smear of wet crumbs.

'I thought we'd lost you!' Caroline's cheeks were red, and her eyes the frantic side of sparkling. 'I'm afraid we've opened the fizz already and I just started making some nibbles because everyone was getting peckish.'

Fiona noticed the little tray of cocktail sausages and the squares of cheese, neatly cubed.

Deborah took the shopping from her and lugged it on to the table and Vonnie pressed a glass of champagne into her hands. The door opened. Allan's head turned, then swivelled. Fiona saw his expression change.

'Hello!' He sounded like a bad Saturday night comedian.

'Hi, Uncle Allan,' said Elsa, with a sweet pink smile.

CHAPTER SEVEN

Vonnie grabbed the small gilt poker from the fireplace set and raised it high above her, pointing

148

towards the ceiling.

'I know! I know!' Deborah put her glass down on the floor. 'Radiohead!'

'Radiohead?' Vonnie burst out laughing. 'It's a film, you numpty!'

Deborah laughed and picked up her wine. She seemed to have drunk rather a lot, David thought, which was not like her. She was usually the first to put her hand over the glass when you were refilling. But not tonight. In fact her lips were stained from all the burgundy she had downed. Although it was very good burgundy, rich and rounded with a long, honeyed aftertaste. Allan had brought it and handed it over with his usual flourish. It was a new one he was trying out in the restaurant, he had said. A small collective near Vidauban. He wanted David's opinion.

David didn't think for a minute that Allan would choose a vintage for the restaurant based on his say-so, but he appreciated the gesture. He'd always quite enjoyed Allan's company; he was a witty man and David valued wit. And he was an assured conversationalist, if one of these people who used your name too much probably because a self-improvement manual had told them it was a good idea. Caroline, however, had always been ambivalent about him. She had a pretty sharp bullshit detector, and it often went off where Allan was concerned. She didn't like the way he flirted, said he'd done it even with her and it wasn't appropriate.

David had told her she was being daft, that it was just an affectation. But he had to agree that Allan was someone who sought and received attention. You could be in a room with Doug and be at peace, hardly know he was there. You were always aware of Allan.

He was a good match for Fiona, however, certainly more the type David had thought she would end up with than Jamie's dad, such a caricature of an ad man, even down to the red braces and loud, braying laugh.

David glanced across at Min. She had been placed in the high-backed chair to the left of the fire and padded into place with cushions, but she was listing ever so slightly to the left. Someone must have dressed her because she was in a blouse too fussy for old fingers and a string of black jet beads that had caught in the point of her collar. David had been taken aback at how diminished she looked when he got home.

He had initially ignored the call from Caroline, expecting it would be another stream of instructions. Pick this up. Collect that. He called her back while he was in the New Town and spoke to her above the noise of the street: footfalls and voices, the clang of scaffolding from building work, and the intermittent swoosh of passing cars on wet cobbles. Caroline launched into an overlong explanation of what had happened, which boiled down to the fact that Min had stripped off and sworn at the cleaner.

David had driven home immediately, stopping only to pick up the turkey, a bird so big one of the butcher's staff had to help him out to the car with it.

The doctor was just leaving as he got back, but he took the time to sit down again and go over with David what he had already said to Caroline. He was a young man and very earnest, with nails bitten

150

down to the quick and suit trousers a little too big around the waist. It was all rather non-committal: keep an eye on her over the holidays, if the episodes become more frequent or you are still concerned, there are more diagnostic efforts that can be made. No one actually used the word 'dementia', although David wasn't convinced that that was what it was. She was eighty-eight, didn't it make sense for her to be susceptible to these little shutdowns? Brief moments when the signal got lost. God knows, he'd noticed the small spasms of memory loss in himself, too. He could get his Dimblebys mixed up, and more than once within the last few months he'd found himself forgetting key dates in Scotland's political journey, dates that ought to be seared into his mind.

David had poured Min a Lagavulin, but it sat untouched by her elbow, and while she looked like she was taking everything in, her eyes were fixed on some point in the far distance. She didn't even seem to notice Katie and Daisy, darting back and forth to the bowl of crisps on the table, like sparrows at a bird table.

Vonnie was still frantically mugging in front of the fireplace. David decided to put her out of her misery.

'*Return of the King*,' he said flatly. He'd figured it out almost immediately when she had gone out of the room, come in again and placed an imaginary crown on her head. Much more fun, however, to watch her acting like a loon.

'Finally.' Vonnie threw her hands into the air. 'Can I sit down now?'

'Your turn, Dad.' Deborah swivelled in her seat. 'Vonnie, you need to give one to Dad.'

Vonnie padded across the carpet and bent close to his ear. 'Don't listen!' she shouted back at the others.

David leaned forward.

'It's a song,' she whispered, stifling a laugh. Her breath was warm with alcohol.

'Uh-huh.' David nodded.

She paused for a moment. ' "Drop Kick Me Jesus Through the Goalposts of Life".'

'What?'

' "Drop Kick Me Jesus Through the Goalposts of Life".'

David burst out laughing. 'You just made that up.'

'No, really.' Vonnie returned to her seat. 'It is a song.'

'There is no way,' said David.

'Come on, Dad!' said Deborah.

'Yeah, come on,' said Fiona. 'We've all done one, it's your turn.'

David raised himself out of his chair, shaking his head. How on earth?

He walked to the front of the fireplace and stood for a moment before indicating that it was a song he was about to do. He put his hands together as if in prayer then dropped an imaginary ball on to his foot and gave it a high kick.

' "Like a Virgin"!' shouted Elsa from the depths of the big sofa.

Vonnie burst out laughing.

David repeated the gestures, waving his arms high and perpendicular to indicate goalposts.

' "The Hokey Cokey"!' cried Katie.

It was David's turn to laugh.

'What's with the kicking?' said Deborah. 'It

must be a football song.'

He waved frantically at her to indicate she was on the right track.

'Football song,' she said. 'God, anyone know any football songs?'

' "You'll Never Walk Alone"?' ventured Jamie.

David shook his head. He bunched his shoulders and put his hands to his head, trying to indicate padding and a helmet.

'Not football. Something to do with chimps?' said Doug. 'Chimps. No, hang on, rugby. "Swing Low, Sweet Chariot"?'

David shook his head again, and clasped his hands together, looking upwards piously.

'A religious rugby song?' said Doug.

Vonnie was in hysterics.

'Somebody, please,' said David. 'I'm dying here.'

'I give up,' said Deborah.

'Me, too,' said Allan. 'Not a clue.'

David dropped his hands to his side. ' "Drop Kick Me Jesus Through the Goalposts of Life".'

'What?' Deborah looked across at Vonnie. 'That's not a song!'

Vonnie was still laughing. 'It is. It's a country and western number.'

'How on earth were we meant to get that?' said Fiona. 'How are we supposed to know some obscure Canadian ditty?'

'It's not Canadian.' Vonnie laughed.

'It's not nice to kick,' added Daisy piously. 'Jesus wouldn't kick.'

David picked up his wine glass and patted her on the head as he passed. 'You're right, Daisy. It's not nice to kick and it's not right to force Grampa to make a complete fool of himself. I'm going to

153

find your gran. She's managed to dodge out of this.'

Caroline was in the kitchen with her hands sunk deep in a bowl of pastry mix. Handel's *Messiah* was playing on the radio and something hot and sweet was spitting bubbles on the hob. A half-full glass of wine sat by her elbow, with the mark of her lips on the edge.

'Hey.' David jerked his thumb towards the door. 'You need to get through there. Charades was your idea and I've just humiliated myself in front of everybody. It's your turn. Granny.'

Caroline looked up with a quick, flat smile. 'I'll just be a sec. I need to get the pastry into the fridge and reduce this sauce and then I'll be done.'

David looked at the table, almost every inch of it covered with food of some sort: mince pies, newly sugared; a tower of what looked like filo parcels; a deep dish of sausages smothered in some type of glaze; a bowl of warm milk with a clove-studded onion bobbing in its middle; and a large plate of misshapen Christmas tree biscuits that the children must have made.

'Do you think there's enough?'

'What?' Caroline looked up again with a faintly worried expression. 'Do you think I under-estimated?'

'It was a joke,' said David. He felt the familiar press of disappointment. Caroline's head was down again, and he suddenly remembered her hair as it had been: dark and burnished. Her smile, wry and teasing. That Caroline would have hurled something at him in fun for his cheek and not minded where it fell or what kind of mess it might make. That Caroline wouldn't even have been in the kitchen at all, but through in the drawing room with her stockinged feet on the table and a laugh in her throat.

'Sounds like fun in there.' She didn't look up again, her hands feverishly working the dough. She was always doing something, always busy, as she had been ever since Euan died. At first, it was the girls that kept her going; she spun through the first few years in a rush of ballet lessons and piano and hockey practice and the school run, and then when they started getting a little more independent, volunteering and her painting. It had always been her thing, art. She had thought of going to art college instead of university, but had been talked out of it by her parents. She was good at landscapes, and the house was covered with them, but David found her portraits a little too formulaic. She could spend the whole week now at a class or her art club evenings. And she had the party, which she seemed to need, as if the thought of stopping even for a moment was so terrible she couldn't contemplate it, because then she would have nothing to do but think and be still and remember.

He knew it wasn't special occasions that hurt the most. It was the unexpected. A boy in the street the very double of him; an odour, resin from a violin case, the smell of hot sun on hair. The memory of the weight of him, a small boy, asleep in your arms. The dreams in which he was always alive; grown sometimes, fine and strong, but always a vague figure, never fully there.

'At least we won't be up until 2 a.m. wrapping presents for stockings,' said Caroline, glancing up again. 'Remember that?' She smiled.

155

David nodded. He had moved over towards the fridge to find another bottle of wine but reached out, almost without thinking and put his hand on her shoulder. He sensed the little jerk of surprise at his unexpected touch before she laid her head briefly against it. Her cheek was warm. It was so familiar to him, the feel of her skin. So long since he had touched her. She moved her head away slowly and he lifted his hand, but he stayed close to her, their arms touching. He could smell her scent, even above the cooking. Warm wool and something fragrant but unmistakably Caroline. Her hair had fallen over her eyes, so he could not see them. He reached up again and lifted the strands away, tucking them behind her ear. He saw her mouth tighten, and was suddenly embarrassed.

'Well, you look like you've got it all under control.' He moved behind her to the fridge, opened it, and pulled out a new bottle of white wine. It was blessedly cool in his hands. 'So you'll be through shortly?'

She nodded. She had stopped stirring and was looking at him again, her eyes wide and bright. She offered a little smile. 'In a sec. Promise.'

The game was over when he returned to the drawing room and Katie and Daisy were lined up on the couch with Doug in between and about to read 'The Night Before Christmas'.

David settled back into his chair and listened. Vonnie had disappeared, as had Elsa and Jamie; gone to the garden to look for owls, Deborah had said, and Fiona and Allan were settled on the small couch like mannequins in a window display, glossy and still. Min had fallen asleep, her head awkwardly settled against the wing of the chair.

156

Doug cleared his throat. 'Right, here we go. "'Twas the night before Christmas, when all through the house not a creature was stirring, not even a mouse—"'

'We had a mouse,' said Daisy.

'Really?' said Doug.

Daisy nodded. 'Birgit hit it with the end of the hoover.'

'Daisy.' Fiona raised her finger to her lips.

'"The stockings were hung by the chimney with care",' continued Doug. '"In hopes that St Nicholas soon would be there. The children were nestled all snug in their beds, while visions of sugar-plums danced in their heads. And Mama in her 'kerchief and I in my cap, had—"'

'What's a kerchief?' asked Daisy.

'Daisy,' said Fiona again.

'It's a hat as well,' said Doug patiently. 'Kind of like a cap.'

Daisy looked up at him. 'Does Aunt Deborah wear a kerchief?'

Doug shook his head, trying not to smile. 'No.'

Daisy pointed to the picture before her. 'Is that all she wears? Just a hat?'

'Daisy. Shoosh!' said Fiona. 'Listen to the story.'

Doug swallowed a laugh. 'No. Well, maybe. I don't know.'

Daisy sat back. 'Some people don't like to wear pyjamas,' she said.

David saw Fiona lean forward.

'Daddy doesn't, do you, Daddy?' Daisy looked across at Allan and grinned at him. 'Daddy likes to sleep with nothing on at all.'

*　　　*　　　*

157

The summerhouse smelled, as it always had, of weather-worn wood and creosote and mouldy canvas from the old deckchairs propped in the corner. Vonnie perched herself on the far edge of the wooden bench and laid the bottle of wine at her feet, separating out the three paper cups she had lifted from the kitchen table. There was just enough light from the moon and the back door for her to see. Caroline still kept some of her gardening equipment in here, even though she had little use of it now with Charlie and Boyd. There were some coir pots, an old waxed cotton and leather kneeler and two pairs of stout gloves. The watering can she remembered, an old green metal affair that always seemed to have spiders nesting in it, had been replaced with a bright red plastic one that looked as though it had never been used.

She poured a half-measure of wine into each of the cups and handed them over. Elsa, who had settled herself on the other side of the bench, and was rubbing her hands together to try to keep warm, took hers quickly, but Jamie hesitated.

'Go on,' said Vonnie. 'If you were French you'd have been drinking since you were three. Your mum won't mind. It's just a splash.'

Jamie gave a nervous smile and took the cup, but he didn't drink any.

'Seriously,' said Vonnie. 'Your mum used to have a sly drink in here when she was a teenager. Maybe not exactly your age but not much older.'

'Really?'

'God, yeah. She'd get half-bottles of vodka and keep them . . .' Vonnie looked round. 'It's not here any more, but there used to be an old plant pot

158

that had a crack down the side so it didn't get used. She kept it in there.'

Jamie took a sip of his wine.

'Did my mum do anything like that?' asked Elsa.

Vonnie shook her head. 'No, not that I can remember.'

'Figures,' said Elsa.

'What else did my mum do?' Jamie leaned back against the wall.

'She was pretty bad actually. Especially when we had people over. We had these cousins, we only ever saw them once a year and they were foul, really foul kids. Anyway, she put laxative in their blackcurrant juice. She found it in the bathroom cabinet. Cascara Evacuant. They'd all had diarrhoea on the way home. Your gran got a phone call to say it must have been her cooking. To this day she thinks she gave them food poisoning.'

'Are you sure my mum didn't do anything?' Elsa held out her paper cup for more wine. 'Smoking? Staying out late?'

'Sorry,' said Vonnie.

Elsa gave a little snort.

'What was Euan like?' Jamie's question came out of the blue and Vonnie saw Elsa glance across at him.

'It's okay,' she said. 'I don't mind. I was just five when he died, so I don't really remember him all that well. He was fun, though. I think.' She gave a flat little laugh. 'Do you know? This is awful. He had been in the loo just before he left to go off, the day it happened, and there was a smell. That's what I remember. How bad is that? My last memory of my brother was that he made a smell in the loo.'

They were quiet, trying to see her face in the near dark. She could tell Jamie was worried he shouldn't have asked. But she really didn't mind. Euan was such a vague figure in her life. Her grief was for her parents, what it had done to them.

'Was it a car?' asked Elsa.

Vonnie shook her head. 'A lorry. An animal feed lorry. He was out on his bike, coming back from a friend's. He was late so he was rushing, and it was on a corner. We were all waiting for him. He was late for lunch.'

'Was it near the house?' asked Jamie.

'No,' said Vonnie. 'He was about two miles away. There was a woman who stopped her car. She was just behind the lorry, I think, and she got to him first. And our GP lived not too far and he got there, too, but he was dead already, before the ambulance even came. It was the GP's wife who phoned my parents, so they wouldn't hear from the police. Actually I'm talking like I was there, but it's just what I've been told.'

She felt cold suddenly, and pulled her sweater down over her fingers. She might not remember much but she did remember the day—hot and sticky—and the noise from the house when the phone call came.

Jamie opened his mouth as if he were about to ask another question, but Fiona was already calling from the back door. Vonnie saw the look of panic on Jamie's face. She reached over and took the paper cup from him.

'Stuff some Twiglets in your mouth when you go into the kitchen,' she said. 'The smell masks everything. She'll never know.'

160

The presents spilled out into the hallway from under the tree in a spread of bright paper. Fiona's knees were hurting from kneeling on the hardwood, so she sat up on the bottom step and propped Jamie's stocking alongside her. He'd had it since he was four and the felt was pilled and faded; the button wheels long since snagged from the appliqué train stitched on to the front. She wouldn't have dreamed of replacing it, though, because every year it came out of the Christmas box, she saw, in her mind, her lovely boy: a small, excited face, dark eyes lit with anticipation. She stifled another yawn. Five more minutes and she'd check again. Allan had told her just to leave the stocking propped outside Jamie's door, but that didn't seem fair. Every year she laid it on the end of his bed when he was asleep and this year should be no different.

She looked back at the tree. Caroline had strung it with all the old baubles they had made as children and the freaky little fairy made out of a small plastic doll to precise *Blue Peter* instructions. It had been Deborah's idea to make the fairy, although she had been unsettled by the doll's eyes, and Fiona had told her that it was possessed.

Allan's present to her was at the back against the wall, still in the same bag, but he had stuck a bow to the side of it and even a tag. She'd already been through them all and noticed that there were plenty for Vonnie. But then there always were. She had at least four from Caroline and David, all of them interesting shapes, compared to Fiona's one small rectangular parcel, which was clearly a book,

161

and a paperback at that. She had felt the familiar pinch of envy, wondered why they didn't notice how unfair it was.

Of course, it had always been that way with Vonnie. Born to be indulged. Born with her hand out.

She glanced round at the grandfather clock. It was ten past midnight.

'Merry Christmas to me,' she said.

*   *   *

Katie woke. It was still dark; the really thick kind of dark that makes you feel like someone had put a sack over your head. She stretched out her leg and sensed the weight just below where her feet had been; heard the crinkle of paper, felt the flare of excitement in her tummy. They'd been in at last. It had taken ages for Daisy to get to sleep; even Dad had come in to be cross, after Mum and Aunt Fiona. Dad had eventually given them a clock with very bright green numbers and said there had to be a six showing before they could get up, but Daisy had seen loads of sixes because she didn't understand about big hands and little hands properly yet.

Katie knew there wasn't a Santa. She'd known for ages, mostly because Elsa had told her but also because of two years ago when Mum, putting her to bed, suddenly said, 'Can you hear Santa? I think that's the sleigh.' But after Mum had gone, Katie had got up to look out of the window and had seen Dad down by the wheelie bins, shivering a bit and shaking some bells, and then she heard Mum at the front door telling him to come in or he'd catch

162

his death. Dad wouldn't have minded the cold, though, because he liked pretending to be Santa. Last year he'd put big welly footprints in the hall, stretching all the way from the front door to the tree, but Mum had got a bit cross, Elsa had confided, because he'd used icing sugar instead of flour, and the floor was all sticky for days.

Katie sat up slowly and stared at the end of the bed. She could just make out the bulk of her Santa sack, the one she'd made at the garden centre with sparkly glue spelling out her name. Grampa had offered her one of his old hiking socks just as they were going up to bed. He said that's what her mum had used when she was Katie's age, but Katie thought it was kind of gross, having your presents where an old person's foot had been. She'd been nice about it, though, and had just said, 'No thank you, Grampa,' instead. She leaned down and felt the oddly shaped packages at the top of the sack, and the surge of pleasure in her tummy again. She lay back down and curled the edge of the sheet tightly around her neck. It would take ages to get back to sleep now. She hoped she'd got the hair straighteners she'd been wanting, and some crop tops even though Mum thought they were inappropriate, and the sweets in the silver wrapping that she'd seen in Jenners, and the necklace shaped like a dog's bone which she'd asked for because a puppy, as Mum had said, was totally out of the question.

She was wakened for a second time by Daisy's excited yell. It was still dark, but it must have been morning because no one was shouting to be quiet. Daisy was out of her bed and the light went on, sharp and fierce. Katie blinked. Daisy leaped on her stocking—hers was a really fancy one, knitted with tinselly thread and her name embroidered into it, and stuffed so full that everything was spilling out of the top. All the paper was the same, silver and shiny.

'Santa's been!' she shouted excitedly.

Katie nodded encouragingly and allowed herself a yawn and a stretch before she dived into hers. She'd thought last night about telling Daisy the truth when they were whispering together in the dark, but she was quite an excitable person and might not take it well; at least not as well as Katie had done.

CHAPTER EIGHT

FRIDAY, CHRISTMAS DAY

'I swear they put these things in just to torment sleep-deprived parents.' Katie watched as her dad twisted the last of the small metal wires that fixed her Bratz doll to the cardboard box. He should complain. She was way too old for dolls, even Bratz ones, and she had never imagined Mum would get her one because she'd once heard her telling Dad they were horrible and looked like 'miniature hookers' when they were in Toys R Us. Katie had asked what hookers were and Dad had said rugby players, but what that had to do with Bratz Katie didn't know.

'There.' Dad peeled the last wire from round the doll's ankle and handed it over. His hair was still all sticky-up because he hadn't had his shower yet. He and Mum had got up just after Katie had burst into the room they were in, finished with her stocking and ready to go downstairs.

She'd actually been a bit worried they were having sex, because they were lying so close together. But Dad was facing Mum's back which was the wrong way round. And they weren't making any noise. In the bits of films she'd seen when Elsa was watching TV they always made noise, and generally someone was on top of someone else. So it must have just been a special Christmas cuddle.

They were always a little more huggy at Christmas and they never minded that she'd been eating Haribo before her Weetabix and might not clean her teeth. Even Grampa was all jolly, and still in his dressing gown. Although Katie didn't like to look at his legs and hoped he would go upstairs to put some trousers on. Aunt Vonnie had handed round a tray of tall glasses with something orange and fizzy and Grampa had made a toast and then kissed Granny twice on the cheek. It was funny the way old people kiss, quick and dry like a bird pecking through leaves. All the grown-ups opened their presents from each other and seemed quite pleased, although Katie felt pretty sad for them because they only got one or two and they were generally quite small, and often books.

Aunt Vonnie got a really nice watch, though, from Gran and Grampa that told you how fast you were running and even when to get up in the morning, and Uncle Allan had given Aunt Fiona a lovely coat, which she was still wearing because the fire hadn't lit properly yet. Riley had a squeaky bone and a tinsel collar. Hector had got a tinsel collar too but his had mostly come off and was trailing behind him. Just like an intestine, Elsa whispered, as she did Katie's hair.

She had got her straighteners, which were the best present ever. They were long and black and had ceramic plates which Elsa said was important because it meant she wouldn't get split ends. Mum had told her to be careful using them because she'd known a girl who burned her finger so badly it had got infected and almost had to come off. Mum always knew someone something awful had happened to: someone who got their eye poked out with a stick; and once someone who'd gone orange because she'd drunk too much Sunny Delight. Katie wondered if she should say something to Aunt Vonnie because she'd had more glasses of the orange fizzy drink than anyone.

Katie sat back on her heels and looked down at her Bratz. She ought at least to look like she was playing with it because her hair was as straight as it was going to get and Mum had said she couldn't use the straighteners on the dogs, not even on their necks where the fur was sticky-up. Over near the fireplace, Daisy was still opening her presents. She had loads. Katie had tried to count them and had got to twenty-three before she had to go to the loo. Daisy was still unwrapping when she got back. Mum always said it wasn't how many or how big, but the thought that counted. Katie thought it was a pretty dumb thing to say because you would have to think more to buy more.

'Aren't you going to open this one?' Aunt Fiona shoved a square package across the rug to Daisy. She had probably left it until last because it was small and didn't look as interesting as the others.

166

Daisy lifted it up, tore off the paper and frowned.

'It's a phone,' said Aunt Fiona.

Daisy's eyes widened. 'I got a phone!'

Katie felt suddenly sick with envy. Mum had said she would have to wait three more years till she got one, and Daisy was just seven! How was that fair?

Daisy opened up the box and pulled out the phone in its small plastic bag. It was pale pink and a slide-up one, like Elsa's, but even nicer. Uncle Allan took it from her.

'It's all set up, poppet,' he said. 'Listen.' He pressed a button and it started to sing, a proper tune like you hear on an iPod.

'Cool phone, Daisy,' said Elsa, who was up on the sofa with the money she had got in a fancy gold envelope.

Mum was picking up all the empty glasses. 'A mobile phone!' she said. 'Goodness me, aren't you a . . . lucky girl?'

Katie glanced at Daisy to see if she'd noticed that Mum's voice sounded a bit high. Aunt Fiona must have noticed, though, because she gave a little sniff and said something about Daisy going to all these different after-school things and needing to be able to keep in touch. Mum nodded and said, 'Mmm, mmm,' with a big fake smile on her face, the way she did when she didn't agree with you at all.

That seemed to annoy Aunt Fiona even more because she ended up saying, 'Each to their own, Debs,' and Mum had said, 'Indeed.' And Dad had stood up and tried to be extra jolly, and Katie had given a little sigh and pretended to like her Bratz.

167

Because that was the other thing about Christmas. Sometimes you tried so hard to be nice you could end up wanting to be nasty instead.

* * *

Charlie stood by the sink and held the kettle under the tap. The blind was up, and out in the garden the inflatable snowman that Gail had insisted they buy for Annie sagged against the cotoneaster bush like a benign drunk. Annie was still asleep, as well she might be because she'd been up twice, once at midnight and then again at 3 a.m. Gail had then woken at 6 a.m. and bleated sleepily for tea. He'd stumbled downstairs, eyes still unfocused and lit the tree lights and the gas fire and angled the doll's house so it would be the first thing Annie spotted when she came bursting in. The kettle clicked off and he poured the steaming water into the two mugs, and then left the tea to infuse while he went to find his toolbox in the utility room. The box was on the third layer, where he kept the rawlplugs and the superglue. He had moved it from the loft and wrapped it in an old nail packet, just to be sure.

Gail was propped up against the pillows. Her fringe was pushed up at one side like an elaborate quiff and she had switched on the small sidelight.

'Is she awake yet?'

Charlie shook his head. 'She's sound, leave her.'

He handed her a mug of tea and laid his own on the bedside table, then fished the box from the pocket of his dressing gown. He held it out, flat on the palm of his hand.

'Merry Christmas, love.'

Gail took a sharp little breath and looked up at

168

him, realising the smallness of it meant something really special.

'Go on, then.' He was grinning at her.

'Charlie.'

'Take it. Open it!' He wanted to see her face.

He slipped in beside her as she lifted the box from his hand and pulled at the ribbon. The soft gilded paper fell away like the skin of an overripe fruit. The box was thickly velvet; midnight blue. The lid opened with a satisfying snap and she screamed with surprise and delight. If he had thought about it he could have had the overhead light on because they were downlighters and the diamonds would have caught the beams and sparkled furiously. They still looked pretty impressive, though, pinned to the white silk interior, bigger even than he'd remembered.

'Oh, my God. Charlie. Oh, my God!' She turned and threw herself on to him, no mean feat given her size. A little fart escaped as she moved.

'Now, that doesn't happen in the adverts.' He started to laugh.

She blushed furiously and swatted at him with her free hand, holding the box out at arm's length with the other. 'Oh, God, Charlie, don't. Oh, Charlie. They're really gorgeous.' Tears sprang into her eyes and she looked back at him again. 'Can we afford them?'

'Well . . .' He sucked at his teeth.

'Charlie.'

'We're fine,' he said. 'Are you going to put them on?'

Gail lifted the jewels one by one from the box and fitted them quickly and deftly into her ears, then eased herself out of bed and padded over to

169

the mirror to look, twisting her head to each side and pulling back her hair with a hand. Her pyjama trousers had fallen below her bump, revealing the silvery streak of stretch marks, like a mollusc's many trails. She rubbed them religiously, and pointlessly, Charlie suspected, every night with cream that smelled like a pina colada.

She turned back to him, her eyes bright with tears. 'They're gorgeous. They're absolutely gorgeous. I love them,' she said. 'I love you, babe.'

'Love you too.' He took a sip of his tea and lay back on the pillow. Outside, the sky was growing light. He felt the warmth creep over him. No work today. It was Christmas. Annie was asleep, and Gail was happy. He looked back at his wife. She was transfixed by the girl in the glass before her. The big girl in the baggy pyjamas, with the skewed fringe and the dancing eyes, and two bright jewels gleaming icily against her sleep-warmed skin.

*   *   *

'Almost done.' Deborah twisted the last small covered button through the buttonhole, trying not to notice the stale smell emanating from Min's favourite blouse, the deep burgundy silk with the high collar and fussy, drooping cuffs, utterly unsuitable for Christmas dinner, but the one she had insisted on.

'It's just this fiddly one near the top,' said Min. 'Stupid old hands.'

'You should see Katie with the buttons on her school blouse,' said Deborah. 'I swear there's not a day when they're all done up right. There.' She stood back. 'Lovely.'

170

'Thank you, puss.' Min leaned over and touched Deborah's cheek. Age had curved her fingers into an awkward angle, but her skin was baby soft, papery and translucent, like the kind of silky tissue they give you in fancy shops. 'Are you having a lovely Christmas?'

Deborah thought it best to lie and nodded. For a second, she thought about telling Min about Doug, but Min's gentle moments were so few and far between these days that she was as likely to blurt it out in the middle of lunch as give her a hug and tell her everything would be okay. Which Deborah knew she could not.

She turned back to Min's dresser, so her face wouldn't give her away, and took another deep glug from one of the two glasses of champagne she had brought through. She intended spending the day in a faintly alcoholic haze, anything to dull the steady buzz of anxiety in her gut.

'A brooch?' she said. 'Or some beads?'

Min bent her head to one side and laid a hand up near her throat, looking at herself in the broad mirror. 'Brooch or beads?' She gave a sudden, mischievous smile. 'What do you think Tyra would suggest?'

Deborah burst out laughing. She knew Min's penchant for *America's Top Model*. She rifled through the large wooden jewellery box in the desk, the one she had loved rummaging in as a child, and picked out the spangliest paste and diamanté concoction she could find.

'I think . . .' She held up the brooch. 'I think Tyra would probably say, "Pile it on, girl."'

Min sat back, reached for her own glass of fizz and bared her throat. 'Then pile it on, girl!' she

171

said.

*   *   *

'I don't know,' said Caroline. 'Maybe another few minutes?'

'It's fine,' said Fiona. 'The juice is clear on the thigh and it's actually coming away from the bones now.' She looked down at the turkey, the skin curled and darkening under the strips of streaky bacon. 'Honestly, Mum, if anything it's a little overdone.'

Caroline peered closer. 'Well, if you're sure.'

'I'm sure,' said Fiona. She slipped on the oven gloves before her mum could argue and eased the giant bird, as heavy as a small child, to the edge of the shelf. Caroline took the other end with a folded teacloth and they settled it on to the hot plate. Caroline handed her the foil and she pulled off two large shiny stretches and wrapped them around the roasting dish.

'Right. That needs to rest for about twenty minutes. What next?' Fiona tried not to look at the sprouts on the hob, boiling into a bland green mush. She'd offered to steam them, but Caroline didn't possess a steamer, and had insisted they be well cooked so Min could manage them with her dentures. Although Fiona had already found and toasted some almonds to sprinkle over the top at the last minute. She leaned across and topped up Caroline's wine glass, and then her own, trying not to think of goose with lemon and apple stuffing and Savoy cabbage, honey-roast parsnips and Elizabeth David's best bitter chocolate pudding.

'What about dessert?' she asked.

172

'The Christmas pud is microwaveable and the trifle is pretty much done. Just the whipped cream.' Caroline leaned back against the range. 'And I think that's us.' She pushed her hair off her face.

'I can whip the cream for you,' said Fiona. She bent across suddenly and kissed Caroline on the cheek, feeling churlish. She had so loved cooking like this when she was a child. Just the two of them in the kitchen. Trays of misshapen scones and uneven biscuits. Spills and sticky patches on the table, dishes in the sink; the air warm and sweet.

'What's that for?' asked Caroline, looking pleased.

'It's nice to be home,' said Fiona.

'It's lovely to have you here,' said Caroline.

Fiona lifted the whisk from the rack by the fridge. 'Do you want anything on the top of it? The trifle.'

'Mmm, we probably should,' said Caroline. 'What do you think?'

'How about some sprinkles?' said Fiona, and hid her smile.

*   *   *

Elsa folded the After Eight Mint case into a thin brown sliver and laid it with the others on the edge of her plate.

She blew upwards into her fringe. The dining room was really warm now with the heat of all the people crammed round the big mahogany table and all the hot dishes that had been brought to the table. She wouldn't have minded another coffee because the cups were so tiny but the coffee pot

173

was long since finished and she was too stuffed to think of getting up to make some more.

Katie, Daisy and Jamie had been excused to go and watch *Willy Wonka's Chocolate Factory*, as long as they took Ben, but everyone else was hanging around waiting for Min who was still working on her Christmas pudding. Ever since the main course she had had a smear of bread sauce on her chin that no one seemed to have the heart to tell her about. It took her an age to chew and Elsa noticed that sometimes her mouth kept moving even when she had stopped eating, like a baby trying to suckle.

She wondered how Matt was doing. He'd phoned her just after they'd sat down to lunch, in the middle of pulling the crackers, and asked her what she was wearing. She said, 'A paper hat, and I'll call you later,' and smiled sweetly at her mum's disapproving stare.

She was trying to be extra nice, because she'd need to tell them soon and because they'd been really generous this year: £200 in cash and the promise she could go into town tomorrow and then stay over at Matt's, although her mum couldn't quite bring herself to say that, so had said, 'We'll expect to see you the next day,' instead.

At the far end of the table, Allan was leaning forward. He caught her eye and smiled. He was still wearing his paper hat, but he must have had a pretty big head because he had to rip it part way down the side to get it on. She'd been trying to avoid looking at him. Earlier, when she'd been playing Twister with the girls, he'd come into the room and said, 'I haven't done that for ages, can I have a go?' And while she was trying to put her

174

hand on a green circle she saw he was looking down her top. It was a weird feeling. She was used to men looking at her; she liked it. But when it was your uncle, even if he wasn't a blood relative, it was kind of repulsive. When he'd talked to her over lunch, she'd seen Fiona glance over a couple of times. Elsa hoped she didn't think she was flirting because she wasn't.

Min appeared to have been defeated by the pudding. She sat back, raised her napkin to her lips and gave a loud burp.

'Pardon you,' said Caroline.

'Better an empty house than a bad tenant,' muttered Min.

Elsa stood up, grateful that the meal was finally over. On the way out she passed Daisy, her face streaked with tears, her new phone clutched in her hand. She ran into the dining room and over to Fiona.

'I've said please and I've asked for ages and he still won't.'

Fiona slipped her arm round Daisy's waist. 'Who won't what, honey?'

'Jamie,' said Daisy. 'I've left him lots of messages on his phone and he won't check they got there. And I want him to phone me too and I've asked nicely and it's really mean.'

Fiona got to her feet with a sigh. 'It is really mean,' she said. 'Come on. I'll sort him out.'

*   *   *

The small moustachioed figure leaped from the ledge and landed neatly on the stone pillar. Jamie kept his eyes fixed to the screen and tried to block

175

out the voice, sharp and insistent.

'Jamie, I said why won't you go and get your phone and give Daisy a call. Everyone else has done it.'

He didn't look up. 'I'll do it later,' he said. 'Call Elsa again.'

'No. You said that ages ago,' whined Daisy. 'And I sent you a picture.'

'Jamie,' said Fiona.

'I'll do it later. I'm doing this just now.'

Fiona gave a spitting breath. 'Oh, for heaven's sake. Where is your bloody phone? I'll go and get it myself.'

He propelled himself out of his chair so quickly that Fiona had to take a step back.

'Fine.' He threw his DS down on to the chair. 'Fine. I'm going. See.'

He climbed the stairs quickly and angrily. Everyone else was still at Christmas dinner; he could hear loud rattles of laughter from the dining room. Why couldn't his mum have just stayed through there with the others and got plastered?

The dead boy's room was cold because he had left the window open. The pile of wrapping paper was still on the bed from his stocking. It had been a good stocking this year, some new games, a really neat solar torch, a tiny digital camera, and a pendant on a leather thong that looked like a spinning scythe, as well as all the usual stuff of sweets and boxer shorts with Homer Simpson on them. He shut the door and took a deep breath and lifted his phone down from the shelf. He would have to switch it on or else Fiona would. And maybe there was nothing; there had been no emails after all. It might be okay.

176

He slid open the phone and pressed the 'on' button, clearing a sit-down space on the end of the bed as he did so. The screen lit after a moment and it made the little fanfare noise. A list of words appeared: 'welcome' in five different languages. Welcome. *Wilkommen. Bienvenue. Bienvenuti. Bienvenido.* His hands felt clammy. There would be something, he told himself, because Daisy had left messages. It would say there were messages.

The first ring was a shrill Diverted call. He lifted it to his ear.

'You have three new messages.'

He blew out a breath. Daisy must have called that many times. He pressed 121.

'Hi, Jamie, it's Daisy on my new phone! I got a phone!'

'Hi, Jamie. It's Daisy, merry Christmas. It's pink.'

'Hiyeeeeee!'

'You have no more messages.'

He exhaled. At the top of the screen, in the middle, was the little white envelope. She'd been trying to learn to text; maybe she'd managed to send one.

'Five new messages,' read the screen. He looked at the numbers. Only one of them was from Daisy.

He felt the lurch of panic in his stomach.

The first he looked at was from Vodaphone. The second wasn't.

merry xmas wank!

There was another. He pressed again.

fckn bender bent job

The third they had used before. It was a picture with text underneath.

fuck off & die

You couldn't really tell it was him, just a hunched back in a blue blazer and a stupid pathetic arm raised up like a claw, trying to get his bag back. Feeble idiot. Fucking feeble idiot.

He felt his face flood red with shame and rage. His fingers were shaking. He dropped the phone on to the covers. The woman had said to keep them all, as evidence, but he could never bring himself to. He picked it up again and went to delete, then stopped. Keep them. Evidence. Keep them. He started to cry and brushed the tears angrily from his eyes.

It took ten minutes for Fiona to come looking for him. She walked in, cross.

'Jamie. Did you find your phone?'

He was lying back on the covers and shook his head.

'What do you mean? It's right here.'

She bent to pick it up and he sat up and grabbed it and held it in his hands.

Fiona shook her head in disbelief and her eyes went cold. 'Jesus, Jamie, what's up with you? It's Christmas Day. Get downstairs now and play with your sister. Did you get her messages?'

He nodded.

'Well, go down and tell her and phone her back, for God's sake.'

He shook his head.

'Jamie.'

'No, Mum.'

'Get downstairs. Now. Or I'll get Allan up.'

He almost laughed. Compared to his mum, Allan was the easy option. For a second he thought that might be okay. He might be able to tell Allan. But Allan would have to tell his mum and then that would be it. He felt the tears of hopelessness spring into his eyes, hot and stinging, and turned his head away so she wouldn't see.

'Leave me alone. Just . . . fucking well leave me alone.' It just came out. He hadn't meant to swear.

Fiona's mouth opened and shut like a guppy. 'You will not speak to me like that! What on earth is wrong with you? Jesus, Jamie, this has got to stop. Sometimes I . . .' She struggled for the right word. 'Downstairs. NOW!'

He shook his head once more and lay back again and put his arm over his face. He heard her exhale in fury and then turn to leave. The door shook in its frame long after her angry steps had receded downstairs.

*   *   *

'Hey.'

'Hey.' He sounded sleepy.

'Merry Christmas,' said Vonnie. 'Did I wake you?'

'Merry Christmas,' said Mike. 'And yes.'

'Sorry.'

There was a long pause. She guessed he was stretching; could imagine him starfishing across her side of the bed, the light still grey through the slatted wooden blinds, no traffic on the street below.

'So, how's the family Christmas?'

'It's fine. It's good,' she said. 'It's family.'

He gave a little assenting snort.

'We just had Christmas dinner,' she said. She lay back in the chair and pulled her knees up tight to her chest. 'I'm a bit pissed. What are you getting up to today?'

'Dunno. Lunching with Lil, I guess.'

'How is she?'

'Ask her yourself,' said Mike.

The line went quiet.

'Can't hear a damn thing,' said Vonnie.

'She's washing,' said Mike.

Vonnie smiled. He was even more fond of the cat than she was and had been less of a cat person to start with. Lil wasn't technically theirs, but belonged to the lady in the ground-floor apartment. She was a snowbird and took off for Arizona at the first hint of chill, usually around mid-October, returning a deep burnished orange and full of the joys at the end of March. For those months, Lil, who was as old as the hills, moved upstairs and in with them, commandeering their balcony, where she would sit and stare out for hours with polite disinterest like a monarch surveying the Mall.

'You're not dressing her up, are you?' said Vonnie. 'You know, little Santa hat or something.'

'Fuck off.' Mike laughed.

The line went quiet again and then he said, 'I've been thinking about London.'

'Really?'

'Yeah. What do you think?'

Vonnie blew out a soft breath. 'Up to you.'

He didn't say anything. She put her free hand to

her mouth and started to bite gently at her nails.

'Yeah, I guess,' he said eventually. 'Money's good.'

'Uh-huh,' said Vonnie. She hadn't planned on having this conversation today. She knew she would have to have it when she was home, but he still had two months to make up his mind. She changed the subject.

'Did you open my present yet?'

'Nope.'

Vonnie giggled. 'You're such a slacker. It's Christmas Day!'

'It's quarter past eight,' said Mike. 'What time were you up this morning?'

'Early,' she lied. 'And thanks for my bangle. I love it.' She'd opened it on the plane over, not wanting to wait. It was a twist of rich brown leather with gold beads threaded through it. Very boho and much coveted by Elsa when she saw it.

She heard him yawn again.

'Right, dozy. I need to go and help with the washing-up. Love you.'

'Love you too. I'll call you later once I've opened the prezzie.'

'You know what it is,' said Vonnie.

Mike laughed. 'Okay. Thanks for my new bike computer.'

'You're welcome,' said Vonnie. 'Give Lil a kiss for me.'

'I don't kiss the cat.'

'It's Christmas Day,' said Vonnie again.

She heard an exaggerated smooching sound.

'There,' said Mike. 'Now I've got a freakin' hairball.'

'You and her both.' Vonnie laughed. 'Bye.'

181

'Bye,' he said. 'And Von, London. Have a think. Okay?'

'Okay,' she lied. 'I will. Bye.'

*   *   *

'Sean Connery,' said Deborah. 'Has to be. No one can touch him.'

'No.' Fiona shook her head. 'Far too hairy. Daniel Craig. Definitely.'

Behind them on the TV, the credits for *Casino Royale* rolled upwards in a blur of white lettering. Not that anyone had really been watching. They were scattered around the drawing room like fallen dressmaker's dummies, slouched low in chairs, legs stretched out in front of them, hands hung over the sides. The dogs were comatose before the fire, tummies swollen by turkey trimmings and the chipolatas no one had wanted. All the children, bar Elsa, were in bed, and the coffee table was cluttered with empty port glasses and the decimated remains of a large box of Thornton's chocolates. Caroline felt slightly sick.

'Dad.' Vonnie turned towards David. 'Pussy Galore?'

'I was always more of a Moneypenny man,' said David.

Allan let out a grunt. 'Barbara Bach,' he said, and gave a low whistle.

'I quite liked Jane Seymour,' said Doug. There was a pause and then everyone burst out laughing, rather unfairly, Caroline thought.

'Jane Seymour?' said Allan. 'Doug.'

'What?' Doug looked hurt and Deborah reached across and patted his knee.

182

'Jane Seymour's lovely,' she said. 'And so like me.'

'Actually, there is this game you can play,' said Vonnie with a laugh. 'Where it's your weirdest crush. You know, the one you don't like to admit to.'

Fiona shook her head. 'Not a good plan, Von.'

Vonnie sat up. 'No, it's really good. Mike and I were at this party once, and this woman came out with George Bush. I'm serious! And now that's all anyone can think about her. That she's the woman who has the hots for George Bush.'

'Junior or senior?' asked David.

'Junior,' said Vonnie. 'She said it was the way he walked. The Texas swagger.'

'That's why it's not a good idea,' said Fiona. 'Let's not go there. Really.'

'Well, we all know Doug's,' said Allan.

'Jane Seymour's not weird,' said Doug. 'She's—'

'Lovely,' said Deborah again. 'Yes, we know.'

'Well, I would have to say Julie Walters,' said Allan. He leaned forward and poured himself another glass of port.

'You are having me on!' Fiona swivelled to look at him. 'Julie Walters?'

'Way to go, Allan.' Vonnie started to applaud.

Allan grinned at her and shrugged. 'It's her . . .'

'What?' said Fiona. 'Liver spots?'

'Twinkle,' said Allan. 'I was going to say twinkle.'

'And so like you, Fi.' Deborah laughed.

'Bugger off,' said Fiona. She looked again at Allan. 'Julie Walters?'

'Yup,' he said and smacked his lips.

'Well mine is that guy who played Gollum in
183

Lord of the Rings,' said Vonnie. 'You know, what's his name? Andy Serkis.'

'You fancy Gollum?' It was Doug's turn to laugh. 'And you make fun of me for Jane Seymour?'

'Not Gollum,' said Vonnie. 'The guy who played him. He's got this really mobile face.' She put her hands up to her cheeks. 'Just a lovely, squishy, mobile face.'

'You're sick,' said Fiona.

'Yeah, and yours would be . . . ?' said Vonnie.

'Mine would be nobody's business,' said Fiona. 'I'm not playing.' She still seemed tetchy after her row with Jamie about his phone. He had stayed in his room for a good couple of hours before Daisy went to tell him *Shrek* was on and he'd come down, but had sat as far from Fiona as humanly possible without actually being out of the room, and with his face sheltered from everyone, perhaps, thought Caroline, so they couldn't see he had been crying.

'Spoilsport,' said Vonnie. She turned to Deborah. 'Debs?'

Deborah put her head to one side. Her hand was still on Doug's knee.

'I would have to say Danny DeVito.'

'It's all coming out tonight.' David laughed.

It was nice to see him so relaxed. Caroline watched him from across the room. His cheeks were flushed, perhaps from the fire, perhaps from the drink. She thought of his hand on her shoulder in the kitchen on Christmas Eve, and the emotions that had shot through her. Panic and pleasure. It had been her who pulled away and part of her had not wanted to.

'Danny DeVito?' Doug was spluttering in mock

184

horror. 'You never told me that?'

'It's not the kind of thing you bring up.' Deborah laughed. 'I just think he's really funny. Cute and funny.'

'You've got that hirsute thing going on there, Debs,' said Vonnie. 'Danny DeVito, Sean Connery.' She sat forward again. 'Actually you could have used Connery for your weirdest. Remember that blue romper suit thing he wore in *Goldfinger*.'

'God, yeah.' Deborah nodded. 'It was a bit like the one you used to wear in your modelling days, Fi, wasn't it?' She grinned at her older sister.

'You did modelling?' said Doug. He must have realised he had sounded too surprised, because he added, 'Not that you couldn't or anything, but . . . you did modelling?'

Vonnie was giggling. 'Knitting patterns,' she said. 'She was the girl in the Fair Isle sweater with the bobble hat.'

'It wasn't just knitwear,' said Fiona starchily.

'No, it was towelling too.' Deborah laughed.

'It paid good money.' Fiona turned towards Caroline. 'Didn't it, Mum?'

Caroline smiled and nodded. It hadn't paid much at all, and it had only been three sittings at most for a small-scale catalogue company, at the suggestion of a family friend. But Fiona had been so proud, and she was taking a bit of a hammering from her sisters tonight.

'See.' Fiona looked at Vonnie and Debs. 'I don't remember you paying your way when you were eight.'

'You weren't exactly Kate Moss, though, were you?' said Vonnie.

'Bugger off,' said Fiona.

'You should get your portfolio out, Fi,' said Vonnie. 'Give us all a laugh.'

'I might just do that,' said Fiona. She sat back, her lips flattened in a fit of pique.

Caroline noticed Allan leaning forward. 'Elsa, have you never thought about modelling?' He gave what he must have thought was a winning smile. Caroline saw Fiona's expression change.

Elsa blushed. 'Eh, no, not really. No.'

Caroline would think later that Min must have been taking everything in and had spoken to save the day, or at least break the awkward silence that had descended on the room, because she sat bolt upright in her chair and said, 'Katharine Hepburn.'

'Pardon?' David looked across at her.

'Katharine Hepburn,' repeated Min. She was smiling. 'Weirdest crush,' she said. 'Katharine Hepburn.'

'Whose?' said Vonnie. 'Yours?'

'Yes,' said Min. 'And why not? She was a fine-looking woman.'

Laughter returned to the room. Vonnie picked up her glass and raised it in Min's direction. 'Absolutely no reason, Min. No reason at all.'

*   *   *

Fiona lay in the dark and felt the faint, swelling throb of an oncoming migraine behind her left temple. She was almost guaranteed one if she started drinking before lunch and she'd started before breakfast. Add to that the onset of her period, too much over-cooked food and Jamie. She'd tried to explain to Allan, tried to get him to go upstairs and remonstrate with him, but he'd just shrugged it off and said, 'Leave the boy be; it's hormones.' Except she wondered now if it was. There was no end to it and he just seemed to be getting more and more withdrawn. And the way he had sworn at her and then looked at her, as though he hated her with all his being. But when he had thrown himself back on the bed she had seen that he was crying and, even through her rage, she felt her heart break for him.

And now Allan wasn't talking to her either. She had asked him to help her clear the glasses and had hissed at him the moment the kitchen door had closed.

'What on earth are you doing?' She mimicked his voice. '"Have you never thought about modelling?"'

'I'm being nice,' he said flatly.

'You're actually being a bit of an arse,' Fiona had replied. 'She's eighteen, Allan. She's my niece.'

'She's my niece too.'

'Well, treat her like one. Instead of being . . . seedy Uncle Al or something.'

'Fuck off,' he had said coldly, and left the room, and now he was as far away from her as possible in the bed, but still too close for comfort. She shut her eyes, felt the faint jerking motion start. She turned to the side, tugging at the sheet as she moved. Sometimes it made him stop, made him realise that she wasn't asleep and she knew what he was doing, but not tonight. He couldn't have cared less tonight. The motion became stronger, more rhythmic. She pressed her head hard into the pillow. He made a noise in his throat and she

187

clenched her fists. She knew who he was thinking about. Pert breasts in a tight top. Pink lips and shiny hair. You pervert. In her head she said the words out loud. You absolute fucking pervert. Stop it. Stop it. STOP IT! STOP IT!

CHAPTER NINE

SATURDAY, BOXING DAY.

'You have all that fluff from the rug on your jumper now.' Dyta leaned down and picked a piece of lint from the shoulder of Hanna's black polo neck. 'You should go and change.'

'I'm fine.' Hanna sat back on her heels and waved Dyta's hand away. 'It's just your boyfriend, for heaven's sake. Not the Holy Father.'

A few feet in front of her, Marek was still engrossed in the racetrack that twisted around the legs of two of the chairs in a neat figure eight. It was a pretty impressive racetrack, even though she said so herself. The present had been Dyta's, so lovely, but without a thought for how it was to be assembled with no man, or Allen key, in the house. They had been up late on Christmas Eve, with a bottle of wine, trying to put it together, until their shrieking had merited a hammering on the floor from the old man upstairs who had a face like he had never known fun and a rather haphazard display of teeth. Dyta had eventually given in and gone off to bed. Hanna had finished it and wound it around the chairs and had charged the adaptor and put batteries in the two small cars, one red and one yellow, and had collapsed into bed with such a feeling of satisfaction and a desire to tell someone how clever she had been.

It had been a lovely Christmas, though. When she had got back from the Haldanes they had spent the afternoon of Christmas Eve decorating the tree and then when it got properly dark they had taken Marek to the window to see if he could see Gwiazdka, the little star, that meant it really was Christmas. The sky was cloudy, so Hanna had pointed to the star on top of a tree in the Meadows. It was flashing and blue, a bit brassy, but Marek had played along. Then they had sat down for Wigilia, the Christmas supper. There was enough food to make Mamo proud, although she wouldn't have approved that half of it was ready-made, and since they both hated carp they had salmon steaks from Marks and Spencer with a honey glaze. They set two extra places as they were supposed to do, one for Mamo and one for a spirit who might want to join them. And they made their peace with each other, made their apologies and gave words to their love. Then Dyta had told Hanna to put her hand under the tablecloth. It was paper, not a proper one, but she had managed to hide some pieces of straw. Hanna pulled one out and it was green, which meant she would marry before the year was out. Dyta let out a little cry of pretend surprise, but when Hanna lifted the cloth all the straws were green, as she had suspected they might be.

'Again!' shouted Marek, and Hanna flopped back down on to her stomach and picked up the red controller, trying to look enthusiastic about another spin around the plastic track. As nice as

189

this time had been she was starting to feel a little stir-crazy in the flat, just sitting around and playing and eating. There was a small square of common ground at the back of the close that held the clothes lines and the bins, but not enough room for Marek to run around, and there was always dog shit from the two dogs on the ground floor.

'Okay, speedy boy. One more run and then lunchtime. And then maybe we'll go to the park before your mama explodes with all the food she's eating.'

Marek giggled and made a face like a fat person, puffing out his cheeks.

Hanna gave him a pretend glare. 'Hey, don't be mean to your beloved mama.'

Dyta was bustling around behind her, carrying pots and dishes to the table. She had made a lot of food.

'Do you want a hand?' shouted Hanna from the floor.

'No, you can do the—' She was interrupted by the doorbell and left the room to answer the door.

Hanna was still on her stomach and on her final lap when she realised there were more than two voices in the hall. She let Marek win again and stood up, brushing down the front of her jumper as best she could. She was still wearing her funny slippers, the ones like giant bare feet with painted toes that had been Marek's present to her.

The door opened and Dyta walked in looking defiant. She was followed by two men: Peter, her boyfriend, and another man, shorter and broader with expectant eyes that widened in relief and delight when he saw Hanna. A blind date. Hanna's heart sank. She tried to convey her annoyance to

Dyta who wouldn't meet her eyes.

'This is Hanna,' she said brightly, smiling at a point above her head.

Hanna smiled politely. 'Hi.' She tried not to sound too bright. She didn't want this man to get ideas from the off. Marek had crawled out from under the chairs and was watching the two men. Hanna lifted him up and pulled him in front of her; her little bodyguard. Normally when men realised he came with her, their smiles weakened and they tried a little less; if at all.

'Hello, wee man,' said the second man. He was wearing a leather jacket that squeaked as he bent down. Now that she had been here for two years, Hanna was able to distinguish Scottish accents and he was definitely west coast, almost a drawl, leaving every sentence with an upturn, like a question he was asking himself. He wasn't as good-looking as Dyta's beau; blind dates never were, but he wasn't exactly horrific either. He had brown hair, cut short, and a broad friendly face, with pale blue-grey eyes. His build was stocky, but not muscular. She might have passed him in the street without a second glance

'Is that Scalextric you've got there?' He grinned at Marek. 'That's the best Christmas present ever. I never got a Scalextric. Maybe I could have a shot later.'

Marek shook his head. 'No.'

'Marek!' Hanna gave him a little shake. 'I'm sorry,' she said, on his behalf.

'That's okay,' said the man. 'He's just shy. You're just shy, aren't you, wee man?'

No, thought Hanna, he's just sensible.

She smiled weakly and tugged at the hem of her

191

sweater. 'Well, I should, eh, go and . . .' She gestured to the hallway and Dyta nodded enthusiastically. She knew she was in big trouble, but also knew that any row was a couple of hours off, because Hanna would never be rude in company.

She had no intention of getting changed, but she did swap her giant foam feet for ballet flats and ran a brush through her hair. Her polo neck was still flecked with lint, so she grabbed the embroidered waistcoat that Mamo had sent over, the one that Dyta had laughed at. This could be her little protest. It was too big; the size Mamo wished she was, and was the colour of bad soup, a pale mustardy yellow with fussy dark green stitching that would give you a headache just from looking at it.

'You look pretty,' said Marek, who was sitting on the end of the bed swinging his legs.

'Don't I?'

'Do I look pretty?'

'You look handsome. And edible.' She bent down and bit his ear gently and he squeaked.

'Who's that man?'

'The man with the squeaky jacket?' Hanna smiled.

Marek grinned.

She didn't want to say she hadn't a clue; not a good message for a child, so she said instead, 'A friend of Dyta's.'

He nodded solemnly and she took him to the bathroom. One of the men had already been in, and the seat was still up. She sighed and laid it down. One day she would have a house of her own and a say in who came to visit.

192

Once they had both washed, she fixed a smile and led Marek through to the sitting room with a silent promise that they would both try to be nice.

*   *   *

Perhaps she had tried too hard, or perhaps Dyta was cross about the waistcoat or had drunk a little too much wine, because just after dessert, a not-yet defrosted cherry cheesecake, she had disappeared into the hall with her boyfriend and reappeared with her coat on. She took Marek by the hand and said they were off to the park for some fresh air and would Hanna get the coffee on? Hanna's mouth was already sore from her steady smile, but she forced a fresh grin and let her eyes blaze at her sister as she swung out of the door.

He was nice enough, the man. He worked for one of the big hotel chains and liked rugby; played with a Sunday league, and his favourite film was *Die Hard IV*. It took Hanna half an hour to find all that out. He asked her what she did, and didn't do that frantic energetic nodding that some people did when she mentioned the cleaning jobs and the ironing.

The coffee grew cold. He sat on the sofa, his left knee juddering slightly up and down.

'Would you like another . . .?' She gestured towards the cafetière.

'No, no, fine.' He glanced around, maybe looking for a clock so he wouldn't have to be so obvious about checking his watch.

She stood up. 'I should probably start on the dishes.'

It worked, as she had hoped it would.

'And I should probably head off.'

She smiled kindly. 'They're taking an age, aren't they? I think Marek has maybe got them into the playpark. It could be hours.'

He nodded again and picked up his jacket. Hanna guessed he had got it new for Christmas because it smelled strong, like the animal was not long dead. They shook hands awkwardly at the door and she exhaled as she shut it.

*　　　*　　　*

It was another hour before Dyta returned. Peter had stopped off in the pub and Marek had fallen asleep. Dyta carried him into Hanna's room and laid him on his bed. Hanna had left the dishes and was lying on the sofa with her eyes closed, enjoying the strange peace of an empty home.

'Well?' Dyta sat on the sofa's edge.

Hanna opened her eyes. 'We had sex. It was great. We did it in the kitchen. I came three times. He's gone home now.'

Dyta's eyes widened then narrowed. 'You're kidding.'

'Of course I'm kidding.' Hanna sat up. 'I'm really cross with you.'

Dyta made an apologetic face. 'I met him with Pete the other night. They're good friends and he seemed really nice.'

'You should have told me he was coming.'

Dyta raised an eyebrow. 'Like you would have agreed.'

'Well, fair enough, Dyta. But I don't like blind dates. I don't need you to bring me home a man.'

'But you need someone.'

'It needs to be the right one.' Hanna put her hand on Dyta's arm.

'But how are you going to meet anyone with the work you do?' said Dyta. 'What, Mr Robertson with his porno magazines under the bed, or that weird guy with the big eyebrows who comes for his shirts?'

'He's married,' said Hanna.

Dyta gave a little laugh. 'Otherwise you'd be after him.'

'For sure.' Hanna squeezed Dyta's hand. It was hard to be angry when she meant so well.

'So you didn't like this one so much?'

Hanna shrugged. 'He was okay.'

'Just okay?'

'Just okay.'

'Did you see the size of his hands?'

'Dyta,' said Hanna warningly.

'Well, you know what they say, big hands . . .' Dyta gestured to her groin.

Hanna giggled. 'I thought it was meant to be the nose.' She paused. 'Peter has quite a little nose, doesn't he?'

Dyta swatted at her, then leaned forward and gave her a hug. 'I just want to see you happy,' she said.

Hanna lay back against her. 'I am happy. I have Marek and you, and Mamo.'

She couldn't see, but she suspected Dyta was pulling a face.

Hanna patted her arm. 'You should go. I've still got the dishes to do.'

She spent a few minutes tidying the sitting room after Dyta had left, and then made her way into the kitchen. She stood at the door for a moment, and

195

looked at the piles of dishes covering every inch of surface space and even the windowsill. It was lovely when Dyta cooked but she always left the kitchen looking like the bears had been in.

*   *   *

'Did you keep them this time?'

Jamie pressed his phone closer to his ear and plucked absently at the blue bedcover with his free hand.

'Yes.'

'Good.' The voice on the end of the phone was calm. 'Okay.' She sounded round and soft; younger than his mum. Her name was Sheila. He liked that she didn't get upset; none of them ever did.

'And do you not think you could tell your mum or stepdad? Because what is being done here is wrong and there are steps you can take, all of you, together. You could ask your mum and stepdad to let you deal with it your way, with their support.'

'No.'

'Why do you not want to tell them?'

Jamie found himself shrugging even though he knew she couldn't see. 'Because they'd go nuts. Well, my mum would. She'd be really angry. And Allan, my stepdad, would tell my mum if I told him.'

'But that's okay for a mum to be angry about something like that, isn't it?'

'No, she'd be angry with me.'

There was the slightest of pauses. 'Why would she be angry with you?'

Jamie bit his lip. 'For not standing up for myself, or something like that. For getting picked on.'

'But this is not your fault. You know that?'

Actually, he didn't. All the websites and all the talks they'd had at school said it was never your fault, but it must have been because why else would they have chosen him? It must have been something he had done, or said, or the way he looked, or something. He had gone over everything in his mind so many times, trying to figure out what it was. The first time, at the bus stop, they were just mucking about, jostling and mugging in the way that they did, even when they were in class. And then the bus came and everyone was getting on and one of them tripped him and he had done a stupid stumble and had to put his hand out on the bus to steady himself. But they were doing it to other people too. He'd wanted to say 'fuck off', or 'tossers' or something, but he didn't say anything; just climbed on. Even his friends had laughed, in that fake, weak way that people do when they're really relieved it's not them.

And then one of them had said 'bent job' to him in the playground and he had said 'fuck off' under his breath, but had gone red too, which was the worst thing because it was as though he were embarrassed; as though it were true. And after that it was every day. Bender. Bent job. Wank. Fuckwit. He had started biting his nails. He'd only noticed when his mum had said to stop and that he was as bad as the Prime Minister, but at least he had an excuse because he had the country to run. He'd wondered if it was because he was thin and had asked his mum for some power shakes, but she said they were like taking steroids and why would he want to look like a circus freak.

He knew his friends felt bad for him. They had

197

always been a group of five but two of them were drifting away and he knew it was because they didn't want to be associated with him, in case they turned on them too. He had understood just before half-term when they'd gone to the wildlife park at Chessington and there were these wolves and one of them had blood on its back, and kept turning round to snap at it because it was so sore. One of the girls had got upset and the man showing them round said it might look bad but it was just that it was at the bottom of the pack and that's what the pack leader did. And none of the others went to help it, or stood up for it, they just slunk around, glad it wasn't them being bitten on the arse. The man said it would be fine because it wouldn't be at the bottom of the pack for ever, just until the cubs had grown then one of them would be the target. It's how they keep order, he had said. It's the way they live. It's okay.

'Jamie,' said Sheila again. 'You know it's not your fault?'

'Mmm,' said Jamie.

'Well, it's not and you need to remember that. Okay?'

'Okay.'

There was another pause. He wasn't sure what else to say. He hadn't really wanted to phone, but sometimes when he thought about it a lot he felt like he might explode if he didn't tell someone. It felt better to know that someone else knew, even if they weren't allowed to do anything.

'How did they make you feel, when you saw these latest ones?' He noticed how she changed her voice depending on the question. It had gone really soft.

He swallowed. Sick, angry, small, rubbish, pathetic, weak.

'Not good,' he said. 'A bit kind of angry, and . . . on my own.'

'It's very isolating, Jamie. If you still don't want to tell your mum and stepdad or a teacher, is there anyone else you could speak to? Another relative or a friend?'

'I'm at my gran's in Scotland,' he said. 'For Christmas.'

'Could you tell your gran, maybe?'

Maybe. He thought about it. 'Probably not. She's got a big party to do for my grampa.'

'Is there anyone else? Do you have a brother or sister?'

'They're small,' he said. 'Daisy's seven and Ben's just a baby.'

'Okay. Well, maybe an aunt or an uncle.' She didn't want to give up.

For a second he found himself thinking of Vonnie. Doug was really nice but he would tell Fiona for sure, but Vonnie could probably keep a secret because he hadn't told about her giving him wine the other night. Then he thought about saying the words to her and he felt his cheeks go red again with the shame and hurt of it.

'Maybe,' he said.

Sheila must have realised she had perhaps pushed it a bit far because she said, 'Well, you have a think, Jamie, and if you think there is someone, then tell them and we can get this stopped. Okay?'

He said, 'okay' back but he didn't mean it. He didn't think it would ever stop. Not like the wolves and not like Sheila said.

'I need to go now,' he said.

'Okay,' said Sheila. 'Take care, and you know you can phone any time. Any time at all.'

He switched off his phone and put it back up on the shelf behind the carved wooden duck and the *Swallows and Amazons* book, and made his way downstairs.

Fiona was in the hall with Vonnie and Deborah because they were all going into town for the sales, and Elsa was going to see her boyfriend. There was a lot of perfume and scarves. Allan was going to play golf with David and Doug, except they didn't have enough clubs and David was trying to sort his set into three bags, including one that used to be Min's and was falling to pieces it was so old. Caroline was standing by the door to the drawing room insisting she would be fine looking after all the kids. 'I raised four children,' she said, in a tight voice when Fiona asked her again if it was okay, and everybody looked a little awkward. Caroline turned towards Katie and Daisy.

'We'll be fine, won't we?'

Jamie had spotted Ben on the floor near the kitchen door, chewing at something he was clutching in his hand. He bent down and pulled it out of his fist. It was damp with spit, a piece of wrapping paper with some Sellotape attached.

'Ben's eating wrapping,' Jamie said.

'Great,' said Fiona. 'Can you do something useful for Gran and keep an eye on him? No sharp objects and keep him away from the toilet, remember. Little horror.' She gave Ben a beaming smile, and smiled at Jamie too and said, 'Thanks, love,' so she must have forgiven him for swearing at her, or maybe she was just pretending to in front of everybody.

200

He looked down at Ben, who was shuffling on his bum across to the golf bags. Jamie had been really embarrassed when his mum said she was pregnant because everyone would have known she'd had sex with Allan. At first Ben had seemed like a nothing, just this really small person who smelled of sick or crap, or had to be propped up because he'd fallen over. But as he'd got bigger, he'd taken a liking to Jamie and got all wriggly when he saw him and sometimes he held up his arms to be lifted. He still couldn't say much. His favourite word was 'Pah!' which meant pretty much anything really. Fiona was worried that his speech wasn't developing properly and had asked Deborah about it because she knew about these things but she said it was fine and the words would come. Ben was a terrible biter, too, and had once taken a lump out of Jamie's cheek. It had been really sore and Jamie had more or less dropped him and Ben had howled the place down. And he smelled, pretty much all the time.

'No, you don't.'

Jamie slid across the wooden floor and caught Ben just as he was about to topple one of the golf bags. He lifted him up and balanced him on his hip the way Fiona and Birgit did and took him outside to wave everyone off. Caroline said they were going to watch a film, but it was a really old one and he didn't fancy it, so he took Ben up to the dead boy's room and let him have a look around. Ben had pointed to the wooden duck and Jamie had lifted it down and given it to him to look at, but he had stuck it in his mouth and Jamie had to take it away. He didn't want him to leave tooth marks on it because that would have been

201

disrespectful. Ben gave a big sigh and steadied himself against Jamie's knees.

'Pah,' he said, and bounced up and down.

'Pah to you too,' said Jamie and Ben chuckled as if it were the funniest thing he had ever heard.

Jamie found himself smiling. The feeling of being idolised, even if it was by a small smelly boy who was your brother, was pretty nice.

CHAPTER TEN

'Where first? Debenhams or Marks and Sparks?' Deborah clutched her coat around her and settled her bag on to her shoulder, bending her head into the stiff wind bowling down the length of George Street. The town was packed with sale shoppers and they had been lucky to get a space in the St James Centre multi-storey, several floors up and a tight squeeze next to a bulky 4x4, but a space nonetheless. Elsa had bolted when they emerged on to street level, with just the quickest of kisses for Deborah and a cheery, 'See you,' to Vonnie and Fiona. Deborah had watched her until she was across the road, hair and coat flying, mobile clamped to her ear, thrilled to be free.

'I'm not setting a foot in Marks and Spencer,' said Fiona. 'It'll be utter bedlam and the only stuff left will be control pants or size 22 or something like that.' She folded her long cardigan across her chest and tucked a strand of hair behind her ear. 'Vonnie, where do you fancy?'

Vonnie bent down to rub a mark from the toe of her boots. They were long and grey, finishing just above her knee. She had teamed them with a little cord mini and her navy pea-coat. She pulled a soft blue beanie hat on to her head and grinned at both of them.

'How about cocktails at the George?'

'Maybe later,' said Fiona. 'How about we start at Harvey Nichols and work our way along from there?'

That will be that, then, thought Deborah. They walked briskly along the narrow lane that led towards St Andrew Square and trooped one after the other through the broad glass doors of the shop, held open for them by a man in a smart long coat and top hat, who said, 'Ladies' in a deep baritone.

They rose on the escalator to a floor where the clothes were set out like museum pieces: one or two at a time, posed and well-lit. Deborah liked a shop where you could rifle through the racks and knew your size by the small square of plastic on the neck of the hanger.

'You should try this.' Fiona held out a jersey dress in dark, loden green with a flippy hem and long draped sleeves.

It looked like it might fit Deborah's left leg. She reached for the price tag.

'You'll still be wearing it years from now.' Fiona gave it a little shake. 'It's an investment piece.'

'So is my mortgage.'

Fiona tutted and hung it back on the rack but not before she had held it against herself and instantly dismissed it, most likely for being something she could see on Deborah.

Vonnie had wandered over to a display of gaudy belts, coiled on a table, like a tangle of exotic snakes. She had picked one up and held it against her tummy, so flat it was almost concave.

'Nice,' said Fiona. 'You should get it.'

'I'm going to go and look at the cosmetics,' said Deborah. 'I'll see you down there.'

She spent a few minutes marvelling at the price of handbags, even in the sale, then wandered over to the make-up counters where she whiled away a good ten minutes testing lipsticks on the back of her hand and batting off the assistants. All but one, who managed to persuade her to have a skin assessment with the promise of a small bag of goodies at the end. It was here that they found her, perched high on a stool as the girl stared at her pores through a giant magnifying glass.

'Your skin's very dehydrated, and you've got some scaly patches in your A zone,' said the girl, as Fiona and Vonnie stopped beside her, both clutching bags.

'My A zone?' said Deborah. 'Where's my A zone?'

'Here.' The girl gestured to her forehead, nose and just under her eyes.

'Oh,' said Deborah. 'I thought that was my T zone.'

'In the more mature lady we call it the A zone. You need to take account of the delicate area under the eye.'

'Your bags,' said Vonnie. She leaned across and picked up one of the lotions the girl had laid out on a little tray and sniffed it. 'Nice.'

'I would recommend our microdermabrasion peel and our mineral hydration gel.'

I'll bet you would, thought Deborah. 'No, thank you,' she said.

'I'll get it for you,' said Fiona. 'A present. I've just treated Von to a belt.'

Deborah shook her head. 'No, really. It's fine. I'm getting some samples.'

'She'll take it,' said Fiona to the girl. 'As well as the samples.'

'No, really,' repeated Deborah. 'I'm fine.' She suddenly felt the urge to cry. Doug might have cancer, her A zone was scaly, and Fiona saw her as a charity case.

The assistant gave a hesitant smile.

Fiona whipped out her purse and handed the girl a card. 'The peel and the hydrating lotion, please.'

Vonnie was looking at Deborah. She reached over and put her hand on Fiona's elbow. 'I think it might be time for cocktails after all.'

*   *   *

The lounge bar of the George was surprisingly quiet given the hordes outside. Deborah sank into the small leather chair and put her smart little bag of toiletries on the glass-topped table, as Fiona picked up the drinks menu. The lighting was soft, Michael Bublé was crooning and the ferns in the deep terracotta pots were lush and real. Deborah had brushed them as she came in, just to check.

'Debs? Still or sparkling?'

Deborah looked up. She wanted a cup of tea and for everything to be different.

'Doug's got a lump.' She hadn't meant to blurt it out; hadn't meant to say it at all.

'What?' Fiona put down the menu.

'He found a lump, well, not a lump but a

205

swelling.' Deborah lowered her voice to a whisper. 'In his testicle. He's going in on Monday to the Western to have it checked. Please don't say anything. He didn't want me to.'

'Oh, honey.' Vonnie got out of her seat and bent to give her an awkward hug. 'I thought something was up.'

'Debs, you must be worried sick,' said Fiona.

Deborah felt tears prickle in her eyes again. She nodded.

'It'll be fine,' said Vonnie. 'It's probably nothing. Men get lumps all the time, well, not all the time, otherwise they'd be covered in them, but you know what I mean.'

Fiona glared at her. 'Even if it is . . . you know, it's really treatable,' she said. 'It's the best kind to get, really.' She paused. 'If there is such a thing.'

They were both looking at her, nodding sagely. She suddenly wanted to laugh. She was glad she'd told them, glad that someone else knew, but she'd forgotten how bad they were at condolence. They always had been. If she'd fallen over when she was younger, Fiona shouted her concern from a safe distance, freaked out by the thought of blood. Vonnie wanted to know how badly it hurt and to have a closer look. When she had got braces, Fiona had given her a hug and said she shouldn't worry because it wasn't as if boys were interested in her anyway. And when she failed her cycling proficiency test, Vonnie asked if she could have her bike because she wouldn't need it any more.

'It's really you who should be having a drink,' said Vonnie.

'Yeah, I'll drive,' said Fiona.

'Fiona will drive,' said Vonnie.

'Tea would be fine, actually.'

'You are not having tea,' said Vonnie. 'Come on, what do you fancy?'

Deborah sighed. 'A white wine then.'

'Crap,' said Vonnie. She raised her hand at the waiter who was hovering just a few feet away.

'Two Long Island Iced Teas, please, and a . . .' Vonnie looked at Fiona.

'Sparkling water,' added Fiona. 'San Pellegrino. No lemon, thanks.'

They sat without talking until the drinks arrived. Vonnie had pulled her new belt from its bag and had threaded it through the loops on the waistband of her skirt. She had dropped the bag on the floor and it was left to Deborah to lean down and pull it into the side and out of the waiter's way.

There was a lemon slice curved on the edge of Fiona's glass and she pulled it out and laid it on the table with a little snort.

Vonnie passed one of the iced teas to Deborah and raised her own.

'Right. Merry Christmas, girls, and Doug's good health.'

'Doug's good health,' repeated Fiona. She took a little sip of her fizzy water. 'Has he had it long? The swelling.'

'No, not long. He thought it might go down but it hasn't.'

'One of our partners had it a good few years back,' said Fiona. 'He just got one ball off and he's been as right as rain ever since. He did the Iron Man in Hawaii last year.'

'Good for him,' said Deborah weakly.

'Have you told Mum and Dad?' asked Vonnie. 'You should tell them. They'd want to know.'

'No, Doug doesn't want anyone to know really, until . . . you know, until we have it checked out. We haven't even told the girls, so you mustn't say a thing. Promise?'

'Promise,' said Fiona. She swiped a quick cross over her heart with a face as solemn as a six-year-old.

'How do you like the drink?' asked Vonnie.

'I have had one of these before,' said Deborah. 'I'm not a complete nun.'

'I never said you were.' Vonnie looked hurt. 'So do you want another one?'

Deborah shook her head. 'No, I'm fine.'

'Fi?' Vonnie turned to Fiona.

'Well, it depends.' Fiona hesitated. 'Are we going to do more shopping or not?'

They sat and looked at each other.

'Nah,' said Vonnie. 'Drinkies instead.'

*　　　*　　　*

It was an hour and a half later that Fiona checked her watch and found that it was 1.30 p.m. She threw down enough money to pay for the drinks, and the very expensive plate of oatcakes, olives and cheese that Vonnie had ordered, and shooed them all back to the car.

There was a moment of panic when Deborah couldn't find the parking ticket. She was sure she had given it to Fiona, but retrieved it finally from her coat pocket, in the torn bit where the lining had come away. She pulled back the seat to let Vonnie in and smelled the alcohol off her as she squeezed past.

'Vonnie, you're absolutely reeking. Mum and

208

Dad are going to think you've just been in the pub all day.'

'Well, we pretty much were.' Fiona stuck the ticket between her knees and pulled on her seat-belt. 'Although you can certainly pack it away, kid.' She laughed. 'Remember you told Mum and Dad you were going to a gospel concert and you got brought home in a police car?'

'That should have been a clue right there,' said Deborah.

'I was just experimenting,' said Vonnie.

Fiona smiled at her in the rear-view mirror. 'When are you going to stop?'

'Ha, ha-ha, ha-ha.'

'You will have to watch, though,' said Deborah. 'Did you not see that thing about hazardous drinking levels in the middle classes? Your liver could be in a right old state.'

'My liver's fine,' said Vonnie.

'And there're all these people whose bladders are bursting,' added Deborah.

Fiona burst out laughing. 'Is that the medical term for they peed themselves?'

'No, their bladders actually burst. Ruptured. Perforated.'

'Why did they burst?'

'Because they didn't pee.'

'That doesn't make sense,' said Vonnie.

'It makes perfect sense,' said Deborah. 'They drank so much their bladders were full, but they were so drunk they didn't know they needed the loo. So their bladders burst. Anyway, it's happening more often. There was a thing on the news about it.'

Vonnie leaned forward and put her hands on

209

Deborah's shoulders.

'What?' said Deborah. 'It's true.'

'I'm sure it is. And I love you. For always knowing something uniquely horrible.' Vonnie sat back. 'And Doug will be fine. Even if he has to have an op. Plenty of men only have one tentacle.'

'Testicle,' said Fiona.

'Pardon?' said Vonnie.

'Testicle. You said tentacle.'

'Did I?' Vonnie sniggered. 'God, imagine eight testicles.'

'I'd rather not,' said Fiona.

'Imagine the bulge.'

'The what?' asked Deborah.

'The bulge. The trouser bulge.'

'That would be quite disgusting,' said Fiona.

'They wouldn't be able to walk,' said Vonnie. 'It'd be like a bunch of grapes. No, plums. Eight plums.'

'Vonnie,' said Fiona.

Deborah laid her head back against the seat and closed her eyes. 'Can we stop talking about testicles, please.' She heard Fiona slide the ticket into the exit machine and then the car emerged into the hurtful glare of the afternoon.

* * *

It was Daisy who had noticed the dark, spreading stain on the seat of Ben's dungarees and advised Caroline that his nappy had reached capacity and needed changing. Caroline had meant to try him on the potty but it had been chaos since all the adults had disappeared. It had started well: they'd watched *Jason and the Argonauts* and then she'd

210

got them all into their coats and almost out into the garden, but then Katie had told Daisy that the molehills were made by dead people pushing up through the ground and she'd had hysterics and demanded they stay inside.

Then Caroline had suggested they make some fancy biscuits but she'd forgotten what kind of mess four children and a bag of self-raising flour can make. Goodness knows what would greet her when she got back downstairs with his lordship.

Ben was enjoying the sensation of an unbound bottom, lying back on the changing mat with both legs straight in the air and his hands holding on to his knees. He was taking an age to potty-train. Fiona seemed a little blasé about it; he only seemed to be changed when someone noticed his nappy was so full it had leaked.

She bent down. 'In my day, young man, you'd have been on the potty from about ten months on. Wouldn't you?'

He gave her a wide-cheeked smile.

She kept her face close to his and he reached up a fat fist and grabbed her hair.

'Ow,' said Caroline gently.

'Ow!' Ben gave a little snorting giggle.

Caroline bent closer and kissed his cheek, breathing in the smell of him. She had seen so little of him since he was born, maybe three times in all. It was lovely to have him all to herself.

She fixed on a new nappy, wrestled him into a fresh pair of trousers and lifted the small scented sack that held the old nappy, slinging it round her wrist, like a strange little evening bag.

Ben had got himself to his feet and was holding on to the edge of the travel cot. He turned a little

211

and raised his arms instinctively towards her and she felt the jolt. It had never gone. Every child she lifted or embraced; a memory of the one she couldn't touch.

She raised him up and settled him on her hip. He was heavy; a solid boy, not like Euan, who had been such a wisp, nothing to him at all.

'Who's Gran's best boy?' she said. She only said it because they were alone. In truth, she had no favourite. She loved them all, but none so much as Euan. She had called him her 'best boy' too and had meant it with every fibre of her. My best boy. My only one.

Ben, perhaps sensing her change of mood, headbutted her gently. She laughed.

'All right, buster, let's go and see what kind of disaster awaits us in the kitchen.'

It wasn't as bad as she'd feared. Katie and Daisy had made up and were playing with the decorations from the top of the Christmas cake, biting off the hard little edges of icing that clung to their bases. Jamie was slumped in the seat at the end of the table.

Caroline settled Ben on the floor and checked in the oven. The biscuits were still a while off from being ready.

'So.' She turned round. 'What do you all want to do while we wait for the biscuits to finish?'

'Can I go on Paper Dolls?' asked Daisy.

'What's that?' said Caroline. 'I've not heard of that.'

'It's these real people but they look kind of like dolls and they just have their underwear on and you get to dress them up,' said Daisy. 'You do it on the computer. Britney Spears is one. You can put

212

hair on her.'

'Oh, I really don't think so,' said Caroline. 'Does Mum let you do that?'

Daisy nodded. 'She sometimes does it with me. But she gets cross when Dad looks over her shoulder, because she says he's just looking at the pants.'

'Daisy,' said Jamie.

'I don't think we'll go on the computer,' said Caroline.

'Can we play in the big tent?' asked Daisy, who must have overcome her terror of the molehills because there were plenty that had popped up around the tent in the last two days.

Caroline shook her head. 'No, sweetheart, because I need it to be all ready for Tuesday.'

'Is it a big party?' asked Katie.

'There will be a lot of people.'

'How many?'

'Maybe about a hundred?'

Katie's eyes widened. 'Will they all bring presents for Grampa? Can we help open them?'

Caroline laughed. 'No, it's not his birthday. It's because he stopped work. Because he retired.'

'Why did he stop working?' asked Katie.

Daisy pre-empted her. 'Because he's old. You have to stop work when you get old because you start to drop things and stuff, don't you, Granny? You can't do as much and you forget things.'

Caroline tried not to smile. 'Kind of,' she said.

'Have you retired?' asked Katie.

That threw her. 'Well, I didn't really work, as such. I looked after your mums. That's a really hard job too.'

They looked at her kindly. 'So Grampa doesn't

213

have to go out to work any more?' said Katie.

'No,' said Caroline. 'He doesn't.'

Daisy gave her a lovely smile. 'That'll be nice for you, Granny. You won't be nearly so lonely now.'

Caroline turned back towards the cooker and gave the biscuits another, unnecessary, check. When she turned back, Daisy and Katie were holding their noses.

'Ben's smelly,' said Daisy.

'He can't be,' said Caroline. 'I've just changed him.'

'No, it's a poo.'

'Oh, gross!' said Katie, waving her hand under her nose.

Daisy nodded. 'I have to live with it all the time,' she said. 'It's quite disgusting. He should be trained by now to do it on the potty. Mum says it's just that boys take longer but I don't think it's normal. He'll probably do poos in his pants until he's well old.'

Katie started to giggle.

'Girls!' said Caroline. She turned to look at Jamie, whose face blanched. She couldn't ask him. But it suddenly occurred to her she hadn't checked on Min for a while and she could ask him to do that. She turned off the oven—the baking was too close to time for her to take the risk of leaving it— lifted Ben again, who was indeed stinking, and opened the door.

'Right. Girls, you just sit tight here. Ben, you appalling creature, you're coming with me. Jamie, would you mind going to check on Min? She's in the drawing room. See if she needs anything. I'll be back in a minute if she does.'

In the high-backed chair by the window, Min laid her book down on her knees and waited. She'd been listening to the chatter in the kitchen; not the words, she couldn't make them out, but the tenor of the voices. The children loud and questioning; Caroline, by turns patient and harassed. She had, however, heard Caroline ask someone to come and check on her. She watched the door to see who it might be. She could do with some company. She hadn't had much interaction with the children this holiday, and suspected Caroline was keeping them at a distance because of what had been happening. She knew something was wrong; that she had been forgetting things. Your episodes, the doctor had called them. He was a skittish thing, young and eager and was trying to be polite, she could remember that much. And he was right in that there were times when she could find herself in a place with no recollection of having got there or even wanting to be there in the first instance. That was the most unsettling thing. To move, function, talk, and not to be aware that you are; oblivious to it all. She would not let on to anyone how much it frightened her, the loss of control.

The door opened slowly. It was the boy. He poked his head round hesitantly as if he expected to find her asleep.

'Hello.'

'Hello.'

'Have you been sent to keep an eye on me?'

He gave an embarrassed smile. 'Ben needs his nappy changed again so Gran's had to go upstairs,' he said. 'She asked me to come in and see if you wanted anything.'

Min nodded. 'And you are?'

She saw him frown. 'Twelve?' he said.

'No, your name?'

The frown deepened. 'Jamie.'

'Of course you bloody well are.' She had always been rather good at names. 'I knew that. Jamie. Fiona's boy.'

He smiled again, weakly.

'So, Jamie, are you having a good Christmas?'

He moved round from behind the door and stood awkwardly in front of her. 'Eh, kind of.'

'Kind of? What does that mean?'

He shrugged before folding into himself again like a collapsing umbrella. Not a good sign in a boy of his age, thought Min, something more than the awkwardness of puberty; a lack of confidence, maybe, deep and building. She'd seen boys like that before, as hesitant and unsure as whipped dogs. And the poor little sod had been left to drift around the entire time he'd been here. She'd noticed that. Hanging around in the background like Banquo's ghost.

She sat a little more upright and looked at him. 'Do you know how to play canasta?'

'No.'

'Poker? Do you know how to play poker?'

There was a flicker of interest. He said 'no' again, but his voice was different.

'I thought you were all playing it online these days now, when you're not surfing for pornography. No?'

He flushed bright red and shook his head vehemently, but his posture had changed, a slight shift, a little more upright, and a hint of an

216

embarrassed laugh was curving at the corners of his mouth. He was a bonny boy when he smiled.

'Right,' she said. 'Would you like to learn?'

'Poker?'

'Yes, poker.'

He nodded enthusiastically.

'Well, go and get me a pack of cards. There are some in the bureau drawer in the dining room. If you don't know what a bureau is, then ask your gran. And while you're at it, once she's finished changing nappies ask her to get an old lady a cherry brandy with just a dash of lemonade. And whatever you're having.'

It was a while before he was back, carrying the tray with the cards, the brandy, something fizzy for himself in a tall plastic tumbler and a small bowl of snacks. He set it on the small side table at her elbow as she instructed and folded out the card table she pointed out, slotted in behind the tallboy.

'Did you tell her we were playing poker?'

'No.' He smiled. 'I just said cards.'

'Clever lad,' said Min, as he pulled up a chair opposite. 'Right.' She laid her hands on the table. Texas Hold'em or Omaha High?'

He blinked. 'Em . . .'

She burst out laughing and pushed the pack of cards towards him. 'You'll have to deal. We'll start with Texas Hold'em, it's the simplest version. Two down cards for each of us. That's your personal hand, you call it your hole or pocket hand, okay? Hole or pocket hand. Take them out and put them face down. Two each. We should have more players but we'll just have to make do.'

He eased the cards from the pack and Min caught their familiar waxy scent as he shuffled them inexpertly and pulled four cards from the top, laying two each down on the baize.

'How much money have you got?'

He looked up, slightly panicked. 'Well, em, I got some money for Christmas but . . .'

'I'm fooling you,' said Min. 'You need to learn how to bluff. We'll play for these just now, and if you're any good, we'll move on to cash.' She picked up a handful of pretzels and shared them out between them.

'Okay,' she said, popping a pretzel into her mouth. 'Listen up.' He was sitting forward in his seat now, his eyes keen, glancing between the cards and the snacks and her hands. His shoulders had lifted. She smiled to herself. Rena would have loved this had she been here. See, Min would have whispered to her, that's all it takes. Just a little time to find something that piques them; engage them, and they'll be eating out of your hand.

And Rena would have said, 'Yes, my dear,' from behind the pages of her book, as if she hadn't heard. But there would have been pleasure in her voice anyway, just at the sound of Min's and the small kindness she was about to do.

*   *   *

Gran had a way of fastening up your coat that made you feel like you might never get out of it again. Katie tugged at the zip, which was grazing her chin, and pulled it down to the middle of her chest, popping the press studs as she went. It wasn't even raining or cold but Gran said they couldn't go outside without a coat and hat, if they had one. Katie didn't have a hat but Daisy did, a pink woolly one with a green cloth butterfly on it that was now pulled down so low on her head that it looked like she didn't have any eyebrows. She peered up at Katie from beneath it.

'What do you want to do?'

Katie shrugged. 'Dunno.'

They'd already had a look in the big tent; Gran had finally relented, but it was really just a big empty space with lots of chairs and tables piled in one corner. Daisy had wanted to dance on the wooden bit that had been put down for a floor; she had copied the moves from the *Disney Girl* magazine and had showed Katie. It was a bit jerky, really, but Katie hadn't wanted to say. Daisy said she was going to do it at Grampa's party. Katie hoped she didn't or people might laugh. And not in a good way.

They'd checked on the hens, but only Pinky was visible, strutting around the enclosure like she was showing off. Katie thought her feathered legs looked like long frilly knickers. They watched her for a while in case she decided to lay an egg, but she just pecked about for ages until they gave up and wandered away.

And now they were bored.

'We could play homes, I suppose,' said Daisy. 'I could be the mum—'

'I want to be the mum,' said Katie.

Daisy thought for a moment. 'We can't both be mums. If we're both mums that would mean we were lesbians.'

'We can't do that,' said Katie.

Daisy nodded. 'Some people think Jamie is a lesbian,' she said.

'A boy can't be a lesbian,' said Katie scornfully.

219

'It's not possible. You have to be a girl. A boy is just gay.'

Daisy glanced up at her. 'Well, some boys at school think Jamie is gay but he's not. He's just not popular.' She pushed her glasses up her nose.

'How do you know some people think that?' said Katie.

'My friend's big sister goes on the bus. She said they say it all the time and that he cried when they said it once.'

'That's horrible,' said Katie.

'It's why he gets sad, sometimes,' said Daisy. 'He doesn't know I know, but that's okay. Mummy says he's a very private person.'

'Does your mum know?' said Katie.

'No,' said Daisy. 'Jamie doesn't like people knowing anything.' She gave a dramatic sigh, then her face brightened. 'It's okay to be gay, though,' she added.

'Is it?' said Katie.

Daisy nodded vigorously. 'Graham Norton is gay.'

'Is he?' asked Katie, not terribly sure who Graham Norton was, but not wanting to say because Daisy was younger.

'But Jamie's not,' said Daisy.

'No,' said Katie.

'And you're not to tell that I know. Or tell Mum.'

'Okay.'

'Swear.'

'I swear.'

Daisy looked satisfied that the secret was safe. She glanced over again at the molehills.

'Is it really dead people?'

'No,' said Katie kindly. 'It's the animals. The moles. I was just kidding.'

'Why do they do that?' asked Daisy.

Katie sighed. 'It's like their graves when the old ones die. They can't see so they don't know they're pushing all the earth up when they dig it.'

Daisy nodded, then her face brightened. 'We could put some flowers on them. If they're graves. That's what you do.'

'I suppose.' Katie looked around. There were some snowdrops over by the back door, a little crop with a curly dog poo right next to them so they would have to be careful when they picked them.

They had just finished when the car appeared through the trees. They ran over. Aunt Vonnie was in the back and had obviously just woken up. Katie's mum got out of the passenger seat and gave her a big hug. 'So, have you girls had fun?'

'We put flowers on the moles' graves,' said Daisy, who was up in Aunt Fiona's arms. Katie could tell that her mum and Aunt Fiona were trying not to laugh.

'Okay,' said her mum.

Katie glared at her and her shiny little shopping bag. She ought to know that if you go off somewhere interesting and don't take your children with you, then putting flowers on the graves of moles is the kind of thing they have to end up doing.

CHAPTER ELEVEN

SUNDAY, 27 DECEMBER

His first instinct was: why hadn't they phoned? David reached out and turned up the volume on the radio. He had come into his study for some peace and quiet after breakfast but the noise had followed him: squeals and yells, a dog's excited yelp, the rumble of running feet up and down the hallway.

'The System Three poll for the Sunday Herald *was conducted in the two days before Christmas Eve. Forty-four per cent of those questioned said they were minded to vote "yes" for independence, thirty-seven per cent would vote "no" and nineteen per cent were undecided. A spokesman for the SNP has welcomed the . . .'*

Now that was significant; that would be the first poll that had shown a majority for a yes vote, and outwith the margin of error. He sat back, feeling the familiar rush of adrenaline. It would not have been enough to take him into the office, but he would have been on the phone by now with the duty editor and the political editor, considering what tack to take, reaction from the parties, the tenor of their leader column, should they run one at all? It was rare he ever had to go in on a Sunday. It had to be big: a train wreck, a plane down, a political resignation. Normally he would just monitor and wait for the calls that would tell him how the paper was shaping up. It was the best of all worlds, a Sunday, the power to have the final say without the need to be there.

The noise in the hall faded and the bulletin moved on: two dead in a car crash on the A9, a stabbing in Elderslie, a rise in calls to a festive domestic abuse helpline and the weather, 11 degrees in Aberdeen; still unseasonably warm.

He leaned back again and looked out of the window. The study was at the back of the house next to the dining room. It had one window that faced on to the garden, but where the dining room was square on to the biggest lawn, with its borders and neatly cut grass, his office faced the drying green and the whirlygig, which today was hung with a pennant of small clothes: vests and trousers and tiny socks. Ben's, he guessed. He was an engaging little boy but David found it difficult to be around him. It was the same with Jamie, and it wasn't their fault; far from it. But he would watch them and sense what felt like resentment. Their whole lives ahead of them. No chance of lightning striking twice. It was different with the girls, with Elsa, Katie and Daisy. He could delight in their company without ever thinking what might have been.

He looked away from the window. It wasn't a particularly big room. There wasn't space for much beyond the broad desk with its faded green leather blotter that he had picked up at a sale in Stockbridge and the bookcases that lined two of the walls. Even if he read from now until he was ninety he would never have as many books as his father had done: encyclopaedias, collected works, novels, gardening books, paperbacks, and rows and rows of academic journals, sorted by topic and date and packed so tight that David could remember the pinch in his fingers if he tried to dislodge one. He used to love going into his father's study when he was allowed, and sitting at the big roll-top desk, fiddling with the fountain pens, spinning in the chair and pretending to work.

Which was, he thought, looking down at the tightly shut laptop, exactly what he was doing now. Pretending to work.

He had the book, of course, or rather 15,000 words of notes, roughly assembled into chapters. And three large foolscap files with cuttings which he needed to date and sort. Such a huge undertaking. And on dark days, like today, a pointless one. He had no doubt it would be politely received, maybe a couple of warm reviews, perhaps even a modest ranking on the Scottish bestseller chart for a week or so. But he expected that there would be numerous apologies for absences at his launch and soon it would be an anonymous spine on a back shelf at Waterstones, and then a library book with not so many date stamps on the fly-leaf.

He really ought to be working on it today. The deadline was August, and he had had a few nights of waking in the early hours with fright at the task ahead. He also ought to be working on ideas for the *New Statesman*. He knew Caroline was telling people he had the promise of a column, but that wasn't strictly true. They had suggested one piece for early in the New Year and who was to know if there would be anything after that? And it was so long since he had actually written anything. He had been good at one time, but not spectacular. His skill had been in extracting information from people, asking the right questions. He was a competent wordsmith, but not a beautiful one.

After the party. He would start then. Or maybe 2 January. He switched off the radio and opened the top drawer on the right of the desk. It held his spare binoculars, a hole-punch he had appropriated from the office, the headed notepaper that Caroline had ordered and that he loathed. It was too thick to fold easily, and the colour of days-old cream, with Fortune House picked out in unnecessarily ornate script. He never used it. And at the very back, lying next to some unopened packs of Post-its, his BlackBerry. He had put it there in a fit of pique on Christmas Day, hating the way it stayed so silent. No texts, no calls. Hating the way he still sought it out and checked it often and reflexively, like an anxious mother.

He turned towards the window. It had started to rain and Caroline was out at the whirlygig, plucking off clothes and laying them over her shoulder as she went along, face scrunched tight against the smirr. The wind caught the drier and spun it. David watched her move with it, unpegging and lifting, unpegging and lifting. A sock fell to ground and she stooped to retrieve it, giving it a hearty shake before she added it to the pile building against her neck.

He felt the same rush of loss and longing as he had on Christmas Eve. He used to be able to tell what she was thinking, could pre-empt the next line of her conversation, a question she was about to ask. Not now. Now they talked as if there were a time delay between them, so out of tune that they would cut across each other and sink into awkward pauses.

She picked the final piece of washing from the line and turned for the house, head bent, hair lank and wet. He watched until she disappeared back into the house. Such a beautiful girl, she had been. Challenging and beautiful.

*   *   *

'You didn't have to bring that through.' Charlie lifted the plates from Gail's hands and laid them on the counter. 'I was just going to do it.'

'Yeah, and pigs might . . .' Gail laughed. 'Annie's showing Boyd her skipping rope through there and I didn't want them ending up on the rug.'

She moved over to the sink and pressed the lever for the hot tap. Charlie came up behind her and slipped his arms round her as the steam rose in the heaped basin.

'He's not going to be here long,' he said, lowering his voice.

'I know.' She leaned back against him.

It wasn't that Gail didn't like Boyd, Charlie knew she did. But sometimes she worried that Charlie was carrying him; that he didn't pull his weight, at work and in the friendship. And when he commandeered the sofa and the TV after being invited for lunch, it didn't help. The fact that he was supposed to come on Boxing Day but didn't turn up because he'd forgotten or was still too lashed from Christmas Day didn't help either.

'He's great with Annie,' offered Charlie. 'She loves him.' Which she did, hurling herself at him as he came through the door and insisting he inspect and admire her entire haul of Christmas presents, including a doll that pissed itself when you squeezed it, which Boyd had pronounced 'freakin' weird', and had earned a hard stare from Gail.

226

'I know.' Gail switched off the tap and squirted some washing-up liquid into the sink.

'There's a lot you know,' said Charlie. He bent and kissed the back of her neck. Her skin was hot and her earrings glinted through her hair, which was half pulled back in a large black claw-like clip. She only took off the earrings at night, and touched them often as if she still couldn't quite believe they were there.

'Do you have to work tomorrow?' Gail exhaled softly against him.

'' 'Fraid so. I need to finish up before that big bash at the Haldanes and I've got a couple of quotes to do.'

Charlie stood back and moved over to the fridge, pulling two bottles of beer from the shelf in the door.

Gail turned and raised her eyebrows at him. 'No, really, it's fine, you get pissed with your pal and I'll do the dishes and then go and clear out the pit that is your daughter's room.'

'I can do that later.'

'It's fine. I'm not incapacitated. And I don't want to watch footy. Keep an eye on Annie, though, and don't let him wind her up. See if you can get him to take his boots off—he's going to leave marks on the rug.'

She turned to leave the kitchen, then stopped and put a hand to her side.

'Another twinge?' asked Charlie, shutting the fridge door with his hip.

'Mmm,' said Gail.

'No twinges,' said Charlie. 'He's a 2010 boy, the year his country votes to win its freeeedum! Aren't you, son?'

Gail shook her head. 'How do you know it's a boy and how do you know the vote will be yes?'

'Because it will.' He bent forward towards her stomach. 'Stay in there, pal. You've got another two weeks before your release date. Okay?'

'Yes, Daddy,' said Gail, rubbing his head with her hand.

'Can you say that to me later?' Charlie grinned at her.

'No. I am with child and you can't touch me.' She turned and caught hold of the banisters as Boyd started to sing, accompanied by Annie's high-pitched warbling. 'You got me into this state and that's your punishment. And now can you get through there before your friend turns my girl into Kerry Katona?'

*   *   *

Elsa laid her bag at her feet and turned the key in the lock. She'd remembered about the alarm— probably because her mum had mentioned it so many times—and once the door was opened, she lifted the small grey panel above the desiccated spider plant and quickly typed in the numbers. The frantic beeping stopped.

The hallway was cold because Doug had turned down the heating before they had left, to save money and at Katie's insistence. She'd seen a documentary about polar bears on Animal Planet and had become the family's green conscience as a result, albeit one who always left lights on in a room she had just left. The cat appeared and wound himself round her legs and she bent down to stroke him. He felt fat. But then they had left loads of food for him, and he would have been scrounging from the neighbours as well.

There was one letter on the floor, a card with no stamp and the kind of feathery, angled writing that meant it had been written by someone old. It was probably from the elderly lady two doors down. She'd become something of a pet project for her mum when they first moved in. Deborah had always been popping round, getting her messages, checking she was okay. Which was all very nice, but as the girls grew older she started asking them to do it, and they hated it, because the house smelled of piss and something burned and the woman always tried to give them the little rectangular tokens from old cigarette packets that she kept in a big wicker basket. Embassy tokens, her mum said they were, and made them put them in the bin and then wash their hands. They had only got out of it when it turned out that Deborah wasn't the only one buying her a bottle of sherry with her weekly shop. Deborah had been at a coffee morning and another neighbour had mentioned that she'd been buying her booze, too, and then another, and it turned out that she had four people in the street doing the same thing and she was actually a raging alcoholic. Elsa and Katie never had to go back.

Elsa lifted the card and set it on the shelf with the house keys. In the kitchen she switched on the immersion heater, refilled the cat's food and water dishes and filled the kettle. She found a tube of Pringles in the cupboard and took them through to the sitting room, turning on the gas fire and the TV and pulling the throw from the sofa over her to keep warm. She checked the clock: 12.30 p.m. She could maybe have two hours before Deborah would be calling to see where she was, and Elsa didn't want to be in her bad books, especially as she was planning to ask about leaving uni tomorrow.

She'd had another long chat with Matt last night, fuelled by a box of wine and a muglai korma, and he had said there was no point in delaying it. He'd asked Elsa how she felt about going back to law and she'd thought about foundations of criminology on a Monday, then two hours of business entities, and she couldn't face it, not unless she knew there was an out. Law hadn't really been her idea, after all. Her parents had got so excited about it when she'd mentioned it after a careers day at school, and it had all just snowballed from there.

Matt said it would be best to get it all done by Hogmanay. They had tickets to the street party and it would be great to have it a done deal and to start planning. A fresh start. Her dad would help, he was bound to see her side, even if her mum didn't. And it might be easier doing it at Fortune House with everybody else there.

She finished the Pringles watching half an hour of *Who Wants to be a Millionaire?* and then went for her shower, delighted to have no one banging on the door needing in. She had always loved the house, but it seemed to have shrunk as she'd grown. She hated Dad's spiky little shavings in the sink from where he had tapped out his electric razor; the laundry basket, stale and always filled to overflowing; Katie's fruity soaps congealing on the bath's edge; the medicine cabinet filled with bottles and cotton buds and boxes of wax earplugs and laxatives and Imodium, and so stuffed that she had to keep her Tampax box in her room.

At least the water was hot. She stood under the shower for ages, until the skin on her chest and stomach had reddened, working out her exact phraseology for what she would tell her parents.

It's like this. I'm really struggling. I'm just not enjoying it. It was too soon to choose. I'm not convinced it's for me. I need some time to figure everything out. It's not even a year; just a few months. Please.

She dried herself and changed into clean clothes, switched everything off and phoned her mum to say she was just leaving for the 3.10 p.m. train. The dutiful daughter; at least for now.

*   *   *

There must be dried thyme. Fiona pulled over one of the kitchen chairs and kicked off her shoes, stepping up on to the seat to peer into the top two shelves of the cupboard. She'd already been through the spice rack, an ancient affair bolted to the wall and holding twelve small wooden-topped jars that looked like they had never been opened. Eight of them were more than two years past their sell-by date. Fiona had lifted them off and grouped them on the counter to go out, but suspected Caroline would stick them right back on once she'd mentioned it.

It wasn't so surprising that they were out of date, because the kitchen itself had hardly changed over the years. It was still dominated by the large Rayburn range, its cream frontage marked and blackened near the door's edges. Fiona still bore a scar on her wrist from one of the hotplates. She must have been about eight, and had only leaned on it for an instant, but it was the hottest one and it seared her skin so badly that she had to be taken to the doctor. It was a good-sized room and Fiona had often imagined what it would look like if it was gutted and replaced with something bespoke and classy. Her parents had kept the old free-standing units, topped with oak, which bore the marks of many years' use: scores and scratches and half-moon stains from hot pans. Only the linoleum had been replaced, and the wax cloth that Caroline liked stretched across the table at all times, greasy and unyielding, like the skin on a cheese. There was one sash window, directly behind the sink with a confusion of plants on the sill.

Fiona peered at the shelf in front of her. Cornflour, baking powder, some vegetable stock cubes, a vanilla pod in a glass tube, oregano, sticking plasters, self-raising flour, a tin of treacle that was stuck to the shelf, and some cupcake cases. There was a small plastic basket with a green handle in the way. She lifted it down. On the top, opened and with the torn foil insert poking out, was a packet of Zantac. Deborah had been right.

Fiona stepped down and laid the basket on the countertop, pushing the Zantac gingerly out of the way with one finger. There was a tube of aloe vera cream, and another of arnica, some dispersible aspirin, more sticking plasters, some tablets for gas and bloating and two small brown bottles. Fiona turned them so the labels were showing. Diazepam and Imovane. To be taken as needed. Mrs Caroline Haldane.

Happy pills and sleeping pills. Everything you need to keep you going; stacked among your

232

basics. She slipped the Zantac packet back where it had been and lifted the basket back into the cupboard, feeling suddenly guilty, wondering how long Caroline had been taking them. She hadn't looked at the date. Maybe they were old. There were certainly some pills left. Or maybe that's what you got after forty-plus years of marriage. Matching china, and rampant anxiety.

The door opened and she jumped, even though the basket was safely stowed above her head. It was Allan and he had his coat on.

'Car keys?'

'What for?' Fiona moved back over to the cooker to check on the stewing tomatoes.

'I'm going to run in to Fortune to get some ciggies and pick up Elsa.'

Fiona turned round to look at him. They hadn't spoken about Elsa since their fight on Christmas Day. 'Are Debs and Doug not about?'

'Yeah, but they asked if I wouldn't mind, seeing as I'm going in anyway,' said Allan, his eyes darting around the countertops looking for the keys.

Lucky you, thought Fiona.

'In my bag, in the hall,' she said. 'Do you know where you're going?'

'Sat nav.' He smiled and put his hand on the door. He had nice hands, long tapered fingers, but masculine for all that. It was what he did with them that she didn't like.

She gave him a flat smile. 'Actually, can you get me some thyme when you're in? Doesn't matter if you can't. I'll try to work around it.'

'Thyme,' he said. 'Okay. Anything else?'

She shook her head and he slipped out of the door. On the hob, the tomatoes spat angrily in

233

their copper-bottomed pot. She thought of the pills in the cupboard and Elsa waiting at the station. 'Maybe a divorce,' she said in her head, and was a little taken aback that she had.

*　　　*　　　*

The Renault Mégane passed in a sputter of exhaust. Vonnie had waved, recognising it as Fiona's hire car, but whoever was driving—it was too dark for her to see—hadn't spotted her. She stepped back out into the roadway and picked up her pace. She ought to have started earlier, because the light was almost completely gone. And she should have planned out her route, as David had suggested, because her lower back was hurting and it only ever hurt if she went further than six or seven miles. She was almost at the row of cottages near the crossroads. They were less than a mile from the house. It was the time of day when people start to think about closing the curtains, but haven't quite got round to it yet because it feels too soon to shut out the world. She slowed as she passed the strip of bright windows, each a different tableau: an empty lounge, fussily papered, with a fringed lampshade and a crucifix on the wall; a man bending to tend to a fire; two figures on a sofa, faces blank and immobile, staring at a TV screen.

She took the left fork at the crossroads. There was a slight dip and she lengthened her stride, hoping she didn't hit a pothole. At the barn conversion a small dog followed her progress along the bottom of the leylandii hedge, growling nervously. She tried to whistle, but didn't have the

234

breath for it. If Mike was here, he would make her sprint the last half-mile, but he wasn't, and she slowed to a plod until she reached the cattle grid, where she stopped. Her walk up the drive would be her cooldown. She tiptoed over the metal bars, the ones that Fiona had broken her ankle on when she was about ten. They had been holding pretend Olympics and Fiona was being Daley Thompson in the long jump, but she'd fallen short and landed between the last two struts. Vonnie thought she had heard her ankle break but Euan said she was lying. Fiona was lucky she pulled her foot out in time because her ankle swelled up horribly, all white and knobbly, like the painted rocks that David had put along the edge of the drive. She had the cast on for ages and everyone drew on it and Caroline even let her paint her toenails—which she'd been wanting to do for ages—because her foot stuck out the end.

She came out of the trees, hands on her hips, still breathing heavily. Like the cottages, the downstairs windows in the house were lit. She could see Fiona in the kitchen, wearing the silly kilt apron, so it must have been someone else in the car. Allan possibly, escaping from his in-laws.

'Good run?'

'Jesus!' Vonnie put her hand to her chest.

Deborah laughed. 'Sorry. Didn't mean to make you jump.'

Vonnie walked towards the figure by the summerhouse door. 'What are you doing in here?' She spotted the glass of wine in Deborah's hand. 'Secret boozer, I knew it. Better watch your bladder, might pop at any moment if you keep that up.'

'I just needed some time out,' said Deborah, 'and Mum said you'd gone for a run. I thought I'd wait for you. Allan's gone to get Elsa.'

Vonnie sat down in front of her on the summerhouse step and settled her elbows on her knees.

'Your phone's been going,' said Deborah.

'Has it?'

It would be Mike wanting to know about London. She'd sent him a couple of breezy texts, but hadn't yet answered his question, mostly because she didn't know how.

'Where did you go?'

'Further than I meant to,' said Vonnie. 'Is Fiona cooking?'

'Yeah,' said Deborah. 'Italian. Smells good.'

Her voice was flat. Vonnie turned, even though she couldn't properly make out her sister's features. 'You okay?'

'Kind of.'

'It'll be fine,' said Vonnie. 'When's he going in again?'

'Tomorrow.'

'I know, but when?'

'Eleven,' said Deborah.

'I'd give you a hug, but I'm stinking,' said Vonnie.

'I'll pass,' said Deborah. 'But thanks.'

Vonnie stood up. 'You coming in?'

'In a moment,' said Deborah, still leaning against the door.

Vonnie started towards the house. She turned, walking backwards. 'He'll be fine.'

She could tell that Deborah was nodding. 'I hope so,' she said.

CHAPTER TWELVE

MONDAY, 28 DECEMBER

'We should have taken the stairs.'

Deborah raised her eyes to the light display above the lift, trying not to notice the large green sign beside it, the one that said Oncology, two lines down, in bright white letters. She reminded herself they were going to a different floor.

An orderly pulling a large metal crate full of sharply folded linen stopped beside them and flashed an apologetic smile. 'Takes an age,' he said.

Deborah nodded and tried to smile back but her lips stuck to her teeth. Beside her, Doug was standing very straight, clutching the white card the GP had given him. They'd told Caroline and David they had some errands to run, and managed to persuade Elsa and Katie that they were doing nothing more interesting than picking up the mail and maybe doing some food shopping. They stopped at the house only briefly to empty the cat's litter tray and then headed across town to the Western General.

The main car park was full and the man at the gate waved them past, with no instruction as to where they might find a space. There were cars on verges and in loading bays, double-parked and crammed together. They circled for a while, with Deborah growing increasingly frantic until an elderly woman reversed out of a space in front of them in one of the furthest lots. They walked quickly back to the main door and through the cloud of cigarette smoke coiling around the small knot of patients outside.

A loud rasping squeak signalled that the lift had arrived, and the doors juddered open. The laundry man stood back to let them in and pulled his cart in after them.

'Three, please,' said Deborah.

The lift smelled stale and there was a crushed tissue balled on the floor in the corner. They rose in silence and she reached across and took hold of Doug's damp hand.

At the reception desk in the Urology Department, Doug handed across his white, crumpled card and they sat in the waiting area under a faded print of Tobermory Harbour. Deborah watched the nurses and auxiliaries move to and fro, at ease in their surroundings. There were two other men in the waiting room, both on their own, both younger than Doug. Deborah tried to catch their eye to give them sympathetic smiles, but one was buried behind the *Daily Record* and the other was flicking idly at the buttons on his jacket. Neither of them looked particularly perturbed.

It was a good twenty minutes before a nurse appeared from a side door and said, 'Mr Warrender?' Doug gave her hand a quick squeeze and followed the nurse through the door into a narrow corridor.

She should have brought a paper or a magazine, anything to distract her. She glanced at the clock. He would probably be examined and then discuss the blood tests that the GP had taken if they were back, maybe even have a scan. He had promised he would call her in if there was anything she needed to hear.

She looked at the pile of magazines on the table. There was nothing that would interest her, not that she would be touching them even if they had. She considered, for a moment, running back down to the shop at the entrance and buying a paper, but she didn't like the thought of Doug coming out to look for her and her not being there.

In the end, she could have gone to the shop. In fact she could have driven to John Lewis and queued in the sale and still made it back because it was ages before he reappeared. She told herself they were just being thorough, but by the time the door opened she was sick with nerves and dread. It couldn't be good. Not to have taken so long.

Doug didn't speak until she reached him and they were in the corridor on the other side of the waiting room door.

His face folded. 'Not looking too great,' he said, and she felt her insides turn to jelly. She grabbed for his hand and followed him into a small room on the left.

The consultant, Mr Swann, was younger than she had expected; maybe late thirties with a thin, pinched face and an electric-blue tie. Behind him, Deborah caught sight of two family photos: a small girl somewhere sandy, and a family shot. His wife, if that's who it was, was prettier than he deserved.

He extended his hand to her and then motioned her to sit.

'As I was saying to your husband, Mrs Warrender, the best option is for us to conduct an inguinal orchiectomy . . .' He paused, realising he had got ahead of himself. 'I've examined your

239

husband and I think in all likelihood that the growth is cancerous. That's certainly backed up by the bloods; there were increased markers of both AFP and LDH.'

Deborah nodded as if she had a clue. 'The growth?' she said. 'There is a growth?'

'There is a small mass that showed up on the scan, yes.'

'And it's cancerous?' she said.

'In all likelihood,' repeated the consultant. 'As I was saying, an inguinal orchiectomy is the best response. Mr Warrender will be in and out in a day. It's all done under local anaesthetic. Basically, we make an incision above the pubic bone and remove the testicle through the inguinal canal. There is the possibility of a prosthesis—'

Deborah held up her hand. 'But if you don't know absolutely that it is cancer, then why are you removing it?'

He must have explained all this to Doug because he was sitting quietly in his chair, hands folded, protectively, in his lap.

'It really is a necessary procedure, Mrs Warrender, where testicular cancer is suspected.'

'Can you not do a biopsy?'

The consultant steepled his fingers and leaned forward on the desk. 'Technically, yes, but it's almost as invasive, and in this case . . .' He tailed off.

She turned to look at Doug. He gave her a weak smile. She wanted the doctor not to be there, so she could pull him to her.

'I realise this is a lot to take in,' said the consultant. 'If you have any questions?'

She turned back to look at him. Any questions?

240

So many, but none that she could ask. Is he going to die? How will the girls take it? If it comes back, what then?

'It really is a relatively minor procedure,' said the doctor again. 'After which we will examine the tumour to see if there's been any spread.' He must have seen the blood, what was left of it, drain from her face.

'Spread is unlikely,' he added. 'The growth is small and we appear to have found it early. And testicular cancer has one of the highest cure rates, essentially a hundred per cent if it has not metastasised. Even in cases where there is spread, cure rates are around the eighty-five per cent mark. It's not a death sentence, Mrs Warrender, not by any means.'

He sounded now like he was quoting from a manual: how to pacify devastated wives.

'But I thought it was younger men . . .' said Deborah.

'Thanks.' Doug gave a flat little laugh. He was trying to make a joke and it didn't work. It never did. He was useless at jokes. She felt the catch in her throat. Her Doug.

The consultant had ignored her last remark and was looking down at some papers on his desk.

'Now, we can schedule the orchiectomy for Wednesday the 6th, if that suits . . .'

'Do you not have anything sooner?' Deborah blurted out. 'Tomorrow.' She suddenly wanted it out of him. Gone. Unable to grow. Stuff David's party and the bloody marquee and everyone coming.

The consultant looked up as Doug reached over and patted her hand. 'The sixth is fine; preferable, actually. A little more time to get organised.'

'Of course,' said the consultant. He scribbled something in the margin. 'So 2.30 p.m. on Wednesday the 6th. Nil by mouth ten to twelve hours prior. Reception will give you all the details.' He sounded as if he were arranging nothing more arduous than a haircut.

They took the stairs down, saying nothing. Deborah even forgot not to touch the banisters and held on to them like a child. There was a new batch of smokers by the front door including a man in a wheelchair with an IV drip towering over him like a cheap lampstand. His skin was pale and waxy and his eyes ringed by deep grey shadow. You could always tell with the eyes, thought Deborah. When people had given up, when the end was close. She felt a sudden wave of nausea. They hurried past.

She paid for the parking at the ticket machine as Doug unlocked the car. He didn't start the engine and she slipped into her seat and gathered him quickly into her. He clung on, his head against her neck, his breathing short. He wasn't crying. Doug never cried. Not at anything. She cradled his head and whispered to him; meaningless words. A woman walked past the bonnet and glanced in, then looked quickly away. The worst possible news, she must have thought. Which in her head Deborah knew that it wasn't, but in her heart felt very much that it was.

Ever since Euan, she had waited her whole life for the other shoe to fall, and now it had. Every cough, every twinge, every one of Elsa and Katie's childhood ailments, she had worried herself sick, and when everyone said, don't be silly, she knew that she was not. She knew that you can lose someone in an instant, and had told the girls so when they chafed at her constant anxiety. And it had been constant, an indelible shadow on a lovely, ordinary life. Long after the accident she would lie at night and imagine Euan had left a few seconds later, that the lorry driver had gone a little slower and she saw in her mind that they passed each other on the road, and carried on, safely home. Euan would have dropped the bike on the gravel as he always did and would have earned another row, and he would have tugged her hair as he always did, and would have called her 'podge', which she never minded, because it was said with warmth.

She felt Doug's hair between her fingers and bent her head again on to his. It could not take him. She wouldn't let it.

*   *   *

Fiona lifted the large tray of chicken breasts from the chilled cabinet and studied the label. She couldn't have liked what she saw, because she put them back down almost immediately and moved on.

'No chicken?' Vonnie followed her with the trolley. 'I thought we were having chicken.'

'No free-range,' said Fiona. 'We're in the middle of one of the best agricultural areas of the country and all that's available is battery-farmed crap. We're going to have to stop by the butcher's.'

'We could use one of Mum's. Pinky's nice and plump.'

'Vonnie! Anyway they're bantams. You can't eat them.'

'I was joking.' Vonnie sighed. The supermarket shop was taking far longer that she'd expected. She'd only agreed to come because Fiona had mentioned a pub lunch afterwards. But it would have to be a fine lunch to make up for this interminable trawl around the aisles of the local co-operative.

'Can you go and find some fresh basil for me?' Fiona spoke over her shoulder. 'I'll get the pasta and the crème fraîche.'

Vonnie veered off towards the fruit and veg. She doubted there would be fresh basil and she was right. She got some pre-packed rocket instead, then took herself off up the crisps and snacks aisle and loaded up on Pringles and Twiglets, and the strange little Japanese rice crackers that she knew Min liked.

'You are as bad as a toddler.' Fiona appeared behind her and dropped a tub of crème fraîche and three large packets of fresh pasta into the trolley. 'Basil?'

'Didn't have any,' said Vonnie. 'Can we go now?'

'I guess so. Although how I'm going to get a meal out of this I don't know.'

The tills had long queues, so Vonnie left Fiona with the trolley and moved over to the newspaper stand. It was still all politics as far as she could see, at least in the broadsheets. The tabloids were exercised by a minor soap star caught on a camera phone making racist comments. She picked up the *Scotsman*. It looked the same. There was nothing about it that would suggest it was being run by somebody new. She wondered if David could stand to look at it; if he even had since he had left. Caroline had emailed Vonnie the weblink to the short piece the paper had run when David's retirement was announced. The picture that accompanied it was good, a black and white shot of him behind his desk, looking serious and important. The copy, however, had been another matter.

The editor of the Scotsman, *David Haldane, has announced that he is to retire at the end of the year. Mr Haldane, 63, one of Scotland's most experienced and influential journalists, said: 'It has been a privilege to have edited this great organ for the last five years, but it is time— at this historic moment in the nation's history— to pass on the baton. I am very much looking forward to new challenges, both personal and professional.' Mr Haldane, a former foreign correspondent, will publish a history of devolution at the end of next year.*

It was crap. Far too clunky for David to have voiced it, let alone written it. And such a bare-faced lie. No one in the profession could have been fooled by it. Vonnie had been so cross on his behalf; wished he could have told the truth. 'Mr Haldane, 63, one of Scotland's most experienced and influential journalists, said: "The bastards shafted me."'

Fiona had reached the till, so Vonnie wandered back over and helped her put everything in bags and was grateful when Fiona paid without asking her to chip in.

*   *   *

The pub was quiet and they chose a seat beside the wood-burning stove, which was mercifully unlit. Vonnie chose steak and ale pie, and Fiona opted for venison, and ordered a bottle of wine, but then only had a glass herself, leaving the rest for Vonnie. They talked about calling Deborah to see how Doug was doing, but decided that wouldn't be appropriate. He would be fine, either way, they were sure of that. Nobody died of testicular cancer these days, if that's what he had. Fiona didn't want dessert, so she ordered espresso while Vonnie demolished a cranachan, a delicious mix of oatmeal, cream, whisky and raspberries.

The waitress had tucked the bill in between the sauce bottles and Fiona picked it up and glanced at it.

'Shall we split it?' She reached down for her bag. 'It's just over £20 each.'

Vonnie sat forward. 'Actually, Fi, I don't have any cash.'

'Well if you put it on a card, I could give you some.' Fiona pulled a couple of notes from her purse. It was an expensive-looking purse, with the solid gilt buckle on the front and rows of cards tucked neatly in the silk-lined interior.

'I don't have a card, either.'

Fiona looked confused.

'I didn't bring them all with me, and the one I have is maxed out.' It was a lie, they were all maxed out, but Fiona wouldn't know. Vonnie swallowed. 'I was actually hoping you might be able to lend me some cash.'

'God, Vonnie. What on earth have you been doing?'

'Christmas,' said Vonnie. 'It's been an expensive

246

time.'

'So you don't have anything at all?'

'A tenner maybe and some change.'

'How much do you want?'

'I don't know. I would ask Dad. But he's already helped out with the flight and everything.' It was so much more than that, but Fiona needn't know.

'Okay.' Fiona looked mildly annoyed, but she glanced again in her purse. 'I've got fifty quid. Would that do?'

Nowhere close, thought Vonnie, but she was embarrassed now.

'Yeah, that would be great, if you don't mind.'

'Are you okay, though, with your cards?' Fiona handed across the cash. 'It's not good to get maxed out, Von.'

'I know.'

'You need to keep on top of it. It can get out of control really quickly. Some of these APRs are just horrendous.'

'I know.' Vonnie tucked the money Fiona had given her into her pocket. 'I'm on it. It's going to be a frugal year.'

Fiona gave a thin smile. 'I suppose you'll be wanting me to get lunch.'

'If you don't mind.' Vonnie sat back. She would have to ask David again now; there was no way £50 would last her until she was home.

Fiona stood up and shrugged on her coat. 'Right, come on, cheapskate. We need to go.'

'I'll pay you back,' said Vonnie, a little petulantly. She scraped back her seat. Even David never lectured her this much.

'Yeah,' said Fiona. 'Whatever.' She made to head for the till. 'By the way,' she said suddenly, 'I

247

like your boots.' Almost as if she knew.

*   *   *

David always stood like Prince Charles, his hands clasped tightly behind his back, one leg in repose. It probably came, Charlie thought, from years of not being allowed to put his hands in his pockets. He knew David's mother, she was a fierce old biddy, and a stickler for manners and a straight back at all times.

'I've got a mallet.' David bent his head to one side and watched as Charlie forced the metal peg through the guy rope and into the grass. 'If that would help.'

Charlie smiled to himself. David was always keen to help out. He would appear out of the house within minutes of them arriving, coat on and ready to go. To be fair, he could be quite handy, especially when they had been working on the hide when he'd lugged wood and sanded as well as any of the lads. Unlike some clients, who fancied themselves as handymen but were as useless as a tit on a truncheon.

Mostly, though, he liked to talk. Politics and sport—although Charlie guessed he wasn't as interested in the latter as the former—the weather, anything, really, apart from the one thing that they had in common, which was Euan.

They had been at the same primary school, and even though Euan was a year ahead of Charlie, it was small enough for them to have been friends. They weren't close friends, if boys that age ever are, but they were part of the same loose-knit group who played football at break, and swam in the river when the weather was fine, and traded blows and jokes and football coins.

Charlie remembered a skinny boy with a quick mind and a double-jointed thumb and the knack of making people like him. He was a really good swimmer, and everyone said that he might swim for Scotland one day in the Commonwealth Games. His sisters were at the school as well, Fiona and Deborah and Yvonne, but none of them could match him in the pool. Euan went up to the High School in North Berwick before Charlie did and they saw each other infrequently after that, but picked up fine each time they did.

Charlie had been on holiday when Euan died, in the caravan over by Oban that his parents took every year. They found out when they got back and the woman over the back wall had bustled up to Charlie's mum as they unpacked the car and told the story with such relish that Charlie had felt quite sick. He had gone inside and his mum had come in and put her arm around him and said it was perfectly okay if he cried. They'd missed the funeral. It had been the day before, but his mum had taken a card that she'd written up to Fortune House. Charlie had gone with her because she had asked him to, and he remembered that it was David who opened the door and invited them in. Charlie's mum said they wouldn't, they'd just come to say how sorry they were and if there was anything they could do he had only to ask. They never saw Mrs Haldane that day; just David, with his bewildered eyes and empty smile.

It was Charlie's first experience of death, though he'd seen plenty of it since. At first, he had avoided the spot on the road where it had happened, not like some of the boys at school who said they had gone down and seen the blood, so much that the police had to put sand down to cover it. Over time, Euan passed into memory, a cautionary tale. Remember the Haldane boy and watch how you go.

Charlie looked back up at David. It had just been over a year ago that David had phoned him and asked him to quote on maintenance and clearing work up at Fortune House. They had employed a gardener for years, an older man who was retiring, and the grounds were too big for David to manage. He remembered Charlie and knew that he had been in the army, but didn't know that he was married and a dad. He always asked after Gail and Annie; seemed genuinely interested. But it must have been hard for him, all the same, wondering how his own boy would have turned out, what he would have been doing. He had never mentioned Euan explicitly, but sometimes, when he talked about something that happened way back, he would say 'we' in such a way that Charlie knew he meant Euan and himself. It didn't unsettle Charlie. He had been around loss and suffering enough in the years in between to handle it well.

He realised he hadn't responded to David's offer. 'A mallet,' he repeated. 'I'm fine, actually. I've got one in the van anyway but the ground's so soft they're just pushing in.'

'Queer weather.' David looked up at the sky.

'It is that,' said Charlie. 'Great for business, though. Wasn't that much call for marquees last December.'

'Don't imagine there was.' David smiled with

250

him. 'It is a bit of a monstrosity, isn't it?'

'Oh, I don't know.' Charlie stood up and wiped his hands on the thigh of his trousers. 'Just about the right size for you and 100 of your closest friends.'

David laughed. 'This was not my idea!'

Charlie grinned. 'It never is our idea. As long as we understand that.' He stretched his arms out in front of him. 'Should be a good night, though,' he added. 'If the rain holds off. A good send-off.'

'Mmm,' said David.

'Must be nice,' Charlie persisted. 'Not to have to be in the office on Monday morning.'

'Not actually all it's cracked up to be,' said David.

'No?'

'No.'

Charlie watched him. He'd heard about this before, men who gave up their jobs and felt they'd given up on life. Yet David hadn't ever struck him like that, not someone who would keel over within a year of stopping work, as some men did. He knew he had a book to write and he must be set up financially. No worries there.

David still hadn't said anything else so Charlie said, 'I'm going to try to retire early.'

'Really?'

'Yeah. I'll sell the business—God willing—and Gail and I can plan some trips.'

'Where to?' David seemed interested.

'Don't know. South America maybe. Australia. Gail's got relatives in Tasmania.' Charlie smiled. 'Are you and Mrs Haldane off anywhere after New Year? A cruise or something?'

'God, no.' David adjusted his stance, as if he

251

were uncomfortable. 'No plans,' he added. 'At least not at the moment.'

Charlie nodded and wished now he hadn't mentioned anything. He and Gail loved to talk about what they'd do if the business did well and he could sell up. Hamilton Island on the Great Barrier Reef—Gail had seen it on a travel show. And he'd always wanted to go to Peru. But you settled for less as you got older; he'd seen that with his own mum and dad. Moving in ever decreasing circles until you barely left the house. Maybe he and Gail would be the same. Maybe David and his wife already were.

'Are you coming down tomorrow?' asked David. He'd invited Charlie and Boyd a few weeks ago; insisted, really, that they come but they'd both been non-committal, Charlie because of the baby and Boyd because he was generally non-committal.

'I'd like to,' said Charlie. 'But Gail's pretty uncomfortable at this stage. Do you mind if we say maybe?'

'Of course,' said David. 'Love you to come if you can, but don't feel any pressure. How is Gail?'

'Ready to pop,' said Charlie. 'And fed up with it.'

'Do you know what it is?'

Charlie shook his head. 'No. But it's a boy.'

David smiled. 'That would even things up,' he said. 'Is Annie excited?'

'Nah,' said Charlie. 'But we've got a big present that should soften the blow.'

'Bribery,' said David. 'Works every time.'

'Hope so.' Charlie got to his feet to stretch out and David made as if to move off. Charlie felt suddenly churlish. What harm in letting him help out a little?

252

'Actually, if you don't mind, I could probably do with a hand to finish this off. It's just the smaller pegs. We need to angle them in the way so there's less chance of anyone tripping over them.'

David was probably smart enough to know that Charlie was being kind, but gave no indication that he did. He looked pleased.

'Right. So if I take the right side and you can finish up here?'

'Perfect.' Charlie bent back to the task, then stopped and looked up again. He smiled. 'You might want to get your mallet,' he said.

*   *   *

Boyd lifted the bin liner and swung it into the wheelie bin with one quick, fluid motion.

'Thank you.' Hanna smiled at him. He was still a little red, but not quite as crimson as when he'd first come over and offered to help.

'It's a dirty job,' he said.

'Yes.' Hanna caught his eager eyes and looked down at her feet. 'Thank you,' she said again.

'Do you need anything else?' Boyd was still looking at her hopefully. She had forgotten how to flirt; wasn't sure anyway if she wanted to.

'No.' Hanna smiled. 'Just the loos to clean.'

'Oh. Okay.'

Hanna smiled. 'I'm guessing you don't want to help with that.'

'No, it's fine, it's just—'

Hanna burst out laughing. 'I'm having a joke,' she said.

'Oh.' Boyd's colour deepened. 'I . . . I should get back.'

Hanna nodded and turned for the kitchen, then turned back and watched him make his way across the lawn. He was tall and not bad-looking and hard-working. Maybe Dyta was right. Maybe she was being too fussy.

'Thanks!' she shouted again and he turned with a smile. 'Thanks, Boyd.'

She finished cleaning the loos, singing to herself all the while, and Caroline laughed at her when she came to find her for the train.

'Someone's happy,' she said.

Hanna didn't reply. She wasn't sure what the Haldanes would think if anything happened with Boyd. She knew they liked her, but maybe they would think it was unprofessional.

Caroline drove like someone twenty years older, more upright than she needed to be and with both hands tight on the wheel. They talked about Christmas, and whether the weather would hold for David's party, until Caroline said suddenly, 'I really am terribly sorry about my mother-in-law. You know, the other day.'

'It's okay,' said Hanna. Caroline had already apologised and had even called Hanna at home to say how sorry she was. Hanna had been a little nervous about seeing Min again, but the old lady had shown no sign of remembering what she had said or done, and had greeted her with her customary, 'Morning, young lady.'

'She would be mortified if she knew what she had said to you.'

'Really, it's fine. It happens.'

'It's a worry,' said Caroline.

'I'm sure,' said Hanna gently. 'Have you . . .' She wasn't sure how to word it. 'Have you spoken to

254

the doctors about it?'

'Yes,' said Caroline. 'They're reluctant to put a label on it, though.'

'Maybe it's just old age,' suggested Hanna.

'Maybe,' said Caroline. 'But I'm not convinced. So hard to diagnose. Anything definite.'

Hanna knew better than to tell Caroline about the old lady in their apartment block in Lodz. They had stopped seeing her after a while and then a new family moved into the home she had occupied. For months afterwards, letters for her would gather by the postboxes at the door, falling from the shelf on to the floor where people would stand on them, leaving grubby smears on the envelopes.

'Well, she has a good family around her,' Hanna said finally. It was the best she could come up with.

'Thank you.' Caroline turned and gave her a fleeting smile before fixing her eyes back on the road. 'Anyway, how is that beautiful boy of yours? It's such a shame he couldn't come down today. The children had such fun with him. You're bringing him to the party, though, aren't you?'

'If you're sure,' said Hanna. 'Is it not more of a grown-up thing?' She suspected Marek would be bored out of his mind, and tired, because the party didn't start until 7 p.m.

'No, no, no,' said Caroline. 'He has to come.'

Hanna felt a little prickle of irritation. No, he doesn't *have* to come, she thought, and then felt immediately guilty. 'Well, if you're sure,' she said. 'That would be lovely.'

All the parking spaces were filled outside the station, so Caroline pulled up directly outside the door. She dug in her pocket and pulled out a bunch of folded notes and pressed the cash into

Hanna's hands. She always did it this way and always said the same thing. 'And there you are.' As if it were a gift, as if she were worried Hanna might be embarrassed.

Hanna had never been embarrassed about earning money. She said, 'Thank you,' and tucked the cash into her purse and dropped it into her bag.

*   *   *

They weren't making it easy for her. They had been an absolute age, virtually all day and now five minutes in the door and they'd gone up to the bedroom, and still hadn't come down.

Elsa stood outside the closed door and clenched and unclenched her fists. She couldn't wait any longer. She'd rehearsed until she was blue in the face and she might lose her nerve. She raised her arm and knocked.

'Uh-huh.' It was her dad's voice.

Elsa opened the door. Doug was sitting on the end of the bed, and Deborah was over by the sink.

'Hi, sweetie.' Deborah turned, looking a little distracted.

'Have you got a minute?'

'Yeah, sure.' Doug stood up and Elsa came in, closing the door behind her. If there was going to be shouting, it would be better if it was muffled.

'I was wanting to talk to you both.' She walked over and perched on the edge of the small chair by the bed's end. It was old and covered in a faded stripe and made a noise like a sigh as she sat on it. She'd been careful to wear one of the tops that her mum had bought her for Christmas, a navy henley

256

that made her look about eleven, and not too much make-up. She figured that the more innocent she looked, the better.

'What is it, honey?' Doug's voice was as warm and concerned as she'd hoped.

'Well.' She twisted her hands together. 'It's just . . . you know I've been struggling a bit on my course . . .'

'Struggling? What do you mean?' Deborah moved away from the sink and came to stand beside Doug, who was still at the end of the bed.

'Well, I'm just finding it all hard going, really tough, and you know I failed jurisprudence.'

'But you're re-sitting that?' The warmth went out of Deborah's voice and Doug glanced at her, a warning look.

'I know, well. Actually.' Elsa took a deep breath.

'What?' said Doug.

'I was wondering. I'm thinking about maybe taking some time off.'

Deborah looked taken aback. 'Taking time off. What does that mean?'

Elsa dug her nails into her palm. 'I'm just thinking about postponing things. It wouldn't even be a year. I mean, we never really talked about a gap year and I'm just wondering if law is what I want to do. I don't really know that it is. And actually it wouldn't be a whole year, maybe even just nine months until next session . . .' She tailed off.

Deborah was shaking her head. She held up her hand. 'Whoa. What? Back up here. You're thinking about dropping out?'

'No,' said Elsa. 'No, just a break, a year off. Not even a year.'

Deborah's head was still shaking. 'No, no. Not tonight, no.'

She turned her face away and Elsa felt the prickle of anger. 'What do you mean, "no"? You can't just say "no," Mum. I've got a say in this, too.'

Deborah was still shaking her head, 'No, no, no.'

Doug reached out and got hold of Deborah's hand. 'Deborah, we need to talk about this,' he said. 'It's important.'

'No,' said Deborah. She walked over to the window, even though the curtains were shut. Elsa got up off the chair. 'There's a project in Quito. It's a kind of charity thing. And you do some travelling after—'

'Quito?' Deborah swivelled. 'Where the hell's Quito?'

'Ecuador,' said Elsa.

'What!'

'Debs,' said Doug.

'It's a really good project,' said Elsa. 'It's something I really want to do. Matt's going and a couple of others, and—'

'Matt.' Deborah gave a hollow laugh. 'So that's who's behind this.'

'No.' Elsa twisted her hands tighter together. 'No, it's my idea. I just need some time to sort things out. I'm really not enjoying law. And I don't know if it's what I want to do . . .' She tailed off and looked beseechingly at her dad.

'Oh, honey, I don't know,' he said.

'I'm not throwing anything away,' she added quickly. 'I'm finding out what I really want. And that might be law, or it might not be, I don't know. I need some time to sort it all out.'

Deborah held up her hand like a school crossing

258

guard. 'We are not talking about this.'

This was so much worse than Elsa had imagined. 'Please, Mum. It's important.'

'Not tonight.'

'Yes, tonight.' Elsa felt her temper snap. 'Now! I've been waiting all day.'

It was then that Deborah burst into tears.

'Oh, great.' Elsa turned for the door. 'Just bloody great. Really mature response, Mum. Well, I've actually decided. And you can't make me stay. Okay?' Her heart was hammering. 'Thanks a lot,' she said over her shoulder. 'Thanks a bloody lot for all your support.'

CHAPTER THIRTEEN

TUESDAY, 29 DECEMBER

Caroline reached for the radio in the dark and eased the dial round until it crackled into life. She really ought to get one of these fancy digital affairs that David was always extolling the virtues of, but she'd had this transistor for almost thirty years and its scratchy commentary had informed her life. Plays and bulletins and quiz shows and concerts. It had started off, shiny and new, in the kitchen where it became spattered with cooking fat and water from the sink and, later, was appropriated by the girls, who would re-tune it to Radio 1 or one of the commercial stations and sing along to its tinny rhythms. Over the years, the aerial had been snapped in two and there were deep scratches along its facia, where the little red line spun back and forth searching for voices or music.

The alarm had been set for 6.30 a.m., but Caroline had wakened, like a startled baby, long before. There was so much still to do. Frances would be down at 8 a.m. with the non-perishables, and the glasses and crockery were due to arrive at 9 a.m. and would need to be laid out. The serving team would arrive at 4 p.m. and the rest of the food an hour later. The invitations had said 6.30 p.m. for 7 p.m., so everyone would need to be washed, dressed and gathered by 6 p.m. at the latest, because there was always someone who turned up early.

The presenters were discussing one of these interminable end-of-year lists. The forecast, she thought to herself. Just give me the forecast. She felt the dull buzz of panic flare in her stomach, and lay back, trying to stretch the tension out of her body. The house was quiet apart from Ben's faint, intermittent chatter from the room down the hall. He would be standing up in his travel cot, fat fists holding on to the edge, talking to the two sleeping forms a few feet away from him. Fiona and Allan never seemed to wake with him. They were lucky he was such a contented boy. He could talk to himself for hours before he got upset. Caroline could never have left Euan like that. He was always on the go. The minute his eyes were opened he needed to be up and on the move. Such a quick mind, her lovely boy.

'And now a look at the weather.' Caroline waited, through Wales and the south-east of England and a slight depression in the Channel. And there it was. Scotland and Northern Ireland, light winds and mild, growing unsettled as the day went on. Unsettled was all right. She could live with unsettled. She swung her legs out of bed and reached for her robe. Min had been wrong. The frost had not come.

*   *   *

The hand came up over Fiona's hip and tugged at the waistband of her pyjama bottoms, the fingers working, damply, towards her crotch. She covered the hand with her own and held it steady.

'Ben,' she whispered. She didn't need to pretend she was asleep.

'Massage,' Allan whispered back, plaintively. He pressed himself into her; rigid and insistent.

'Ben's awake,' she hissed.

'Just quickly.' He sounded petulant and her heart sank.

She held on to his hand and tried to pull it up towards her neck in a forced cuddle. She made a snuggling sound. 'Can't,' she whispered back. 'Ben.'

There was a pause and then he pulled away from her, curling right to the other edge of the bed. Fiona peered over the covers. Ben was standing up in the cot but he was babbling at the door. His nappy ballooned around his rear like a small airbag.

She felt the movement start across the bed and pushed back the covers angrily on her side. Jesus, Allan, give up, would you?

'Hey, small boy,' she said loudly, and Ben turned with a dazzling smile. She felt the bed go still. 'Who's got a cuddle for Mummy?'

261

Katie dug her spoon into her cornflakes and tried to look like she was enjoying them. She hated cornflakes. She hated the way they didn't taste of much and went wet really quickly, like soggy little leaves. On holidays Mum let her have Frosties or Coco Pops or those little individual boxes. She always had first pick because Elsa didn't care. She just wanted something that wouldn't make her bum big. The options at her gran's were pretty bleak, however, just plain cereal, mostly cornflakes, and not even the proper packet with the chicken on the front, but pretend ones from the supermarket. The only other choice, though, was the porridge that Grampa ate, but Katie couldn't even think about because it reminded her of dog sick.

'Come on, eat up.' Mum didn't look up from her own bowl to say it. Sometimes she would say it even when you had finished, especially on school mornings, when she just issued instructions in a steady stream of words. 'Finish up, drink your juice, have you packed your bag, where're your shoes, find your hairbrush, you've got something on your nose.' She seemed a little funny this morning, though, probably because of the row with Elsa. Elsa had told her she'd had a big fight with Mum and Dad. She didn't say what it was about, but she said as soon as Grampa's party was over she was 'out of here.' She probably didn't mean for ever but she had made it sound that way.

Katie looked back at her plate. Some of the cornflakes had stuck to the edge. She pushed some more over to join them, then loaded another lot on to the spoon, turned it over and sank them into the milk.

'Please may I leave the table?'

Mum looked up. Her eyes were red and quite small. She gave an unexpected smile.

'Okay. Toilet and teeth.'

Katie winced. Her mum always said that, even in front of other people. When Mum was really old she would say that to her, just to get her own back. 'Toilet and teeth, Mum, and I'll be up in a minute to smell your breath.' As long as she didn't ever have to wipe Mum's bum. One of the girls in her class had said her mum had to wipe her gran's bum because she was eighty. That's what happened when you got very old; you turned into a baby again and forgot everything you'd ever learned.

*   *   *

Min stood by the back door and watched Hector totter across the gravel towards the drying green. He didn't quite make it and squatted on to the stones. Min waited until he was done then walked over and kicked some of the gravel over the small steaming pile. It didn't cover it all, but it would do. Caroline had given her a lecture before the family arrived about always scooping and had even provided some ridiculous scented bags and a fancy plastic grabber thing with a long handle, which had actually come in handy for reaching cobwebs in her sitting room. But Min had never stooped to pick up dog shit in her life and she wasn't going to start now.

Riley had disappeared round the corner like a hare at a racetrack, probably with the scent of a

263

pheasant in his nose. He'd killed one just a few weeks back, a male in full plumage. Min had told Caroline to pluck and cook it but the dog had made too much of a mess of its breast apparently. There were feathers everywhere. Min had pulled out the two largest tail ones, and they were now in a dry vase on her dresser with blood and small bits of flesh still attached to the tips.

She stood for a moment, savouring the air. There was a faint hint of salt from the sea, but no wind, the cloud hanging low over the fields.

Hector had gone as far as he could manage, halfway across the drying green, and was now making slow progress back to the house and his bed. Min called for Riley, and waited. There was no sign of him. She hoped he hadn't gone over the wall and down to the barn conversion by the road. They had a bitch, the family that lived there, a small terrier, and Riley could seek her out even when she wasn't on heat. It had caused a bit of a fuss just a few weeks back because he'd mounted her during a birthday party, and a roomful of under-fives had had hysterics, by all accounts.

'Riley!'

'Do you want me to find him for you?' The voice came from the back door. Min turned. It was the boy and he was smiling at her.

'Thank you. He might have gone after a bird. Have a look down by the far hedge. If not, he's probably got out.'

'Okay.'

She saw a change in his face, the flush rise on his cheeks. She glanced down. There was a darkening stain on the upper leg of her trousers. Now that was unexpected. She had felt nothing.

264

She looked back up. 'It's rude to stare.' She spoke sharply to cover her own discomfiture and the boy took off, shouting for Riley, as if nothing else had happened.

Min walked back quickly to the house, now aware of the damp chafing. Caroline had been rushing around like a dervish this morning. The last thing Min needed was for her to fall upon her and make a fuss. She had reached the back door when Riley appeared at her feet. He must have done a loop and come up through the vegetable patch. Min turned and scanned what she could see of the garden. There was no sign of the boy but she could hear his voice, faint in the distance. She opened the door and the dogs went in before her. He was a pasty lad. A run about in the open air would do no harm at all.

*   *   *

'We need to talk about this. We need to say something to Elsa.' Deborah folded the towel and laid it over the back of the chair.

'I know. We will.' Doug was over by the window, holding back the curtain with one hand. 'The kids are running about daft in the marquee,' he said. 'Do you think Caroline knows?'

'Doug,' said Deborah.

He gave a sigh and turned to face her. 'When she gets up,' he said. 'I'll talk to her then.' He had stopped Deborah from going to Elsa's room last night. Sleep on it, he said, you're too upset for anything to be gained. But sleep had produced no solutions, just a fresh buzz of panic when Deborah woke.

265

'She can't throw it all in,' said Deborah. 'She can't.'

Doug said nothing and turned back to the window. They had talked well into the night. Deborah had wanted to tell Elsa and Katie straight away about the diagnosis. She'd managed to let Fiona and Vonnie know what had happened. Doug was in the loo and they pulled her into the kitchen and hugged her when they heard.

But Doug didn't want the girls to know. Certainly not yet. He wanted the party over before anything was said, and was even talking about not saying anything at all until after he had been in for the op. In case, he said, it wasn't cancerous after all and they all got worried for nothing. Even if it was, he said, he didn't want Elsa to feel blackmailed by his condition into doing anything. That worried Deborah immensely because it suggested he might give in to her idea, and he couldn't.

She watched him at the window. 'You're going to cave in on this, are you?'

'No.' He paused for a moment. 'I just think we need to hear her out.'

'Oh, God, Doug.'

He sighed. 'I'm not saying we should agree. I'm just saying we should hear her out. You know she's not been enjoying it as much as we thought. She seems pretty certain it's not for her.'

'How does she know it's not for her? She's hardly given it a chance. It's just her fly-by-night attitude to everything. It's not a piercing, Doug, it's her career. And there's no way she's going off travelling with this Matt character. We don't know the first thing about him.'

'Deborah. She's eighteen and she's known him

266

for a while.'

'How many times have we met him? Twice? And you're okay with that? Her heading off with a virtual stranger? Anyway, with everything going on with you, she needs to be here.'

'No.' He spoke quickly. 'No. I've been clear on that. Okay? We don't use that as an excuse. For anything.'

'Doug.'

'No. We're not putting our lives on hold because of this.'

Deborah went to open her mouth, but he held up his hand. She couldn't remember him ever putting up his hand to her.

'I'll talk to her,' he said.

Deborah sank on to the end of the bed. 'Tell her she's got to see it through.'

'I'll *talk* to her,' repeated Doug. 'When she gets up. I'll talk to her.'

*   *   *

Daisy tucked her feet through the back of the chair and leaned forward on to the table, pushing her glasses up her nose like a diminutive professor. She poked a small finger towards a carefully arranged platter of hors d'oeuvres.

'What are those pinky ones?'

Caroline, leaning back against the warmth of the range with her cup of coffee, swallowed her smile.

'Pinky ones?' Frances looked confused. 'These ones? Oh, that's salmon. And asparagus. Salmon and asparagus croustades.'

She gave Daisy a tight little smile, one to match her tight little top. It was a sage-green affair with a

267

small insert of lace at the point of the V. Frances had already said she would need to leave about 4 p.m., 'to go home and change' so there would be a new outfit for tonight and Caroline expected it to be spectacular.

'I'm allergic to fish,' said Daisy. 'Salmon is fish.'

'It is,' said Frances briskly. She seemed awkward around small children, but then she had never had any of her own. Caroline had always wondered why. Bob would have made a wonderful father. But Frances had never said and Caroline had never asked, wary of touching on something private and painful.

'And asparagus makes your pee smell funny,' continued Daisy.

'Well, you probably ought not to have any then,' said Frances.

'It's not just me,' said Daisy. 'Asparagus makes everyone's pee smell funny. Doesn't it, Gran?'

Caroline didn't have time to react before Daisy had turned back to Frances.

'Do you want me to help pass out the plates tonight? I'm very good at passing out plates. Mum lets me do it if it's not her really fancy ones and Dad said I might get a job as a waitress when I'm bigger. I'm quite strong. I won't drop them.'

'That's very kind of you, and I'm sure you won't,' said Frances. 'But we've got lots of waiters to help out.'

'Grampa lets us have red wine with lemonade in it as a special treat. But my mum says it's just to knock us out in case we get annoying. Are we having red wine tonight?'

'Oh, I don't know,' said Frances. 'Maybe just lemonade. Are you allowed lemonade on its own?'

'Sometimes, but it's bad for your teeth and it makes you hugely fat,' said Daisy. 'And some children get fizzy madness, don't they, Granny?'

Caroline nodded sagely.

'That's a pretty top,' continued Daisy. 'Are you Granny's chef? My daddy has a chef.'

'Really?' said Frances. 'Em.' She glanced again at Caroline. Two bright red spots had appeared on her cheeks. 'No, em, yes, I suppose I am Granny's chef. Sort of.'

Caroline intervened. 'Daisy, toots, we need to let Frances get on. Can you run out to the tent and count the tables for me? I've forgotten how many there are.'

Daisy slipped off the seat and twirled out of the door, delighted to have been given an important task.

'She's a bright little spark,' said Frances, with a laugh.

'She is.' Caroline set down her coffee. 'She's very excited about tonight. They all are.' She hoped Frances wouldn't notice that she hadn't said, 'we all are'.

Frances nodded and returned to her task. The table was laden with platters and dishes, piled high with the hors d'oeuvres that could be left out until the evening. Once Frances was done arranging them, they would sit out in the larder until they were needed.

'And the wine company delivered?' Frances spoke without looking up.

'Yes,' said Caroline. 'The reds are all still in the dining room and I got David to put the whites in the extra fridge in the garage. He's had a look through and it all seems to be there.'

The door opened and Min appeared. Caroline thought she had already seen her in trousers that morning, but she was now wearing a skirt. And socks. Caroline's heart sank. She had obviously changed but forgotten to put on her tights.

Min offered a curt 'hello' to Frances and moved across to the coffee machine.

'I'll need to make a fresh pot,' said Caroline. 'Vonnie's just finished it off.' She gestured downwards with her eyes. 'Are you not cold?'

Min didn't notice the cue. 'Cold? It's like September out there.' She pulled out a chair and sat down with her legs stretched out in front of her and reached over for one of the salmon and asparagus croustades. She popped it in her mouth. 'I'll have tea,' she said. 'Seeing as there's no coffee.'

Caroline saw Frances look up, then double-take as she caught sight of Min's legs: pale and spindly, veined like old cheese. She looked back quickly at the platter she was working on and said nothing.

'Tea was it, Min?'

'That's what I said,' muttered Min. She reached out for another of the hors d'oeuvres, a little mousse-filled pastry, and stuffed it into her mouth.

'Right, no more.' Caroline laughed. 'Or there'll be none left for everyone else.' She put the mug of black tea in front of Min and the old lady got to her feet to take it through to the morning room, where she would sit with the paper and peruse the death notices until her drink grew cold. Min loved obituaries, mostly because she was delighted to have outlasted others her age. She moved over to the door, still chewing, glanced again at Frances and then down at the tray of croustades. 'These are

270

really rather good,' she said, and was gone before she saw the flush of relief in Frances's pink-cheeked face.

CHAPTER FOURTEEN

'No. Like this.' Dyta grabbed the waist of Hanna's dress and yanked it upwards, slipping the belt that she had fastened around her waist lower on to her hips and pulling the material over. 'You have good legs, Han, you should show them.'

'Yes, thank you.' Hanna stepped back and rearranged the frock, pulling the belt back up and the hem back down. 'I think this is fine.'

Dyta shrugged. 'You're not going to get a date if you dress like the cleaner.'

'I am the cleaner,' said Hanna. 'And I have a date.' She glanced over at the sofa where Marek was slumped on the cushions, digging in his left nostril. He looked strange in the button-up shirt Dyta had bought him in Primark and he wasn't terribly enthusiastic to be going. A coach had been laid on for everyone coming from Edinburgh, and Caroline had kept two spaces for them.

'It'll mostly be friends of the Haldanes,' said Hanna. She had said nothing to Dyta about Boyd, mostly because there was nothing to tell. He would be there, but it wasn't like they had arranged to meet or anything.

Dyta had turned her attention to Hanna's hair, fluffing it out at the sides.

'I'll stay up and hear all about it.' She stood back and eyed Hanna the way she did when she cleaned the windows, looking for flaws. Hanna half expected her to lick her fingers and wipe some imagined mark from her cheek, the way Mamo liked to do.

'We won't be late,' said Hanna. 'We'll just stay for a couple of hours.'

'You've not to work,' said Dyta. 'Have a drink, flirt, okay, but no work. No tidying up.'

'No tidying up. I promise.' Hanna grinned at her. Caroline had said the same. 'You'll come as a guest.'

'And you never know . . .' Dyta handed Hanna her bag, a small beaded affair, which looked a little out of place with her jersey dress but was the smallest they had between them.

Hanna bent forward and gave Dyta a peck on the cheek and a smile, for lending her the bag and for always hoping for the best. And she was right. You never did know.

*   *   *

Her mum never did her own dirty work. Elsa watched her dad make his way down the path towards her. She'd been waiting all day to be summoned.

'Gotta go,' she said quickly into her mobile. 'My dad's coming.'

'Good luck,' said Matt. 'Let me know.'

She tucked her mobile into the pocket of her Puffa jacket and took a deep breath. As soft as her dad could be, she didn't expect it to be a particularly comfortable conversation.

'Hey.' He ducked under the lowered branch. 'Your gran said she thought you were out here.

You'll need to go in soon and change for the party.'

Elsa gave him a wan smile.

He sat down on the bench beside her and looked out of the gap. 'This is quite a place your grampa's got. I could do with one of these at home.'

'Couldn't we all?' said Elsa.

Doug gave a chiding laugh. 'Don't be like that.'

Elsa followed Doug's gaze out over the stubble field. 'I never saw the appeal of birdwatching,' she said. 'No offence to Grampa, but it's a bit . . . pointless.'

'Oh, I don't know,' said Doug. 'It would be quite nice to take time out every day just to sit still and stare at something. It's a form of meditation.'

'Like trainspotting,' said Elsa.

'Don't be mean,' said Doug. 'Each to their own.' He turned and glanced at her. 'Look at the size of you,' he said suddenly.

'Not the best thing to say, Dad.'

'It's gone so quickly,' he added. 'My little pooch.'

It had been his pet name for her when she was growing up. She dug her hands into her pockets and looked at him, worried suddenly that he was being too nice.

'Did Mum tell you to say "no"?'

'No,' said Doug and smiled.

'No, she didn't or no, I'm not getting to do it?' said Elsa.

'We're just worried you've not thought this through. I meant to talk to you first thing, but I'm still trying to get my head around it.'

'I have thought about it. Really, Dad. I've thought about it loads.'

273

'What would you do for money? We couldn't afford to subsidise you for something like this, love.'

'I know,' said Elsa. 'I wouldn't expect you to. I've got my savings account and I would work for a couple of months here before we go. I'd get enough. And once you've paid, it's pretty much all covered, food and everything.'

'What do you know about the company that's running it?'

'They seem pretty good. They've been doing it for ages; about fifteen years. Matt knows some people who went with them last year, not Ecuador, but Indonesia, and it was great.'

'When did you start planning?'

Elsa exhaled. 'I don't know. Just when I realised I wasn't enjoying the course, I suppose. I'm really not, Dad. Enjoying it.'

'Could you not give it more time?'

'It's been a whole term. I don't want to get to the end of a year and decide I don't want to keep going.'

'Well, what would you do instead?'

'I don't know. I need to figure that out.'

'Well, that's the worry,' said Doug. 'Running off to the other side of the world isn't necessarily going to help you to figure that out.'

'It could. It's a break, a complete break. I came straight out of school and into uni and it's just been exams, exams, exams.'

'And what about Matt?'

'What about him?'

'Was this his idea?'

'No.'

'Because if it was, it's not fair on you, because

274

he's finished his course. He can afford to take the time.'

'I know. But he didn't push, really. If anything, I pushed him. Just to find out more about it.'

'Your mum and I hardly know him.'

'He's a good guy, Dad.'

'Some people thought Peter Sutcliffe was a good guy.'

Elsa almost laughed. 'That's what Mum said, isn't it?'

Doug gave a sheepish grin. 'Actually that was mine. The point is, love, we're very far off from giving this our blessing. You need to know that. We need a lot more information.'

Elsa felt her heart sink. 'Like what?'

'Well, like university for a start.'

'I could get a deferred placement. It means I'd start again in October.'

'For the same course?'

'No. Yes. Maybe, or maybe something else.'

'Well, that's something you'd need to have straight. A plan.'

Elsa nodded. It was sounding a little more hopeful. Although she knew that whatever her dad said could be blown out of the water by her mum.

Doug rubbed his hands across his face. 'Look, it's your grampa's party tonight. We'll all sleep on it and then we can have another talk.'

'With Mum,' said Elsa.

'Yes, with your mum.'

Elsa shifted herself along the bench and gave him a hug.

'Thanks, Dad.'

'I haven't promised anything,' he said, as if he were reminding himself, but he held on to her for a little longer than she had expected. 'Pooch,' he said, against her hair.

In the pocket of her Puffa her phone started to sing. Doug pulled away and shook his head. 'You're a menace with that thing,' he said. He stood up. 'Go on, answer it.' He bent and kissed the top of her head as she dug the phone from her pocket.

It was Matt.

'Can you hold a sec,' said Elsa.

She gave him another hug. 'Thanks, Dad. Love you.'

'Love you too,' he said.

Elsa waited until he had clambered out of the clustered bushes and was halfway back up the path to the house.

'Hey,' she said into the phone.

'I thought you might need rescuing,' said Matt.

'No, it's okay.'

'So, are we set?'

'Don't know.'

'Okay,' said Matt. 'But heading the right way?'

Elsa watched her dad stop at the back step to ease off his outdoor shoes, then disappear inside. 'Maybe,' she said.

*   *   *

The tent looked very different with the tables set and candles lit and the heaters glowing orange like streetlights. The waiters and waitresses were all about Elsa's age, clad in black trousers and shirts with short white aprons tied round their waists.

Katie watched them from the doorway. There wasn't much for them to do yet because not many

276

people had arrived. Just some neighbours from a house nearby. Katie didn't like them already. The woman had hair that was too long and she wasn't wearing a bra. She could have done with one because her breasts weren't where they should have been, but much lower down. It had been hard not to notice. The man, meanwhile, had put his hand on top of Katie's head when Grampa had introduced her. Katie hated when people did that. It was so rude and you never knew if they'd just been to the loo or something and maybe not washed afterwards. Mum said lots of people didn't, especially men. That's why you were never to have the mints in restaurants, because Mum said that they almost always had pee or poo on them. The neighbours had, however, commented on how pretty her dress was and she was pleased about that. She liked her dress. It was stripy black and silver, and brand-new. Mum had had to pull off the tags just before she put it on.

Katie and Daisy had already planned to help themselves to lemonade and crisps, find a good vantage point, and give everyone points for how good they looked. Judging by the ones who had arrived first, the winners might actually turn out to be Aunt Fiona or Aunt Vonnie, They were all quite pretty, and their breasts were exactly where they should have been; in Aunt Fiona's case, maybe even higher.

Katie took a final look at the tent and then turned and ran back towards the house. Aunt Fiona had asked her and Daisy to keep an eye on Ben while she finished getting dressed, which was taking an awfully long time. They had put his travel cot in the den and Katie had left him sitting

277

blinking through the mesh like a big gerbil. He had started to cry by the time Katie got back, so she and Daisy half lifted, half dragged him out of the pen and put him down on the rug. He scooted off across the room and got hold of the television remote before they could stop him. They managed to get it away from him and followed him, giggling, out into the hall. There were some guests there, standing at the dining room door and Ben scuttled over to them.

'Hello!' One of the ladies had a very posh voice. She looked down at Ben, who had stopped by her feet. He stuck out a hand and pulled at the bow on her shiny patent shoes. His hands were damp and sticky and Katie saw that his palm had left a mark. He tried to raise himself using the woman's leg as a ladder. She gave a little nervous laugh and said, 'Oh, goodness.'

'I am so sorry.' It was Aunt Fiona. She skipped down the rest of the stairs with jewels sparkling at her neck, her lips bright red and shiny. 'Come on, Baby B.' She bent and scooped up Ben. 'Bedtime. Say night night.'

Ben didn't say anything, but struggled a little as he was carried away. It didn't seem fair. He missed out on everything because he was so small. Katie waved at him and he rewarded her with a big smile.

*   *   *

'Can you zip me up?'

Deborah turned her back to Doug and put her hands on her waist to hold the two edges of the dress together. She'd tried it on only a couple of weeks ago and it had been fine, verging on snug.

278

Now, after a few days of Baileys Irish Cream and cheese footballs, it was snug, verging on tight. But she would be standing most of the night.

Doug tugged the zip to the top and bent to kiss the back of her neck. 'Lovely,' he said.

She lay back against him for a second, and fought the urge to cry. She couldn't be without him. She wouldn't be able to keep going.

'Now, me.' He held out his wrists, the cuffs of his shirt dangling over them like a dandy. She turned to fasten them, folding the cuffs back briskly and slipping the cufflinks through the buttonholes. It was a pink shirt, not a colour he normally wore, but Elsa had persuaded him to buy it in a pre-Christmas sale and he quite suited it. He hadn't yet tucked it in and it hung out over his tummy. She gave him a little pat when she had finished.

'Wall of steel,' he said with a smile.

It never had been, and she didn't care. She raised herself on her stockinged feet and kissed him.

*   *   *

From his vantage point at the top of the stairs, Jamie watched the people criss-cross the hall below. Caroline, in fancy black shoes, carrying what looked like presents; David checking his tie and then his teeth in the hall mirror; a couple he didn't recognise, holding glasses of wine and looking a bit lost. He could smell soap and aftershave from the bathroom down the hall, and hot food from below. The sound of voices was multiplying and he could hear the music from the

279

marquee, something Scottish and a bit frantic.

He had one hand on the banister. It was decorated all the way down with thick brass studs to stop people sliding. He would quite like to slide down it. It was the perfect kind of banister, broad and smooth with a curve towards the top. He'd seen people do it in films and it looked like fun.

'Hey.' A pair of hands descended on to his shoulders. He didn't get a fright. He knew Allan was still upstairs getting ready and he had been waiting for him. He turned and smiled. Allan was in a suit and a blue striped shirt with an open neck. He smelled clean and strongly perfumed, and his hair was still a bit wet.

'Looking sharp,' said Allan. 'Ready to go down?'

Jamie shrugged.

'Come on,' said Allan. 'It'll be fun.'

He kept his hands on Jamie's shoulders until they were at the bottom of the stairs, and then walked beside him out into the garden. His mum had said he could watch TV or go back to his room and play his DS but only after he had made an appearance, which he took to mean just wandering around until most people had seen him. He followed Allan down towards the marquee. Fiona was over at the bar talking to a woman with red hair, but Allan didn't make his way over to her. Instead he just kind of launched himself into the nearest group of people and held out his hand. 'Allan Fleming. David's son-in-law.' He was very good at it, probably because of the restaurant, and Jamie liked to watch him. Sometimes he would shake people's hands and put his other hand on their shoulder as well and he would kiss the women. Twice, one on each cheek, even when he

280

didn't know them at all. Jamie stood and waited. After a little while Allan turned and pulled him into the group.

'And this is my boy. Jamie,' he said.

It sounded a bit corny, and it wasn't really true, but Jamie still liked to hear him say it.

*　　　*　　　*

He hadn't expected presents. David laid the bottle of wine with the bow around the neck beside the other parcels piling up on the desk in his office. It hadn't even occurred to him to stipulate no gifts on the invitation. He turned the wine until he could see the label. It was Californian and not very good, but there were at least four others, one of them from the restaurant critic, that would have to be laid down to do them justice. The literary editor had brought a pile of new hardbacks. She would have got them for nothing, but it was a nice thought all the same. And there was a carved wooden bird call from one of his reporters. He tried it out, the distinctive chirrup-cheep of the siskin. It was a sharp, sweet sound and for a moment he wanted to be out at the far end of the garden, away from the growing gaggle of people, nothing but the wind in his ears. He had answered so many questions about how the book was going and had lied convincingly to every one.

The door slipped open, and Caroline came in, with Hanna's little boy in front of her.

'Here we are,' she said, as Marek walked shyly to the desk and put down the two gaudily wrapped presents he had been carrying. 'Marek's my special helper tonight, aren't you, sweetheart? He's the

281

official present collector.'

'I had no idea people would bring anything,' said David. He smiled down at the small boy, who was looking around his study with wide grey eyes. 'Thank you. You're doing a grand job.'

'I know. I didn't even think to say,' said Caroline. Her cheeks were flushed. She was wearing a navy dress with a necklace of large purple stones. There was a small dark smudge of mascara just above her left eye. He wondered if he should point it out.

Her smile interrupted him. 'Oh, and Min has managed to find the political editor. I think he's regretting having a go at the First Minister in his last column.'

'Do I need to intervene?' said David.

'No, she's fine,' said Caroline. 'She's enjoying herself. I'll keep an eye on her. And the girls will too.' She took Marek's hand. 'Right, my love, back we go. Do you think any more people will have arrived?'

Marek grinned up at her and nodded, obviously relishing his role. David watched them leave, and noticed as he did the tightening in his throat. A lovely boy, but not their boy.

*   *   *

Katie carried the two glasses of lemonade carefully across the marquee. The waiter had filled them almost to the top and some had already sloshed out stickily over her hands. She held them out straight in front as she curved around the edge of the dance floor hoping no one would bump into her and make it spill on her dress.

There were quite a few people dancing, the kind of Scottish country dances they did at school when you were supposed to have outdoor games but it was raining, and the boys were made to ask the girls. Katie hated that bit. It wasn't that she was always last to be asked, because she wasn't, but she was never first, either, and there was never a rush to get to her as there was with some of the prettiest girls in the class.

She and Daisy had been forced to abandon their competition to see who looked the best, because not a lot of them did. They were mostly old people and a bit dull. All they seemed to talk about was the election and the weather. Katie knew all about the election because they were studying it in school, but it didn't mean she would want to hear about it if she was at a party. All it would mean really was that Scotland wouldn't have to get involved in wars if it didn't want to, and for people like Daisy, it would be the same as arriving in another country when they came to visit. Which made it sound more exciting than it actually was.

She reached the door of the marquee and handed one of the glasses to Daisy who was waiting outside. She hadn't wanted to come in because Aunt Fiona had made her dance with a really old man, a friend of Grampa's, who had a kilt on, and scratchy hands.

They stood by the door for a moment. It was just as well that Daisy hadn't come in, because Aunt Fiona had made Jamie get up and dance, and he was standing in the line for Strip the Willow, looking like he wanted the ground to open up and swallow him whole. The woman across from him was quite big and when it was their turn to twirl, she spun him round like he was a wet shirt in a washing machine. Elsa was dancing too but she was enjoying it, tapping her feet and clapping. The man she was dancing with looked like he'd won a prize.

*　　　*　　　*

'Are you sure I can't help?' Hanna stood by the kitchen door, as Caroline frantically sliced the last of the lemons.

'No!' Caroline shooed her away with her hand. 'I said no working tonight, just enjoy. I'll be done in a sec.'

Hanna must have seen her through the window and made a point of coming in. But it was only a few lemons because the caterers were running short.

'Is Marek still with Deborah and Doug?'

Hanna nodded. 'They're watching the dancing. He's having such a nice time.'

'I hope it's not too dull for you,' said Caroline, scraping the lemons on to a side plate. 'All these old fogeys.'

'No way.' Hanna let go of the door and came all the way into the kitchen. 'They're really nice people and it's a lovely party; I've heard so many of them say that. The house looks beautiful.' She was close to Caroline now, ready to take the plate of lemons outside, to help even though she had been told there was no need. Caroline reached over suddenly and slipped her arm around Hanna's waist. No one else had uttered such reassurance; no one else had been quite so lovely.

'I am so glad you came tonight, you and your

284

boy,' she said.

*   *   *

All in all, and somewhat unexpectedly, it had been a good night's work. Charlie tucked the rest of his business cards back into his inside jacket pocket and picked up his glass of water. He had at least four serious expressions of interest, and one 'you absolutely must come round' from a middle-aged woman who had applied her lipstick like a child who couldn't keep within the lines. David had been a champ about introducing him around. He had made a point of coming over and getting both him and Boyd a drink and then squiring Charlie through the throng. It had been curious for Charlie to watch him; so assured, so different from the man with the mallet and the lost boy. He had a really infectious laugh, something Charlie hadn't noticed before, a deep rumble that came from his chest and bubbled up into his throat. A lot of the people there seemed to be former colleagues or journalistic compatriots. Charlie recognised one of the reporters from the TV news: a seriously overweight man, whose pudgy face ballooned from the neck of his shirt like rising bread. Gail always complained that if a woman looked that bad she wouldn't be allowed on TV. Charlie had pointed out, not unreasonably, he thought, that if a woman looked that bad she shouldn't be allowed out of the house. He'd got a pillow in the face for that one.

He looked through the crowd at Boyd. He had moved over to the edge of the lawn because the fireworks were about to go off and because it took him nearer to Hanna. She was talking to Fiona,

285

wine glass in one hand, the other waving animatedly as she spoke. She had pulled her little boy in front of her, probably to shield him if the bangs got too loud. She was looking good, although you could see her hip bones through the stretchy material of her dress. Maybe Boyd didn't mind, but Charlie liked his women with a little more flesh.

He felt the shudder against his hip and pulled the phone from the waistband of his trousers. It was Gail again. She had phoned twice already: once to tell him that Annie was finally asleep and then again to let him know some inconsequential nonsense about the American crime drama that she had been following religiously and whose final episode was tonight.

'Hey. Who have they killed off now?'

'Charlie.'

He knew instantly.

'You need to come,' she said.

'God. Now. Is it now?' He felt the fizz of panic.

'I think my waters have broken.'

'You think? Are you sure?'

It was only about a week ago that she'd brought him home from a job, convinced her waters had gone. It had turned out to be stress incontinence and she'd been so embarrassed.

'No, it's real. It's everywhere.' There was a pause and then a giggle. 'It looks like Niagara.'

He gave a panicked laugh. She sounded so calm; his Gail, his amazing Gail.

'I'm on my way. Do you need to go in? God, Gail, I'm about forty minutes away. And Annie. Have you called your mum? You need to call your mum.'

'I'm just going to. And drive carefully. I'm not too sore. I don't think it's like right now. But soon. Okay?'

'Okay, okay.' He started moving through the crowd towards Boyd. Turn, man. Turn so you can see I need to go.

'I'm on my way,' he said again.

There was a laugh. 'She's not going to be a 2010 baby, your girl,' said Gail. 'She didn't listen.'

'Boy,' he said. 'I told you it's a boy.' He was running now, weaving between the little clutches of people. Just off to his left, the first of the fireworks shot into the sky and burst above his head in a sparkling spray of light.

'Try to watch them without saying "woooo!"' said Deborah.

Fiona leaned back and craned her neck as the rockets spat into the sky. As each one burst, the throng of people around her let loose a whoop, directly proportional to the size and brilliance of each explosion.

'Wooooo!' shouted Vonnie and toppled gently against her. Fiona braced herself and hooked her arm around Vonnie's waist, feeling Deborah's hand shoot out in support as she did so. Fiona caught hold of Deborah's fingers and squeezed.

At the far end of the lawn, she could just make out Allan and Doug moving around, positioning and lighting the fireworks. She wondered now if she'd ordered enough; they seemed to be disappearing fast.

She looked round to make sure David was watching. He was at the mouth of the marquee, whisky tumbler in hand. She'd had one dance with him and he'd held her like a tailor's dummy, which was much the same way he held Caroline.

Although she'd told him she could only waltz because of her black Stella McCartney pencil skirt. Anything more strenuous and she would have a split up to her navel. She'd teamed the skirt with a white silk shirt, and her best black Boudiche bra underneath. Min had already told her that her slip was showing, which was pretty rich from an octogenarian who regularly seemed to forget her pants.

'Where did you get the fireworks?' asked Deborah, repositioning herself to get a better grip of Vonnie.

'Allan uses this place in Muswell Hill. They deliver countrywide so we got them couriered up.'

'Is Mum even out here?' asked Deborah. 'I hope she doesn't miss them.'

Fiona saw Allan raise his hand to her through the gloom.

'Wait till you see this one,' she said. 'It's the finale. It spells out "Good Luck". We got it as a surprise.' She turned and raised her glass to David.

'Happy retirement!' she called out.

There was a rushing noise from the far end of the lawn, then a loud bang and the word 'Goooood' exploded into the clouds and then dropped, dissolving like letters falling from a computer screen.

There was a rattle of applause, then another fizz. Fiona looked upwards. The firework exploded, higher than the first. Maybe it was the wind; a freak gust. She heard Deborah's sharp intake of breath, muttered confusion from the crowd behind.

'What's that say?' Vonnie was still leaning

against her, her head flung backwards.

' "Luck",' said Fiona tartly, her heart sinking. 'It says "Luck".' The word fell to earth and the hesitant ripple of applause behind her died out.

Vonnie straightened herself. 'Was that . . . ?' She started to laugh. 'Was that an "f"?'

'Vonnie,' said Deborah.

'It was an "f",' persisted Vonnie. 'It said "Fuck". "Good Fuck".' She nudged Fiona in the ribs and gave in to her giggles. 'Nice one, Fi. "Gooooood fuuuuuuck".'

Deborah shook her head. 'It was an "l",' she said. 'It must have been the wind. Don't pay any attention. That was amazing.'

Fiona didn't know whether to laugh or cry. She glanced round. David was talking again, caught in the middle of a small huddle of guests. Maybe he hadn't noticed, maybe nobody had.

Allan appeared at her side, rubbing his hands and smelling faintly of sulphur. He grinned at Doug who had joined Deborah. 'That beats barbecuing, eh? Nothing like a spot of pyrotechnics to release the inner caveman.' He pretended to beat his chest.

'Did you see what it said?' said Fiona.

'What?'

'The last one. Did you not see?'

'It was fine,' said Deborah.

'It wasn't fine,' said Fiona. She lowered her voice. 'What it said was "Good Fuck".'

'Nooo,' said Allan.

Fiona nodded. 'How could you not see? That's what it said: "Good Fuck"!'

Allan shrugged. And right there, in front of her sisters, he reached over and took her glass of wine.

'Really?' he said, raising it to her in a mock toast. 'Chance would be a fine thing.'

*　　　*　　　*

'That's so exciting.' Hanna turned a little to the side and held her arms out backwards as Boyd slipped on her coat. She felt the skin of his hands on her neck, warm and roughened.

'Yup. A brand-new wean.'

'Wean?'

'Baby,' said Boyd. 'Sorry.'

She smiled at him. He was genuinely pleased for Charlie. He had come across to tell her, just after Charlie had rushed off. There had been a bit of a panic because Charlie's van was hedged in by another car and Mr Haldane had to dash around the guests until he found the owner.

The pile of coats was growing smaller, so she wasn't the first to leave, and she'd stayed longer than she meant to. Marek was propped in the corner of the sofa. He had been asleep when she had laid him down and was still sound, his lips slightly parted. She found his coat, a small fleece-lined cagoule, and tucked it under her arm.

'Right. I think that's me.'

Boyd's hands were in his pockets. He had on a suit but it looked like it was wearing him, rather than the other way round. He had not asked her to dance.

'Actually.' He shuffled his feet. 'I'm going to need to get a cab back too. Do you mind . . . ?' He looked down at her sheepishly.

'No, of course not. I should have said. We can share.' She dipped her eyes, realising she had

290

spoken quickly. All their previous conversations had been somewhat disjointed, short and snatched. But it would be nice to have someone to chat to in the taxi. Marek would be sleeping and she found the benign intolerance of taxi drivers wearying. Every conversation followed a similar track. Where are you from, love? Poland, is it? There's a lot of you over here, isn't there?

She moved round to the front of the sofa and bent to lift Marek into her arms.

'Do you want me to carry him? He looks a ton weight.' Boyd flushed. 'Well, I don't mean . . .'

Hanna laughed. 'No, it's okay, but could you get my bag?'

Boyd bent down and lifted the small beaded purse and held it self-consciously in front of him.

Hanna shifted Marek on to her shoulder. She had no idea where Boyd lived but suspected he would do the decent thing and drop her first. If Dyta was true to form she would be at the window when she heard the taxi engine idling. Boyd might even see her up the stairs and Dyta would love that. Hanna could see her face now. Eyes bright with mischief and hope.

They made their way through the small groups of people in the garden until they found Caroline.

Hanna bent in to give her a hug, and Caroline planted a kiss on Marek's head.

'Thanks so much for coming,' she said. 'I'm really glad you could. I hope he's not exhausted tomorrow.' Her hand came up and gently touched Marek's hair.

'Thanks for asking us,' said Hanna. She noticed Caroline glance at Boyd, still clutching Hanna's little jewelled bag.

Caroline turned back to Hanna and gave her a warm, conspiratorial smile. 'Bye, you two,' she said, with the emphasis very much on the last word.

*   *   *

Caroline stepped through the front door and slipped off her shoes. They were new and higher than she normally wore and pinching terribly. She padded across the hall. She would have liked nothing more than to have retreated to the drawing room, where she could shut the door and sit perfectly still and not have to smile or talk. Not long now. People were starting to go. She went upstairs and found a cardigan to drape round her shoulders, then stood at the window for a moment, watching the people moving around by the marquee. It had gone well. The weather had held.

Someone had put off the light in the downstairs hall and she had to come down the stairs holding the banister. The switch was over by the dining room door, which was propped wide open to let the catering staff move to and fro with ease. Caroline crossed the parquet, her stockinged feet slipping on the polished wood. She went to reach up her hand, and saw, as she did so, two figures. She had moved without sound. They did not know she was there.

They were over by the lazy Susan, David pressed against Frances. They were facing away. Caroline couldn't see Frances's face but saw her hand reach up and back to the side of David's head. He caught it with his mouth; almost a bite.

Caroline wasn't aware of moving away but found herself in the kitchen, dry-mouthed and shaking.

292

She closed the door behind her and held on to the handle and let out a little sob of shock and rage.

Oh, God. Oh, God.

She moved across to the window. There had always been a problem with the kitchen blind, a sticking point in the cord not quite halfway down. If you didn't know how to pull it, you could bring the whole roller down on your head. Caroline tugged, and the bale of faded flax linen slid to the windowsill, shutting out the movement of shape and light from outside.

She turned towards the kettle. She didn't want tea. It was just instinctive to fill it, settle it back on to its base and switch it on.

She could hear the faint lilt of music from the tent. Someone laughing. She put her hands on the edge of the sink. Her head felt light.

She could tell from their posture that this was nothing sudden. There had been an ease to their intimacy.

Oh, Christ. David.

When? When did it start? After Bob died? Before? She remembered when Frances had arrived that afternoon. David had given her a perfunctory kiss on the cheek, as he always did, but Frances's hand; her hand had gone to his chest and rested there, just below the breastbone and just for a second. Caroline had noticed that. A friend would reach instinctively for the shoulder or the elbow; the breast was where a lover would lay their fingers.

She stood for a long time, with the steam from the boiled water dissipating around her. Then she heard voices in the hall and the door opened. It was David. He was smiling. 'Here you are,' he said.

'That's some more folk leaving.' He held the door for her. She moved across and past him, aware that she was nodding, terrified that she might brush against him, wanting to scream. On the driveway, a small car was about to pull off. Caroline fixed a fresh smile and said her farewells. The man, a colleague of David's, leaned out of the window as they pulled away.

'Have a good life!' he shouted.

'I intend to,' said David, and laughed. Then he turned and walked back quickly to the garden and the marquee. Caroline stood for a moment watching the tail lights disappear down the driveway.

Soon there would be a flood of cars and then, in a matter of days, the girls and the children. And Min. Min was going too. They were all kidding themselves if they thought she wasn't. It was more than old age, Caroline was sure of that. Soon, she would be beyond their reach.

She thought of David's hand hovering at the small of her back as it had done on occasion throughout the evening, not quite touching. Frances's hand at his mouth. His lips on her flesh. She couldn't bear it. A sob rose again in her throat and she turned for the house.

The kitchen was still empty, and she pulled out a chair and sat down. The table was surprisingly tidy: the extra plates and glasses that hadn't been needed were stacked according to size; the left-over hors d'oeuvres were covered in clingfilm and lined up along the table's edge. Frances had asked her if she wanted to keep them and Caroline had said 'yes', even though there was no space in the fridge or on the shelves in the larder. She looked at the miniature quiches and tartlets and skewers sealed under the tight plastic. They had been just right. In fact, everything had been just right. Absolutely perfect.

She felt empty, hollowed out. This was it. Too much. Too much to take. After everything. The pain was building in her chest. She stood to find her tablets, and as she did so heard the muffled exclamation in the hall.

She had closed both doors when she had come in, the one that led to the corridor to the back door, and the one off the hall. She stood for a moment; heard someone say something that sounded like, 'Christ.' She crossed the room, opened the door to the hall. Fiona was bending down near the Christmas tree, or as much as she could in her tight black skirt. She turned at the sound.

'Shit,' she said. 'Mum.'

'What is it?' Caroline started towards her

'I tripped over him,' said Fiona. She got to her feet. 'He was just lying here.'

Caroline looked down. Hector was stretched out on his front near the tree, where the presents had been, his hind legs splayed awkwardly behind him. A small piece of silver tinsel had stuck to one of his paws.

'He's not moving,' said Fiona. 'What's wrong with him?'

Caroline bent down on to her knees and put her hand on his head. His skull was small under his fur.

'What's he doing here?' said Fiona. 'I thought they were supposed to be shut in because of the fireworks.'

'I don't know,' said Caroline. 'Min's away to

bed.'

'Is he okay?' Fiona bent behind her. Caroline could smell perfume and the warm breath of wine.

'He's dead,' said Caroline simply.

'Shit, Mum.' Fiona reached out a tentative hand. 'Are you sure?'

Caroline nodded. She looked up. 'Could you go and get your dad, love?'

'Oh, shit. Min's going to be devastated,' said Fiona. She straightened up. 'Should I get her too?'

Caroline shook her head. 'No. Just your dad. I'm going to move him into the den. In case someone comes through.'

Fiona nodded and disappeared across the hall. Caroline slipped her hands under the small prone form and stood up. He was surprisingly heavy. She carried him across the wooden floor and nudged open the den door with her hip. She laid him down on the rug by the cold fire, moving his limbs into a more natural position, as if he had fallen asleep on his side. This would kill Min. He had been a present from Rena; a puppy to replace another old dog, a gift from someone Min ached for every day.

The heat was going from his body. David was coming. Caroline bent down suddenly and buried her face in the thick, wiry fur at his neck.

CHAPTER FIFTEEN

WEDNESDAY, 30 DECEMBER

Vonnie laid her arm across her face and tried to keep her eyes from opening too far. Not that it was sunny. In fact the light that had flooded into the bedroom when she had pulled the blind aside was dark enough to threaten rain.

It was a little after 9 a.m., and she was surprised to have woken so early, her head still thick from last night. Although everyone had sobered up when they heard what happened to Hector. They had sat round the kitchen table once the last of the guests had gone, wondering how and when to tell Min. Caroline had argued it should be sooner, but David thought they should let her sleep and tell her in the morning, and everyone else had agreed. So Hector had been moved into the utility room, and wrapped in a Hunting Stewart blanket, and would hopefully not be too stiff for Min to see him when she woke. Katie and Daisy had both got noisily upset and Vonnie had taken them in to say goodbye to him. She had planned just to stand by the door with them, but curiosity had taken over and they had both knelt and had a little poke at him and asked a series of inappropriate questions about body fluids and whether dogs turn into ghosts.

Vonnie lay for a while listening to the noises of the house. There was no way she was going to get back to sleep so she slid her legs out of bed and slipped on her jeans and yesterday's jumper and went downstairs. She wasn't the first up: there were two milky rings on the kitchen table, two empty bowls by the sink and a packet of Rice Krispies opened on the countertop. She scooped out a handful while she waited for the kettle to boil. Frances's catering crew had taken most of the food away, but had left some platters covered in clingfilm on the kitchen table. Vonnie lifted an

297

edge and eased out a small tartlet and popped it into her mouth, then thought better of it and spat it back into her hand then dropped it into the bin.

She opened the blind. Outside, the lawn bore the marks of so many party shoes, flattened and muddied. A paper napkin flapped across the big flowerbed like a wounded gull.

The marquee doors were still tied back and Vonnie saw the flash of movement among the neatly stacked tables and chairs, two small figures dipping and weaving.

She carried her tea outside, slipping her feet into Caroline's wellies in the scullery as she went. The wind hit her like a slap in the face and she hurried across the lawn towards the tent.

It was Katie and Daisy. They bobbed up from behind a serving table as she came in.

'Hey,' said Vonnie. 'Is this a private party or can anyone join in?'

They both shook their heads and she pulled out a chair and settled herself on to it.

'So.' Vonnie looked at them both. 'Did you enjoy last night?'

They both nodded again.

'I think everybody did,' said Vonnie.

'Well, not Min,' said Daisy. 'Because her dog died.'

'She doesn't know that yet,' said Vonnie.

Daisy nodded. 'It's really sad.'

'It is sad,' said Vonnie, 'but he was very old.'

'Will Min get another one?' asked Daisy. 'A puppy?'

'I don't think so,' said Vonnie. 'She's still got Riley.'

'Hector was the nicest,' said Daisy. 'Riley tries

298

to have sex with your leg.'

'He does,' said Vonnie. 'And it's not very nice.'

'We're going to bury him today. In a hole.'

'Are we? In a hole,' said Vonnie. She rested her elbows on the table.

'Grampa's going to dig it. In the flowerbed where he does his poos.'

Katie burst out laughing. 'Not where Grampa does his poos!'

Daisy giggled. 'Then it would be in the toilet.' They bent their heads together and for a second Vonnie saw her sisters in a moment of shared laughter. Deborah's eyes in Katie and Fiona's heart-shaped face in Daisy.

She saw Daisy raise her head and turned. David was making his way across the grass towards them. He must have showered already because his hair was wet and slicked back. He wore a thick roll-neck and his binoculars were strung around his neck. He looked pale. He wandered into the marquee and stopped in front of them.

'Are we going to bury Hector now, Grampa?' asked Katie

David seemed a little taken aback. 'Em, no. Not right now. But I tell you what you could do. You could get some stones so we can put a cairn on top of his grave. I'm sure Min would like that.'

'What's a cairn?' asked Daisy.

'A pile of stones,' said David.

'How big?'

'Oh, pretty big,' added David. 'And they need to be quite small stones. Lots of them. Do you think you can manage that?'

Katie and Daisy nodded and Vonnie watched them run off. She shook her head.

'I remember you used to do that to us. Give us a task to make us feel important when it was just a ruse to get rid of us for an hour. I'm wise to you now.'

'How long do you think it will take them to collect enough?' David laughed.

'Well, seeing as they don't have any containers, at least an hour and a half. And you'll have no gravel left on the paths.'

'Small price,' said David. He pulled out a seat next to her and leaned across to ruffle her hair.

'And how's my best girl this morning? A little fragile?'

'I wasn't that bad,' protested Vonnie.

'You were that bad,' countered David.

Vonnie pulled a face. 'But not outrageous.'

'No.' David smiled at her. 'Never outrageous.'

'It was a good crowd,' said Vonnie. 'Good fun.'

'Mmm.' David lifted the binoculars from around his neck and laid them on the table. 'The conscientious and the curious.'

'Dad!' Vonnie turned to face him. 'Why would you say that? Everyone wanted to be there.'

He shrugged and Vonnie reached for his arm and gave it a squeeze. 'I thought you had a great time.'

David looked a little shamefaced. 'I did. No, I did. Really. I've just never been one for these full-blown affairs.' He gave a forced laugh. 'I'm sure half of them just wanted to have a nosey around the house.'

'You should have said something to Mum,' said Vonnie.

'It's fine,' said David. 'Your mum likes organising and it was a good night.'

Vonnie smiled. 'Did you see the last firework?'

'Yes, that was a little unexpected. I suspect it will turn up in a diary column somewhere.'

'Fiona was so embarrassed,' said Vonnie. 'I think they paid a small fortune for them.'

'They should get their money back,' said David. He sat back in the seat and stretched.

'Is Min awake yet?'

David shook his head. 'I've just checked. I want to get to her before anyone else.'

'Do you think it was the fireworks that killed him? The stress?'

'God knows,' said David. 'He was as old as the hills. It could have been anything.'

'She's going to be gutted,' said Vonnie. 'Really.'

'I know.' David sat forward and rubbed his hands across his face. He sat like that for a moment, not lifting his head.

'You okay?'

'Yeah. Just a little . . .' He couldn't seem to find the word.

'Flat?' said Vonnie.

'Mmm,' said David.

Vonnie watched him. It must actually be really strange, to be in such a high-profile job one day, and then the next to have no say, no influence. Out the door. And he was such a news junkie. Vonnie knew he would still be listening to every bulletin, sorting stories in his mind, trying to anticipate what might come next. And everyone last night had been acting like he'd won the lottery, or at the very least his freedom because he was retired, when it's not something he would have chosen.

'I'm really proud of you,' she said suddenly. 'Really. I used to love telling kids at school what

301

you did. Their dads were bankers or accountants. But you had this amazing job. A different story every day. And I always knew stuff before they did. All the gory bits, too.'

David looked up. 'Thanks, love.' He reached across and put his hand on her knee. Maybe no one else had said that to him. She hoped someone had.

'I'm going to make toast,' she said. 'Do you want some? I could bring it out here.'

He shook his head. 'I'm going to go down to the hide for a bit. If you hear Min up, come and get me, okay, love?'

Daisy appeared at the door of the marquee, with a handful of white gravel pooled in the folded edge of her jumper. 'Grampa, look!'

'Perfect,' said David, and Daisy beamed and hurried off.

'I think it's going to be a very small cairn.' Vonnie pushed her chair back and stood up.

'He was a very small dog,' said David.

*   *   *

Annie sat on the plastic chair at the foot of the bed trying to force-feed Minstrels to the large doll with the cupid's bow mouth, and studiously ignoring the small bundled shape just a few feet away from her. She had come into the ward hesitantly, clutching Charlie's hand and, after a cautious cuddle with Gail, had stood peering politely through the sides of the small cot, exactly the way she did with the less remarkable animals at the zoo.

'This is Jack.' Charlie had bent down. 'This is your baby brother.'

Annie had stared hard at the small frowning face above the wrap of white blanket.

'Why is it all red?'

Charlie swallowed his smile. 'He's just been born. Everyone's red just after they've been born.'

Annie wrinkled her nose and looked closer. 'I can see its eye. It's got an eye.'

'Jack,' said Charlie. 'He's called Jack. And he has two eyes. I hope.'

Annie nodded again. 'When will it wake up? Will it wake up soon?'

It was Gail who had sensed that might be the right moment. 'Here, Annie, wait till you see what Jack got you.' She had motioned to Charlie who lifted the large wrapped box from a plastic bag by the side of the chair. 'It's for being his big sister,' said Gail.

Annie fell on the present with delight and Charlie had backed on to the chair at the side of the bed and reached for Gail's hand.

In the end he had been home in plenty of time, even with that stupid arse who had blocked him in at the Haldanes'. Gail had been in the bath with a cup of camomile tea, looking surprisingly serene. Her mum had arrived to sit with Annie, and was being unnecessarily busy in the kitchen. He had time to change out of his suit into jeans and a long-sleeved T-shirt.

They had driven to the hospital with the Proclaimers playing on the radio. And it hadn't taken so terribly long. Gail had opted for gas and air and Charlie had sat at her head watching her eyes widen in terror at the certain pain. She had told him off for singing along to U2's 'Beautiful Day' on her CD, even though the Geordie midwife

303

had insisted she honestly couldn't tell the difference between him and Bono. Then a little after 2.20 a.m. the midwife motioned to him and he let go of Gail's restless hands and moved from her head, and watched as the small form was guided from her, damp and smeared, and laid on her belly like a new-landed fish.

'A boy,' pronounced the midwife and Gail had laughed.

'Told you,' Charlie said gently.

The pain ebbed from Gail's eyes, bright now with tears. Charlie would remember the look on her face for a very long time.

He looked across at her now. She had closed her eyes, although she wasn't asleep. Her hair lay flat against her head and her skin still had the sheen of exertion. The top two buttons of her pyjama top were undone. She'd been a little tearful when he got back with Annie because Jack hadn't latched on properly. And she had cried more when Annie clambered on to the bed for her careful cuddle.

He let go of Gail's hand and leaned forward in the chair to look down again at his boy. He had a faint feathering of black hair—Gail's hair—and, somewhere beneath the covers, long tapered fingers. A boy. His boy. He knew he wouldn't have cared had it been another girl. Not a jot. But this was his boy. His little boy. He had a sudden image of David Haldane, and a sense of unfathomable loss. How could you bear it?

He felt Gail's hand in his hair and realised she was motioning him towards Annie, who had lost interest in the doll and was staring at the family across the ward. The girl in the bed could have been no more than nineteen. She lay with her baby

304

in her arms, studying it with numb astonishment as her relatives clustered around. They were making a lot of noise and had taken most of the spare seats in the ward, but who had the heart to make a fuss?

Charlie reached out with his foot and tapped Annie's leg.

'Hey, nosy p, do you want another look at your brother?'

Annie slid off the chair and peered again into the Perspex box.

'It's awake!' she cried.

Charlie turned and grinned at Gail. 'It's awake,' he said.

Gail slid herself gingerly up the bed and gestured to Annie, who clambered on. Charlie lifted Jack and placed him on Annie's legs, tucking Annie's arm under his neck.

'No. Careful.' Gail bent forward awkwardly. 'A bit further up. There. You need to make sure his neck is supported.'

Charlie saw a flash of consternation on Annie's face. 'You're doing great, toots,' he said. He tried to catch Gail's eye to warn her to ease up, but she was looking down and adjusting Annie's grip on her brother. He turned and dug the camera from the bag.

'Right, after four, all say cheese!'

'Cheeeeeeezzze,' shouted Annie, as Charlie pressed the shutter.

When he looked at the picture later, among all the others he had taken that day, he would notice that Annie was laughing, Jack was squinting, but above her lovely smile, some of the light had gone from Gail's eyes.

Maybe dogs didn't care that much when their best friends died or maybe it was Riley's way of saying goodbye. Katie watched him dance across the lawn as Grampa carried the small bundle, still wrapped in the tartan blanket, towards the biggest flowerbed. Min wasn't crying but Katie could tell that she had been; her eyes were really small and quite red and Gran was standing very close to her, as if to catch her if she fell over.

Katie thought it was a bit rude that Elsa and Jamie and Aunt Fiona and Uncle Allan hadn't turned up. Everyone else was there, just standing around and looking solemn. Grampa got to the edge of the hole and laid Hector on the ground and unwrapped him from the blanket like a present you didn't want. He was stiff, like the dogs on wheels in the Argos catalogue that Katie had wanted when she was small but had never got. Min made a funny noise in her throat, and Grampa put Hector in the hole and started covering him up with the earth.

Katie didn't feel like crying which was a good thing really because she wanted to be a vet. And if you were a vet, you couldn't afford to cry over dead dogs, or you'd spend a lot of your time in a bit of a mess.

Once the earth was all back in, Katie and Daisy helped Grampa pile the stones into a cairn. It was a bit wobbly and not very high and bits kept falling off. Riley must have thought they were playing because he came over and started to dig. Grampa kicked him with his foot and shouted, but Riley kept coming back. Katie hoped he didn't come

306

back again when everyone had left and dig Hector up. Riley was good at digging and Katie had seen him dragging a dead rabbit around the garden. It had been pretty gross.

*   *   *

In the bathroom, Fiona turned on the tap and settled herself on the loo, peeling her pantyliner from her pants. She tore it in half and dropped it into the bowl between her legs. She knew she really ought to have put it in the bin, but she was in a hurry. She figured she had maybe fifteen minutes. She flushed, washed her hands and checked her teeth in the mirror. She took a deep breath and opened the door. Back in the bedroom, Allan was sitting on the end of the bed. He'd just assumed she was ready when he had reached for her; he always did. He didn't think about pantyliners or unshaven days or the fights they had had, or the fact that she didn't want to.

'Quickies,' he had whispered.

'Quickies?' She had caught his hand and turned to look at him. 'You want quickies? Allan, they're burying the dog.'

But he was heading back south tomorrow and she had held him off until now. There would be five full days when he was on his own without her. If she capitulated, he would leave in better humour and she wouldn't have to worry. She knew it was fucked-up thinking; that he had never given her any real reason to doubt his fidelity; that it was no way to exist as a couple. But she also knew, maybe more than most, how compromised a marriage could become, the little deals you had to forge just

307

to make it to the end of the day.

He held out his arms but she moved past him to the small radio at the bedside and switched it on for background noise. It was *Gardeners' Question Time*. Black spot on roses. It would have to do. She went across to him and pulled him up by the hands and slipped her arms around his waist.

'Mmm.' She tried to give him a dreamy smile.

Allan lifted her hand to his mouth and made her touch his lips. He stared at her. She reached for his crotch with her free hand. He was hardening. His other hand went for her breast under her jumper, pushing up her underwired bra and searching for her nipple. She bit her lip. He liked when she did that, didn't realise it was to distract her from the other sensations that his hands on her skin provoked.

'Need to be quick,' she whispered and closed her eyes. He pressed her back against the wall and she felt his hand on her jeans. He reached for the zip and started to talk. She kept the smile on her face but laid her arm up against the wall and pressed her fingers through her hair and into one ear. He never seemed to notice when she had done that. She found it dulled the words a little, and the noises he made. The little grunts and moans, the muttered, breathy questions. Did she want it? She wanted it, didn't she? And she would agree because that made it go quicker. Yes, she wanted it. She really did. She really, really, really did.

*   *   *

The car eased round the corner and down the track. In a little while the trail of sand would start,

308

carried on the wheels of all the other vehicles that had come this way. When they were small the girls would watch for it, then argue over who had seen it first, the first proper sign that they had arrived at the beach. Caroline shifted into a lower gear to ease over the potholes. The rain had started, just a smirr, but enough to bring the wipers on. Beside her, Min sat silently, her hands clasped in her lap, her face obscured by the waxed rainhat she was wearing. She had been terribly upset about Hector, but it was she who had insisted that they get him in the ground 'pretty damn quick', seeing as he had been lying overnight and it was warm enough that it could be April.

Jamie was in the back seat, a little slouched but looking out of the window with apparent interest. Caroline had been surprised when he had volunteered to come. She had offered to take Min out for a run in the car and had then thought of the beach, because Riley could come too and she could take her sketchpad.

It would have been best if she could have come away on her own, that's what she needed. Space and time to think. It was so strange to watch David behaving as if all was exactly as it should be. He didn't know. He had excused himself from the trip to the beach without realising that he had not been invited. Boyd had called to say Charlie's baby was a boy, and all was well, but no one would be down to dismantle the marquee until tomorrow. David thought he could make a start, unhooking the outer layer of pegs and lifting the wooden floor.

Caroline had watched him as he explained this to her and wondered how his face would change if she said, 'I saw you.' She had hardly slept, and had lain in her quiet room and heard him come upstairs a little after 2 a.m., whistling. The shock of what she had witnessed had given way to a blank numbness. She felt hollowed out, incapable of feeling. Frances. Frances Fletcher.

The car park was almost empty, just a small red Citroën Saxo and a camper van. Caroline got Riley out of the boot and attached him to his lead, then asked Jamie if he would take him down on to the sands and let him go, but only if there were no other dogs in the immediate vicinity. She and Min would take their time. Jamie moved off, his arm outstretched as Riley surged forward, pulling the lead as taut as a wire.

There was a small patch of woodland to walk through before you reached the sands, with tall, thin Scots pines that soughed gently in the wind as you passed, like a sigh of regret. Caroline had tried to sketch them several times, but she could never get the sense of movement, the gentle dip and nod of each one. The path was broad and well-trodden, but Caroline took Min's arm anyway, and she didn't complain, as she sometimes did.

She did tut, however, when they passed a discarded plastic bag, stuffed with take-away dishes and Coke cans, and pierced by a small wooden fork.

'Dirty buggers,' she said. 'Is there a bin?'

'I'll pick it up on the way back,' said Caroline.

By the time they had come out of the trees, Riley was off his lead and in the water and Jamie was standing at the edge. Neither he nor Daisy seemed to possess a pair of wellies, or anything stouter than baseball boots. He turned and gave a half-hearted wave as he saw them.

Min stopped. 'He's not a happy lad, that one.'

Caroline turned to look at her. 'I think it's just hormones,' she said. 'He's at that age.'

'Maybe,' said Min. She let go of Caroline's arm. 'Are you walking? Because I don't think I'll walk.' She nodded her head towards Jamie. 'I'll keep an eye on the boy. You go off. We'll be fine.'

Caroline smiled. The whole point of this jaunt had been to keep an eye on Min and she was having none of it.

'I might just go out to the rocks,' said Caroline. 'There and back. I won't be too long.'

She stood for a while to make sure Jamie realised that Min was heading his way, then turned for the far end of the beach. The wind was offshore, sending the water scudding out into the estuary in great billowing sheets. She passed a young couple with two boxer dogs. They were wearing matching waterproofs. She smiled at them and they smiled back. They weren't touching but something in their body language meant you could tell they were together; an awareness, a sense of each other, their arms swinging close enough for an easy, unthinking clasp of the hands should their fingers brush.

When had she and David lost that? Long after Euan, but she couldn't remember exactly when it had started to change, just that there came a time when it felt odd that he touched her at all. She could remember the last time they had made love, although that was such a fraudulent expression for what had passed between them; in the dark and under the sheet, the perfunctory movement of limbs, her utter rigidity, nails dug into palms, the awful effort on his part to finish and finish quickly.

311

Afterwards he had said a quiet 'thank you' and she had turned her head away and stared, unseeing, at the bright numbers on the clock.

Some months later, David had developed a bad cough that turned into a chest infection. He moved into the spare room, so as not to wake her, he had said, and he had not come back. Was that when he had gone to Frances? She wondered what story he had told himself, what excuse, what justification. She felt a sudden stab of anger. Frances. A friend. Someone who knew what they had been through, who was there on the day. Such a betrayal, and of Bob, too. Decent, solid Bob who had doted on both David and his wife. She found herself wondering about Christmas Eve. His hand on her shoulder, her cheek against his skin. Had that been guilt? He had been away for hours that day. Had he been with her? God, what a mess. What an utter bloody mess.

She had reached the start of the rocks and turned to check on Jamie and Min. They were a good distance away and still by the water's edge, and Jamie seemed to be throwing in a stick for Riley, doubtless under instruction from Min as to the perfect speed and trajectory.

Caroline climbed gingerly over the rocks, slick with seaweed. She stopped well before the water and stood looking out. There were quite a few ships in the distance, giant freighters headed for Leith or Stavanger, but tiny on the horizon like a child's bath toys.

Directly across from her was the low curve of Fife. She could just make out the spread of villages, from Buckhaven and Methil and round the tip towards Elie and the East Neuk. She knew

312

Elie. That was where the woman who had found Euan had moved to, when, like Min, she grew too old to live by herself. She'd been from Dunbar originally, a maths teacher at North Berwick High. She was behind the lorry, on the way to see her sister in Tranent. She must have been a careful driver because she had time to stop and pull in to the side before she got out and started to run.

She was still there when Caroline and David arrived. The ambulance had turned up and the men were down on the road with him, as was the woman. And she had stood up and looked at them both with such pain and such horror, knowing already that he was gone. Caroline remembered that her knees were bloodied, maybe from kneeling so long on the road, or maybe it was Euan's blood. She never found out.

They had met her again almost a month after; had asked the police to put them in touch, so they could say thank you and she had agreed. And they had sent cards at Christmas every year until one year hers had come with a change of address and the news that she was moving in with her daughter. A few years after that the cards stopped altogether. Caroline had continued to send them, but heard nothing more. It bothered her. She had no idea if the woman was still alive and she ought to know. She was the woman who had seen the life go out of her boy, the woman who had held him, tight and dead in her arms, until someone who loved him could come.

She slipped her notepad from the pocket of her jacket and the small end of a pencil, sharpened to a soft grey point. She would sketch now, lose herself in the scratch of lead on vellum, empty her mind of

313

David and Frances and Euan, and all that was to come, everything except the lines and shapes of sea and land.

She finished three small studies before she stood to walk back: the curve of the far coast; a slack coil of seaweed; the tiny, curving comma of an anemone in the rock pool in front of her. She closed the book and slipped it back in her pocket. Min and Jamie had started out towards her, followed by Riley who was dragging what looked like a small tree. They were making slow progress and she met them more than halfway back.

'I was just explaining about the sewage spill we had here last year,' said Min. 'Faeces as far as the eye could see.'

Which must have been delightful for a twelve-year-old, thought Caroline. Jamie was looking bored and cold, but then he was only wearing a sweatshirt, the one with the red dragon on the front, the one that Min had worn when she lost her coat.

'Right,' said Caroline. 'I think we should head back. I need to stop and get some bread and milk.' She took the lead from Jamie and clipped on Riley, and they walked back together towards the trees and the start of the path. When they were off the sand, she handed the dog and the car keys to Jamie.

'You're on drying duty. There's a towel in the boot.'

He gave a half-hearted nod and moved off, dragging Riley this time, because the dog knew the walk was over. Min had stopped a little way back and had turned so she was facing the water again. She lifted her fingers to her mouth and gave a piercing whistle, as she had always been able to do.

'Min?'

She turned her head to look at Caroline. 'You shout him for me,' she said. 'I can't see him.'

'Jamie's got him. They're off back to the car.'

'Got who?' Min looked irritated.

'Riley.'

'No,' said Min. 'Hector.' She turned back to the beach.

Oh, God. Caroline took a step towards her. 'Min, he's not here. He's not with us.'

'I know he's not with us,' said Min. Caroline saw the fingers on her hand start to fold into each other in agitation. 'But he doesn't go far.'

'No.' Caroline stepped in front of her. 'He's not with us, Min. Hector's not with us. He died. Last night. Remember? We just buried him.'

The words sounded so brutal. She took Min's hands. The old lady's eyes were confused, watery with the wind. How could she have forgotten? Just a few hours.

'He doesn't. Go far,' said Min, haltingly, but with purpose, as if the words might anchor her.

CHAPTER SIXTEEN

Jamie could tell something had happened. Caroline had been too brisk when she got back to the car with Min. She had settled her into the front seat and clipped on her seat-belt like she was a small child, talking loudly the whole time. She didn't even say thank you for drying Riley, which he had, and had been nipped in the process as the

315

dog wrestled with the towel. At first, he thought they might have had a fight and just not been speaking, because his mum and Birgit could be that way sometimes. But then Min started making small noises, like little 'oh!'s as if everything were a surprise. He couldn't see her face once he was in the back seat, but he could see her hands and they were moving all the time, twitchy and clutching. She fell asleep before they were back at the house, at least he thought she had because her head kept dunting off the window, near the sticker on the window that said 'Islay: And it's Goodbye to Care.' Caroline didn't stop for food as she had said she would but headed straight home.

She gave Min a little shake when they got into the driveway and helped her out of the car. Min seemed pretty out of it, Jamie had thought. He had asked if there was anything he could do and Caroline had said, 'No,' and then, 'Actually, yes,' and could he go and find his mum and see if she would do the shopping. Bread and milk and bacon and toilet roll.

Fiona was in the kitchen, slicing red peppers into thin wedges with the kind of big shiny knife that serial killers use. The radio was on and she had been singing as he came in. The best place to find his mum happy was in a kitchen, especially if there was no one else in it. She was really bad at singing, though, like the worst people you ever got on the *X Factor*. She smiled at him and kept slicing, piling the finished peppers neatly on to an oiled tray.

'Hey,' she said. 'How was your walk?'

'Fine. Kind of.'

'Kind of? Where's your gran?'

316

'She's helping Min. She wondered if you could go and get some bread and milk and stuff.'

'I thought you were going to get it when you were out?' said Fiona. She paused and, still holding the knife, pushed back a strand of hair with her arm.

'I think Min wasn't too well,' said Jamie. 'We had to come back.'

'Really? What happened?'

Jamie shrugged. 'Dunno. She just seemed to get kind of upset.'

'Another one of her turns, probably,' said Fiona.

Jamie pulled out one of the chairs and sat down. 'What's wrong with her?'

'Old age,' said his mum. 'It's a shame, but it happens.'

'She was fine most of the time,' said Jamie. 'It was just at the end.'

'And Gran wants me to get the milk?'

Jamie nodded.

'Do you know where Vonnie or Deborah are?'

Jamie shook his head. 'Haven't seen them.'

The last pepper was sliced and she placed her knife down. 'Well, I suppose I better go now, no point in sticking anything in the oven just yet.'

'Could I come too?' He wasn't sure why he had asked. Maybe just the thought of hanging about the house for another afternoon or lying in the dead boy's room trying not to think about his phone.

Fiona paused for an instant. 'Em, yes, I suppose so. Yes. If you want. Can you run and tell Allan? He's having a little lie down upstairs. And give Daisy a shout. She's been out in that bloody marquee all day with Katie. I doubt she'll want to

317

come but we should ask.'

Neither Daisy nor Allan wanted to come, so Jamie got to sit in the front of the hire car. Fiona sped along the lanes so quickly that anything interesting she pointed out was always behind him by the time he turned to look, including two cows who were on top of each other, a burned-out car, and a standing stone in the middle of a field which helped you get pregnant. Fiona said it had been there for thousands of years and for it to work you had to walk round it three times. 'And have sex, obviously,' she added and laughed at her own joke. She slowed down when she got into the town and then got a bit confused about the one-way system and ended up giving the finger to a man who tooted his horn at her. 'You didn't see that,' she said, like she always did.

There was a car park at the station, but it was small and completely full. The main street of the town was pretty busy, but most of the people seemed to be old. Men in beige, women in hats, and a couple of small dogs with coats on. There were several small shops: a butcher's, a baker's, a chemist and a newsagent that was also a post office. The supermarket was at the end of the street and set back a bit with a small car park. Fiona let out a hoot of delight when someone pulled out of a space in front of her. Once they were inside she sent him off to find bread (brown granary) and eggs (free-range organic), and some of the wheat-free cereal that didn't bring Daisy out in a rash, and toilet paper that wasn't so thick that it would clog up the septic tank. They didn't have any of the wheat-free cereal, and Fiona pulled a face at the till when he told her and muttered

318

something about where was Waitrose when you needed it, which Jamie thought was a bit rude.

In the car park, they stowed the shopping in the boot of the car, but instead of opening the front doors, Fiona paused suddenly and looked over at him.

'Shall we go for a coffee?'

Jamie shrugged.

'I'll take that as a yes,' said Fiona. 'Come on.'

She locked the car and they headed down a small lane. Fiona said the town had not really changed since she was young. She found a coffee place that she said had been there for ages and they ducked inside, past the revolving racks of birthday cards and shelves full of ornaments and candles and small tartan things that tourists might buy.

Fiona found a table and pushed the dirty dishes that were still on it to one corner, then slung her coat over the back of the chair. There was a tall, greasy menu decorated with teapots balanced between some sauce bottles and she ran her eyes down it.

'I used to come in here when I was your age. We'd get off the bus after school and come in here for a hot chocolate. This is where all the kids hung out.'

He wanted to laugh because it sounded really old-fashioned and dull. He tried to imagine a crowd of teenagers, his mum in the middle, thinking she was all grown-up.

'So, what are you having?' asked Fiona. 'Hot chocolate?'

'Can I have Coke?'

'Well, I suppose.' She must have been trying to

be nice to him because she was usually pretty strict about anything fizzy, saying she didn't want him to have 'Scottish teeth'. He wasn't exactly sure how they were different from English teeth but she made it sound worse.

The waitress was about Fiona's age but with short hair and very pudgy legs under her striped apron. She was really nice, though, and wiped the table with a cloth and told him he wouldn't taste better chocolate cake anywhere, when he said that's what he would have.

'So. Are you having a nice holiday?' Fiona leaned her elbows on the tabletop and rubbed her hands together. She had that condition that leaves your fingers all cold and pale because the blood doesn't reach them properly. Even on the hottest days, her fingers could be icy.

'Uh-huh.'

'Are you not absolutely bored?' said Fiona. 'Not having another boy about.'

'No, it's fine.'

'We should go into Edinburgh to the cinema one day. Would you like that? In fact, we need to give Allan a run up to the airport tomorrow so we could go then.'

Jamie nodded again. 'Yeah. Okay.'

'Or you should phone some of your friends,' said Fiona. 'See what they're up to. Is anyone away overseas this holiday?'

Jamie shrugged again. 'Dunno. Maybe.'

The waitress came back with their drinks and set them out on the table, then a few moments later reappeared with a thick wedge of chocolate cake for Jamie and a shortbread round for Fiona. Fiona reached across and swiped a curl of icing from the

320

cake and popped it in her mouth.

'Not bad,' she said. 'But not the world's best ever.'

Jamie hoped the waitress hadn't heard.

'Well,' Fiona continued. 'When we get back, you could have them over, your friends. Sleepover, you haven't had one for ages.'

'Nobody really does sleepovers,' said Jamie. He wished she would stop asking about school and friends.

She dunked the teabag around in the little metal teapot then lifted it out and laid it on her paper napkin. Jamie watched the dark brown stain seep outwards into the fibres.

He looked up. Fiona was staring at him. She reached up suddenly and smoothed his fringe out of his eyes. Her fingertips were cold.

'What's going on in there?' she said, tapping his forehead gently. She pulled her hand away and curled it back round her teacup. 'Eh? What's going on in that head?'

He gave her a smile but he didn't answer. She didn't really mean it as a question anyway. She wasn't really expecting him to tell her.

*　　　*　　　*

David picked up the book that Min had left open and upended on the edge of the coffee table. It was a biography of Stalin, a new one she had got just before Christmas and she was already halfway through. He smiled. Rena used to get so cross with her, the way she treated books. Rena treated hers like fragile children. Min sucked the information from them, leaving them with spines split by overuse, pages thumbed thin, margins laddered with scribbled notes.

The door to the bedroom opened and Caroline backed out, pulling it shut carefully behind her. David laid the book back down and sat on the edge of the armchair. On the floor, in front of the fire that was yet to be lit this winter, Riley lay in an exhausted stupor, paws flicking intermittently in his remembered run.

'Is she asleep?'

'No, but she's settled.' She sat down at the far end of the small couch, lifting away one of Min's cardigans as she did so. David wondered if she realised she had given it an instinctive sniff.

'Do you think we should get the doctor back out?' she said.

David exhaled and shook his head. 'I don't know. I mean, I didn't see the worst of it, but it's been a pretty emotional day for her. She might just need a rest.'

'I suppose so.' Caroline dropped her head.

'What?' said David.

'It's getting worse,' she said. 'More frequent. These little turns. She called me Rena.'

'She's eighty-eight, Caroline.' David stood up and walked over to the fireplace. Riley wakened momentarily and raised his head, eyeing him dolefully.

'It's more than that,' said Caroline. 'I'm a bit worried.'

'Well, what do you think it is? Dementia? Alzheimer's?' He spoke more sharply than he meant to.

'Shhh!' Caroline looked up at him quickly. 'I don't know. Maybe. But if they are little strokes,

322

like the GP said, then each one must be doing more damage.'

'Well, there's no point in doing anything now until after New Year. The doctor said to wait and see. Let's do that. Okay? If we're still worried in a week or so, then we can get him back and take it from there. Let's not imagine the worst.'

They both fell quiet.

'What if she needs care?' said Caroline suddenly.

David sighed. It wasn't that he hadn't thought about it. 'Well, we're here, aren't we?' he said. 'And we could get someone in.'

Caroline looked away from him just as the door opened. It was Vonnie.

'Everything okay?' she said.

'It's fine,' said David. 'We're just trying to sort out Min. She's still a bit upset over Hector.'

'Well, sorry to butt in, but, Dad, Charlie just called to confirm he can come down tomorrow and take the marquee away then.'

'Charlie?' David felt his smile come. 'How's the baby?'

'Oh, shit, I forgot to ask.' Vonnie pulled a face. 'Sorry.'

'I'll phone him back,' said David.

'Okay.' Vonnie ducked back through the door and David went to follow her. Caroline was still on the sofa. In fact she hadn't moved an inch. She was still looking into the far distance.

'Caroline?'

'Hmm?' She turned to him, her expression blank.

'Are you okay? Is there something else?' He wondered if she'd given him the whole story about

Min's episode at the beach.

She shook her head slowly and offered him a thin smile. 'No.' She made to stand up. 'There's nothing else.'

*   *   *

Charlie stretched his feet right to the end of the bed and wondered if revelling in the feel of clean sheets meant he really was a closet metrosexual, as Gail had often claimed.

He rolled on to his side and peered at the clock: 10.45 p.m. Early for him, but it had taken a good two hours after Annie had gone down to get the house tidy for Gail and Jack coming home tomorrow, and he was knackered. He yawned deeply. One last night of unbroken sleep, if Annie stayed put, then down to Fortune to dismantle the marquee in the morning and over to the infirmary in the afternoon. He flopped over again on to his back and stretched his limbs out indulgently. He'd had a couple of beers and watched unapologetic crap on the TV. A car show, and half an hour of utterly unsatisfying soft porn on Bravo.

'Daddy.'

He hadn't even heard her come in. He leaned up on his elbows. Judging by her outline she was carrying a large toy.

'Hey, bun, what's up?'

She said nothing and clambered across the duvet and down in beside him, dragging the toy after her. A long plush ear fell across his face.

He knew he should send her back but from tomorrow on, there would be no room for her. She'd watched him patiently just after tea as he'd fixed the temporary cot to the side of the bed, so that Gail only had to roll over to breastfeed. He'd been careful to point out that it used to be Annie's cot and she was lending it to Jack now she had her own big girl bed.

She turned on to her side and he turned to face her.

'Are you missing your mum, pet?'

She shook her head.

'Did you have a bad dream?'

'Mmm.'

He reached over and cupped his hand around her head. 'What was it about?'

'Bad dogs.'

'Okay,' said Charlie. 'And what were they doing to be bad?'

'Biting. And scratching.'

'Oh dear,' said Charlie. 'I better check they didn't do too much damage.' He put his hands below the covers and grabbed her arms and legs.

Annie squealed.

'Nope, not too much damage. They can't have been that bad.'

Annie giggled and curled closer towards him.

'Right, miss. It's very late. This is probably not a good plan but you can stay here tonight, but tomorrow, no. Mummy will be very tired. Okay?'

Annie didn't answer.

'I tell you what, why don't we say night night to Mummy,' said Charlie. 'Night night, Mummy.'

'Night night, MUMMY!' yelled Annie.

'And why don't we say, night night, Jack,' said Charlie. 'Night night, Jack.'

There was a pause. Annie gave what sounded like a sniff.

'Go to sleep, baby,' she said.

CHAPTER SEVENTEEN

THURSDAY, 31 DECEMBER, HOGMANAY

Katie rolled to the side and pressed her hands tighter between her pyjama legs, pulling her knees up as far as they would go and willing the pressure to ease. She shut her eyes, hoping sleep might come back but it hadn't for ages now. Mum had said not to have so much water just before bed and she would be furious to know Katie was clutching. But she had been so thirsty after rushing about all day with Daisy. And now she was bursting for the loo. Daisy was sound asleep; you could only hear her breathing if you lay really, really still. Katie had almost got used to the other noises, the creaks and hisses that the house made with all its pipes and floorboards and draughty corners, but she'd never had to get out of bed in the middle of the night to walk about in it.

She turned on to her front, twisting her head sideways on to the pillow so she could breathe, but that was worse. It felt like she might wet the bed at any minute. The thought propelled her out from under the covers and into the cold, still air. She hurried across the room, past Daisy's bed and pulled open the door, thankful that Mum had remembered those plug-in lights which she always took with her on every holiday in case anyone 'tripped and broke their neck'. It was really dark at Gran and Grampa's. Mum said it was because they

326

weren't in the city and didn't have the streetlights. Katie had a streetlight practically outside her window at home, so her room was filled with a thick orangey glow no matter what time she woke.

The bathroom was down the hall and then kind of round a corner, off the bigger hallway where most of the other bedrooms were. Katie followed the lights and tried not to think of the film Elsa had let her see when she had babysat. The one where the man had sliced at the woman with the biggest knife she had ever seen and it had made this awful sound, the same kind of sound that Mum made when she was cutting up potatoes that were too big to go in the pot. She reached the bathroom and didn't lock the door but pushed it over as far as she could. She pulled down her pyjama bottoms and sat down quickly on the loo seat and just in time. The noise she made was so loud that she had to put up her hand to her mouth to stop giggling. She sounded like the horses at the riding stables when they stopped and put their legs apart and it all just gushed out. It took an awfully long time, right up to the last dribbly bit.

The toilet was one of these really old-fashioned ones with a chain above your head that you pulled. Katie hesitated. It was very noisy and she might wake everyone else up. If she left it, it would save water and it would probably be a grown-up who would be in first and they wouldn't mind so much. Anyway, she'd found a poo in the toilet just a few days ago, a big slug-like one, so there was someone else who wasn't flushing either.

She washed her hands and dried them as best she could on the small embroidered handtowel that always seemed to be damp, switched off the light and tiptoed back along the corridor.

She was almost at the bedroom door when she heard it. She put her hand on to the wall instinctively. It was a sob, kind of gulping and quite soft, and then another one. Crying. Katie closed her eyes to try to hear better. It was up the other end of the hall where Gran and Grampa and Jamie's bedrooms were. She took a couple of steps forward and tried to locate the sound. There was another one. It seemed to be coming from the room that Gran was in. Why would Gran be crying? Maybe she was having a bad dream. Maybe that was it. You could cry in your sleep, and shout, and laugh. Mum had once come rushing through to Elsa's room because she heard her laughing, but found her fast asleep. It seemed to go quiet and then there was another one.

It was then that Katie thought it might not actually be Gran having a bad dream, but it might be Euan. That was right by where his room had been. Maybe that's what he did, cried at night because he was dead. She felt herself go cold with terror and threw herself back into the room, making such a noise that Daisy flopped over and went 'whmaa!' before going straight back to sleep. Katie stayed under the covers straining to hear, but the door had closed after her and she couldn't tell if the noise was still there. She knew ghosts weren't real and that it wasn't really Euan but it was still one of the scariest things that had ever happened to her. She couldn't wait to tell Daisy.

*   *   *

'There's no point in putting any feed on it now.'

328

Charlie kicked the small, muddy divot back into place on the edge of the lawn and tamped it down with the toe of his boot. 'First week in March, but no earlier. It'll come back.'

'All your good work undone,' said David ruefully. 'You must have been cursing us the other night.'

'Naah, you're all right,' said Charlie, surveying the flattened and pitted lawn. 'It seemed to be a good night.'

'Yes, it was. I'm glad you enjoyed yourself, although I'm sorry you were down here when it all happened.'

Charlie smiled. The Haldanes had all made a big fuss of him when he'd arrived and insisted he have coffee while the lads made a start on the marquee.

'A boy,' David had said, shaking his hand warmly. 'You were right.'

Charlie had brought out his phone and shown them the pictures he'd taken of Jack in the hospital, and Mrs Haldane, who was still in her dressing gown, had remarked how well, but tired, Gail looked. 'You take care of her,' she had said kindly. They had a gift for him, a soft receiving blanket, the colour of a blackbird's egg. 'Just a minding,' Mrs Haldane had said as Charlie thanked them.

It was good coffee she had made too, strong and aromatic, none of the instant crap that most people offered in mismatched china mugs you knew they'd pulled from the very back of their cupboard because they didn't like you using their best. The house had been chaotic, with people coming and going, some dressed, some still in pyjamas, children and a dog, dishes clattering, shouts from the hall. This was how it should be, Charlie had thought. A house full of children and grandchildren, healthy and happy and all together.

'Well, I better let you get on,' said David. 'What time do you have to be up at the hospital?'

'Early afternoon,' said Charlie. 'Gail's desperate to get out. Not getting much sleep in the ward, I think.'

'I imagine not,' said David. 'Look, there's absolutely no rush to come back. Just in your own time.'

Charlie nodded. 'I'm going to take a good few days clear, but I'll be doing bits and pieces after that. I'll call and let you know.'

'Of course.' David turned to go. He had his binoculars strung around his neck. He looked back. 'You enjoy being with that boy of yours,' he said.

'Thank you,' said Charlie, in as heartfelt a manner as he could. 'I am. I will.'

*   *   *

'I can give you a run up. It's really not a problem.' Fiona leaned against the door jamb and watched Allan scoop up the last of his toiletries from the top of the dresser. He had a lot of toiletries. Aftershave and moisturiser and serum and hair gel, all with different fragrances. Sometimes he smelled like pot-pourri.

'No, no.' He spoke quickly and automatically, his mind already on the flight and everything he would have to do when he got back down to London.

330

'I thought I might take the kids up to the pictures or the winter fair in Princes Street Gardens or something,' said Fiona. 'So we'll be going anyway. We could cancel the taxi.'

'Mmm.'

'And you're okay for me to stay up here until the 4th?' She leaned down and righted Ben who was making slow but steady progress back around the edge of the bed, but had started to tilt backwards and was pulling the duvet with him.

'Yeah, yeah, yeah.'

'And you've got an arse like Michael Douglas.'

'Hmm?' Allan looked up.

'Nothing,' said Fiona. She was right. He hadn't been listening.

'TAXI!' It sounded like Vonnie, bellowing from the bottom of the stairs.

Allan swept up the last of his stuff, bent down and kissed Ben's head, then turned to Fiona with his mouth puckered. His kiss, wet and open, slid off on to her cheek. She fought the urge to wipe, picked up Ben and followed him out into the hall.

Downstairs Daisy clung to him. He had already said his proper goodbyes but David shook his hand again, the kind of shake where you grab the elbow and hold on. Everyone else hugged him, apart from Elsa. Fiona noticed that. She stood by Deborah and Doug, with a polite smile, but made no move towards him.

Fiona went with him out to the taxi. The driver hadn't even bothered to get out, but had popped the boot and was sitting, chewing methodically and staring out at the men taking down the marquee.

Allan swung his case into the boot and shut the lid.

He bent forward and gave her another kiss. Dry, this time, and on the cheek.

'Bye, darling,' he said. He was much happier with her after yesterday, as she had known he would be. She was much happier with him now that he was leaving.

'Bye. I'll call you tonight after the bells.' She stepped back and let him slide into the back seat. She could smell the fragranced trees clustered on the rear-view mirror, just before she shut the door. 'Be good,' she said, not even sure that he could hear.

*   *   *

'So what are we doing tonight?' Vonnie bit into the apple and propped her feet up on the seat of the chair beside her. She was wearing odd socks and her hair was wet from the shower and stuck to her forehead in thick, damp strands.

'What would you like to do?' Caroline slipped the last of the plates into the dishwasher and closed the lid. She didn't feel like doing anything beyond going to bed or finding somewhere that she could sit completely still. She felt absolutely drained; empty, and there was a dull buzzing in her head, the way it was when water got in your ears at the swimming pool.

Vonnie shrugged. A small piece of apple skin was stuck low on her chin and Caroline reached out instinctively and flicked it off. It was strange how as a mother you never lost that: the instinct to touch, correct. Only she had no one to do that for her now. It was a parent's or a lover's touch and she had neither.

332

'Dunno,' said Vonnie. 'Are you all partied out?'

Caroline smiled. 'I think so.' She turned to Deborah who was putting away the last of the clean breakfast cups. 'What do you and Doug feel like?'

'Do you know I might not even stay up for the bells,' said Deborah. 'I'm still knackered after Tuesday.' She pushed her fringe back from her forehead.

Vonnie gave a disbelieving snort. 'Debs, you have to stay up! What's going on here? C'mon, everybody, where's your party spirit?'

The door swung open and Fiona appeared with a crush of sheets in her arms. 'Mum, can I just run these through the machine? I've got some towels as well.'

Caroline nodded, wondering why she needed to.

'Hey, Fi. You'll be up for a bit of a party tonight, won't you?' Vonnie looked beseechingly at her.

'Sure,' said Fiona. 'What are we doing?'

'This pair are off to bed, so it sounds like it's you, me, Min and Dad.'

'You can't go to bed,' said Fiona. 'It's Hogmanay.'

'I'm not—' Caroline started to remonstrate but Fiona interrupted her.

'Here, before we get that far, I'm going into Edinburgh in a bit to take Daisy, Ben and Jamie to the Winter Gardens. Anybody else want to come?' She turned to Deborah. 'Debs?'

Deborah furrowed her brow. 'Actually, would you mind taking Katie with you? Elsa's heading into town to meet her pals so Doug and I can meet you there when we've dropped her off.'

'I'll come with you,' said Vonnie. 'It's years since

I went to the Winter Gardens. They still do the skating rink, right?' She turned to look at Caroline. 'Mum?'

Caroline hesitated. It was on the tip of her tongue to say 'no', to find some reason why she ought to stay. But in a few days they would be gone. She untied her apron and lifted it over her head. 'Actually, I will. Vonnie, can you go and tell your dad we're off. He's down in the hide and he'll need to keep an eye on Min.'

* * *

Princes Street Gardens had been busier than any of them expected, but then it was a lovely afternoon, and often people didn't know what to do with themselves in the daylight hours of Hogmanay, waiting for night and the year to turn.

The queue for the ice rink had been too long, snaking the full way along the edge of the rink and out on to the cinder path. There was no point in joining it; those at the very end said they had been told it would take an hour at least to reach the front.

The line for the giant Ferris wheel beside the Scott Monument didn't look much shorter, but seemed to be moving more quickly. Doug held their place while they had a look round the Christmas market. They bought crepes and coffees and returned to him with chocolate moustaches. It was another ten minutes until they reached the front.

Caroline held Ben tight on her lap as the cage juddered forward to let on another group behind them. He was wearing a little Peruvian hat with bobbles the size of his fists. Vonnie had been holding him, but had handed him over before they started to move. In the cage immediately in front of them, Deborah was going through a list of dos and don'ts with Katie and Daisy who had both been made to sit up straight and hold on to the sides, even though they weren't moving properly yet. Fiona and Jamie were on the next one up. Fiona was checking her mobile, and Jamie was biting his nails. Doug was standing with Ben's pushchair by the entrance, looking relieved that someone had to look after it.

The last cage was filled and the wheel lifted slowly into the sky, until they were rising above the high neon of the shop signs. The air was cold, chilled by an easterly wind. To her right, Caroline could see the old Royal High School building and Calton Hill with its distinctive Greek columns, the sea to the east. She twisted in the seat as the wheel rose towards the tipping point. Up, over the North Bridge, she caught sight of the dome of Old College with its gold statue: Youth Bearing a Torch of Knowledge. Why she remembered that particular fact, she didn't know—when she'd forgotten much of everything else that she'd learned in the lecture halls that lay below.

She would have been Elsa's age. Eighteen and invincible. She had met David in the second week in an English Literature tutorial. He was wearing a jacket that had been his father's with leather on the elbows and a collar he had turned up. She didn't like it, or the way he crossed his legs over at the knee, almost like a girl. But she liked his shoes: sleek black suede, and the way his hair had curled down over the back of his neck. Light brown and

335

wavy.

He had loved the city as much as she did and when it became clear that they were going to be together, in the third year, and before the moment of carelessness that brought them Euan, they talked about the flat they would have. Top floor with a view; New Town, South Side, whatever they could afford. It didn't have to be big, but it had to be high; with windows that looked on to sky, not stone. They ended up in Joppa in a basement flat with bars on the windows and just enough room outside the door for David's bike—which they chained to the railings—and two mismatched chairs they found in a skip. They would sit there in the evening, beside the bins, with a blanket wrapped round them in winter and wine in the summer, toasting their happiness. It wasn't the best time of their lives; *that* came with Euan. But it had been lovely.

Caroline felt the wind and something else catch in her throat. She couldn't reconcile that boy with the man she knew now. Nor the girl she had been.

Ben was wriggling on her knee. He wanted up. She lifted him until he was standing. The tip of his nose was red from the cold and his eyes bright and watery. He stared out over the spreading city, a look of wonder on his face.

'Edinburgh,' said Caroline. 'Isn't it lovely?'

Ben bounced up and down on his fat little legs and clapped his hands in cold delight. And Caroline laughed. She looked across at Vonnie who smiled at her. She was grown. They all were. Whatever had to happen now, it would be all right. They could cope with whatever had to come. The wheel slipped over the apex and carried them slowly back down towards the ground.

*   *   *

'Hey!' Elsa pushed her way through the crush of bodies in the bar and let her bag fall at her feet.

'Babe.' Matt turned and scooped her off the floor and put his mouth on hers, warm and beery. His jacket smelled of smoke. She snaked her arms underneath and up over his shoulders and held on. Their tongues twisted together.

'Jeez, get a room.' One of Matt's friends nudged into them, grinning broadly and balancing a cluster of shot glasses.

Matt bent and picked up her bag and carried it over to the table then sank on to a stool and sat back. Elsa settled on to his knee and his hand slipped round her back and down into her jeans, resting on her right buttock. She put her hand on his neck and twisted it into the thick waves at the nape of his neck.

'So.' He looked up at her. 'Where are we?'

'Close. I think.' She leaned down and kissed him again and then pulled an apologetic face. 'But you might have to come and see them, you know, tea or something. Dad was kind of hinting.'

Matt shrugged. 'Yeah. Whatever. Let me know.' He reached over and handed Elsa a glass.

Elsa crossed her fingers and held them up then took the glass and tipped the vodka into her mouth. Matt bent his face up towards her and they kissed again, the liquid slipping between them. Elsa felt the bite of the alcohol and the warmth of his body beneath her. It could be like this all the time, if they would just say 'yes'.

*　　*　　*

Hanna lifted Dyta's hot-pink boy-shorts from the drier and laid them on top of the neatly folded pile. Maybe it was all the practice she got with the ironing because her washing was stacked as precisely as the sweaters in Gap. Three piles. Her own, Marek's and Dyta's. They took turn about for the laundry and today it was hers. Not that she minded. She found the launderette strangely calming and hypnotic. She loved the heat of it, the clean, soapy smells. She unzipped the long nylon bag and slipped in the clothes. At the far end of the bench, Marek was sitting, legs dangling, twisting the limbs of a Transformer and talking to himself. He gave another hacking cough, the kind that comes up from your boots, and Hanna winced. It seemed to have come on very quickly, but at least his temperature had gone down.

'Bad cough, that.' A large woman in a white nylon cardigan nodded towards Marek and made a sucking, disapproving noise with her teeth as if Hanna herself had brought it on.

Hanna nodded. He was fine. Although he should be playing with someone, not sitting waiting for pants to dry. That was her New Year's resolution: to make more friends. She would have to work at it. Maybe get out of the flat and into somewhere a little bigger with a garden where she could have other children round to play.

'Covonia syrup,' said the woman. 'It'll shift anything. My man had a really bad chest October past. Antibiotics didn't make a whit of difference. No bloody use at all, but Covonia . . . That got the

338

phlegm moving. Should have seen the—'

'Thanks,' interrupted Hanna. 'I'll remember that.' She stood up and turned to Marek. 'Ready?'

He nodded and jumped up and gave another cough just as he passed the woman, almost as if he knew.

'Try some of that syrup!' she shouted after them. 'Shift anything!'

On the pavement, Hanna gave Marek one of the handles of the bag. It was heavy enough to drag at his side, but he liked to help. It was lovely outside, bright and sunny with hardly any wind and a sharpness to the air that she had not felt for weeks. There was a café across the road with steamy windows and a sunflower painted inexpertly on the door.

'Chocolate?'

'Yay!'

They crossed the road together, and Marek hopped over each of the white stripes because Dyta had once told him if he stood on them the bears would come. Hanna hopped too. Because it was a beautiful day and there was a whole new year to come. And the day after tomorrow Boyd was taking her out. And maybe it would be the start of something or maybe not. Who could tell?

*   *   *

There were two things Deborah noticed as they emerged from the trees. The marquee had gone and so had David's car. Caroline had arrived just in front of them. The children had all wanted to go with her and were piling out of the back of her silver Honda Jazz.

339

Katie and Daisy ran across to where the marquee had stood, but Caroline headed straight for the back door. By the time Deborah got there, she was in the hall, shrugging off her coat and calling Min's name.

The response came from the drawing room. Min was in her chair with a book on her lap, and Riley curled at her feet, but they could barely make her out, because none of the lights was on.

'Hello,' said Min. 'Did you have a lovely time?'

'Where's David?' said Caroline sharply.

Deborah, who had started switching on the table lamps, stopped and glanced at her mum.

Min looked as if she was trying to remember. 'Edinburgh,' she said finally. 'Yes, Edinburgh. To the office, I think.'

'It wouldn't be the office, Min,' said Caroline. 'He's retired, remember?'

'Of course,' said Min. 'Of course he is.'

Caroline's lips were pursed.

'Maybe he was coming to meet up with us,' suggested Deborah.

'Yes, maybe,' said Caroline. She moved across to the windows and pulled the curtains shut with an angry twitch, even though there was still light in the sky.

'Right,' she said. 'Who's for a cup of tea?'

'Lovely,' said Min. She beamed at Deborah. Riley had stood up and was stretching indulgently.

'We should probably call him, shouldn't we?' said Deborah. 'Let him know we're back.'

'I don't think so.' Caroline made her way over to the door. 'He'll be back soon enough.'

*   *   *

340

David stood under the stream of warm water with his face upturned. There was an assortment of expensive shower gels in the metal rack that hung from the shower attachment, but he was always careful not to use any of them and leave their scent on his skin.

Frances had set him out a towel—dark green and thickly piled—and had lifted his clothes from the floor and set them on a chair beside the bed. He dressed quickly, but left the curtains shut.

Frances was at the sink, swirling the teapot under the tap. He came up behind her and linked his hands round her waist, bending to kiss the back of her neck and glance down the loose V of her robe. He whistled and she gave a little laugh.

'Mr Haldane,' she said.

He moved away and sat at the table. She had set out some food but he wasn't hungry.

'Are you next door tonight?' He watched her spoon loose tea from an ornate tin and stir it vigorously into the pot.

'Yes,' she said, without turning. It had become her tradition since Bob had died. A neighbour's party and home just after the bells. He found himself fretting occasionally that someone else would catch her eye, and was ashamed of himself for even entertaining such skewed logic. He shouldn't be with her, and sometimes could not quite believe that he was. She had seemed an odd choice for Bob, who had been quiet and stolid even at university, where he and David had met. They had socialised as families for years before anything had happened. She had always been attractive in a bosomy kind of way, with a quick mind and an easy

341

manner, but David had never felt himself tempted, not in the least. Caroline had always occupied all his thoughts. So when it happened, on a wet Saturday after a dinner dance six years ago, his response to her had taken him by surprise, a sudden, fierce rush of need and longing. She had drunk too much and so had he—good whisky—and she had leaned up to give him an inconsequential peck on the cheek as they took a lift together to the ballroom of the Caledonian Hotel, where Bob and Caroline were waiting.

He had stayed away from them for months afterwards, until it had started to look odd. When they had met up again—Caroline had insisted they come down for dinner—he knew it would develop; he had wanted it to. Just over a year later, Bob had died. At his funeral, as everyone else bent their heads for prayer, David had kept his straight and steady, and said his own heartfelt apology; but one with no promise attached.

He had told himself at first that it was purely physical, but knew it was more than that. She was uncomplicated and appreciative, engaged with him and what he did in a way that Caroline had not been for years. He could tell her things that he could not now imagine articulating to Caroline, fears and insecurities, hopes and small triumphs. At the beginning, she had often grown upset, Frances, at what they were doing, and he had tried to reassure her as best he could. It happens. It is not a deliberate hurt. She doesn't know.

Frances gave a luxuriant yawn. 'I'll phone,' she said. 'After the bells.' She always did, and Caroline expected it.

She lifted the teapot over to the table and sat

down opposite him.

'It's almost 2010,' she said. 'Who would believe it?'

He nodded.

'You're going to have a lot more time on your hands.' She gave a small smile and poured the tea into two tall china mugs.

She meant time for her, he knew that, but he didn't respond. Just reached for his tea and cradled it, gingerly, in his hands because it was still too hot to be drunk.

He left at 3 p.m. with light still in the sky. He drove up over the Mound and past the court buildings and the National Library, towards the university. At the far end of the Meadows, he took the left turn on to South Clerk Street and then curved round by the old Commonwealth Pool and down towards Holyrood Palace, where he parked, and walked towards the low path that skirted the base of Salisbury Crags. There were plenty of other people out, students and couples and dog owners. The path rose steadily at the base of the cliffs and he found himself quickly out of breath. He stopped when it levelled out, almost directly opposite the *Scotsman* offices. They were in near darkness because there was no paper on New Year's Day. It felt strangely comforting to know there was no one there, as if they had all left when he did and had never been back. He walked a little further until he was climbing again and the wind strengthened and blew away his dark thoughts. He stood for a while on the top and looked for the kestrel but she wasn't there. He dug his hands in his pockets and started back to the car.

CHAPTER EIGHTEEN

Vonnie lifted the lid of the piano and laid her fingers on the cold keys. She couldn't remember the last time she'd played. She must have been a teenager practising chords or arpeggios. She tried to recall the music for 'Oh, Can You Wash a Sailor's Shirt?' and gave it a bash, but she hit more wrong notes than right. Five years of lessons for this. Such a middle-class thing to do. Piano and ballet and speech and drama and she'd used none of it. Her music teacher had been a hoot, though, a benign German lady with a towering beehive and a raging drink problem. She'd always kept a glass of something on the piano top; gin, probably, because Vonnie could remember the distinctive, berried aroma from the tumbler as she lifted it down. Sometimes the teacher even fell asleep if it got very hot in the room at the top of the school. Perhaps that's why Vonnie had never got beyond Grade 3. She tried a quick chord but her fingers tripped over themselves, so she shut the lid and looked round the room.

It had always had a mish-mash of furniture, this room, the place where you put anything that didn't fit elsewhere. So there was a Welsh dresser with an assortment of fancy plates, the kind you never eat off; and a dark wood writing desk pushed against the far wall; and a sofa with faded covers that was face-on to the gas fire. At some point a new carpet had been laid, a pale beige wool affair and not the dark blue one that Vonnie remembered. It had been a nylon mix because you could raise sparks from it if you rubbed your socks along it. Deborah used to hate that. Vonnie would sneak up behind her and touch any exposed skin, feeling the sharp snap of electricity. Deborah used to go crying to Caroline, and Vonnie would point out that she felt the pain too, although Caroline always said pain was easier to bear when you were inflicting it.

There was a wall of family photographs, and Vonnie picked up the vodka and tonic she had brought through with her and walked across. There were other photographs elsewhere in the house, but these she liked best, because they were mostly the informal shots, snaps in every sense of the word, captured behind the cheapest of frames. There was one of Euan on a rope swing over a river, on a holiday she couldn't recall. It was faintly out of focus, or maybe it was just his movement but you couldn't make out his features. He was on the point of jumping, and his limbs were tensed and tanned. He tanned easily. She remembered that about him now. That his skin was always burnished. She looked closer. There were slight smudges on the glass where someone had touched their fingertips.

There were plenty of her and Fiona and Deborah as well, including the three of them posed in a row like ducks on a wall. Vonnie looked at herself. It must have been after Euan died because she was about eight, hair parted severely to the left and fixed with a kirby that looked as though it hurt. You could tell that Fiona liked having her picture taken because she was beaming at the camera. Deborah had her forced Wallace and Gromit grin, all teeth and stiff, stretched lips. There were several when they were older and adolescence had speckled them with spots and dissolved their smiles and they stood sullenly apart from each other like band members on an album cover.

Her favourite photo was in the middle of them all. It was of her parents' wedding, or rather the immediate aftermath. They were standing outside the Leith registrar's office, with a chip shop half in view to the left. Caroline in her cheesecloth dress, with her hair in a messy up do, David in his skinny suit. They'd not had a proper photographer, partly for money reasons, partly because they didn't want anything so formal. They were surrounded by friends, people Vonnie didn't know. Caroline was laughing loudly, her mouth wide open, maybe in shock at what she had just done. David was grinning at a youngish man with an exuberant beard and a kipper tie. You could tell their hands were joined, even though you couldn't see, just by the angle of their arms. And everyone was looking at them with such surprise and delight. They were living in a flat in Joppa at the time and their honeymoon had been two days in the Highlands because David had just joined *The Scotsman* as a reporter then and Caroline was expecting Euan.

So strange to know now the path their life had followed. An editor and housewife. A son and three daughters. The loss of your first-born, your beautiful boy. A mortgage, a pension, an ulcer, five grandchildren, a cleaner, and a garden that grew too big for you to manage.

Vonnie stood back. Was it really inevitable? That marriage mired you in domesticity and convention with separate bedrooms and a Welsh dresser and good sets of china that gathered dust in a room you left cold?

346

She perched on the sofa and tried to imagine herself and Mike in a wedding photo and found that she wanted to laugh. It was then she noticed the tennis ball rolling past her feet. She looked round. The door was further ajar than she had left it and Ben was gripping on to its edge, wobbling like a tiny drunk.

'Hello,' said Vonnie.

He ignored her and sank to the floor and scuttled forward towards the ball. He didn't crawl as such, but he could work up quite a speed by shuffling on his bottom. He reached the ball, picked it up and raised it to his mouth. Vonnie pulled a face. It looked like Riley's ball, the one he carried around the house and garden and gnawed on when he wasn't licking his balls or chewing his arse. She wasn't exactly Deborah but she knew that it probably wasn't a good idea for Ben to be using it as a pacifier. She leaned down and took it out of his hands.

'Why don't I hold on to this?'

'Pah!' Ben raised his arms indignantly towards her. 'PAH!'

Vonnie laughed. He was a funny little chap. She bent down to pick him up. He wasn't shy around her, or anyone for that matter. He settled into her arms and pointed towards the door.

'Okay. Let's go and find one of your own toys.'

He chattered away at her, garbled baby nonsense, with the odd half-formed word. 'Daw' was apparently 'dog', uttered when he spotted Riley pattering across the hall, and he said 'Mam' when he saw Fiona.

She was in the kitchen, with Deborah and Caroline, clearing away the dishes from the

347

children's tea, or rather Deborah and Caroline were and Fiona was standing at the head of the table with a wine glass. Vonnie handed Ben over.

'He was chewing the dog's ball,' she said.

Fiona sighed and put down her wine. 'Not a good plan, BB.'

'Should you rinse out his mouth or something?' said Deborah.

'No.' Fiona rolled her eyes at her. 'He'll be fine.'

'He could get worms,' added Deborah.

'Well, that wouldn't be the end of the world, would it? We might get rid of some of these chubbles.' Fiona grabbed a small fat thigh and Ben shrieked with delight.

'Fi!' said Deborah.

'Oh, Debs, it's fine. He's not got worms. Stop worrying.'

'Does he need to be changed?' said Caroline. 'I could take him up.'

'Would you mind?' Fiona smiled at her. 'He feels okay, but there's no harm in checking.'

'Pass the parcel,' said Caroline and gathered the small boy into her arms. Fiona waited until she had left the room then turned back to Deborah.

'Anyway, the real point is whether she's got the means to do it. She can't expect you to pay.'

'What are we talking about?' Vonnie pulled out one of the high stools and sat down, wishing she'd brought her drink through with her.

'Elsa,' said Fiona.

'What about her?'

'She's decided she wants to take a gap year.' Deborah gave a dramatic sigh, managing to make it sound as though she wanted to shave her head and join a cult.

348

'And?' Vonnie leaned forward and lifted an apple from the fruit bowl and started to polish it on her sweater.

Deborah looked confused. 'Well, it would mean jacking in her course, chucking it all away.' She sat down opposite Vonnie.

'Doug's going to cave in,' whispered Fiona.

'No, I didn't say that,' said Deborah. 'He's just more open to the idea than I am.' Her face was very flushed.

'Are you okay?' Vonnie looked across at her. 'You've gone bright red.'

'Thanks for noticing,' said Deborah sharply.

'God, you're so tactful,' said Fiona, shaking her head at Vonnie.

'What?'

'It's the menopause,' said Fiona.

'It's the perimenopause,' said Deborah. 'It comes first.'

'Really?' Vonnie sat back.

'Yes, really.'

'God, sorry, Debs. That's a bit early, isn't it?'

'Vonnie!' Fiona was staring at her.

Vonnie held up her hands. 'Okay! I'm just asking.'

'Anyway,' said Fiona pointedly. She turned back to Deborah. 'It really surprises me that Doug's even considering it, you know, with his . . .' She made a shape with her hands in the air, but whether she was trying to draw a 'c' for cancer or sketch a gonad, Vonnie wasn't sure.

'Well, I think you should let her go,' Vonnie said. 'Where's the harm? Everyone's doing it.'

Deborah shook her head. 'She's just started at uni. It's nonsense, Vonnie. It's just a whim.'

'Well, she can go back,' said Vonnie. 'It's just a year. That's the point of it. Gap. Year.' She bit into the apple.

Fiona snorted. 'It's not that easy. There's so much competition for jobs now, especially in law. She's got a place at a good university, on a good course. What happens if she gives that up? She might not get another place and then what? Do you want her to end up still living off Debs and Doug in her thirties?'

That was deliberate. Vonnie was sure of it. She burst out laughing.

'What?' said Fiona.

'Thanks, Fi.'

'What?'

'Are you talking about me? You think my life is one long gap year? You think I'm still living off Mum and Dad?'

'No.' Fiona looked at her blankly. 'No, I'm just saying until you have kids you can't understand . . .' She rolled her eyes at Deborah and lifted her shoulders into a shrug.

'Bollocks,' said Vonnie. She slipped off the stool and lifted the bottle of wine in the middle of the table and poured it into a dark ceramic mug that she pulled from one of the hooks under the cupboards.

'Anyway, don't be so touchy,' said Fiona. 'This isn't about you. It's about Elsa.'

Vonnie swallowed the wine and looked at her, then turned to Deborah. 'Do you know anyone who's had a gap year and not benefited from it?' she asked.

'Well, I know people who never came back,' said Deborah. 'There were those two girls from

350

England who got killed in Australia and that girl in Thailand. The one who was teaching and I think it was a fisherman or something—'

'For Christ's sake,' said Vonnie. 'She's not going to get hacked to death by a homicidal maniac. It might be the making of her. Have you thought about that?'

Deborah stood up and pushed in her chair. Her cheeks were still very red.

'I would think about it Debs,' said Vonnie. 'It's not the end of the world. Really.'

Deborah shot her a look that suggested that was exactly what she thought it was, although *everything* was the end of the world for Deborah. She left the room without saying anything else.

'Nice one, Von,' said Fiona sarcastically. She didn't wait for Vonnie to respond, but followed Deborah out of the door.

Vonnie topped up her wine and sat back on her stool and exhaled slowly. What a great start to the evening. She should have stayed in the study with the girls in the pictures; girls who didn't insinuate or snipe, or even speak. She suddenly missed her own space, and Canada, and Mike. She dug in her back pocket and pulled out her phone and shot off a text. Just one word:

homesick

*   *   *

Jamie hooked his legs over the chair and glanced up from his DS screen. Ben was still traversing the big sofa, naked from the waist down. Caroline had

351

said he needed to do some potty training and had asked Jamie to keep an eye on him while she changed. A small plastic potty was positioned at one end of the couch, near the laid-down towels, but Ben didn't seem to know what it was for because he'd already had it on his head and used it like a hammer against the edge of the fireplace. Jamie really hoped he didn't do a pee or anything. He was supposed to get him on to the seat if he looked like he was going to, but how did you know when he was going to? It wasn't as if he could say.

'My goodness me!'

Jamie turned. Min had stopped by the door and was eyeing Ben, or rather Ben's bum, with a horrified expression. 'Is there any need for that?'

Jamie started to snigger. He was glad it was Min who had come in and relieved that she seemed to be okay. He liked that she was funny. Although it was strange how she could switch from being fine to being really odd so quickly.

'He's potty training,' he said by way of explanation.

'I can see that,' said Min, 'but we don't all need to be witnessing it, do we?' She walked slowly into the room, holding on to bits of furniture as she passed, a little bit like Ben did. Ben had turned at the sound of her voice and was beaming at her, but then he beamed at everybody.

'I don't know what you're smiling at, young man, flashing your bits at all and sundry. That's a habit you'll need to grow out of.'

'He doesn't like his nappy,' said Jamie. 'He gets a rash from it.'

'Nappy,' said Min. 'He shouldn't still be in a nappy. What age is he? Three? Four?'

'He's thirteen months.'

'Still,' said Min. She reached the chair with the high back and sat down slowly, holding the edges as she did so.

'Where is everyone else?' she asked. 'This house is like the *Marie Celeste*.'

'I think they're all getting ready,' said Jamie.

'What for?' asked Min.

Jamie hesitated, wondering if she was about to have another funny turn. 'The New Year,' he said.

'Mmm,' said Min. She peered over at him. 'And what are you doing?'

'I'm just playing. My DS,' said Jamie.

'I didn't understand a bloody word you've just said.' She held out a beckoning hand. 'Here, let me see.'

Jamie got up reluctantly and carried the computer game player over to her. 'It's Super Mario 4,' he said lamely.

'Well, you'll need to show me,' she said, when he laid it in her lap.

He picked it up and angled it so she could see the screen, then moved the figures around.

'What a load of utter crap,' said Min, and Jamie stifled another giggle.

'I've got other games,' he said.

'Like what?'

'Brain training.'

'Brain training? Now that I would like to see.'

He left Min holding the console and went over to his bag, pulling out a new cartridge.

'I need to put this one in,' he said.

She watched him intently as he swapped the games. Her eyes were bright blue and watery and she was a little bit smelly when you were up close.

353

He felt bad for thinking that way. He knew she was trying to be nice to him, even though it was a bit annoying to have had his game interrupted. He'd been on level eight and he hadn't had time to save it.

'Do you want me to show you?' he asked, when the game was in and ready.

'Well, I'm hardly going to know how to do it myself, am I?' she said testily.

'Okay. Em, well, this one is about adding up. It shows you lots of coins and you have to add them up really quickly in your head. Like this, this would be . . .'

'Two pounds forty,' said Min, quick as a flash.

Jamie looked at the screen. 'Yeah. Wow.'

She tapped the side of her head. 'Mental arithmetic. I was always a whizz. Next.'

He pressed the next screen.

'Eighty-five pence,' said Min.

'You're really good at this,' said Jamie. He bent down on to his knees and leaned on the edge of the chair. 'There're puzzle ones as well.'

'Okay,' said Min. 'Let's have a go at them.'

'Do you want to hold it?' asked Jamie.

'No, you do the dirty work. I'll come up with the answers.'

'Well, for this one, you have to use the pen thing.'

'Pen thing?'

'This.' He held out the stylus. 'You just tap it on to the screen where you think the bits should go.' He handed the stylus and console over. 'Like this one. There.'

'I'll give it a go.' Min held the console away from her as if she were reading a song sheet from a long

354

way off, and he sat back on his heels and watched her. Her mouth was moving as if she were talking to herself, but she did that quite a lot.

'What in God's name?' Min stabbed the stylus at the screen. 'Why has it gone away?'

Jamie peered over her shoulder. 'You've got to be really quick,' he said. 'It's moved on to the next one.'

'There's quick and there's demented,' said Min.

There was a laugh from the doorway and they both turned.

'Now, this I never expected to see,' said David.

'David!' Min's face lit up. He walked across to her and bent to give her a kiss. She put up her hand and touched his cheek.

'We were wondering where everybody was,' she said. 'Is it raining?'

David looked puzzled. 'No.'

'Your hair is wet,' said Min.

David straightened up and put his hand to the back of his head. 'Is it?' He turned and smiled at Jamie and looked down at Ben. 'Gosh,' he said, 'we seem to have lost our trousers.'

Caroline must have heard his voice or maybe Ben's chuckling, because she poked her head round the door and said, 'Oh, you're back,' in the flat way Jamie's mum sometimes did when she'd been waiting for you to appear. David didn't have time to respond because Fiona and Doug and Katie all appeared and David clapped his hands and said, 'Right, let's get some drinks on the go,' and Min said, 'About bloody time.'

It was Katie who noticed that Ben was peeing. She shrieked and everyone turned to look. He'd got to his feet again so the arc of yellowy liquid

355

went quite high and landed nowhere near the potty but on the sofa cushion instead.

'Well, we could see that coming, couldn't we?' said Min.

*   *   *

Charlie carried the small tray carefully through to the lounge, flicking off the kitchen light with his shoulder as he went. Two mugs of tea and the chocolate layered biscuits that Gail loved.

It had been a struggle to get Annie into bed and settled. She had suspected—rightly—that Jack was still up and getting attention, and had been down twice, once in angry tears. Charlie hoped she would warm to her brother soon. She still called him 'it' and had spent the entire journey home from the hospital staring pointedly out of the window rather than at the small form in the brand-new car seat.

The Moses basket was still on the floor by Gail's feet but Jack was up on her lap, pressed against her exposed right breast. From the look on Gail's face and the colour of Jack's it wasn't going well. The baby broke away with a sputtering wail and Gail burst into tears. Again. That would be the third time since she'd got home, at every attempt to feed.

'I can't do it. He's just not latching on.' She lifted her top higher and raised Jack back to the nipple. He was obviously hungry because his little mouth started to suck even before he'd reached the reddened flesh. Gail bit her lip and held the back of the baby's head steady. Even Charlie knew the noise he was making was too loud. When it was

356

working well you heard almost nothing. He remembered that from Annie.

'Ow!' Gail pulled Jack back and laid him down on her lap. 'It's too sore. I can't.'

'Hey.' Charlie put the tray on the coffee table. 'It'll be fine. Here, let me take him.' He lifted Jack up and over his shoulder, not an easy task given that he was as stiff and rigid as a plastic doll. 'He'll be fine, babe,' he said above the racket. 'It just takes time.'

'But he's hungry.' Gail threw her head back against the sofa. 'I'm going to have to give him formula if it goes on like this, and then he'll get loads of colds and stuff and . . .' She tailed off and looked at Charlie helplessly.

'He won't get tons of colds,' said Charlie. 'C'mon, calm down. He'll get the hang of it.' He patted Jack on the back and felt the warmth suddenly on his shoulder blade, the faint sour smell of spit-up. He grinned.

'Well, he must have got something because it's all down my back now. That's my boy. Won't be the last time you puke on your dad, now and when you're a teenager.'

Gail gave him a wan smile that stretched immediately into a yawn that doubled her chin.

'You should have a lie down.' Charlie raised his voice to compete with Jack's frantic warbling.

Gail shook her head. 'He needs a feed.'

'Okay,' said Charlie. 'C'mon. Let's get you locked on, young man.' He bent on to both knees and lifted Jack off his shoulder and towards Gail, trying to achieve the angle he had seen the midwife do in the hospital. Gail lifted her top again and squeezed her breast between her fingers,

357

positioning the nipple in anticipation. Charlie felt the flicker in his crotch and tried to ignore it. She had gorgeous breasts and he'd loved playing with them when she was breastfeeding before. Once, a good few weeks in when her milk was flowing and Annie was sleeping for longer than thirty minutes at a stretch, they'd seen how far she could squirt the milk across the room, giggling hysterically when she hit the lampshade. It was the first time she had let him at her breasts since the birth, the first time they had made love since Annie had arrived.

But Charlie knew better than to try anything this early. She was veined and sore and miserable and it would be a long time before the breasts she was offering up inches from his lips were his again.

'Okay?'

Gail nodded and leaned forward. She was wearing velour jogging bottoms that stretched high over her still-mounded stomach, like the trousers old men wear. She plugged Jack on and he saw her wince, and supported the small straining body until he felt the fight go out of it.

'He on?'

'I think so.' Gail laid her head back against the sofa again and motioned for a cushion. Charlie stood up and propped one under the baby.

'Your tea's going to be cold.' He picked up his own mug and sat down carefully next to her.

She shook her head. 'Doesn't matter.' She seemed weak with relief.

'Do you wanna watch TV?'

She shrugged.

'I could sing to you.'

She mustered another small smile. 'TV,' she

358

said.

He picked up the remote and flicked through the channels. It was too early for the Hogmanay shows and the only film he could find was *Brokeback Mountain* where Heath Ledger and Jake Gyllenhaal were grappling with each other in a tent.

'Gay porn?'

'Yeah,' said Gail flatly.

She'd loved the film when it first came out. Charlie could take it or leave it. He had always been more of a *Blackhawk Down* man himself.

He opened the biscuits and fed her one, wiping away the crumbs that fell on Jack's head. He seemed to have the hang of it now; his hand had stopped gripping the flesh of Gail's breast and was just resting on it, curled and pink and perfect. Charlie felt the tension go out of him. He was done in. The marquee should have been a two-day job, but he'd had to get it done today and done early, so he could get to the hospital and the other lads could get to the pub. He closed his eyes. Gail would nudge him if she needed anything.

When he opened them again, a good half-hour had passed, Jack was asleep and the film was still on. He glanced over at Gail. She was staring at the screen and her cheeks were wet with tears. Charlie reached for her hand.

'It's fine,' he said, knowing it wasn't the film that had moved her. 'Everything's fine.'

*   *   *

'She'll be so cross she didn't make it, especially with Daisy still up. Maybe we should just wake her?' Doug staggered up the stairs under the weight of Katie, who had finally given in to sleep and keeled over on the big sofa at a quarter to midnight.

'No.' Deborah followed him, carrying Katie's slippers which had dropped from her feet. 'She's done in. There's no point.'

She was actually glad of an excuse to get out of the drawing room. It was far too hot after Min had complained of the cold and David had put on the fire. And Vonnie was getting outrageous. She had found some small ornamental glasses in a display cabinet and was trying to persuade Deborah and Fiona to switch to vodka shots. And the television had been turned up too loud to let those who were watching it hear while various conversations went on in other parts of the room.

If it hadn't been rude, Deborah would have quite liked just to head off to bed herself. She'd never really been a big fan of Hogmanay, maybe because it had always felt a bit of a letdown. She'd always quite envied people who took a cottage up north with a gaggle of friends and made a real event of it. She and Doug never had. They always seemed to be at home, just the four of them until Elsa started wanting to go out with her friends and they were down to three. And they had fallen into the pattern of letting Katie stay up and waiting for the neighbours to pop round. They were nice people, Pringle sweater types with noisy laughs, and kisses that left you wanting to wipe your cheek.

Doug had reached the girls' room and laid Katie on the bed. They bent together and shuffled off her dressing gown. She woke as they did so and mumbled something and Deborah put a hand on her hair and said 'Shhh,' and she settled again.

'What about her teeth?' she whispered to Doug.

'One night's not going to make any difference,' he whispered back. 'She'll be up in a few hours anyway. Do them then.'

She nodded reluctantly and made to follow him out of the door. Katie had curled on to her side and a strand of her thick hair had fallen across her cheek. Doug was right: she would be cross tomorrow, but right now she was perfect.

Deborah pulled the door closed gently but made no move to go downstairs.

Doug was at the end of the hall, but walked back up towards her. 'You coming?'

'We should have had another one,' she said. 'We should have had three.' They'd always talked about three, but she'd had two miscarriages between Elsa and Katie and decided not to risk fate by trying again. And now it would never happen because she was shutting down inside, and Doug was ill.

He smiled at her and pulled her in. 'That's because you come from a three,' he said.

Deborah pressed against the curve of his belly. 'I come from a four,' she said quietly.

'So you do.' He kissed the top of her head. 'But we're fine as we are with our two. Our lovely two.'

She looked up at him with one eyebrow raised. 'What do you think your elder lovely is up to right now?'

'Enjoying herself,' said Doug.

'I'll bet,' said Deborah. She put her head back on Doug's chest and curled her arms around him.

'Do you not want to go back down?'

Deborah shook her head. 'I want everything to be okay.'

'It will be,' said Doug quietly. 'We'll get through this.'

She nodded and they stood for a moment in silence.

'Come on,' said Doug finally. 'It's not much longer. Let's go and celebrate. You're not going to have everyone together like this again for a while.'

Deborah reached up and kissed him on the mouth; a deep kiss. 'Happy New Year,' she said. 'I love you.'

'And you, darling. Happy New Year.'

Almost everyone was on their feet when they got back to the drawing room, apart from Min who was issuing orders from the depths of her chair. 'Turn it up. I can't hear a damn thing she's saying.'

On the television, a woman in a spangly top had bared her teeth in a frantic smile. 'A momentous year,' she said. 'In a matter of seconds we will be into a *momentous* year! Are you ready, Scotlaaaand?'

'We've been ready for three centuries,' shouted Min. 'Get on with it!'

Deborah reached for Doug's hand and held on. David brought over two glasses of champagne and pressed them into their free hands then returned to the back of Min's chair where he stood next to Caroline. Daisy was bouncing on the sofa, Vonnie swaying slightly by the standard lamp. Deborah saw Fiona slip her hand around Jamie's shoulders; noticed that he didn't move away.

'So, here we go,' shrieked the woman. Behind her, the hands of Big Ben were almost completely merged at midnight. 'Ten, nine, eight, seven, six, five, four, three, two, one.'

The screen erupted in a flash of fireworks.

Deborah turned to Doug, felt his mouth on hers.

'Happy New Year!'

Everyone was moving. Hugs and kisses. Riley was barking, roused by the noise. Vonnie toppled into a chair in a fit of drunken giggles. Daisy was shrieking and Min started to sing.

'Should auld acquaintance . . .'

'God, here we go,' muttered Fiona under her breath. Which probably was, thought Deborah, as she bent in to return her sister's kiss, a more appropriate greeting for the year to come than anything else she could think of to say.

*   *   *

The last firework dissolved into the clouds above the castle and the great unsteady crowd started to shift, pushing Elsa, still singing, away from the Princes Street bandstand and right to the gardens' furthest edge. Matt's hand was in her back pocket. They passed the pathway that led to Hanover Street. At the top, near the turnstile gate, was a billboard for the referendum with a giant question mark. They were all over the city, these signs, a rash of unanswered questions. The crowd was thinning out and the girl in front of her had started to dance, a little conga step. She had a streak of purple in her hair and a deep, raw-edged laugh. Elsa suddenly felt ridiculously optimistic. Everything would work out; she was sure of it. Her mum and dad would come round. They wouldn't deny her this. She leaned forward, caught hold of the woman's waist and danced her way into a whole new year.

CHAPTER NINETEEN

'But I'm not tired!' Daisy stopped on the fifth step and renewed her grip on the banister.

'No. You're exhausted.' Fiona slipped her hand round the front of Daisy's forehead. Sweat had frizzed her fringe into spiralling ringlets.

'I don't want to go up. I want to go back down.'

'No,' said Fiona. 'It's too late. It's morning actually. We're all ready for bed.' She thought of clean sheets and a gloriously empty space.

'Can I call Daddy again?'

'No,' said Fiona. 'He's busy.'

It had taken three calls to his mobile before Allan had phoned back. Fiona knew she could have called the restaurant direct, but she didn't like to. Allan's front of house manager was a rather severe Lithuanian, who always managed to make her feel like a phone pest, even though she rarely called the main number.

Allan had sounded stressed, as well he might, with a roomful of festive drunks in gold paper hats. He was open until 2 a.m. and had laid on a young Celtic fiddler; a nod, he had said, to Fiona's Scottish roots. Fiona suspected it was more of a nod to his libido.

She was in her early twenties, the fiddler, and studying at the London School of Music. Fiona imagined someone lovely with glossy hair and pale, slender arms.

'Pleease,' said Daisy.

Fiona nudged her up the stairs. 'No. Bed.'

Daisy finally reached the landing, but stopped

suddenly and put her hand to her mouth.

'I forgot my reservations!'

'Your reservations?'

'My New Year reservations! Katie said I had to write them down.'

'Res*olutions*,' said Fiona. 'And you don't have to write them down. You just have to do them.' She put her hands on Daisy's shoulders to guide her to the loo. 'What are they anyway?'

'I'm not going to pick my nose so much and I'm going to use a ruler when I draw lines,' said Daisy.

Fiona nodded, concealing her smile. 'Those sound pretty achievable.'

'Katie's resolution is to get a dog and a crop top,' said Daisy.

'Not a dog in a crop top,' said Fiona.

Daisy laughed. 'Noooo!' She stopped at the door to the bathroom and turned to look at Fiona. 'What are your reservations, Mummy?'

Off the top of my head, thought Fiona, becoming celibate and sorting out your brother. She went for the white lie instead. 'I don't think I have any this year.'

'Do you not make them when you're old?' asked Daisy.

'Old*er*,' said Fiona. 'And no, not always.'

'Is that because you do everything right anyway?' Daisy stifled a small yawn.

'Something like that.'

*   *   *

Someone had made an attempt to stack the dishes on the sink's edge, but had not thought to wash them. They were mostly glasses, the good crystal,

365

flutes and tumblers, some with lipstick marks and greasy fingerprints. Caroline reached for the tap and placed the plug in the sink. She should get them done now. Done and out of the way. She stood back and closed her eyes. She could still hear the pucker of David's empty kiss as the bells had sounded midnight. Happy New Year.

The door opened behind her and David came in with a tray of small plates and crisp bowls and plastic tumblers, sticky with lemonade. He placed it at her elbow and she could smell the drink on him. Whisky: sharp and woody. He said nothing but he reached past her to switch on the kettle and she heard him yawn as he moved back out through the door. Frances had called, a little after midnight. It was Caroline who had answered and she had heard her own words as if someone else were speaking them.

Happy New Year.

'All the very best,' Frances had said warmly. 'Hope to see you soon.'

The room was busy with chat and laughter. Caroline had handed the phone to David. 'Frances,' she said, and saw the flicker of something in his eyes, and knew then that she could not go on.

She put her hands into the warm, soapy water and swirled them around. It didn't take long to finish the dishes and she left them in wet, glistening rows on the drainer, then found her tablets in the high cupboard and took one. She would need to renew the prescription soon, she was taking too many. You need to learn to unwind, the doctor had said. You need to change the way you live.

The door had not closed properly, sometimes it didn't, and she could hear David whistling through in the drawing room. She made two mugs of tea, stacked the last of the plates in the dishwasher, and left the room to end her marriage.

He glanced up as she came in. He was in his favourite chair and was annoyed at being disturbed, she could tell that by the faint furrowing of his brow, his flat, fleeting smile. There was a book on his lap.

She handed him the mug of tea.

'I thought you were off to bed,' he said.

'In a minute.'

'I'm just going to read for a while,' he said pointedly. He placed the mug on the table beside him. 'I suspect it'll be lunchtime before anyone's up.'

'Mmm. I expect so.'

She perched on the far end of the sofa, not wanting to sit too close. He had switched off the television and the only noise in the room was the dying spit of the fire and the soft click of a carriage clock she had always hated.

David looked over at her, puzzled that she was still there.

'Can we talk?' she said.

A look of exasperation settled on his face. 'Now?'

She nodded.

'Is it about Min?' He picked up his tea, and she saw him eye his book.

'No. Us.'

'Us?' That got his attention. 'What about us?'

'I think . . . I'm thinking we should have a break. For a while.'

'A break?'

He didn't get it. He probably thought she meant a holiday. She set her own mug on the floor at her feet and a little spilled out. She wiped it from the back of her hand.

'I need to leave. I need to go.' She said this with her head down, but lifted it to see what his reaction was. He was frowning.

'Caroline, what's going on?' He shifted round a little until he was properly facing her.

'David . . .' She stopped, struggling for the right phrase.

'What?'

'I'm not happy.' It sounded so childish when she said it, so petty, but she didn't know what other words to use.

'Not happy?' He sounded almost contemptuous.

'No. It's not right,' she said. 'It doesn't feel right. Us. Not any more.'

'What on earth has brought this on?'

The night of your party, she wanted to say, that's what brought it on, but before that, so many things.

'Nothing specific,' she said. 'Well, that's not exactly right.'

He didn't seem to have heard. 'Are you serious?'

'Yes.'

'Huh.' He pressed his hands down on to his knees.

The silence between them was excruciating. She dug her nails into her palm and felt the bite of pain. She wanted it over.

'Should we be seeing someone about this?' He probably felt he had to say it, but there was no purpose in his voice.

'Maybe,' said Caroline. 'Maybe we should.' She

368

had no heart for it, either.

He turned his head slightly as if something had just occurred to him. 'Is there someone else?' It wasn't said with any kind of accusing tone but she felt the urge to laugh out loud.

'What? No. Well, yes. Yes, there is.' She looked straight at him. 'Frances.'

His brow furrowed as if he didn't understand, but she saw his expression change.

'I know,' she said flatly.

'Know what?'

She had wondered if this was what he would do, but it felt so shabby that he had. 'David, don't. Please.'

There was a flash of defiance in his eyes. He lifted the book from the table and gripped his hands round the cover.

'I saw you both.' She felt as though she were reading a script. 'I saw you on the night of the party. In the dining room.'

His fingers blanched white and he looked away and after a while he murmured, 'I don't know what to say.'

'I've been wondering when it started,' said Caroline.

He didn't reply, so she sat and waited.

'Was it before Euan?' she asked finally, when it became clear he was not going to speak.

'No, God, no. No.' He looked round at her and she felt a strange sense of relief. 'No. After. Long after.'

She nodded, as if that made sense.

'I'm sorry,' said David flatly. It was a statement rather than an apology, and it was not heartfelt. She flinched.

'The thing is, it's not just that,' she said. 'It's not been right for a while. A long time. You must know that.'

He nodded his head, but it seemed an instinctive response rather than a considered one. They sat in silence again. The blackened wood in the fire collapsed in on itself, sending out a spray of embers.

'What do we do now?' said David. He had fixed his eyes on the fire.

'I've got my painting course,' Caroline said haltingly. 'And after that, well, we could see where we are, and then I was thinking I would move out. Back into the city, maybe. I don't know. I haven't really thought that far ahead.'

He was quiet again for a moment, as if he was trying to visualise it, and then he said, 'Min?'

'I'll help,' said Caroline. 'Any way I can. But I can't live like this, David. We can't. It's not . . . honest.'

'Honest?' He gave a little snort. 'What the hell does that mean?'

'I don't know,' said Caroline. 'Do you love me?'

She wondered if he would say, 'Of course.' He had once brought her home an article one of his colleagues had written, early on in his career, a piece of frippery for the women's page, on how you know if he's the one. It was a series of questions to ask your fiancé. If he said 'of course', when you asked if he loved you, that meant he didn't. They used to joke about it, when the words of attachment, of adoration came easily to them. Do you love me? Of course I do.

But he didn't say 'of course', he just said, 'Caroline,' and reached out a hand which stopped well short of her knee.

Caroline watched his hand withdraw and bent to pick up her tea. She held the mug in her hands, feeling the heat go out of it into her stiff, clenched fingers.

Just a few feet away from her, David laid his elbows on his knees and lowered his head into his hands. 'Christ,' he said.

*   *   *

Jamie reached for the hard little plastic baton at the top of the lampstand and pressed it in. The dead boy's room went dark. He pulled up the covers and stayed to the left of the mattress because there was a dip in the middle of it that you could roll into, and it felt deeper than it looked. The duvet had started to smell more like him than the washing powder, but that made sense because he'd slept in it for nine nights. His hands were shaking. He should have known better than to look at his phone. How stupid he had been to look. They would never forget. They had not forgotten tonight.

happy new year wank

He could see them, lying around in one of their bedrooms, music on loud, laughing as they pressed 'send'.

It would be bad when he went back, he knew that now. Four days to go. Four days for something to change. Maybe someone new would have started and they would turn on them, like the wolves at the wildlife park. Or maybe something would happen; something would happen to him like it had to Euan. Maybe he would have an accident. Dead in a roadway, with people white with shock and on their knees, and a lorry stopped. And there would be a special assembly at school and some of the girls would cry and put flowers wrapped in plastic at the scene. There would be messages and Chelsea scarves and shirts, because that's the team he followed, and the teachers would lie and say how great he was; how missed he would be. Then maybe it would come out that he had been bullied, and people would start to wonder if he had stepped out on to the road. And the school would start to ask questions and they would panic, his tormentors, waiting for someone to point and say: It was them. It was because of them.

He tasted blood in his mouth and realised he was biting his nails. He propelled himself out from under the covers. Standing in the centre of the room, he felt his skin contract with the cold. He slipped into his jeans, reached out for his sweatshirt and wrapped it around him, and then made for the thin line of light at the base of the door.

Someone was still in the drawing room. The door was pulled to but he could hear voices, one of them Caroline's. He crossed the hall and went down the passage towards the kitchen where he got himself a glass of water and stood before the big range cooker. It was nice the way it was always warm. At home, they had a cooker with a black top as cold and smooth as a headstone. The second you stopped using it, it went cool. He felt the lurch in his gut at the thought of home. He didn't want to go home. If he could stay here, move, change schools, never see them again, any of them, but his mum would never let him. It was just shit, just utter shit. All of it.

He was at the back door before he even realised what he was doing. He found his baseball boots under the bench beneath the coat rack and pulled them on, the laces still tied from last time, then lifted his jacket from a peg and shrugged his arms through the sleeves. The door had a metal runner on the bottom that scraped across the flagging. He pulled it open carefully and left it ajar. He moved quickly away from the house, no idea where he was going.

It was cold. When he looked up he could see stars in the patches of sky where the clouds had cleared. He followed the path by the edge of the big lawn until he reached the side gate. It was open and he came through on to the driveway. He started to walk along the edge because the gravel would have scrunched if he had stood on it, then picked up his pace until he was jogging and then running. He could hear his own breath, and see it, like puffs of smoke. Down through the steady trees, no wind to move them. He came out at the cattle grid and jumped it without pausing, his eyes now accustomed to the dark.

The road was empty and he stood for a moment, feeling stupid and tearful. Just a fucking idiot, a fucking feeble idiot. He turned to the left and started to walk. Where are you going? You fucking loser. Where are you going? He put his hand up to his eyes and brushed the tears from them. Loathing surged inside him. Fucking freak. He started to run again, sobs catching in his throat.

Where are you going, you fucking freak?

He only stopped running when a car passed in the distance, somewhere on another road. He didn't know how far he had gone but he could hear water. It sounded like the drain at the back of their house in London when someone was having a shower. He slowed and moved towards the sound. It wasn't big enough to be a river, but it was bigger than a stream. A tributary, maybe. He remembered this bit of the road. If you went over the bridge quickly in the car, your stomach would leap. Once it had been in spate and they had stopped to watch the churning waters, brown and tumbling. Mum had grabbed him as he bent over the wall and pretended to push him in and he had got a dreadful fright. He was quite far from the house now, further than he realised. He stopped by the low stone wall but it was too dark to see the water below. He climbed down the side, his feet slipping on wet grass, and bent low on to his heels. It was fast-flowing, he could tell that. He reached out and sank his hand into the water. It was only a moment before the ache started, deep and dull, building into real, unbearable pain. He waited as long as he could, counting in his head and biting his lip to try to block the sensation, then pulled out his hand, feeling the burn in his fingertips as the heat returned.

The earth around him was soft and kind of sucky, and he could feel it seeping in through the canvas of his Converse baseball boots.

He plunged his hand back in and counted. He reached eight and had to pull it out.

It occurred to him suddenly that he should have brought his phone. He could have dropped it into the water and maybe the current would have pushed it along the bottom until it came to the bigger river, and it would get scraped over stones until it was all scored and marked and unrecognisable. Maybe, over time, it would go as far as the sea, rolled out into the waves and buried deep beneath the dirty silt.

He looked down at the water again, black and fast, and suddenly imagined himself tipping in. A splash that no one would hear. Maybe he would hit his head on one of the stones or rocks on the bottom and the water would close, coldly, around him, the way it did when you lay all the way back in the bath.

*   *   *

Fiona pulled the girls' bedroom door to and wedged it slightly open with a small slipper. Katie was sound asleep when she had ushered Daisy in, read two quick chapters of her favourite pony book, and settled and shushed her. Fiona expected Katie would be cross when she woke and realised she had missed the festivities. She checked on Ben, who was curled in a fat, contented ball in the clean sheets of her bed, then padded back down the hall to say goodnight to Jamie.

The door to Euan's old room was open. Euan used to keep it shut. Fiona remembered when he started doing that; telling her she couldn't come in, putting up a sign. Keep Out. No girls. She had pretended she didn't care, but she did care. He had grown up and left her behind, with Deborah and Vonnie, who didn't like what she liked, who seemed so young and immature.

She looked in. The light was off, but there was enough of a glow from the lamp in the hall to see that the bed was empty. Jamie must still be in the loo, hopefully giving his teeth a good scrub after all the lemonade and Coke David had been foisting on him. She flicked on the top light and went to sit on the end of the bed, smoothing her hand over the rumpled duvet.

Euan had grown a lot the winter he had begun closing his door, and his voice had started to break. He was much more serious, and while he would still laugh with Fiona, it wasn't like before, not the curled-up-on-the-floor belly laughs at something silly or rude. She had teased him about his voice, mimicking the awkward discordant squeak that would come on when he was halfway through a sentence. It bothered him, but not that much. He was sailing through puberty as he sailed through everything else; the awkwardness that dogged her Jamie had not touched him.

She glanced around the room. The book Jamie was reading was upside down on the small bedside table. It was sci-fi, some fantastical tale with a fussy, gothic cover. His case was propped open by the far wall, his clothes, clean and dirty, jumbled in a heap inside. His phone and baseball cap were laid on the high shelf beside a stack of Euan's old books.

It had taken years for Euan's possessions gradually to disappear. At first, the room was left exactly as it had been, even his clothes on the floor. Fiona knew that sometimes Caroline went in and lay on his bed. She only did it when she thought they were all asleep and she cried so quietly you could hardly hear her. And once, months after,

Fiona had walked past and seen David standing by the window with his face pressed into the jumper Euan had worn most. It was the last piece of clothing to be put away, folded and laid in a box and placed somewhere safe.

She didn't often wonder what Euan would have been like as an adult. He was so fixed in her mind as a boy, tall and sinewy with his thick quiff of dark hair. She liked to think they would have stayed close. He would be married by now, a husband and a dad, and doing well because he always had.

She did sometimes wonder, however, if she would have been different. She was meant to be a middle child, not the eldest. Nobody had said anything, no one had said, it's over to you now, step up, but she had found herself changing, trying harder at everything. School, sports, hobbies. But no matter how well she did, she always felt a fraud, as though it wasn't really her turn. When she got her Higher results her parents had hugged her and said how proud they were, but behind their smiles she knew they were wondering how well Euan would have done, the same way they would have been wondering at her wedding and the birth of all her children. She didn't resent that. It was just the way it was.

She let out a breath and stood up. Jamie was taking an age and she was dog-tired now and ready for sleep. 'Happy New Year, Eu,' she said quietly, and pulled the door behind her. It had been her special name for him, one that she had not uttered for very many years.

The extractor fan was still whirring in the bathroom but the light was off. Fiona felt a little stab of irritation. She had been quite clear that he should follow her and Daisy up to bed. She went to the top of the stairs and stood. She could hear Vonnie in her room, clattering about. She had drunk way too much and even David had been a little disapproving this time, refusing to join her in yet another bottle of wine. Fiona didn't want to call out, so she padded down the stairs. She tried the kitchen first, but it was in darkness. When she came back out into the hall, David was by the door to the drawing room.

'I thought I heard someone,' he said.

'Is Jamie still down here?'

'No.' David looked tired. Caroline appeared behind him at the door. Fiona wondered why they were still up.

'He went upstairs,' said Caroline. 'Just after you did.'

'Well, he's not in his room and he's not in the bathroom,' said Fiona.

'Have you tried the kitchen?' said Caroline.

'Not there.'

They stood in the hall.

'Jamie!' called David, but not too loud.

There was no response.

'He might have fallen asleep in one of the other rooms,' said Caroline. 'He looked absolutely done in, poor love. I'll go and have a look.' She crossed the hall and disappeared up the corridor. Fiona and David stood, not talking.

'I'm sorry about this. You can just go on up to bed if you want,' said Fiona after a moment. 'He'll be around here somewhere.'

'No, it's fine,' said David. He looked distracted.

Caroline was back in less than a minute.

'No. No sign.'

Fiona furrowed her brow. What on earth was he playing at?

'Right,' said David. 'You check upstairs again, and I'll have a look through here.'

Fiona took the stairs two at a time. She checked every room, apart from Vonnie's and Deborah's. In the bathroom, she felt the end of Jamie's toothbrush. It was wet. He must have just brushed his teeth.

David was calling from the downstairs hall.

'Have you found him?' She peered over the banisters, her voice still a half-whisper.

'No, but the back door's open.'

Fiona ran down the stairs and followed David through to the back hallway. Caroline was already there and had put on the light in the cloakroom. It was a fluorescent strip light, harsh and unforgiving.

'His shoes aren't here.' Fiona glanced around her. 'He always leaves them here, the baseball boots. And his jacket . . .'

She looked at her parents; saw the fear in their eyes. No. This was nonsense. He'd just nipped outside for some bizarre reason. The door was wide open and they spilled out into the night.

'Jamie!' Maybe he would just appear from the bottom of the garden, slumped and sullen.

'Jamie!'

There was little wind and Fiona's voice carried out across the black space. She shivered. It was properly cold, cold like she remembered.

'I'll check Min's,' said Caroline.

'Why would he be at Min's?' said Fiona.

'I don't know,' said Caroline, and disappeared towards the small annexe.

Fiona walked down across the lawn, shouting as

she went. David had gone round into the front garden and she could hear his voice echoing hers.

'Jamie! Jamie!'

She checked the summerhouse and the hide and stood, hoping she could hear him moving about somewhere. She met David a few minutes later by the side gate. He shook his head.

'Where in God's name . . .' said Fiona. She was still cross but fear was taking over.

Caroline had rejoined them. 'He's not there. Was he upset about anything? Remember Christmas Day?'

'I know.' Fiona ran her hands distractedly through her hair. 'But I think that's just hormones. I mean, he's moody, but they all are. At that age. Aren't they? There's nothing specific.'

'I'll go get Debs and Vonnie,' said Caroline. 'They won't be asleep yet and we can all look.' She disappeared back into the house.

'What about his phone?' said David suddenly. 'Would he have his phone? You could call him.'

Fiona tried to focus. 'No, it's in the room. I saw it on the shelf.' She ran back into the house and up the stairs, just as Doug emerged from Deborah's room. His hair was tufted up behind his ear and his pyjama bottoms ballooned out of the top of his trousers. He stumbled towards her and she flashed him a quick and grateful smile and moved quickly into Euan's room. Jamie's jeans were gone. He must have put them back on. She reached for the phone and lifted it down. Outside, she could hear David calling.

'Jamie! Jamie!'

He must prefer the volume off, because the screen lit in silence. He hadn't personalised his wallpaper, either. She waited until the signal bars appeared and then pressed for the menu as she hurried back downstairs. Come on. Come on. She didn't know what she was looking for. Maybe he had just called someone. Maybe someone had called him and he was upset. A girl? She wouldn't mind if it was a girl.

There was a short list of numbers displayed in the inbox. He had read all of them because the little envelopes were opened. Only one of them was from Daisy's number.

She stopped at the first number she didn't know.

fleming takes it up the arse

Fiona's fingers froze. She looked at it again. A joke? It had to be a joke. One of his friends mucking about.

She pressed again, the most recent message.

happy new year wank

It had come in just a few hours ago. Before the bells. When they were all downstairs.

Her thumb moved instinctively.

merry xmas wank!

fckn bender bent job

Oh, God.

She pressed again. A photo slid into view with text below. She leaned closer to try to make out who it was, what was happening.

Jamie. Oh, my God. Her hand went to her mouth and rage and fear flooded through her. Bastards. Utter bastards. Oh, Jamie. My boy. My sweet boy.

'Fi?' Deborah was behind her on the stairs, as hastily dressed as Doug, her hair unbrushed. 'What is it?'

Fiona turned, her heart pounding. She held out the phone. 'Look.'

'What is it? Is it Jamie?' Deborah took it from her and looked down, blinking at the words on the screen. Awful, horrible words.

'What?' Deborah put one hand to her throat. 'Did he just get this?'

'One of them,' said Fiona. 'But there are more.'

'Oh, Fi.'

'Shit,' said Fiona. 'Shit. Where has he gone, Debs, what has he done?'

Deborah grabbed her arm and held on. 'He's not done anything. It'll be fine. He's just upset. Honestly. Poor lamb.'

'What do I do?' Fiona's voice cracked and she started to cry, small, noiseless sobs.

Deborah put her arm around her and guided her down the stairs. Caroline and David were by the back door with Doug.

'He is upset about something,' said Fiona when she reached them. She held up the phone. 'I can't go into details but obviously something's not right.'

'I'll get the car,' said David, his mouth set in a grim line.

'David, you've been drinking.' Caroline laid a hand on his arm. Her face was pinched with worry.

'I'm okay,' said Doug. 'I only had one. I'll drive.'

'Where's Vonnie?' asked Deborah, grabbing a coat from one of the pegs.

Caroline bit her lip.

'She's pissed, isn't she?' said Fiona.

'It's not important,' said Caroline.

'Should we not be calling the police?' It was Deborah who asked what everyone was thinking.

'No,' said Fiona. If they called the police that meant it was serious, potentially terrible and it couldn't be. He was just upset. He was just upset about some stupid little bastards. 'We need to look first,' she said. 'Anyway they wouldn't come out. Not so soon. It needs to be hours before they come out. He can't be far. Doug, can we go?'

She pushed through them, still clutching the phone. David and Doug followed her and they piled into Doug's car.

'I'm going to walk down the drive and head up towards the farms,' said Deborah. 'You take the main road. Call me if you see him.'

They took off in a frantic scrape of gravel. David was in the passenger seat. It suddenly occurred to Fiona that this is how he would have sat on the day Mr Fletcher drove him and Caroline down to Euan. Fingers knotting, willing the car to go faster, willing the woman on the phone to have got it wrong. Not Euan. Not their boy. Expecting to pass him on his bike at any point; to give him a row for being late and a hug for being Euan. She shook the thought from her mind and tightened her grip on Jamie's phone. The car was moving fast down the drive, headlights on full, and she stared as hard as she could at the shapes in the trees, praying that one of them would be him, her own dejected boy, coming back to her.

*   *   *

Caroline stood in the hallway. There was no way she could just sit and wait. She had already done another check of all the rooms downstairs. She looked at the phone hoping it would ring. We've got him. It was all a big misunderstanding. Maybe he would come back while they were all away and she could get him warmed up, give him something to eat, a hug. She tried to think why he might have gone. Fiona could be tetchy with him, but not so much that he would have run off. He couldn't have had a clue where he was going. He had hardly been out of the house since he got here. And it was cold. After weeks of the strange tepid weather, it was cold. Let him be okay. Please, God, let him be okay. They were words she had said before and she felt the surge of terror inside her as she remembered repeating them over and over on another day. She reached for the radiator by the hall table. It was cool. She headed for the utility room and opened the small panel on the boiler, pressing down the small levers. The boiler gurgled and spat into life. Soon the warmth would be creeping back into the house, the house that had once withstood the worst a family could ever face. A house that would no longer be her home.

She wondered what David was thinking. He had jumped to his feet when he had first heard Fiona in the hall, desperate to get away from Caroline, from what she had just said. But he seemed to have accepted it almost instinctively, as if she had asked him to agree that an old, familiar object was done

384

and destined to go out. And now this. It was all too unreal.

She headed for the stairs. Fiona had been right about Vonnie. Caroline had barely been able to waken her when she had gone in. The smell of drink was overpowering and she had muttered and giggled when Caroline had shaken her shoulder. She was partially under the duvet, still fully dressed. Caroline would try again. Get her up, get her a coffee and get her sober in case they needed her, in case he couldn't be found.

She had just reached the landing when she saw the figure by Fiona's door.

'Daisy?'

Daisy turned towards her. She was in her nightie and shivering.

'What's wrong, darling?' Caroline moved towards her.

'I've got a sore tummy.'

Caroline bent before her. 'Do you need the toilet?'

'No.' Daisy shook her head. She wasn't wearing her glasses. 'Where's Mummy?'

'Mummy's downstairs with Grampa, but she's a bit busy with something,' said Caroline. 'Come on, let's get you back into bed and Granny will sit with you till you fall asleep again. Okay?'

Daisy nodded and Caroline took her hand.

'Is it morning?'

'Yes, it is, sweetie. It was morning when you went to bed, and it's still morning. It's New Year's Morning.'

'I'm cold,' said Daisy.

'Well, let's get you bundled back under your quilt,' said Caroline.

She pulled over a small wicker chair and settled it beside Daisy's bed. Katie was snoring softly in the far corner. Daisy curled back under the covers and lay looking at Caroline.

'Will Mummy be up soon?'

'Very soon,' said Caroline. She smiled the best she could and then turned and listened to the silent house beyond the door.

*   *   *

It was cold enough for Doug to put the heating on. Fiona kept her face pressed to the side window. They weren't going fast because Doug was trying to keep his eyes on the road and look for Jamie at the same time.

They drove as far as the crossroads and saw nothing. Doug eased the car to a gentle stop.

'Which way first, do you think?'

'I don't know.' Fiona felt sick.

'Maybe he's not on the road,' said David. 'Maybe he went over the fields.'

'He's only got his baseball boots on,' said Fiona.

A phone jangled somewhere in the front and Doug snatched it up.

'Deb? Uh-huh. No. Yeah. No. Okay. Great. That's really decent of them. Okay, darling.'

He put it down. 'She's at Home Farm. She's not seen him, but she got the Caldwells up and they're checking the outbuildings.'

'Okay,' said Fiona. She pressed the button on the door handle and the window slid down.

'JAMIE!'

There was no noise beyond the idling engine.

'Right,' said David, tapping the window with his

386

left hand. 'Let's go this way and then we can double back to the bridge. If we don't see anything by then, I think we should call the police.'

Fiona nodded in the blackness of the back seat.

*   *   *

They drove for another twenty minutes, up towards Athelstaneford and then back past the crossroads where they had stopped. When they reached the crossroads for the third time, Doug turned for home without saying anything.

Fiona sat back in the seat and laid her hands in her lap. They were shaking slightly. She closed her eyes. The police would come. There was no more she could do. The air rushed at her from her opened window, fierce and cold.

'There!'

It was David who reacted first. Fiona threw herself forward and peered through the windscreen.

He was walking along the edge of the road in the direction of the house. He was coming back. Fiona burst into noisy tears. Doug exhaled as if he had not ever drawn a breath and said, 'Thank God.'

Jamie turned at the noise of the car. Even in the fractured light of the headlamps Fiona could see he was pale. She had the door open even before Doug had come to a stop.

'What the hell are you doing? What the fucking hell . . . !' She ran towards him.

He looked at her, his face expressionless, and she grabbed him and pulled him to her. He didn't respond, just lay against her, shaking with the cold.

She could feel the damp and pulled away. The arms of his canvas jacket were soaking, as were his jeans, almost up to his waist.

'My God, Jamie. Did you fall in? What happened? What were you thinking?'

David was out of the car too.

'Come on. In you come. We'll get you back to the house.'

Jamie moved towards the Fiat and slid into the back seat without a word. Fiona followed him and sat as close as she dared. She reached out a hand and caught hold of his and gave it a squeeze. His fingers were freezing, even to her own frigid hands, and stiff, clenched under his palm. His mobile was still clutched in her other hand and she slid it into the pocket of her coat.

'It's okay,' she said quietly, hearing the shake in her own voice. 'It's okay.'

Doug sped off up the road, faster than she had ever known him to drive, holding his mobile to his ear to call Deborah.

'You've given us all a big fright,' said David, without turning round.

Fiona leaned forward and pressed her free hand on his shoulder.

'A big fright,' repeated David.

'Sorry.'

It was barely a whisper and Fiona doubted that David would have heard it above the noise of the engine. She gave Jamie's hand another squeeze and held on to it until the car pulled up at the back door.

Caroline was outside and enveloped Jamie in a huge hug, but knew better than to ask any questions.

'The heating is on,' she said. 'For a bath. And I've just boiled the kettle if anyone wants some tea, or something.'

Fiona nodded and leaned in to kiss her mother's cheek. 'Thank you.'

She shepherded Jamie up the stairs and towards the bathroom.

'Go and get warm,' she said. 'And then we'll talk.'

Back in Euan's room, she settled herself in the chair by the window. Her heart had stopped hammering and she felt weak with relief and bewilderment. She had almost lost him, but she wasn't entirely sure that she had got him back. And she had no idea how to start the conversation she was about to have. She still had her coat on and she dug Jamie's mobile from the pocket. It occurred to her suddenly that she had not checked to see if he had responded to the messages. She went to his outbox, but it held only the texts he had sent Daisy. She checked the call history. Daisy's number was there, but it wasn't the most recent: that was another number she recognised. It had been all over the TV, in the ads about bullying. A helpline. She was sure of it. She scrolled down. He had called it several times; maybe five in all.

She dropped the phone into her lap, trying to keep a hold of her emotions. He had needed help but he had not come to her. Why hadn't she seen? Why hadn't he said? Shame, maybe. Maybe he was worried how she would react. He had been terrorised. His nails. There was nothing left of them and she had nagged him about it, told him it was a disgusting habit.

She realised suddenly that she had not called

Allan. Why was that? Because there was nothing he could do, or because he wasn't Jamie's dad? She glanced at her watch. It was almost 2.20 a.m., but he would still be at the restaurant. He would want to know. She used Jamie's phone, but found herself going straight to voicemail. She punched in the numbers for the main reception, steeling herself for the icy blast of contempt from the Lithuanian, if he was still around.

He was. 'I'm afraid Mr Fleming is with a client.'

'A client?' said Fiona. She had a sudden unbidden image of Allan wrapped around the fiddler in a storeroom.

'Is it an emergency?' He ignored the inference of her exclamation and drew out the vowels of the last word.

She dug her hand into her cardigan and bunched it round her fingers. 'Not an emergency, no, but really very important,' she said, as coolly as she could.

'I can have him call you when he's free.'

'If you wouldn't mind. My mobile. As soon as he's available. Please.'

'Of course.'

She switched off the phone and sat in the quiet room until Jamie appeared, trying to push images from her mind. She had left some pyjamas outside the bathroom door, and had tapped on the door to tell Jamie they were there. They were a little too small and the legs of the trousers hung above his ankles. His hair was wet and tufted and she wanted to cry. He looked so young and so crushed.

She leaned over and patted the bed. 'Come here.'

He walked across and sat down, his hands

clasped together in front of him.

'I'm sorry, Mum.' It was a small voice and it broke her heart more than it had already been broken.

'I know. But you shouldn't have done that, honey. We were all frantic. Where were you going to go?'

'I don't know.'

'How did you get wet?'

He said nothing.

'You know you can always come to me. Always. About anything.'

He nodded, but it was a polite rather than an instinctive nod.

Fiona took a deep breath. 'I know about the messages. On your phone.' She saw the instant stiffening of his limbs. He looked up at her. 'We were looking for your phone. We wondered if you had it with you.'

He didn't respond.

'Jamie, love, what's been going on?'

He had gone very, very white. 'It's just stuff,' he said, his voice flat.

'It's not just stuff. I read what they wrote. I saw the picture.'

He made an expression that she couldn't interpret. His fingers had loosened and were flicking at his side.

Fiona took a breath. 'And I know that you've called the helpline. For bullying. I looked at the numbers. Honey, why? Why couldn't you tell me?'

Maybe it was the softening of her voice, but his face changed. She could tell he was trying not to cry.

'It's nothing,' he said again, as if he were trying

391

to convince himself. He put a hand to his forehead and caught at his hair.

'Jamie, it's not nothing.' She gestured at the phone and her voice rose a little. 'This is definitely not nothing. I need to know how long it has been going on, who they are and what else they've done. And does the school know? Have you told them?'

'No. Mum.' His hand was still at his head. He looked like he was about to bolt.

'Jamie. I'm not having it. This is really—'

'No. Please!' He sounded so panicked.

'What? We have to do something about this, love.'

'No!' He stood up from the bed. 'No. Mum. No. Please don't. Mum, don't do anything. Don't say anything. Please!'

His face crumpled and she stood too and reached for him and pulled him into her. He was almost as tall as she was, tensed like steel against her. She tightened her grip. 'Shhh shhh.' His head went into her shoulder.

'Please, Mum.'

'Shhh.'

He was crying now and she held on to him, and raised a hand to his hair. His thick black hair.

'It's all right,' she said. 'You're all right. It's going to be fine. I promise you. It's going to be absolutely fine. I promise.'

*   *   *

It was the smell that woke him, that, and the sensation of something cold and curdled on his cheek. Charlie opened his eyes. Jack was on his back, stretched diagonally, his face inches from

Charlie's, both hands above his head in sleepy supplication, his perfect mouth, with its tiny sucking blister open slightly for each soft, spaced breath. Charlie didn't remember Jack spitting up after the last feed, but he must have because Charlie was lying on it. He lifted his head and wiped his cheek. His neck hurt and he needed to stretch, but if he did he might wake Annie, whose knees were dug into the small of his back. She'd come through so often they'd finally given up and let her in somewhere around 4 a.m., the same time that Charlie had remembered what day it was and said happy New Year to Gail and blew her an exhausted kiss. He raised his eyes to the clock on Gail's side; she was turned away, almost to the edge, and holding on to her pillow as if it were a new lover. It was 7.50 a.m. So that made an hour between midnight and 1 a.m., then maybe 2 a.m. until 4 a.m., then 6.15 a.m. until now. Almost five hours of sleep.

He shifted himself carefully on to his back. Annie was in the foetal position and still holding the ear of her rabbit, whose glassy brown eyes were level with Charlie's. It looked almost as shell-shocked as he felt. He glanced across at the cot, still strapped to the bed on Gail's side, empty and untouched. In a few days it would probably be filled with washing or boxes of tissues and breast pads; anything save a baby. He closed his eyes again and exhaled gently, willing himself to go under again. It was still early, his girls and his boy were all sleeping and he had no need to be anywhere but here.

*   *   *

Jamie lay back on the bed and watched the light give shape to the room. There was no noise in the house. Mum had left him around 3 a.m. but he had not slept. It was as if there were a motor in him, running and running and he couldn't turn it off. Fear and shock and a strange kind of elation. Mum knew: she knew about the phone and everything they had done, but she didn't know anything else. She didn't know that he had waded into the water, the shock of it taking his breath, the pressure of it willing him forward, pushing him on.

He turned his head into the pillow. Daisy. It had been Daisy. One clear thought in among all the others. How sad she would be. The look on her face when someone tried to explain. How she would become what Mum was now: the Girl Whose Brother Died.

CHAPTER TWENTY

FRIDAY, 1 JANUARY, NEW YEARS' DAY

When she was small, Vonnie liked to think that the leaching stain around the light fitting in her room was in the shape of a butterfly. Then Fiona had pointed out that it had three pendulous curves, not two, and was, therefore, more like a bottom with an extra buttock. Deborah had said that wasn't funny because water might have dripped through the light and on to Vonnie and electrocuted her and how would Fiona feel then, having made a joke about it all? Fiona had said she would feel fine because she wasn't responsible for the missing slate that had caused the leak. Vonnie felt fine too because she had seen someone being electrocuted on *Tom and Jerry* and they had been in good shape afterwards; just a bit singed. David had climbed on to the roof to fix the slate while Caroline held the bottom of the ladder and told him, laughingly, that he was a fool.

The original lampshade had been replaced, so the shape was more obscured than Vonnie remembered. She narrowed her eyes. She used to try to make other forms from the stain, a bit of the Olympic logo, wagon wheels and someone puffing out their cheeks. She could still see them all. She hadn't looked at her watch, but she guessed it was early, by the lack of sound and the grey tinge to the light at the edge of the curtains.

She felt terrible; her head was thumping and her mouth felt dry. She reached out a hand from underneath the covers and lifted her watch. It was a little after 8.30 a.m.

She stretched, and as she did so, slid her mobile from the small table. Mike would still be up, at least he ought to be, and she had promised to call. She shuffled back under the covers and dialled the apartment. He answered quickly.

'Hey, babe.' Her voice was croaky. 'Happy New Year. Call me back. Okay?'

'Okay.'

She ended the call and stretched herself again as she waited for it to ring, which it did almost immediately.

'Happy New Year,' said Mike. She could hear music in the background and some voices, low and laughing. 'You sounded like crap, honey.' He

395

laughed. 'Rough night?'

'Mmm,' said Vonnie. She stretched again. Her stomach was hurting. 'Who've you got there?'

'Some of the guys.'

She heard the music and noises fade. He must be moving to another room.

'How's Lil?'

'She's fine. Enjoying the company.'

'Is she drinking beer again?' They had discovered that Lil was partial to a tipple after catching her licking the tops of the empties clustered around the bin. It was only beer she went for; the wine bottles were always left untouched. It had become her party trick. If they had people round, they would pour the smallest of measures into a saucer for her and she would crouch low, tail flicking in pleasure as she drank.

'Yeah. I'm keeping an eye on her units, though,' said Mike.

Someone must have cranked up the volume because the music suddenly grew louder.

'Is that the Grateful Dead?' Vonnie smiled. 'You sad, sad people.'

'Piss off,' said Mike genially.

Vonnie yawned again. 'Well, you better get back to your stoner buddies and I'll get back to sleep. Just wanted to say happy New Year. Love you.'

'Love you too. Von?'

'Uh-huh?'

'Have you thought about London?'

Vonnie rolled her eyes. He just wasn't letting this go.

'No? Yes?' said Mike, when she didn't respond.

'I don't know.'

'Why don't you know?' His voice became soft

and deliberate, the way it did when she hadn't paid her credit card bill.

'I just don't. It's such an upheaval, I suppose.'

'I know,' he said.

She doubted that he did. London, for him, would be an adventure, a new country, a new start. For her, it would be coming home; going back.

'We can talk about it when I'm back,' she said. She wasn't feeling great at all; now was not a good time.

He didn't reply.

'Mike? When I'm back? I'll have a think in the meantime. Okay?'

'Okay.' There was a pause. The Grateful Dead warbled reedily in the background. 'Would it help if I asked you to marry me?' The words came out in a rush, almost as though he had just thought of it.

'What?' She hadn't seen that coming.

'Would it help you decide if we were married?'

'Oh, my God. Mike.' She propped herself up, and felt instantly sick. 'Shit.'

He gave a nervous laugh. 'Shit was not the response I was hoping for.'

'No, I feel sick,' said Vonnie.

'Neither was that,' said Mike.

'Mike. I . . .'

'What?'

Vonnie held a hand to her mouth. She was stunned. They'd joked about it before, of course; him in one of those hideous powder-blue tuxes, her in the full meringue, but nothing serious, just the will-we-get-round-to-it-one-day conversation that most couples must have when they've been together for a while.

'You don't have to do that,' she said.

'I want to.'

'Really?'

'Will you marry me?'

'Yes.' The word came out before she realised she would say it.

'Well, that's a deal then.' He sounded relieved.

'I better get a ring,' said Vonnie, with a high laugh that sounded like it came from someone else. 'I'm going to need bling.'

'If bling's your thing,' said Mike.

She sat in a daze, the phone pressed tight to her ear, her stomach churning. Yes. She had said 'yes'.

'Are you there?'

'Yes.'

'Are you shocked?'

'Yes.'

He laughed. A door squeaked open and the music grew louder. 'I better go,' he said. 'Tell the guys.'

'Yeah,' said Vonnie. 'Me too.'

'I love you.'

'Yeah,' said Vonnie. 'Me too.'

She laid the phone on the covers and looked at it, her stomach still churning. She wondered if she could take it back. Did she want to? She propelled herself out of bed and just made it to the loo where she was copiously and noisily sick.

It was another hour before she went downstairs. She was sick twice more, brushed her teeth and then showered, standing under the hot water for so long that it grew cool. Married. She couldn't see it, but neither could she see herself without Mike. And what else could she have said? No? She wondered what Mike was doing, maybe nursing a beer and the growing sense that he had just made a monumental mistake, as his friends slapped him on the back. That wasn't fair. He wasn't like that. He wanted her.

She felt a little fizz of pleasure. She would get a ring. She splayed her fingers out on her left hand and studied them. She wasn't into diamonds. Maybe an emerald. She liked emeralds. But it would mean moving, going with him, settling down . . . coming back. She switched off the shower and pulled her towel around her, suddenly cold.

Everyone else seemed to be up and about. She passed Daisy and Katie in the hall, still in pyjamas but wide awake, running shrieking towards the drawing room with Riley in hot pursuit, and Ben, bringing up the rear with his slow bottom-shuffle, clutching half a bagel.

The kitchen was crowded but no one was talking. Fiona sat with her hands clasped round a mug, Deborah close beside her. Caroline was over by the sink, staring out of the window and Doug was tucking into a plate of bacon and eggs. Vonnie's stomach turned at the smell. There was no sign of Min or Jamie or David.

'Morning.' Vonnie yawned.

Fiona and Deborah barely acknowledged her, and Caroline turned from the sink to offer a thin-lipped smile. Doug looked flustered.

She moved across to the fridge. 'How is everyone? Sleep well?'

'No.' Fiona's voice was flat.

Vonnie turned to look at her.

'Do you want coffee?' Deborah was on her feet.

'No thanks, I'm feeling a bit bleh, actually.'

'Really?' It was said so sarcastically that Vonnie

stopped.

'What's going on?' she said to Fiona. 'What's up with you?'

Doug got to his feet, laid his plate on the counter and put his hand on Deborah's shoulder before leaving the room.

'What?'

'We had a bit of an incident last night,' said Deborah.

'What? What kind of incident?' Vonnie moved over and slipped into one of the seats.

'Jamie ran away,' said Deborah. She glanced at Fiona. 'We were up half the night looking for him.'

'Ran away?' Vonnie tried to focus. 'Why? Is he okay?'

'He's fine,' said Deborah. 'He's back.'

'Thanks for all your help,' said Fiona flatly. 'Oh no, that's right, you didn't help because you were drunk. Pissed out of your head. Again.'

'Fiona.' Caroline turned from the sink. She looked awful: pale and exhausted. She glanced uneasily at Vonnie. 'I tried to wake you, do you not remember?' she said. She dried her hands on the towel, but didn't let go of it afterwards.

Vonnie felt a flash of shame. Shit. Had she drunk that much?

'I had no idea,' she said. 'Is Jamie okay?'

'No,' said Fiona. 'He's not okay. He's being bullied senseless at school and he's not okay.' Her voice cracked a little and Deborah, who was standing behind her, laid both hands on her shoulders.

'Christ, Fi, I'm sorry,' said Vonnie. 'That's awful. Did you know it was happening?'

'Yes, I knew and I chose to do nothing,' said

400

Fiona. 'No, of *course* I didn't know!'

'Okay,' said Vonnie.

'We could have done with your help,' said Deborah.

'I'm sorry,' said Vonnie again. 'What time was this?'

'From about 1 a.m., until . . . well, until we found him, which was after 2 a.m., or something.'

Vonnie stretched her hands out on to the table. She felt sick again, but knew better than to say.

'Where did you find him? Were you all out looking?'

Caroline started to speak but Fiona interrupted her. 'No. Mum had to stay here because there was no one to look after the kids and you were out of it—'

'I've said I'm sorry.' Vonnie felt the first prickle of annoyance. She felt bad enough already, no need to make her feel worse. 'I get it.'

'Do you?' Fiona got to her feet. 'Do you get it, Von? You were pissed. You couldn't help. We needed you and you couldn't help.'

'Fiona.' Caroline laid a hand on her arm.

But Fiona shook it off. 'No, Mum, she has to hear this. What is it with this family that we can't tell her when she's behaving like a selfish brat?'

'Hey, steady on.' Vonnie sat back. 'I know you're upset, but don't take it out on me, okay?'

'Fiona, it's not your job to tell her off,' said Caroline.

'Oh, no? Well, someone's got to do it,' said Fiona. 'Because you and Dad don't. You never have. All we get is, "Oh, that's Vonnie." Christ, Mum, she's up to her ears in debt, and she's got a raging bloody drink problem, or are we all just

401

pretending that it's normal to have a vat of wine every night, that it's okay to piss her life away up against a wall?'

'Oh, for God's sake.' Vonnie stood up. 'I don't have to listen to this. I know you're upset but there is no need to be such an absolute bitch.'

'Or maybe I'm just being honest?' said Fiona.

Caroline continued to twist the tea towel between her fingers and Deborah looked at her feet. Vonnie turned for the door.

'Is that it?' said Fiona. 'Nothing to say?' She folded her arms and watched her sister through narrowed eyes.

Vonnie stopped. 'Actually I do have something to say.'

'And what's that?' Fiona's voice was tight with mockery.

'I just got engaged,' said Vonnie. 'Thought you might like to know.'

'Vonnie!' Caroline went to follow her, but Vonnie held up her hand.

'No. Enough. Just leave me be, okay? After all that. Just leave me be.'

At the back door, she pushed her feet into her trainers and unhooked a fleece from one of the pegs. It must have been Doug's because it hung off her shoulders and well past her fingertips. Jamie's baseball boots were on the back step, caked in wet mud. It was cold out, not cold enough for a frost, but enough to make the air sharp. She would walk and let the day clear her head and cool her shame and anger. She had reached the side gate when she spotted David in the hide. He didn't seem to hear her approach. He was sitting perfectly still and staring out over the field. His binoculars were still

402

in his lap, the leather cord woven around them in a neat figure of eight.

'Hey,' she said.

He turned at the sound of her voice. There were bags under his eyes and his hair was flattened down at one side, as if he had just got up.

'Hello.' He raised a hand to her face as she sat down beside him. His fingers were cold on her cheek.

'I just heard about Jamie.'

David was looking at her.

'I'm sorry,' she said.

'It's been an awful night,' he said.

'I wish I'd been . . .' Vonnie tailed off.

David gave a sigh. 'You can't keep doing that, love,' he said gently. 'Drinking that way.'

'I had no idea, Dad.'

'I know, but I'm worried about you.'

'You don't need to be. I'm fine. It was Hogmanay, for heaven's sake.' He was still watching her. 'Honestly, Dad. It's okay.' She smiled carefully. 'Anyway, I've got some news of my own.'

'What?'

'I'm getting married.'

'What!' He turned fully to face her.

'Mike just asked me. I said "yes".'

David held out his arms. She couldn't read his expression, but his voice was warm. 'Darling.'

Vonnie lay against his chest, breathing in the smell of his waxed jacket. She never cried, but all of a sudden she felt that she just might.

*　　*　　*

403

The water was still a little too hot, so Caroline twisted the dial until she felt it cool, then stood back and shook the drops from her arm. She left the shower door open and checked that there was soap and shampoo opened and within reach of the sturdy plastic chair fixed to the corner of the unit. She laid out a fresh bath mat—Min preferred cotton to cork—and draped the towel over the small white stool beside the sink. She could hear Min still humming through in her bedroom. She had been on amazing form, sharp and bright and full of celebration. But maybe, when you get to eighty-eight, the turn of another year holds an added achievement all of its own.

'I think I might take a bath,' she had said loudly when she came in to the kitchen for her coffee. She had always said bath, even though she didn't have one. Caroline knew that was her cue. Min would never ask directly for help, but she did need it, not to wash, but to get everything set up. She hadn't seemed to notice that Caroline and Deborah and Fiona were sitting shell-shocked at the table.

'Ready!' Caroline tilted the blinds a little, even though the window was frosted and Min's privacy guaranteed. But it took the edge off the light, which felt like the right thing to do.

Min appeared in her dressing gown and slippers, one hand fussing at the back of her head.

'There's a pin . . .' She turned her back.

Caroline put her hands into Min's hair. It was soft and lank, as fine as fraying silk. She found the kirby and teased it out.

'Thank you,' said Min briskly.

'Do you want some of your new smellies?' asked Caroline. Fiona's present to her this year had been

404

an extravagant box of Jo Malone, shower gel, body cream and a candle all in lime, basil and mandarin.

Min shook her head. She favoured Vosene and any old soap, and had worn only Joy by Jean Patou since anyone could remember, which Fiona really ought to have known.

'Right, I'll let you get on.'

Min put her hand up to Caroline's cheek. 'Thank you, dear.'

Caroline smiled at her and, as she did so, felt her eyes fill with tears.

'Are you all right?' Min's voice was uncharacteristically gentle.

'Not really,' said Caroline.

'And why is that?' Min tilted her head to one side.

'Jamie ran off. Last night. He's having an awful time at school with some boys—they've been sending him these text messages—and he just took off. David and Fiona and Doug all went out in the car. They found him, but . . .'

'I knew there was something up with that boy.' Min shook her head. She didn't look in the slightest bit surprised. 'Poor sod. Children can be vicious little shites, you know.'

'I don't know if I was meant to say, or not,' said Caroline.

'Better out than in,' said Min. 'No point in hiding stuff. Never made it any better—secrecy.'

Caroline wondered suddenly if Min knew about Frances; if David had told her.

But Min only said, 'How's Fiona?'

'She's pretty cut up about it,' said Caroline. 'Doesn't know how to address it.'

Min nodded.

405

'Oh, and Vonnie got engaged, apparently. She had a fight with her sister and that was her parting shot, so I don't know any more. She's gone out for a walk.'

'Engaged to whom?'

'Mike, her boyfriend.'

'Never heard of him,' said Min. 'Is he a new one?'

'You've met him, Min, a couple of years back.'

'Have I?' Min squinted at her. 'Well, maybe I have. Anyway, that's the way it goes in families.' She gave a thin-shouldered shrug. 'One triumph, one tragedy. It all evens out.'

'Does it?'

Min reached over and clasped Caroline's hand. 'Always. In the end, it all evens out.'

Caroline was suddenly unable to look at the old lady. With Min it felt like the worst betrayal. They would have to get someone in to do what Caroline had just done, the small kindnesses that should come from those you love, not those you pay. And she could get so confused. Would she understand?

'You'd best get in. The water will be getting cold soon,' Caroline said, and turned to leave the room. She would come back and check in half an hour. Min should be dressed by then, or at least decent and ready to have her hair done.

She spent a few minutes needlessly straightening cushions in Min's small sitting room, picking up fallen papers, putting Riley's toys in his basket, which he promptly removed, and refilling his water dish, not sure what to do next.

Min had started to hum again. Caroline stood for a moment trying to identify the tune. It might have been a carol, or the jingle for an ad, she

406

wasn't sure. She took a last look round the room and headed back to the main house.

David was by the car. The boot was open. He turned to look at her, his eyes blank.

'Min's having a shower,' she said, just for something to say.

He nodded. 'Vonnie and I are going for a walk,' he said. 'Get out of the house for a while.'

'Where is she?' said Caroline.

'Getting her walking boots,' said David.

'Did you hear—'

'Yes.' He cut her off. 'Great news.'

Vonnie appeared at the back door, with a jacket hung over her arm, and a plastic bag into which she was stuffing a small bunch of bananas.

Caroline walked towards her and gave her a hug. 'I'm so sorry about earlier,' she said. 'I'm really pleased for you, darling. That's lovely. Just lovely. You mustn't mind Fiona. She's terribly upset, that's all.'

'So I gathered,' said Vonnie. 'It's okay, Mum. It's just Fiona, and I'm glad Jamie's okay.' She accepted Caroline's kiss on her cheek.

'Will you tell me everything when you get back? We can have a little celebration.'

'Would I be allowed champagne?' said Vonnie.

'Vonnie.'

'I'm kidding, Mum,' said Vonnie, in a voice that suggested that she wasn't. She moved past Caroline and over towards the car. Caroline stood back and watched them leave. Vonnie waved to her as the car pulled off, but David didn't. He kept his eyes straight ahead, even when the car curved level with her to drive away.

Deborah lay back on the bed and lifted her arms over her eyes.

'Tired?' Doug was standing by the small sink, trying to shave because both the bathrooms were occupied. One by Fiona, and the other by Katie and Daisy who were waterboarding a Barbie.

'Exhausted,' said Deborah.

Doug dried his face on the small hand towel and came over to sit next to her. She felt the bed dip and she reached out a hand which he caught hold of and pressed quickly to his mouth.

'Has Elsa called yet?'

'No.' Deborah sat up slowly. 'I expect she'll still be asleep.' Doug didn't say anything, and she looked at him. 'What?'

'She's coming down tonight though?' he said.

'Mmm,' said Deborah. 'Matt's going to drop her off.'

Doug nodded.

'You're up to something,' said Deborah. He smiled. There was a small blob of shaving foam just under his left ear and she reached over and wiped it away. 'What are you up to?'

'I've been thinking about Jamie,' he said. 'How unhappy he's been.'

'I know.'

'Why don't we ask Caroline if Matt can stay for dinner?'

'Doug.'

'Well, why not?'

'It would be horribly awkward, that's why not,' said Deborah. She looked down at her hand still caught in his.

408

'It won't be horribly awkward. It'll be fine. And look, we're going to have to thrash this out with Elsa at some point, so . . .'

'We are not doing that over dinner,' said Deborah. 'There's too much going on, Doug. Jesus, you, Elsa, Jamie and now Vonnie.'

'What did Jesus do?' Doug smiled.

'Don't try to be funny.' Deborah leaned over and settled against the softness of his belly, breathing in the smell of him, warm and faintly soapy. 'You're not funny.'

'So you say.' Doug gave her a squeeze. 'Look, it doesn't mean we are going to let her go, love, but he's important to her and we need to get to know him a bit better.'

Deborah sighed. 'I suppose.'

He held her away from him. 'Everything is going to be fine. I know what you're worried about, and it will be *fine*. We'll sort this out with Elsa, and I'll get sorted out. I'm not going to die, and your daughter is not going to become a waster. Jamie will be okay and you can get yourself a fancy hat for Vonnie's wedding. Okay?'

'I don't suit hats,' said Deborah, and felt immediately churlish. It should be her offering these reassurances, not Doug. She lay back against him.

'You never know,' said Doug. 'By the end of the evening you may absolutely adore him; this boy.'

Deborah gave a little flat laugh. 'The way this holiday has been going,' she said, 'I doubt it.'

*   *   *

There was only one other car in the lay-by; a beat-

409

up red Punto with a broken aerial and a half-empty bottle of Lucozade on the back shelf. David manoeuvred the Volvo close to the banking and far enough away from the Punto to allow it to pull away without coming anywhere near him.

Vonnie peered at the sky out of the window. 'Weather's turned.'

David nodded. It was the perfect day for walking in the Pentlands. Apart from some high cloud banked out over the sea, the sky was clear, a watery sun shining full on the contours of the hills.

They got the rucksack out of the boot and Vonnie swung it on to her back. David retrieved his walking stick from the glove compartment. It was more of a vanity than anything. He didn't need it, but he liked to carry it. It was steel and collapsible, light as a feather.

There were several paths into the hills. The one they chose to take started along the edge of a cattle field. The animals were clustered at one corner, in the steam of their own breath, their coats hung about with thick coagulations of dung. Vonnie went in front, the rucksack bouncing a little with each step. It was slick with mud underfoot, but she didn't seem to notice, or if she did, she didn't mind. She didn't baulk at the worst the outdoors could throw at her. Her brother had been the same. Full of curiosity, inured to cold, damp, discomfort.

It was good to be away from the house. They would have to talk more, he and Caroline, he knew that and dreaded the thought of it. They had hardly looked at each other since she had said her piece. Beyond being numb, he wasn't sure how he felt. It had been utterly unexpected, so there was

410

shock at that, but it hadn't felt like a bombshell. But then of course Fiona had come downstairs and everything had kicked off when they realised Jamie had gone.

He had felt so foolish, foolish and angry that she had seen them on the night of the party; seen them and been watching.

He had been consumed with guilt at the start of the affair; could hardly look at Caroline at first, but that had faded over time. The physical side of their marriage had ended long before he and Frances began. It had been a gradual process, born of age and tiredness. They had got into a situation where one would go to bed before the other, usually Caroline first. It would be dark when he went up and the bed was big enough to go the whole night without touching. It had never seemed strange that they didn't talk about it, nor did it seem odd when he moved into the spare room during a bout of illness, and made it, gradually, his own.

It wasn't ideal, he knew that, but their happy-ever-after had died with Euan. And what they had created over time, a benign coexistence, seemed to work. At least, he thought it had. They could still socialise as a couple, make joint decisions, function as husband and wife, but have their own space, their own time. Most marriages, he had assumed, followed a similar pattern.

He felt a sudden little jolt of anger. Why do this now? Why dismantle their lives? And what did she want? What did she think was still to come? Love? Contentment?

'Come on, old man. Keep up.' Vonnie had stopped at the end of the field, where the path

411

took a swing to the left and started to climb across a long, mossy slope.

'You've got thirty years on me,' said David. 'Be kind.'

She stopped to wait for him and held out her arm.

'Bugger off,' he said. 'I'm not that decrepit.'

She laughed and tucked her arm into his and they walked like that for maybe thirty yards, until it became so bumpy underfoot that they were in danger of pulling each other over. Vonnie let go and fell into step beside him, matching her pace to his.

They talked about everything of little or no consequence: other climbs they had done, the weather, politics. Vonnie seemed bemused by, rather than involved in the upcoming vote, which didn't surprise him. She had lived out of the country for so long now that it would have little relevance to her. She spoke a little about Mike and the engagement, which seemed to have come as a shock. David had only met him a couple of times, but he seemed a decent enough man, self-possessed and engaging.

They had reached the flank of the hill—you couldn't really call it a mountain—and they stopped and had a mug of coffee from the flask. The ground was too damp to sit on, so Vonnie perched on a small stone and David stood beside her. They were high enough up to get a good view: Edinburgh and the sea beyond, a great grey sheet; and the sweep of farmland to the south, the fields chequered brown and green. A little further up the track two figures were on their way down; probably the occupants of the Punto. It was two boys, barely

412

out of their teens, as David had suspected from the state of their car. He saw them look at Vonnie the way most men did, but she didn't seem to notice.

He and Vonnie didn't talk again until they had reached the top. It was a deceptive summit. No pinnacle to reach, just a broad, flat expanse with a small cairn at one end. Vonnie got to it first and turned with a triumphant smile. She sat on the furthest edge of the circle of stones and pulled out the water bottle, leaning her head back and tipping it into her mouth.

David's legs were stiff when he sat beside her. It was several months since he had done any proper walking. She held out the water bottle and he took it gratefully. Caroline, had she come, would have brought a bottle each.

To the north, the sun had broken through the cloud, sending shards of brilliant light on to the city.

'Should have brought the camera,' said David.

'Yeah,' said Vonnie.

They both sat in silence, savouring the view.

'Biccie or banana?' Vonnie dug in the front pocket of her rucksack.

'Biscuit,' said David, and prised a digestive from the packet she pulled out.

He watched her as he ate. She was so straightforward, his youngest girl. He felt a sudden surge of sadness and affection. It wasn't right to favour one of your children, he knew that, but with Vonnie it was just instinctive; it always had been. Maybe it was because she was so like Euan; maybe just that their characters were a better fit. He couldn't imagine coming out for a walk like this with Fiona or Deborah. It wouldn't even occur to him to ask.

He wondered if he should say anything more to her about her drinking. He hoped she was right about it; that she was on top of it. He didn't get any sense that she hid it, which was when you really had to start worrying. But she could certainly pack it away.

She turned towards him and held out the packet of biscuits. He shook his head, dusted his hands free of crumbs and shifted his position a little on the hard stones.

'What was Jamie like when you found him?'

'Wet.'

'Wet?' Vonnie turned round.

'I think he'd gone through the burn or something. I don't know. Fiona's still to get to the bottom of it all.'

'Poor lad,' said Vonnie. 'He's been super-quiet since he's been here.'

'Hardly says a word,' said David.

'Was he miles away?'

'No, he was on his way back. Down near the bridge.'

'Can't have gone far then.'

'I don't think it was a serious attempt to run off,' said David. 'He had nothing with him. No money or phone or anything.'

Vonnie nodded. 'You must have been worried,' she said and reached out to cover his hand. It was a simple statement, but beautifully put. He knew what she meant and he loved her for it.

'Vonnie,' he said quickly. 'There's something you should know.' He hadn't even thought that he would say anything, but suddenly it seemed absolutely right that she should be told.

'Hmm?' She turned to look at him.

'Your mum and I are probably not going to be together much longer.'

'What?' She looked confused rather than shocked.

'Caroline thinks we should have some time apart. A separation.'

'What!' She had been about to lift her hand away, but stopped, holding it in mid-air.

'Caroline thinks we should have a break from each other.'

'Oh, my God, Dad.' Vonnie clutched his arm again.

'It's okay. I'm sorry to tell you like this, but I thought you should know. There're going to be implications. For all of us, really.'

'When?' said Vonnie. 'When did this happen?'

'Last night,' said David.

'Jesus.'

'It's okay,' said David again.

'How is it okay?' said Vonnie. She had put down the water and was staring at him, her eyes still clouded with incomprehension. 'What's going on? Where did this come from?'

'It's very complicated.'

'God, Dad. I can't believe this. What? She's just going to go?'

'No,' said David. 'Not just go. She's going off on her painting course to France, so that's almost a month and then we're going to see. But she's probably going to move out. I suspect that's what will happen.'

Vonnie turned completely towards him. 'She's planned this? She's thought it through? And what's this all been about, with the party and us all

415

brought home to play happy families?'

'It's not like that, Vonnie. It's a lot of things.' His throat felt suddenly dry.

'Like what?'

He steeled himself. 'I've been seeing someone else.' It felt odd to say it out loud. It sounded more dramatic than he had imagined, and more real.

Vonnie's mouth was open, but no words came.

'It's not just that. Caroline's not been happy for a long time. Neither of us has, really.'

'Shit. Dad.'

'I know. I'm sorry.'

'Shit.' She was shaking her head.

He waited for her to ask who it was, and he wasn't sure that he could tell her.

'Wow,' she said.

'I'm not proud of it,' he said.

Her hand was still on his arm and she gave it a squeeze. He felt the sting in his eyes. She didn't judge.

'I can't believe this,' she said again.

'I'm so sorry, love. I didn't mean to spoil your news about Mike . . .'

'Stuff that, Dad, this is huge. This is . . .'

Her fingers were cold. 'Look, love, it's just the way it is, okay? Sometimes you need a break, when things have not been right.'

'Have they not been right?'

'Not really,' said David. 'Not for a while.'

Vonnie pulled her arm away and curled it protectively around her knees. 'But now, Dad. You've just retired. And what about Min . . .' She tailed off.

'It'll be fine,' he said again.

'Do Debs and Fiona know?'

'No. I don't think so.'

'They need to know, Dad.'

He sighed. She was right, but how they should be told he wasn't sure. And Min. She would be bewildered by it all. It was getting colder now they weren't moving. Vonnie sat back and zipped her jacket to the neck and rested her elbows on her knees, staring out towards the city and the sea.

'Who is it?' she said finally.

'Frances. Frances Fletcher.'

Vonnie made no movement beyond a short nod of her head.

'I'm sorry,' said David again.

It was almost as if she had not heard him.

'I'm hungry,' she said. 'Let's stop somewhere for lunch.'

She stood and held out her hand to him, and when he was on his feet swung the rucksack round on to her back, said nothing more and and turned her head towards the car.

*　　　*　　　*

Elsa opened an eye. Matt was over by the fridge, holding the door open with one hand, and scratching somewhere below his waist with the other. Her head hurt. Really badly. She rolled over and felt her face press into the old rubbed velvet of the sofa, stale from decades of dust and people's arses, and God knows what else.

She rolled back. Matt had found some bread which he was sniffing. He dropped two slices into the toaster and rinsed out a highball glass, then refilled it with water and chugged it down. On the other side of the room, the prone form of another friend lay cocooned in a sleeping bag by the edge of the fireplace, like a large blue caterpillar.

Elsa shifted herself up into a semi-seated position and laid her head against the sofa's edge.

'What time is it?'

Matt shrugged.

'Should say on the cooker,' said Elsa.

He squinted towards the oven. 'One thirty.'

'Shit,' said Elsa softly. She held out an arm and Matt refilled the glass and brought it over. It was lukewarm, and tasted faintly of Coke. She gulped it down.

'I need to phone Mum and Dad.' She looked around the room for her jeans. She could remember shimmying them off to get into her sleeping bag, but not where she'd thrown them. They were down the side of the sofa, with her suede boots and someone else's jacket. She dug in the pocket and retrieved her mobile

'Can you not belch or fart or anything?'

Matt grunted and stood up and wandered out of the room towards the loo.

There were lots of messages when she switched it on. She scrolled through them, smiling at most of them. Mum's was one of the first and the longest. She hated to use abbreviations, which, as a former speech therapist, was probably understandable, but it meant you got three pages instead of one. She put capitals in as well and all the correct spacing and punctuation.

Happy New Year, Elsa! Hope you are having a wonderful time. Take care! Lots of love, Mum and Dad and Katie.

418

Elsa dialled the number for the house. It was Caroline who answered and she wished her a happy New Year and waited for Deborah to come on the line.

'Are you just up, madam?'

'Not quite,' lied Elsa. 'Happy New Year, Mum.'

'And you, darling. How was the castle?'

'Yeah, good,' said Elsa.

'Well, we're all, em, fine here,' said Deborah. 'Your Aunt Vonnie got engaged.'

'Wow,' said Elsa. 'Who to?'

'Mike,' said Deborah. 'You know Mike.'

Elsa had never met Mike, or even seen a picture of him, but she said, 'Yeah, of course. That's great.'

'It is,' said Deborah. She sounded a little nonplussed. 'Oh, hold on. Here's your dad. Lots of love, see you soon.'

'And you . . .' Elsa tailed off. She heard the phone being passed over.

'Hey, puss, happy New Year.'

'Happy New Year, Dads.'

'Did Mum tell you about Vonnie?'

'Yeah,' said Elsa, stifling a yawn. 'Great news.'

'When will you be down?'

'Later,' said Elsa. 'Maybe teatime?'

'Okay,' said Doug. He paused. 'How's Matt?'

'Fine.'

'Is he there?'

'Yes.'

'Well, I tell you what, why don't you bring him down with you when you come. Stay for supper. Very informal. It would be nice to see him.'

'Are you sure? What about Mum?'

'She'll be fine,' said Doug breezily and almost sounded like he believed it.

419

'I don't know,' said Elsa. Across the room the shape in the sleeping bag turned a bleary face her way and Elsa held up a finger to her lips.

'It'll be fine,' said Doug. 'A good idea. Lots of people. We'll see you for supper. Yes?'

'Okay,' said Elsa slowly.

'Fine,' said Doug. 'Love you lots.'

She sat holding the phone until Matt reappeared from the loo. His hair was fanned up at the front and his T-shirt said: *'Fuck You. I Would.'* There were two small damp circles on the front of his boxers.

She grinned at him, suddenly hopeful. 'You might want to have a shower,' she said.

*   *   *

'I want to be the shoe!' Daisy reached across the board and snatched up the small silver boot. That left Jamie the top hat or the dog, because Katie already had the car. He didn't really care what he was, he didn't actually care if they played the game, but his mum had asked him to keep them busy. He knew what she was trying to do. She was trying to make him feel important, responsible, the big brother. She was watching him almost all the time and when he looked at her, she would give him a big smile that never quite seemed to reach her eyes.

The Monopoly board was the one that Fiona had played with when she was small and when she had opened the lid of the box it had smelled like an old tent, damp and canvassy. Lots of the pieces were missing. There were only three hotels left, and some of the fake money was criss-crossed with

420

yellowing Sellotape where it had ripped in two.

They were in the little sitting room and Fiona had folded out the card table that Jamie had used to play poker with Min. Ben was underneath. Jamie could feel the scrabble of a small fat hand occasionally on his feet and ankles.

His mum had said they wouldn't talk about it again until they were back home unless he wanted to and he didn't. She had told Allan and he had phoned and said they were bastards but he shouldn't have run off because that didn't solve anything. It was kind of nice that they were on his side. But the sick feeling in his stomach was still there. She had said not to worry, everything would be fine, but she had no way of knowing that it would be.

There was a thud from under the table. Jamie bent sideways in time to see Ben, flat on his back and face reddening, open his mouth to wail. It must have hurt because he never cried. Jamie reached out and pulled him up and on to his knee. A gob of spittle landed on his arm.

'Ew, gross,' said Katie.

Ben was still snivelling so Jamie settled him on to his knee and blew a raspberry at him. He liked when you did that. Ben's face creased into an instant smile and he giggled. That was the best thing about him. It didn't take much to brighten him up and make him forget that anything bad had ever happened.

After what seemed like ages, Jamie let Daisy win, which annoyed Katie, and she left in a huff. Daisy followed her and Ben scuttled after them, his tears long since dried, and Jamie was left on his own. He tried to put everything back in the box,

421

but it, too, was held together with tape, and the lid wouldn't go on properly. He squashed it down as best he could and was trying to fold away the table when Min came in.

She stopped at the door and looked at him. Her hair was wet and it had left damp patches on her blouse. Sometimes he wondered if she peered at you because she couldn't see properly, or if she was trying to figure out what you were thinking. She had a book tucked under her arm and her glasses clutched in one hand. She poked them towards him.

'Glad I've caught you,' she said.

He nodded.

'Heard you've had a spot of bother. At school.'

He wasn't sure what to say. He just kind of assumed that no one had said anything to her. It was bad enough everyone else knowing what had happened and having to come out and look for him. They didn't seem to know what to say to him since he'd got up and he had felt so ashamed he could hardly look them in the eye.

'Well?' Min peered more closely at him.

'Kind of,' said Jamie. He could feel the heat in his cheeks.

'Kind of? You either have or you haven't.'

'Yes.'

Min nodded. 'Well, I don't need to know the details. Just wanted to say, you remember your worth, young man. You're a good boy. Don't you mind these ignorant little shits. Okay? Don't you mind them. They'll end up as nothing. Shits, that's all they are. Ignorant little shits.'

She punctuated each of her sentences with a little jab of her glasses and when she was done, she

422

turned and left, and Jamie stood where he was and wondered how it was possible to want to laugh and cry at exactly the same time.

CHAPTER TWENTY-ONE

Two aubergines, some onions and three rather rubbery courgettes. Caroline peered into the vegetable rack. At a pinch it would make the basis of a stew. She could use the shoulder of lamb to go with it. A bit dull but a welcome change from turkey. Doug had just asked if it was okay if Elsa's boyfriend stayed for supper and she had not wanted to say 'no'. It would be good to have a distraction, someone different to talk to.

She gathered up the vegetables and brought them out from the larder and into the kitchen, settling them on the chopping board by the sink. There was a bottle of good red wine uncorked by the kettle and she poured herself a small glass to sip as she cooked. The kitchen was too quiet, so she switched on the radio. It was a discussion and it sounded political, but she didn't care, she just needed voices to drown out the ones in her head. What have you done? What now?

She wondered if David had told Vonnie and suspected that he might have; perhaps that's why he had suggested the walk. If he was to confide in anyone, it would be her. Vonnie would take his side. She always did. Caroline would know the minute they were back just from her face.

She rinsed the vegetables and started to chop. It was growing dark outside. They must have stopped for lunch afterwards, a long lunch.

There was movement in the hallway, a scrape of the back door, and a quick, cool rush of air as the door opened and Fiona walked in. She had on a gilet, a sleek silver-grey one with a fake fur collar.

Fiona rubbed her hands together. 'It's lovely and warm in here.'

'Have you been out for a walk?'

'Just round the garden.' Fiona slipped into a chair and yawned. 'Something's been at Hector's grave.'

Caroline stopped chopping. 'Riley?'

'Probably. Or a badger. Do you still get them? I kicked the earth back over. I mean he's not poking out or anything, but you might want to get Dad to take a look at it.'

Fiona stood again and pulled a glass out from the cabinet behind her, then poured herself a large measure of wine from the bottle behind Caroline. She yawned again. 'God, I'm so tired.'

'I'm not surprised,' said Caroline. She wiped her hands on the legs of her trousers and scooped the diced courgette off the chopping board and into the glass bowl she had placed at her elbow. 'How's Jamie?'

Fiona shrugged. 'Flat,' she said. 'Just uncommunicative, really.'

'What are you going to do?' Caroline reached for an onion and deftly sliced off one end.

'I don't know,' said Fiona. She sat back down, shrugging off her gilet as she did so, and hooking it over the back of the chair. 'I'll need to speak to the school, but he's in a panic about that; terrified it will make it worse. You know, I took a note of the numbers and I feel like just calling them up and saying, "I know what you did, you little bastards; I've got the evidence."'

'I can understand that,' said Caroline. 'But that's probably not the best move. Do you know how long it's been going on?'

'Pretty much since he started,' said Fiona.

'And is it just him?'

'Seems to be. He had some friends from primary, but, well, you know how it is. They feel bad for him, but they're not doing anything.'

'What does Allan think?' Caroline always felt a little awkward asking Fiona about Allan. He wasn't Jamie's dad and she found she thought of him differently because of that.

'He's saying we should let Jamie sort it out himself.' Fiona sipped at her wine.

'And what do you think?'

'I think that's crap,' said Fiona. 'What is he going to do? Take them all on? Turn the other cheek? That's what he's been trying to do and look where it's got him. It's too serious for that. It may not be a specific offence, but it might be covered under the Public Order Act or the Communications Act. I've left a message with my secretary to check when she's back.'

'So you might sue them?'

'No.' Fiona steadied her voice. 'I might have them prosecuted.'

Caroline stopped what she was doing and studied her daughter. She didn't want to say that that seemed extreme, but it did. She couldn't imagine how that would help Jamie, either.

'They've got to be held accountable.' Fiona pre-empted her. 'If you make an example of them, it discourages others.'

'Of course,' said Caroline and continued with her chopping.

Fiona cupped both hands around her glass and watched her. 'Do you want a hand?'

'If you wouldn't mind,' said Caroline. 'Elsa's boyfriend is coming as well.'

'What are we having?'

'I was thinking stew. I've got shoulder of lamb and these veggies.'

Fiona tilted her head. 'How much of the lamb?'

'Plenty,' said Caroline.

'Do you have any apricots and cumin?'

'Cumin, yes. Not sure about the apricots.'

Fiona stood. 'Well, prunes would do, or even raisins. We could jazz it up a bit. Make a tagine?' She posed it as a question but didn't wait for an answer, moving across to the larder. Caroline laid down the chopping knife.

It should be something rather lovely, cooking with your daughter, but with Fiona it always felt like a tutorial. Even when she was tiny, she liked to take over. Fairy cakes done just her way; white icing, never pink. It was their thing, baking, one of the only times that they really connected. It seemed so strange to say that about your own child: that you found it hard to connect, but, with Fiona, it was the truth. She had come out of the womb with a purpose, although quite what that was, Caroline wasn't sure. But she had always been driven, and only became more so after Euan died.

Fiona reappeared after a moment, arms laden with cans of chopped tomatoes and packets of dried fruit, which she deposited on the table.

'We should be able to do it,' she said. She glanced at her watch. 'It needs to slow-cook. What time are we eating?'

'Not much before 7 p.m., I shouldn't think,' said Caroline. She stood where she was, with her wine in her hand, waiting for instruction.

Fiona pulled an apron from the back of the door and double-tied the bow around her waist. 'Right.' She looked around the kitchen. 'Would you mind putting some music on, Mum? Something jazzy, if you can find it. I can't stand all this political crap.'

Caroline did as she was told. She found Louis Armstrong on Radio 2 and gave a quiet smile as her eldest girl began to sing.

The tagine had been in the low oven for half an hour when David and Vonnie returned. Caroline was still in the kitchen, tidying up the dishes they had used. Fiona was upstairs seeing to Ben who had woken from his nap. Caroline watched the car curve round into its normal space, and saw David and Vonnie get out. It was completely dark now and she couldn't see their faces. She stayed at the sink, and kept the tap running.

It was Vonnie who came in first and Caroline could tell as she turned, even before Vonnie had said a word, that she knew. Her cheeks and the tip of her nose were pink and she didn't smile.

'Hi, love, did you have a nice walk?'

Vonnie looked at her. She didn't reply; just moved across to the cupboard, pulled out a wine glass and helped herself from the opened bottle. It was a big glass that she poured.

Caroline took a breath. 'Vonnie, do you think you should . . . ?'

'Should what?' said Vonnie. She raised the glass. 'Have a drink?'

Caroline swallowed. 'Darling—'

427

Vonnie interrupted her with a small and bitter laugh. 'I think I deserve one, Mum. What do you think?' She looked at her for another moment and then turned for the door. 'I'm going for a shower,' she said, and closed it behind her.

Caroline stood where she was for a while, her heart hammering. Then she went to look for David and found him in the drawing room with Min. They both glanced up as she came in.

'What's that odd smell?' said Min, looking at her over her glasses.

'Tagine. Fiona's been making it for supper. It's a kind of Moroccan—'

'I know what tagine is,' said Min sharply. 'Smells like you've used too much coriander. You can overdo it, you know.'

Caroline smiled patiently at her, but Min had already returned to her book, a large-print thriller with a pair of bloodied scissors on the cover that David had found for her in the mobile library.

David was standing by Min's chair. It was an awkward pose and he seemed reluctant to move.

'Good walk?' said Caroline, and he nodded.

'Vonnie seems upset.' She wanted to challenge him, make him admit what he had just done.

'Does she?' His eyes were a little defiant.

'Marriage,' said Min suddenly. She snapped her book shut and took off her glasses and looked, unseeing, at the pair of them. 'Getting married, engaged, it's unsettling. That's why she's upset.' She patted David on the bottom with her free hand. 'Darling, can you get that fire stoked up? It's bloody freezing in here tonight. And that brandy you promised? In your own time . . .'

428

It was bad enough missing midnight but to be the last person to know Aunt Vonnie was getting married was too much. Katie pulled the hairbrush through her hair and wished Daisy would shut up.

'Granny says it means we might have to go to Canada for the wedding. Have you been to Canada? I haven't, but we've been to San Francisco which is near it and we stayed in a really nice hotel with a pool and everything, but I couldn't go in the jacuzzi because you're not allowed in it if you're a child because you might get cooked.'

She was sitting on the other bed, holding her stupid blue rabbit, her feet dangling off the edge, not touching the floor. They were supposed to be getting dressed because Elsa's boyfriend was coming for tea and Mum had told her to 'look nice', without being specific. Katie had changed her top because there was a yoghurt spill on the one she had been wearing, but she drew the line at putting on a skirt or something. She had asked Mum if it was true that Vonnie was getting married and Mum had said, 'Oh, yes,' as if she'd just remembered, That was strange, because Mum loved weddings. She always bought the magazines if anyone royal or somebody from *Desperate Housewives* was getting married.

'She doesn't have a ring or anything because her boyfriend just asked her on the phone,' said Daisy, pushing her glasses up her nose. 'But she'll get one when she goes back to Canada. Mum said she would get carrots, and that would make her happy because it's like being spoiled and Aunt Vonnie

429

likes to be spoiled. Why would she get carrots?'

Katie shrugged, and put down the brush.

'It's a shame you were sleeping,' said Daisy. 'I don't need much sleep. Mummy says I'm like Mrs Thatcher who was the Prime Minister once and stayed awake almost all night, like I did last night.'

Katie stood up. 'Nobody stays awake almost all night,' she said dismissively. 'Unless they're . . . having sex or something.'

It was the only thing she could think of to say. She didn't wait to see what Daisy's reaction was, but left the room. That was the problem with cousins. There was never one your age, who liked the things you did, and while Daisy was okay, she could also be so babyish and annoying, and not just because she had a mobile phone.

Her comment didn't seem to have bothered Daisy though, who followed her out into the hall.

'We might get to be bridesmaids. Have you been a bridesmaid before? I've been a bridesmaid; at Mummy's friend's wedding. It was her second wedding so it wasn't very big, but I got to throw petals and I got a flower bracelet. It's really pretty. And I might get to go to her next wedding because she's not married to that person any more either.'

Katie skipped down the stairs, looking like she didn't care that she'd missed out on everything.

It was much warmer downstairs. There was only one little radiator in the bedroom that they shared and even though it was on full, the room still felt like a fridge when you opened its door.

Everyone was in the drawing room. They looked like the small figures from the doll's house that Katie no longer played with: stiff and unmoving, as if a giant hand had placed them there. Grampa was

430

standing with his back to the fire, which was fierce and sparking. Gran was over by the window, in the smallest seat there was. Min was in her favourite chair with a glass in her hand. Mum and Aunt Vonnie were at opposite ends of the blue sofa, each with a cushion tucked under their arm. Dad was next to Mum, and Jamie was on the window seat, with his feet pulled up. Riley was lying so close to the hearth that it must have felt like he was being baked. Only Aunt Fiona was missing, and by the banging noises coming from the kitchen, she was in there and busy. There was a fancy tray in the middle of the big coffee table with a bottle of champagne with a Christmas napkin tied round its neck.

'You look nice, toots,' said Mum, without even looking at what she had on. Katie went over and sat down next to her dad. She turned and smiled at Aunt Vonnie.

'Congratulations,' she said shyly. 'About your wedding.'

Aunt Vonnie leaned towards her and gave her a hug. She smelled of alcohol and onion crisps, which must have been what was in the little bowl on the table beside her.

'Thanks, honey. That's sweet of you.'

'I told her!' crowed Daisy, as if she were a boss or something.

'It's a special day,' said Aunt Vonnie and held out her glass. 'More please,' she said to Grampa in a little girl's voice, and he looked at her before he picked up the champagne bottle and poured more into her glass.

Mum got up at that point and said she would go and see if Aunt Fiona needed any help. Katie moved over into the space she had left, which was nice and wide and still warm from her bottom. Dad put his arm round her and gave her a cuddle.

'I'm hungry,' said Daisy.

'Are you, darling?' said Granny. 'I'm sorry. It shouldn't be too much longer.'

'We need to wait for the man of the moment,' said Min. 'What's he called again? Mike?'

'Matt,' said Grampa. 'Mike is—'

'Her other half,' said Min quickly, nodding towards Vonnie.

'My other half,' repeated Vonnie. 'My. Other. Half.'

Katie's dad gave a little nervous cough.

'So,' said Min. 'Shall we play a parlour game?'

'What's a parlour game?' Daisy got up from her place on the floor and helped herself to some crisps.

'It's a game you play in a parlour,' said Min witheringly.

'How about cards?' said Vonnie. She sat forward. 'Happy Families?'

'Vonnie,' said Grampa, and then stopped what he was saying, and turned his head.

It was a car. Katie thought it sounded like the engine was about to explode and when she got out of her seat and moved over to the window, she saw it was really old and very small.

'They're here!'

'About bloody time,' said Min, and levered herself out of her chair, as everyone else moved into the hallway. Katie stayed at the window and saw Matt unfold from the driver's seat like a penknife. He put an arm round Elsa as they walked to the door; quite low down, almost at

432

her bum.

*   *   *

He was even taller than Katie remembered. He was at least as big as Dad and towered over everyone else when Mum introduced him by the front door. Mum's voice had gone high and a bit English, which happened sometimes with people she didn't know very well, or she didn't like.

'And this is Katie,' said Mum, as if Matt had never met her before, which he had, when he'd come to pick up Elsa at the house.

'Hello again,' said Matt, who had obviously remembered. He had a nice smile, although he was looking a bit scared.

Katie smiled back and shook his hand because everyone else had. It was warm and a little bit damp and she wiped her own on the side of her dress afterwards, but not so obviously that he would see.

'So,' said Mum. 'I think we better go and eat. Everything is pretty much ready.'

Katie thought it was a bit mean that they didn't put Elsa and Matt together at the table. Matt was down beside Dad and opposite Min, and Elsa was over on the other side beside Aunt Vonnie. Perhaps Mum and Dad were worried they would be touching under the table, like people do in films. She watched them eat their supper and imagined them having sex. There were some people you could imagine having sex, like Elsa and Matt, and even Aunt Vonnie; and some people you couldn't, like Gran and Grampa. But then they probably didn't anyway because they were old and you were bound to stop when you got old because it wouldn't be nice.

Katie could tell that Elsa was nervous because she kept darting little glances around the table. When she looked over at Katie, Katie gave her a big smile to make her feel better, and Elsa smiled back.

It was amazing that Matt managed to eat anything because everyone kept asking him questions.

Grampa asked him what he was studying and Matt said he'd finished studying but he'd done Politics and Chemistry, and Grampa said that was an odd combination and what was he doing with it? Matt said he hadn't made up his mind yet and that's why he was taking a year out.

Grampa then asked him what he thought about the elections and Matt said because he was English he felt a bit removed from it all, and that started Min off and she said that's why they were having the election so that everyone in England could be properly removed from it all.

Matt just smiled, but Gran made a face at Min, who pretended not to see and made extra-fierce sucking noises as she ate.

And then Aunt Vonnie knocked over the wine bottle as she was helping herself, and as Gran helped her to mop up the mess, Aunt Vonnie turned to Matt and said, 'I hear you're thinking of travelling,' and everybody went kind of quiet as though someone had farted.

'Mmm,' said Matt. 'That's right. Yeah.'

'South America, isn't it?' said Aunt Vonnie. There was a giggle in her voice.

Katie saw her mum glance across at her dad.

'Yes,' said Matt. 'Ecuador. And Peru.'

'You're working, aren't you? It's not just travelling?' said Aunt Vonnie, as if she knew all about it already, which she couldn't have because she had never met Matt before. She stood up and reached for the other wine bottle, a white one this time, and poured it into her glass. There was still some red wine in it and it turned a lovely pinky colour.

Mum coughed loudly.

'It's kind of split in two,' said Matt. He put his fork down. 'We start off in Quito, which is the capital of Ecuador. There's a street project for kids. It's an outreach programme, where you go and find them, the kids, and talk to their families, that kind of thing. Find them in the markets . . . Their parents are stallholders. You collect them and get them to the centre, play with them, feed them, a little bit of education, that's all you can do really. Basic hygiene, that kind of stuff.'

Elsa wasn't saying anything, but she had stopped eating too. Katie wondered if she had known Matt was going away.

'Is that an organised programme or do you just turn up and help out?' asked Grampa.

'No, it's organised,' said Matt. 'It's a gap year company that does it.'

'And is there any training?' asked Grampa.

'A little,' said Matt. He looked a bit uncomfortable. 'It's not a full-on social work thing. It's just helping out basically.'

'Mmm,' said Grampa.

'And once you're done with the street children?' asked Aunt Fiona.

'Travel,' said Matt.

'Whereabouts?' asked Aunt Fiona.

'There're lots of options,' said Matt. 'I was thinking of the Inca trail.'

'Machu Picchu?' said Aunt Vonnie.

'You can go that far if you want,' said Matt. 'I've not decided yet.'

'I've always wanted to go to Machu Picchu,' said Aunt Vonnie. 'I've been to Guatemala. But never further south.'

'Tikal?' said Matt.

'Yeah,' said Aunt Vonnie. 'Amazing. Have you been?'

'No.' Matt shook his head as Gran stood up to clear the plates.

'I wish I'd done a gap year,' said Aunt Vonnie. She handed her plate to Gran. 'Why didn't I get to do one?'

'No one was really doing them then,' said Gran. 'Just those and such as those. It was seen as a bit of an indulgence, I suppose.'

'As compared to now?' said Aunt Fiona.

'It's actually quite good for your CV nowadays,' said Elsa suddenly. 'Isn't it?' She glanced over at Matt, who nodded his head in agreement.

'I can imagine it is,' said Aunt Vonnie. 'Elsa, do you not fancy something like that?'

'I'd love to,' said Elsa. She sat forward in her seat. 'In fact . . . I'm thinking of maybe going. With Matt.'

Katie looked up. She knew something had been going on, because everyone was being very slightly weird the way they were talking, but this was a surprise. She stared at Elsa. There were two pink spots on her cheeks.

'Going to South America?' said Grampa. 'But

436

you've just started your course, haven't you?'

'Exactly,' said Mum. 'It's really not the time—'

Elsa cut across her. 'I can get a deferment. But I'm thinking of changing my course anyway.'

'Really?' Grampa looked very surprised.

'I'm not sure if it's for me,' said Elsa. She glanced across at Matt. 'I'm thinking of doing something else.'

'Is that wise?' said Grampa. 'To switch at this stage?'

'Exactly,' said Mum.

'I think that would be a backwards step, Elsa,' said Aunt Fiona. 'You need to give it a bit more time. It does take a while to get used to it. It's a whole new discipline, law.' She turned to Matt and said, 'I did law,' and looked a bit put out when he just nodded, as though he wasn't really interested in what Aunt Fiona had done.

Katie's dad leaned forward. 'Well, nothing's decided, is it?' he said. He smiled at Elsa.

'Why are you thinking of leaving law?' asked Grampa.

Elsa looked as though she were about to cry. 'It's just not turning out the way I thought.'

'But you've only been doing it for—'

'Three months,' said Mum. 'Hardly any time at all.'

'Gosh,' said Grampa. 'This is a turn-up for the books.' But he didn't look cross and he leaned over and put his hand on Elsa's. 'I had no idea you weren't enjoying it,' he said. 'That's a shame. It's a very good school.'

'A very good school,' Mum agreed.

'Well, I think you should go.' Aunt Vonnie sat back and cradled her wine glass between her hands and looked down the table at Gran. 'Life's too short, isn't it, Mum? Just go. Get up and go.'

'Go where?' said Min, as if she'd just woken up.

'South America,' said Aunt Vonnie, speaking extra-loudly. 'Elsa wants to go to South America.'

'With this one?' Min nodded her head towards Matt.

'Yes,' said Elsa defiantly. The spots of pink on her cheek were almost red.

Min gave a little shrug. 'Well, keep your wits about you. Your great-grandfather and I were robbed blind in Puerto Montt.'

'Pardon?' said Aunt Vonnie.

'Where's Puerto Montt?' said Aunt Fiona.

'Chile,' said Grampa.

'That's what I said,' snapped Min.

'When were you in Chile, Min?' asked Aunt Vonnie, who looked like she was trying not to laugh.

'When was I in Chile?' Min looked at Grampa.

'Oh, God, Min, I can't remember. Late sixties?'

'Can't have been,' said Min. 'Allende wasn't in power.'

'Must have been early seventies then,' said Grampa.

Katie stared at Min. She couldn't imagine her going anywhere interesting, or having anything exciting happen to her, like being robbed.

'What took you to Puerto Montt?' asked Matt.

'Eh?' said Min.

'What took you to Puerto Montt?' repeated Matt. He was smiling at Min as if she'd said something really clever.

'A conference,' she said. 'My late husband was at a conference in Concepcion. We travelled a bit too.

438

Lovely country. I remember a big lake, the most brilliant green, emerald, really. Probably algae or something like that, make you sick as a dog if you swam in it, but lovely to look at.'

'Todos los Santos,' said Matt. He sounded excited.

'Pardon?' said Min.

'Todos los Santos,' said Matt. 'That's probably the lake. It's known as the Emerald Lake.'

'Well, there you are then.' Min had obviously forgiven Matt for being English because she beamed at him.

Elsa beamed at him as well. In fact everyone was smiling apart from Mum, who looked cross.

Min turned until she was looking at Elsa. 'And when are you off?' she said.

There was a little pause.

'She's not definitely going,' said Mum, just as Elsa said, 'April.'

*   *   *

Pudding was a big disappointment. Gran brought through a plate of cheese and some grapes for the grown-ups, and said the children could have ice cream if they wanted, but only if it was vanilla.

Katie suspected she was trying to chase them away. No one was talking much, apart from Matt and Min, who were new best friends. He was probably just being polite but Matt kept asking about all the other places Min had visited. It turned out she'd been all over the place, even Africa.

Aunt Vonnie had excused herself and had been away for a very long time. She reappeared carrying

439

a bottle that said 'Port' on it, and had some tiny glasses in her other hand.

She sat down heavily in her seat. 'Anybody want some tawny?'

Min nodded. 'Pour me one. I'll be back in a minute. Nature calls.' She got very slowly to her feet and walked out of the room, her paper napkin still tucked into the waistband of her trousers like a little festive sporran.

Grampa had a strange expression on his face.

'Just a small one,' he said, 'and then I think we should stop.'

'Really?' Aunt Vonnie set the glasses out on the table, as if she were about to play a game. She pulled the cork top from the bottle and poured the dark brown liquid into the glasses, right to the rim. Katie thought it looked like old blood.

Aunt Vonnie was drunk; Katie could tell. Perhaps it was because she had got engaged and she was trying to celebrate, although you would expect her to be smiling more.

'Cheers, m'dears,' she said, and finished the small drink in one gulp.

'Vonnie, enough, love.' Gran spoke so quietly that Katie almost didn't catch what she was saying.

Mum and Dad were looking down at their laps and Matt had started to fidget with his napkin.

'Enough what?' Aunt Vonnie gave Gran a quizzical smile.

'Just enough.'

'Just enough,' mimicked Aunt Vonnie. She looked round the table. 'Mum's had enough, haven't you, Mum? What about you, Dad. Have you had enough?'

Mum pushed back her chair and spoke in the

440

kind of voice she used when she was pretending to be in control, but was actually panicking. 'Elsa, Katie, you can all be excused. Elsa, will you and Matt take the younger ones through to the drawing room, please?'

Katie was annoyed to be leaving. There was obviously going to be a row, and she would miss it. 'I haven't had my ice cream yet,' she said.

'Later,' said Mum sharply. She stood up and walked round to the door, and when they had all trooped through it, shut it firmly behind her.

*   *   *

'What's going on?'

Deborah laid her elbows on the table and stared across at Vonnie. She wanted to reach over and slap her, for initiating the conversation with Matt and Elsa about Ecuador and for drinking as she had in front of the children.

Vonnie was leaning back in her seat and twirling her small, empty glass by its base.

Fiona shook her head and looked between Caroline and David. She was obviously waiting for them to remonstrate with Vonnie, but neither said anything. Doug gave a little, unnecessary cough.

'Vonnie.' Deborah sat back and waited.

Vonnie glanced up. 'Why are you looking at me?' she said. Her eyes were bright.

'There's obviously something wrong,' said Deborah.

'Oh, there is,' said Vonnie. She looked down the table towards Caroline. 'Shall you tell them or will I?'

'Vonnie,' said David. 'No.'

441

Deborah turned to look at her dad. He was grim-faced and had both hands awkwardly in front of him. At the opposite end of the table, Caroline had got to her feet. Deborah would remember that later and realise then that it was the kind of news you delivered when you were standing.

'What is going on?' said Deborah again. She looked at Fiona, who shrugged, and then at Caroline, who was still standing.

'Your dad and I are splitting up,' Caroline said, and put a hand on the tabletop as if to steady herself.

It was Fiona who reacted first. 'What!' She stared, open-mouthed, her gaze swivelling between her mum and dad.

David had put his hands to his head. He rubbed his eyes and glanced at Vonnie. 'You said you wouldn't do this,' he said quietly.

'Dad?' Fiona had turned towards him. 'Dad?'

'We think it's best,' said David. 'A break.'

Deborah sat absolutely still in her chair, her hand smoothing over the faded cotton of the napkin. No one had real napkins nowadays. Why was that? Did everyone eat differently? Was everyone less fussy? She looked down at the floral pattern, so familiar to her she could trace it with her eyes shut. Pale roses and intricately coiled leaves. She didn't want to look up, didn't want to see the stricken faces.

She felt about eight; felt her legs should be dangling, not quite reaching the floor. She didn't understand; couldn't believe it. Everything else, and now this. Mum and Dad.

'Jesus Christ,' said Fiona.

Deborah felt Doug's hand cover hers.

'Gosh,' he said, to no one in particular.

'And you knew?' Fiona was looking at Vonnie.

'A little while ago,' said Vonnie. She was slumped so low in her seat, she looked as if she might slide out of it.

Deborah was still unable to speak. She looked between her parents and it struck her, as she did so, that she had grown used to seeing them like that, at opposite sides of a room or table, always with space in between them. They used to hold hands once, long ago, on family walks, she remembered that. Two figures up ahead, so close you couldn't distinguish where one form stopped and the other began.

Doug squeezed her hand.

'Where on earth did this come from?' said Fiona. It was the last question she posed as a daughter. After that, she went all professional and asked about counselling and intervention and all the other things she must go over with clients.

But this was her parents and it made no sense. After so long. Why would you give up after so long? When she found her voice, Deborah asked them that, and neither seemed able to answer. David seemed to be letting Caroline do most of the talking. His elbows were on the arms of the chair, his fingers locked tight as if in prayer.

So it boiled down to this. It had been coming for a while. There was no good time to do it, but something had to be done. A separation initially. Caroline was going to France for her art course, and then they would talk again when she was back, but in all likelihood she would move out. A flat in Edinburgh, maybe closer, so she could help with Min.

'Who needs to be told,' Fiona said forcefully.

'I'll do that,' David had said. 'She's my mother.'

At which point, Caroline sat forward and said, 'We both should,' and David didn't seem to have the heart to disagree.

Everybody sat silent for a while until Vonnie looked at David, and he seemed to take it as a cue.

'There's another dimension to all this,' he said. 'You should know that.'

Deborah heard her mum breathe in. It was a slow breath, not panicked.

'I've been. I've been, em . . .' He couldn't seem to find the right word. 'I've been seeing someone else.'

Fiona sat back in her seat. 'Wow,' she said. 'Wow.' Everyone sat perfectly still, until Fiona gathered herself enough to ask the next logical question. 'Who? Who is it?'

'Frances,' said David, and Deborah felt a strange little laugh bubble up from somewhere inside her, just before the tears.

*   *   *

Min paused halfway across the bathroom. Now why had she come in here? She found herself glancing down at her crotch; the most ridiculous thing to have to do, but necessary because the accidents were becoming more common and she never had any warning; just someone's embarrassed glance, like the boy earlier this week, or a sensation as she moved. She was dry, so it wasn't that. She looked around. Think. Wash hands? Close the window? Get something? Her watch. That was it. She had left her watch on the

444

shelf. She felt a little flash of triumph. Not so addled after all. She leaned across and picked it up. The gold had grown soft with age and use, as smooth as the coat of a well-loved dog, as she slipped it over her wrist. She could never do the clasp; that would have to wait for a pair of more able hands.

She could hear a voice. It sounded like David. He must have come to get her for dinner. She hadn't realised she was late. She returned to her small sitting room to find David fending off Riley and Caroline standing behind him.

'Hello. Am I keeping everybody waiting?'

'Waiting?' David looked confused.

'For supper?'

'No, no,' said Caroline. 'We've had supper, Min. We were just finishing. Just now?'

'Oh,' said Min. She held out her wrist. 'No wonder I was looking for this. Could you close it for me, dear?'

David moved over and fastened the clasp on her watch. His hands were cold. He glanced at Caroline, who hadn't moved since she had come in.

'What?' said Min. They looked so concerned, the pair of them. 'What? Have I been naughty? Has somebody complained?'

'No.' David smiled, but it wasn't a real smile. He sat down on one end of the sofa and Min settled herself at the other end. Caroline didn't seem to want to sit but David glanced round at her and she moved over and pulled out the small chair from the table and perched herself on the edge of it.

'So,' said Min. 'What's this little delegation all about?'

'Well, we've got something to tell you.' David leaned forward until his elbows were resting on the front of his knees. 'Caroline and I have decided to take some time apart, Mum.'

'To separate,' said Caroline, as if Min might not have understood. 'We've just told the girls. We weren't actually going to say anything, not yet, but it came out and so they know, and we—'

'We wanted you to know, too,' said David.

Min found herself nodding.

'It hasn't all been thought through yet,' added David. 'Caroline's going to be away in France, and once she's back, we'll know a bit more about what might happen and when. So . . .' He held out his hands. 'I know it's all a bit of a shock . . .'

Min swallowed. It actually wasn't such a terrible shock but she felt suddenly quite nauseous. Caroline's head was down, as though she couldn't meet Min's eyes.

'Well.' Min shook her head. 'I don't really know what to say. I'm terribly sorry. For both of you.'

It was then that Caroline stood up and moved over in front of her, bending on to her knees. Min took Caroline's hand and patted it. She couldn't think of anything else to do.

'I'm so sorry,' said Caroline, her eyes pooling with tears. 'I'm really so sorry about this, Min.'

'There,' said Min. 'No need to apologise. Not to me. These things happen. And if you're sure. If this is what you have to do. Well . . .'

'I'll be close,' said Caroline. 'After France. I won't go far. I'll always be close.'

Min nodded again. She knew she had come to rely on Caroline too much; small courtesies had grown into proper caring. She couldn't bear to

446

think of what Caroline's going might mean, but, worse, she couldn't bear to think that she might have stayed out of guilt. She kept hold of Caroline's hand. 'I hope it's not someone else who's brought this about,' she said quietly.

'No,' said Caroline before David could respond. 'No one else has brought this about.'

She bent forward suddenly and enveloped Min in a short, tight hug, then stood and quickly left the room, one hand at her mouth. David sat where he was and only got to his feet when Min did.

'How are the girls?' asked Min.

'Confused,' said David.

'And how are you?'

'I'm all right, Mum.'

She moved over to him. 'And there's nothing that can be done?' she said. She knew as she asked it what the answer would be.

'I don't think so, no.'

Min nodded again, then reached out and grabbed his arm. He pulled her in and folded his arms round her.

'David,' she said and felt the panicked hammer of his heart. 'Oh, David.'

CHAPTER TWENTY-TWO

SATURDAY, 2 JANUARY

'Are you going to tell the kids?' Deborah didn't turn from the sink where she was filling the kettle.

'God, no,' said Fiona. 'Well, not yet, anyway.'

It was mid-morning and obvious that none of

them had slept well. Breakfast was over and the kids were allowed to watch what they wanted on television. Elsa was still sleeping, and David was shoring up Hector's grave, watched by Min, who had appeared a few moments ago in hat and muffler, looked at them all and said, 'Bloody awful business, eh?'

Deborah moved across and settled the kettle on its base. Her eyes were still red from crying. She sat down heavily opposite Fiona and stretched her arms out on the tabletop.

'Frances Fletcher,' she said. Again.

'I know,' said Fiona. 'I can't believe it either.'

'At the party, and everything,' said Deborah. 'I mean, why would you do that? Why did she show up?'

'She was the caterer,' said Fiona flatly.

'I know that.' Deborah rubbed her eyes again. 'But . . . do you think that they'll carry on, now that it's all out in the open?'

Fiona shrugged.

'Or maybe, they might decide to stick it out, Mum and Dad, once Mum's back from France. Maybe Dad will realise and just stop, you know . . .'

Fiona sighed. She knew Deborah was clutching at straws. 'I doubt it,' she said. 'You know, it's really not that uncommon now. You see a lot of older couples calling it quits.'

'Even at Mum and Dad's age?'

'Sometimes older. I had a man last year in his seventies; he'd been married fifty years and just wanted out. People are living longer. Even if you're in your sixties or seventies you could have a good fifteen, twenty years ahead of you. That's a long time to be unhappy.'

'But who is happy?' Vonnie lifted her head. She had come into the kitchen with them and settled herself immediately in a chair, pulling up her knees protectively and curling her arms around them. She had no make-up on and her hair was pushed up into a little quiff at the front. She looked terribly young.

'Some people are happy,' said Deborah. 'Lots of people are.'

'Are they?' asked Vonnie. 'Doesn't everybody live with some level of dissatisfaction? Isn't it just a question of degrees?'

'There's a difference between being dissatisfied and being unhappy,' said Fiona.

'Are you happy?' said Vonnie.

Fiona chose not to answer.

'If you'd asked me, I would have said Mum and Dad were happy,' said Deborah. 'Well, maybe not happy, but content.'

'Clearly not,' said Fiona. She watched the steam from the kettle billow out from under the cabinets and rise upwards towards the pulley.

'Tea?' Fiona got to her feet as the kettle clicked off. Deborah nodded but Vonnie shook her head.

'Oh, my God,' said Deborah suddenly. 'What if Mum finds someone else before they can sort it out? That can't happen.'

'It's not up to you to say what can and can't happen,' said Fiona. She was not surprised at her sister's reaction; if anything, it was more of a normal response than her own. She felt strangely detached about the whole thing, curiously unfazed. She had watched her parents as they talked last night, and all she could think was, What a waste. What a waste to have stayed for so long with

449

someone you don't love. 'If you look back,' she said, 'it's not exactly been a bed of roses. They've been pretty much living separate lives for years.'

'Ever since Euan,' said Vonnie suddenly.

'Do you think that's it?' said Deborah.

'No,' said Fiona. 'It's everything that's happened since.'

'Of course that's it,' said Vonnie. 'Mum's not ever been able to forgive Dad for letting him go out that day. Dad said he could go cycling, after Mum had told him not to. She blames Dad. She always has.'

'Vonnie, that's not true,' said Deborah. 'If it was, they would have split up years ago. And hang on, she's the one who's been wronged here.'

'Is she?' Vonnie put her legs down and sat forward. 'She's pushed Dad away. Maybe not consciously, but she has. She's just withdrawn. She's not supported him in anything, just immersed herself in her crappy painting.'

'Is that what Dad said?' Fiona still hadn't got the full story of Vonnie's conversation with David.

'No,' said Vonnie. 'He's really cut up about it all.'

'I can't believe you're angry at Mum,' said Deborah.

'It does take two,' said Fiona, not wanting another fight. 'It's a cliché but it's true.' She could hear herself saying it and wanted to laugh at herself. Like you've got it all sorted out. Like you know the rules for the perfect marriage.

'And what do we do at Christmas now?' said Deborah. 'Or birthdays? Mum comes one year and Dad comes the next? With Frances?'

Fiona shrugged. 'Maybe, but it doesn't help to

450

think like that. It's too soon.'

'They'll have to sell the house,' said Vonnie.

'No,' said Deborah. 'The house has been in this family for almost a century. They can't.' She looked across at Fiona again. 'Can they?'

'Maybe. I don't know.' Fiona shrugged again.

Deborah sat back. 'This is just crap,' she said. 'And I can't believe it's come up now, with everything else. I mean, Jesus. And just as we're all going home.'

'There's no good time for it to come up at all,' said Fiona. She looked down into her tea, still too hot to be drunk. 'But you're right. It is crap. Utter, bloody crap.'

*   *   *

It struck Caroline, when David was in the middle of the floor, that it was the first time he had been in her bedroom in years. He had knocked before he entered and now perched awkwardly on the end of the bed and said, 'Are you all right?' the way people do when they don't really care how you answer.

She nodded and turned away from the dressing table and towards him.

'Min's awfully upset,' he said. 'She doesn't want to come through.'

'I know.'

He put his hands together and studied them.

'I'm sorry,' said Caroline, because it felt the right thing to do.

He looked up at her. 'Are you sure about this?'

She was taken aback. A frown creased her forehead. 'Yes.'

He nodded. No discussion, no pleading.

She noticed how tired he looked, or maybe it was just his walk with Vonnie. It was a while since he had walked that far.

'Thank you for not saying to Mum . . . about Frances,' he said suddenly.

'It's not for me to say,' said Caroline.

David nodded. 'What happens now?' he asked.

'I'm not terribly sure,' said Caroline. 'I'll be in Carcassonne for the course. And then . . .'

'When does it start?' asked David.

'January 20th,' said Caroline.

David nodded. He put his hands on his knees and levered himself up. 'Now that the family knows, are we telling people?'

She wondered if he meant Frances; had already assumed that she had been told. 'I wasn't going to say anything,' said Caroline. 'Not broadcast it.'

'All right.' He was at the door now, his back to her.

'Should I go and see Min?' she asked.

'No. I would leave her a little while. To let it sink in.'

He left the room and she heard him greet someone in the hall in a quiet voice. A few minutes later there was a light tap at the door. Caroline turned again. It was Vonnie and she was in her running gear. She came in and sat in almost exactly the same position that her dad had done.

'Darling, how are you?' said Caroline. She had sensed a deep hostility from her youngest girl last night, but Vonnie had not actually articulated anything beyond her opening gambit.

'Fabulous,' said Vonnie, twisting her fingers together.

452

'I'm sorry this all came out now,' said Caroline. 'After your news.'

'Is there a good time for it to come out?'

'No.'

Vonnie sat studying her fingers.

'Are you angry?' asked Caroline.

Vonnie shrugged. 'Would it matter if I was?'

'Of course it would matter.' Caroline stood and moved over and sat beside her daughter. She didn't reach out to touch her, but placed her hands together in her lap.

'Why did you bring us all home?' asked Vonnie, looking at her.

Caroline's brow furrowed. 'I don't understand.'

'You drag us all home, insist we come, make a huge and unnecessary fuss for Dad's retirement, and then you land this on everyone,' said Vonnie.

'It wasn't planned, Vonnie.' Caroline pressed her hands together.

'He made a mistake, Mum. One mistake.'

'It's not just that,' said Caroline.

'Then what?'

Caroline exhaled but added nothing to what she had already said. Vonnie was looking around the room, and her eyes settled on the small framed drawing by the light switch. It was Euan, a study Caroline had done when he was about ten, and engrossed in a game, unaware that anyone was watching.

'Is it because of Euan?' Vonnie kept her eyes on the picture.

'What?' Caroline didn't understand.

'You blame him for Euan.'

'What!'

'Because Dad got him the bike and said he

453

could go out on it.' Vonnie's voice was flat.

Caroline was shaking her head. 'Don't bring Euan into this.'

'Why not, Mum?' Vonnie turned. 'He's brought into everything else. Everything we do; everything we've ever done. The way you feel about us all, the way you feel about Dad. Even if you don't say. No one can be as good as Euan. None of us. No matter what we do, so why try? Well, what if he hadn't turned out so great, Mum? Did you ever consider that? What if he was a lousy dad, or a wife-beater, a druggie or a waster, or just didn't like you, didn't want to know you?'

Caroline felt a sob building in her throat. 'Don't talk about him that way. Don't make him part of this.'

'He is though, Mum.' Vonnie got to her feet. 'He's part of everything and he always has been.' She was at the door now and took a last, quick look at the sketch of her brother. 'Perfect Euan,' she said, and was gone.

*   *   *

Vonnie felt as though her limbs were filling with sand. She slowed her pace until she was almost walking, what Mike called her geriatric jog, arms high and tight, feet pattering. It was still cold and she wished she'd brought another layer.

She had come out of the driveway with no sense of where she might go, just needing to be moving and away. In Canada she ran to clear her head, but she would have to run to the border and back to be able to do that today. She expected Caroline had gone crying to Fiona and Deborah. Your sister. So

454

mean. She knew she shouldn't have said what she had about Euan, but she also knew it was the truth. Everything would have been different had he lived. This would not have happened. Mum and Dad.

She headed towards the sea, knowing that she wouldn't reach it. The roads were quiet and she was passed by only a handful of vehicles, one of them a Land Rover with two collies in the back that threw themselves at the window at the sight of her, leaving slavers on the glass. She followed their frantic barking into the distance.

If she could have snapped her fingers and been home, she would have. Back in Vancouver with Lil coiling around her legs and Mike close by. Nothing would have changed. It would be Sunday, so no mail to surprise her, bills or late payment queries. They would rise late and wander down to the deli for brunch and sit in companionable silence with the papers.

She would phone him later to tell him. He would be kind, but pragmatic. His own parents divorced when he was young, so he was used to a disjointed family. He had half-brothers and -sisters and a stepmother called Junie who kissed him so exuberantly that she left her lipstick on his cheek, thick and red, like an angry weal.

But that was his family, not hers. She felt the anger well inside her again. How could Caroline have done this? Just take off and destroy everything? It was one transgression and she had used it as an excuse. Vonnie couldn't get the image out of her head of David on his own in the house, as lost as an echo.

'Fuck,' she said under her breath. She picked up her stride. 'Fuck,' she said again, and again. 'Fuck.'

She realised she was moving faster. The road had dipped slightly downhill. She moved away from the edge and into the middle of the long empty stretch and pushed herself forward, running, running, running until she felt as though her heart might burst.

*   *   *

Hanna settled her heel on the seat of the chair and wedged the foam separators between her toes. Her feet splayed out like a hobbit's. The polish was a dark, inky purple, almost black, and she brushed it on in small, careful strokes, her tongue clamped between her teeth in concentration. Her hair was still wet from the shower and Dyta's expensive straighteners blinked at her from the windowsill. She rarely straightened, but Dyta had persuaded her it would look more sophisticated, especially since she was wearing a skirt.

She tried not to think why she was painting her nails. He would only see them if her tights came off, and it was January so there would be only one reason why her tights would come off. And she wasn't going to sleep with him. It was just a date. Just lunch.

She finished her toes and sat back. It would take ten minutes for them to dry properly, which would leave her just twenty minutes to get to the restaurant, and she had wanted to walk. She stood up and hobbled across the bedroom on her heels. Marek was giggling in the other room and she wondered what Dyta was doing with him. She'd promised to take him out for fresh air and to play with him, so he wouldn't spend the afternoon slumped on the sofa in front of the TV.

Her make-up took no time. Just some tinted moisturiser, a curve of blue liner on the edge of each lower lid and a little more lipstick than she normally wore. She had never got the hang of mascara. Her hands were always at her face, and any time she wore it, it ended up smudged and smeared around her eyes, which made her look even paler than she already was. She switched on the hairdryer and bent her head, rubbing her hair with her free hand, then aimed the nozzle at her toes. It wouldn't look good to be too late. She persevered with the straighteners, because Dyta would make a fuss if she didn't and try to do it for her. It worked fine on her fringe because it was long enough, but made little difference on the rest.

The polish on her toes felt dry, so she pulled out the separators and pulled on her tights, black opaque and new, so there were no bobbles behind the knees. She had worn good underwear: matching pants and a bra with underwiring, which gave her a little more shape under her thin black polo neck.

She ought to have polished her boots. The leather had worn away at the tip of each toe, as had the veneer on the heels, but they were the only ones she had, and if he was looking that closely at her boots, then she hadn't done a very good job of dressing up.

'Nice.' Dyta stood up from the sofa when she emerged into the sitting room. 'Earrings?'

'Forgot.' Hanna ran back into the bedroom and picked up two large golden hoops and slid them through the holes in her lobes.

'Better,' said Dyta when she reappeared. 'Right,

little one, give Mama a kiss.'

Hanna bent towards Marek. His arms went round her neck and squeezed, but his eyes stayed on the television. She'd told him she was going to lunch with a friend and he hadn't asked anything further.

'Hey,' said Hanna. 'Kiss.' She tapped her cheek and he leaned into her face and pressed his lips noisily on to her skin. 'Love you,' said Hanna.

Marek nodded and sat back on the sofa.

'Don't let him watch all day,' said Hanna, leaning over to kiss Dyta.

'I won't. We're going to the park, baby, aren't we?' She took Hanna's shoulders and pushed her towards the door. 'Go. Have fun. And no rush.' She raised her eyebrows meaningfully.

'I don't know when . . .' Hanna tailed off.

'It's fine. Go. Have fun,' repeated Dyta. She held the door open. 'Go!'

It felt like everyone else was still in bed, even though it was almost noon. Hanna crossed Melville Drive without even having to wait at the side or use the green man, and set off down Middle Meadow Walk. There were a few dog walkers about, and she passed one jogger, a middle-aged man in bright white trainers, who was very red and breathing harshly. She gave him a smile of encouragement and swung her bag as she walked.

The path cut directly across the Meadows. She would never dream of taking it at night. It was poorly lit and there were too many trees, but in the day it was lovely. If she could get Marek a bike and teach him how to use it, it would make the perfect run, straight and wide and smooth and surrounded by green space.

458

There was a little more traffic on Lauriston Place, but not much, because it was a public holiday. The Scots liked their New Year. She had lain in her bed on Hogmanay and listened to the shouts and laughing in the street. Dyta had tried to persuade her to stay up; said she would stay in until midnight, but she was just being kind because there was a party to go to, and there was no way Hanna could go with Marek. He had fallen asleep around 10 p.m. and she had gone to bed not much later, which was pretty sad but had not felt that way. She lay and listened to Marek breathing and to the revelry around her and tried to guess the exact moment when the old year had passed and the new one had begun.

Boyd had suggested a restaurant on the Royal Mile, so she turned right at Chambers Street and made her way past the museum and the university lands. It was breezy and more than once she had to dance over swirls of windblown leaves and litter. She checked her watch as she got close. She was five minutes late, but that would be perfect. It was a Mexican restaurant, squeezed in between two knitwear shops, with an elaborate ceramic cactus propped outside the door.

He wasn't there and she felt a little sting of panic. There was another couple in a booth near the back; they glanced at her as she came in. The music was Mariachi and a little too loud.

'I'm meeting someone,' she told the waitress who came forward with menus, and hoped that she was right.

'You can sit anywhere,' said the girl with a small smile.

Hanna picked a table near the door and slung

her jacket over the back of her seat. She laid her bag on the tabletop. She might need her mobile if he didn't show, to get Dyta down here with Marek and rescue her. She glanced at the menu and wondered if she should order a drink, then felt the rush of cool air as the door opened.

'Hi.' He filled the doorway.

'Hello.' She stood up and waited for him to reach the table, then bent in for a kiss on the cheek. She could smell aftershave; a little too much, but that was lovely because it showed he was trying. He had on a shirt and a leather jacket and he had shaved recently because his skin looked pink and smooth and there was a small, still bloody scrape on the left side of his chin, low down, so he must not have noticed.

'I'm sorry I'm late,' he said. 'Didn't realise there would be so few taxis about.'

'It's fine,' she said. 'I just got here.' She sat down again and put her bag at her feet and laid her elbows on the table. He looked good.

'Oh, and happy New Year.' He looked as if he thought he should kiss her again but he didn't. 'Did you have a good Hogmanay?'

'Yes,' said Hanna. 'Quiet, but fun.' She picked up the menu because she didn't know what to do with her hands and she didn't want him to ask any more about Hogmanay in case he thought her pathetic for going to bed. 'How about you?'

'Yeah.' He gave a rueful smile. 'Still suffering a bit.'

'Did you see Charlie? How's the baby?'

He shook his head. 'Nah. I'll leave them be for a little while. Gail's done in. You know, broken nights and all that. Don't think the wee one is

460

sleeping much.'

Hanna nodded. 'It's tough. The first bit.'

'Who's got your boy?' he asked.

'My sister. Dyta.'

He nodded and glanced down at the menu and she felt her toes tighten in her boots. It was getting awkward.

The waitress moved across and stood expectantly. 'Can I get you some drinks?'

'Margaritas?' Boyd looked across at her and Hanna smiled gratefully. Margaritas would do the trick. This was always the hard bit. Just at the start, when you were trying a little too much, and even though you knew it was only lunch you were wondering if it would ever become something more.

He was funny, and more considerate than she had appreciated. It was obvious he adored Charlie. His parents were no longer alive and he had one sister, but she lived in Nottingham. Charlie was like his family, although he didn't phrase it that way because it would sound corny. He had asked a lot about Poland and her family and why she was here, but as though he really wanted to know, not out of politeness.

They had started off with a small pitcher of margarita, but it was so delicious they got another, and then some Corona with the food, until, by the time they paid the bill, Hanna's head was swimming with possibility.

They came out of the restaurant laughing and Boyd said quite quickly, 'Would you like to come back?' and Hanna said, 'Yes.'

His flat was cold and untidy and the duvet, when she lay back on to it, smelled a little stale. He

461

switched on a gas fire that sputtered into life and turned to her awkwardly. She noticed his belly when he took off his shirt, and hoped he had not seen her look. He kissed her and tasted of lime.

It was fine. He went a little fast, but it was fine; lovely, even.

She noticed her toes as she was putting her tights back on, her vampish toes, and felt a flash of shame. Boyd went to the kitchen and made her coffee in a KitKat mug and apologised for the mess.

*   *   *

'What's through there?' Daisy stood on tiptoes by the fence and tried to peer through the trees. She had a hat on because it was so cold, but it was too big for her, and covered one of her eyes, like a patch.

'A house, I think,' said Jamie. He kicked at a loose stone with his left foot and watched it tumble a little way down the slope.

'Can we go and have a look?'

'I think it might be someone's garden. A neighbour,' said Jamie.

Daisy put her hands on the wire. Fiona had made her wear a pair of mitts that threaded through her sleeves, which Daisy hated because she thought they were for babies. She'd slipped them off as soon as they were outdoors and they hung now from the cuffs, white and furred, like rabbit's paws.

Jamie was at a loss what to do. Go and get some fresh air, his mum had said, and take your sister. Fiona was obsessed with fresh air. But as big as the

462

garden was, there was nothing to do. No swing or trampoline, or even a tree with branches low enough to climb. They couldn't watch the hens, which Daisy liked to do, because the cold had driven them inside their hut. And there were only so many games you could invent involving the washing poles.

It was good to be away from the house, though. There had been a lot of shutting of doors and urgent voices in the last twenty-four hours, and he suspected it was about him and what he had done.

Daisy was still looking at him.

'We could go down the driveway,' he said, 'to the cattle grid.'

'Cool!' said Daisy. She let go of the fence and fell in step beside him.

She talked most of the way down, asking him impossible questions, the kind that drove their mum mad when they were all in the car and Daisy was in an inquisitive mood.

Do birds cry? Why do we have fingernails? How far can a frog hop without stopping?

Her favourites were the 'what would happen if?' questions. What would happen if I ate poison? What would happen if there was a storm and the sea came all the way in here? What would happen if my leg was too long?

Jamie didn't mind the 'what would happen if?' questions. He sometimes made up fantastical answers, which made Daisy giggle, especially if he added something rude. And he liked the way that she accepted what he said, even when he wasn't sure of things himself.

When she was satisfied that her 'what would happen if' questions had been answered, she posed

463

him another. 'Do you want to go home?'

'Not really.' Jamie looked down at her.

'I do,' said Daisy.

'Why?'

'I miss Daddy, and Katie's being mean.'

'How is she being mean?'

'She's cross that I got to stay up all night and she fell asleep and that I knew about Aunt Vonnie's wedding before she did.'

'That's not your fault,' said Jamie.

'I know!' said Daisy, with sudden indignation. She pushed her glasses back up her nose and used one of her dangling mitts to wipe her nose.

They had reached the cattle grid, and she stopped and peered down through the gaps.

'Is there water in there?'

'No,' said Jamie. 'Just earth.'

'What would happen if a mole fell in?'

'They'd probably get stuck and have to get another mole to help them climb out.'

'Can I go across?' She slipped her hand into his. She still did that sometimes and he didn't mind. Her fingers felt very small and a little bit sticky.

He guided her over the slippery metal poles.

'Mum said Uncle Euan used to jump acoss here,' he said, when she had reached the other side.

'Before he was dead.' Daisy nodded sagely.

'Yeah.' Jamie hid his smile. 'Before he was dead.'

'Can you jump across?' She stood on the other side and squinted at him, her breath clouding in the cold air in little smoky puffs.

He was about to say that he had done it before, just the other night, but that would have launched a whole series of other questions that he did not want to answer.

'Go on.' She put her hands together in anticipation.

'I'll need a run up.' Jamie walked backwards until he was about ten yards away and motioned to her to stand to the side.

Daisy gave a little stamp with her foot. 'Ready . . . steady . . . go!'

He burst into a sprint and launched himself over the grid, legs cycling as he jumped, so he landed a good three feet from the furthest edge.

'Yay!' Daisy was clapping. 'That was miles! I bet even Uncle Euan didn't jump that far. I bet you jumped further than anyone.'

It was nonsense of course, it was no distance at all, but he laughed with her and took her hand again when she offered it, and helped her back across, and answered some more impossible questions on the way back up to the house.

*   *   *

Deborah leaned against the door jamb and watched Elsa sleeping. She had gone back to bed after lunch without saying and it had taken a little while for Deborah to track her down.

Elsa's hair had fallen acoss her face in loose wisps and one hand was held loosely to the covers. Deborah had a sudden image of her, barely three years old, running past the back door. She was wearing shorts and a little T-shirt on one of the rare hot days of that summer. Doug had just got the paddling pool out and Elsa was desperate to get in. Her hair was up—two small bunches—and

465

she had turned as she passed and given Deborah such a heart-stopping smile that she had had to catch her breath. Her beautiful, beautiful girl.

She and Doug had talked long into the night, lying side by side in the dark, their voices whispered. It was strange to hear him so forceful. If they were to take anything from all that had happened, he said, it was that life was short and there for the grabbing. He had been impressed with Matt and how he had equipped himself, and Deborah had had grudgingly to agree. They talked in circles for a very long while about Caroline and David, and Jamie, and his own prognosis, and then he had said: 'I think we should let her go. She's a good girl, Debs. I think she needs this. I think we should let her go.' And then the most curious thing happened. Deborah found herself unable to offer up any more objections.

Doug had said it should be Deborah who told her. She moved into the room and sat on the bed and took hold of Elsa's hand. She wore three rings on the right hand, one of them a thumb ring, which Deborah had always thought looked a little tacky. Around her wrist was a piece of red wool that meant something Deborah would never know and which Elsa never took off. Her nail polish, a deep red, was chipped, but her hands were soft and unlined, apart from a long thin scratch near her thumb.

Elsa's eyes opened and she gave a soft grunt.

Deborah patted her hand until Elsa shifted herself up in the bed and opened both eyes.

'Your dad and I have had a talk,' she said. 'We need to know what you'll be doing when you get back. We need to know that. Okay? A proper plan.

466

Something in place. And if we have that then, yes, you can go.'

She bent into the warmth of her daughter's hug.

'Thank you! Thank you so much!' Elsa, wide awake now, kissed her exuberantly on the cheek. 'I love you.'

'And I love you.' It was why Deborah had just said what she had. To the girl she had brought this far, safe and unscathed, and who needed to go further, and on her own.

*   *   *

Hanna stood at the edge of the road and waited for the Green Man to appear with his purposeful, pointless stride. She had asked the taxi driver to stop on Princes Street. It would be too expensive to take the cab all the way home, but she hadn't wanted to tell Boyd that. And, anyway, she needed to walk, to be moving.

He had stood with her outside his flat until the taxi came, and had given her a hopeful kiss. 'I'll give you a call,' he had said and she had smiled her assent.

The cloud had lowered, and it felt as though she were moving through a fine spray of mist. She could sense her hair starting to curl at the back of her neck. She crossed the road and made her way up the thin pass of Lady Stair's Close which brought her out on the cobbles of the Royal Mile. There was a small knot of Japanese tourists in matching rain capes by the entrance to a coffee shop, closed and shuttered, like almost everywhere else at this time in the afternoon.

Near the statue of Greyfriars Bobby she was

467

passed by a surge of cyclists in bright Lycra like a flock of exotic birds. She had Middle Meadow Walk to herself, and there was just enough light left for her to take it. She lifted her bag from her shoulder and strapped it across her chest and picked up her pace as she crossed the park. He would call, she was sure of that, and they would just have to see. She was so different from Dyta, who fell in and out of love as easily as she changed her clothes, fleeting passions that tormented and elated her. But Hanna had never felt that sort of connection; of need.

She took the stairs slowly and stopped outside the door. She could hear music; hoped Dyta had remembered to take Marek out.

They were in the sitting room and dancing. Marek rushed at her and threw his arms round her waist and she bent and breathed in the smell of his hair.

'Hey, here's Mama.' Dyta grinned at her.

'Hi,' said Hanna.

Marek detached himself and moved back into the centre of the room, twisting and gyrating like a little old man.

Hanna slipped the strap of her bag over her head and laid it on the sofa.

'So?' Dyta moved across to turn down the volume.

'Yeah. Nice time.' Hanna perched on the arm of the chair. She tried to avoid Dyta's eyes, so full of fun, and hope.

'I think I'm going to go and change.' She turned the music back up as she passed. 'And then I'm going to do some dancing.'

She sat on the edge of her bed and waited. The

door opened. Dyta came in and sat beside her and put a hand in hers. Hanna smiled.

'Good?' said Dyta.

'Yes,' said Hanna. 'Good.'

* * *

'Gently!' Charlie bundled the wet nappy into a nappy sack and dropped it behind him, trying to keep an eye on Annie who had watched him change Jack and was now patting her brother a little too enthusiastically on the head.

'He likes it when you're gentle,' said Charlie. He doubted Jack liked it at all. His face was scrunched up in bewildered indignation at what amounted to a happy-slapping from his elder sibling. But Charlie didn't want to make too big a fuss. Annie's outright resentment of the baby had given way to a sharp curiosity, and they were being very careful to keep her as involved as possible.

'Do you want to help me get him dressed?'

Annie nodded.

'Well, can you go and pick me some mitts?' Best to keep her focused on the hands and away from the fontanelle and any major organs.

'Charlie!' Gail's voice drifted up from the lounge, and he felt a little unbidden flash of irritation.

What now? Gail's mum had not long gone, leaving a lasagne in the oven and the faintest trace of hairspray in the air. The house had been hoovered and dusted; Annie fussed over; two washings done, dried, folded and ready to be put away, which was his next task.

'Chaaaarlie!'

She hardly ever left the sofa and the simplest of tasks seemed to reduce her to tears of exhaustion or frustration. He was starting to get a little twitchy about work, too. He'd managed to get some paperwork done, but he would need to take a couple of hours on Monday to quote on a job that Boyd had brought in—a full garden clearance at a house in Bruntsfield.

Annie had found the scratch mitts and had grabbed one of Jack's hands to try to pull it on.

'Whoa, whoa, whoa,' said Charlie. 'Gentle. Remember.' He helped her ease them on, then aimed a little punch at Annie's face with Jack's tiny white-gloved fist.

'Boof,' he said.

Annie put her hand to her cheek. 'Bad Jack,' she said, and Charlie grinned. It wasn't exactly sisterly love, but it was a start.

CHAPTER TWENTY-THREE

SUNDAY, 3 JANUARY

Katie didn't mind hugs. Except when they came one after the other until you'd been pressed into so many jumpers your face felt sore from all the wool. And Min was wearing a great big brooch that had jabbed into her cheek. The only people she hadn't had to hug were Jamie and Daisy because that would have been too embarrassing. She stood back from the little group clustered in the hallway. Gran had opened the front door to let them go out, but Mum and Dad were taking an age to say all their goodbyes. Elsa had already gone outside and was standing by the car, with a hurry-up smile, impatient to be away. The cases were in, squashed into the boot, with one wedged between her and Elsa in the back seat.

Mum had hold of Aunt Vonnie and was whispering something in her ear and crying at the same time, and Aunt Vonnie was nodding.

Daisy moved across until she was standing beside Katie. They had been a bit funny with each other ever since the other day, which Katie felt bad about but didn't know how to change.

'When do you go back to school?' asked Daisy.

'Wednesday,' said Katie.

'I go back on Tuesday,' said Daisy.

Katie nodded.

'We're going on the plane tomorrow.'

Katie nodded again.

'If you get a phone will you give me your number?' asked Daisy.

'I might get one for my birthday,' said Katie, which was a little bit of a lie because she was pretty sure she wouldn't.

'When's your birthday?'

'July.'

Mum had let go of Aunt Vonnie and moved on to Aunt Fiona.

'You could phone me anyway,' said Daisy. 'On the proper phone.'

'Uh-huh,' said Katie.

'Have you got my phone number?'

But before Katie had a chance to give her answer, which would have been 'no', Dad had put his hand on her head and his other hand in Mum's back and steered them towards the door.

'Bye,' shouted Katie over her shoulder.

'Byee,' shouted Daisy.

And then they were in the car and everyone was gathered about it outside and waving at them. Mum wound down the window as Dad started the engine and twisted round to reverse. He looked quite serious and he didn't wink at her and Elsa as he normally did. Mum held her hand to her ear like a phone and then pointed at Aunt Fiona, who nodded back at her.

'Bye.'

'Bye.'

The farewells followed them down the drive. Mum twisted back round to face the front. They turned left at the cattle grid and accelerated away. Elsa slipped her iPod on and laid her head back against the seat. Dad took one hand off the wheel and caught hold of one of Mum's. Katie waited for him to tell her to start singing so she wouldn't feel sick. But he kept his eyes on the road and his hand in Mum's and he said nothing.

*   *   *

'How about this?' Dyta bent over the paper. 'A late Georgian house with a stunning garden. Three reception rooms, kitchen, morning room, five double bedrooms, study, three bathrooms, three-bay timber garage, walled garden with summer-house and terrace.'

'Sounds a bit small,' said Hanna. 'How much?' She lifted the shirt and repositioned it on the ironing board. Beside her, the iron gave out a little sigh of hot steam.

'Only £1.4 million.'

'But no gym?' said Hanna.

'No gym.'

'I'd like a gym.'

'Fussy, fussy, fussy,' said Dyta. She sat back on the sofa, careful not to topple the neat piles of laundry stacked at the other end. With everyone heading back to work soon, Hanna had been inundated; three bin bags full on Saturday morning alone.

Hanna pressed the iron to the cloth. It was good cotton, this one, almost silky to the touch with long, elegant cuffs and a waist slim enough for only a washboard stomach. She had never seen its owner because she dealt with his wife, an attractive brunette from Trinity with three small children and a fun, spiky nature. He must have been special, though, to snare someone like her.

'Really can't be arsed ironing, isn't that awful?' the wife had said, when she had first phoned, and had given such a naughty laugh that Hanna had joined in. She had become a regular customer and had stuck a £25 White Company token in with the bag just before Christmas, with a handwritten card, which was sweet of her.

Hanna always took extra care with that woman's order, knowing that the effort would be appreciated, but then she had grown so adept that almost everything was done well. When she had first started she had burned herself often, and occasionally the clothes, and always had sore, small scars on her hands. Now she could get through a bag of fifteen shirts in around twenty-five minutes. She grew to know what her customers liked. A sharp crease in the trousers, T-shirts folded flat as handkerchiefs, shirts hung three to a hanger, no

473

more, no less. She learned of their vanities, their habits and insecurities, all from the cloth. One man had his initials stitched into his collars, like a small boy identified by school labels. Another had a secret little pocket stitched into the waistband of his chinos, two pairs exactly the same. She could smell their perfume and aftershave, and sometimes their sweat, on the shirts with yellowed armpits when she would have to hold her breath as the sour steam rose around her. But mostly the smells were clean and comforting, care being taken, a pride in appearance.

She charged £1 per item for the first ten and that dropped down to 75p per item if there were twenty or more. Children's clothes—up to the age of fifteen—were 50p each, and bedding was £2 per piece, apart from pillowcases which were 25p. For curtains she charged £5. The small repairs she did for free, the loose buttons and unpicked seams. Anything else, she tucked a handwritten note into the returned items, offering to help. Most people took her up on her offer.

She liked to add up how much she was making as she was working, especially when she had been going for an hour or more and her back was beginning to ache, and the spit and hiss of the iron was beginning to grate. But she could clean and iron from now until eternity and still never have a house like the one Dyta had just described. She looked over at her sister, curled in the sofa's far corner. She hadn't spoken explicitly to Dyta about renting somewhere else, slightly bigger with a garden for Marek. She had been scouring the property section for weeks, not to buy, she could never afford to buy, but even the rental properties were out of her reach, and just recently she had thought of looking out of the city, maybe even East Lothian where the Haldanes lived. She could afford a small house to rent there. A former council house, maybe. She would need to be settled by the summer because Marek would start school afterwards. But Dyta wouldn't want to come. She was a city girl, her friends, her job, her man were all here.

'Oh, no, no, here it is. This is the one.' Dyta sat up. 'Exceptional listed nineteenth-century castle with outstanding views over the Firth of Forth. Drawing room, cinema. Cinema! Coach house, courtyard and woodland gardens.'

'And all for just . . .' said Hanna.

'Just £2.1 million.'

'Perfect,' said Hanna.

'Lots of room for you and lover boy.' Dyta grinned at her and Hanna shook her head.

'He's not my lover boy.'

'Does he know this?' Dyta got to her feet and stretched like a dancer, arms raised above her head and her hands twining together.

Hanna pulled a face at her. Dyta was having a dig because Boyd had phoned twice since Saturday. He had wanted to see her today, but she had said 'no' because she had so much ironing to finish. She had suggested the following weekend, and he had agreed, but then called her today to say he would be down at the Haldanes on Wednesday and would she be there? She wouldn't; she was going on Tuesday, so they had settled on Tuesday afternoon after she was back. Boyd and Charlie had a job, but it would only take a couple of hours.

Dyta was delighted. She was already talking

475

about a double date, something that Hanna had no intention of doing. 'I'm taking it very slow,' she had said to her sister, and had not shared the fact that she had already slept with him, which was hardly the definition of slow. She still blushed when she thought of it. Next time she would take Marek, so there would be no chance of her losing her head as she had done yesterday, after the pitcher of margarita and the almost perfect lunch.

*   *   *

Fiona bent on to her knees and peered beneath the bed. There were two small socks, inside out and balled up. She reached in and pulled them out, and the gaudy platform boot from a Bratz doll.

She lobbed the socks into the open case beside her and put the small and solitary shoe on the bedside table. Daisy had already 'packed' which meant heaping everything in the centre of her bed, even her shoes and her toothbrush. Fiona had spent a good fifteen minutes straightening out all her belongings and placing them in the case so they would all fit.

She could hear her mobile ringing through in the other room. It would be Allan. She had called him earlier to let him know when they would arrive, but his phone had been off and she had left no message. She closed Daisy's case and returned to her room.

He was at work. She could tell by the muted chatter and tinkle of crockery and glasses behind him.

'All set?' he said.

'Yeah. Just finishing packing up.' She plucked

476

idly at the bare, dimpled mattress.

'Do you want to be picked up from the airport tomorrow?' His tone suggested he would prefer she didn't.

'No, it's fine,' said Fiona. 'We'll get a cab. The flight gets in at 4.30 p.m., so we should be home for supper.'

'I might be a bit late,' he said. 'Staff meeting.'

'Of course.' She wondered if it was true, and noticed, as she did, that she felt no real prickle of panic. What if it wasn't? What if he was being unfaithful? How would she feel?

'And how's our boy?'

She felt her heart give a little. She liked when he said, 'our boy'.

'He's as well as can be expected. We've got a lot to get through when we're home, but he's okay.'

She had not yet told him about Caroline and David, which she knew was odd. Most women would have rushed to phone their spouses; a shoulder to cry on, an intimate with whom to share the burden of knowledge.

'Well, all right then,' said Allan. 'I'll . . . see you tomorrow, I suppose.'

'Yeah, see you tomorrow.'

She laid down the phone and looked at her room. This was where she had mapped out her life, the amazing life she was going to lead: the job she would do, the places she would visit, the men she would love, the children and house she would have. How she would look. Maybe this would be the last time she ever slept here. The house would be too big for David and Min. It would have to be sold, if the split was permanent.

The rush of tears took her entirely by surprise.

She raised her fist to her mouth so that she would make no noise and sat convulsing with sobs. It was over within minutes and she stood up quickly and wiped her face and gave a little cough. It was the thought of the girl she had been, and the woman she had become, and something else, too. It was watching her parents say what they had said less than forty-eight hours ago, and seeing herself, some years hence, but clear as day, telling her own beloved three the same sorry tale.

CHAPTER TWENTY-FOUR

MONDAY, 4 JANUARY

Charlie switched on the engine and turned up the heating full blast. In the passenger seat, Boyd was blowing on his hands. It had taken longer than they had expected to quote on the Bruntsfield job and they were frozen. It was a magnificent garden, or rather it had been, because it had been left to run riot for a couple of years at least. In the biggest of the two greenhouses was a vine that had taken over almost the entire roof, its sinewy branches as thick as Charlie's arm, the unpicked grapes shrivelled and cobwebbed with thick, white mould. It took skill and patience to nurture a vine to this age and the old lady whose garden it had been obviously knew what she was doing. It was her son who was selling it, an impatient man who declined Charlie's offer of cuttings. Just gut it, he had said. The same would be done to the house. People liked a clean slate. And with the market still so tough, you couldn't afford to be sentimental.

They agreed a price and a start date of Wednesday.

The warm air was starting to come through, but not quickly enough for Boyd, who was stamping his feet in the floorwell. Charlie had told Gail he would come straight back, but he was enjoying being out of the house, and not in the middle of yet another breast-feeding crisis.

'You look like crap,' Boyd had said when they met up, and Charlie had to agree. He felt like crap.

Boyd, on the other hand, looked in good form, as well he might. He had had his hair cut, always a sign that there was a woman on the go. Charlie had dug him in the ribs and asked him if it was love, after Boyd had told him about his date with Hanna. Boyd had said, 'Fuck off,' but with a smile.

'Seems a nice lass,' said Charlie.

'Yeah,' said Boyd and looked so pleased with himself that Charlie had started to laugh. He hoped it worked out. Boyd deserved a bit of luck in love.

*   *   *

The curtains were still shut when he pulled up outside the house. He had stopped to get rolls and milk and a paper and fill up the van with diesel and it was gone 10 a.m. before he arrived home. He could hear the television as he opened the door. It sounded like the news, but unnaturally loud. Annie met him in the hall with Coco Pops stuck to her pyjama top and the palm of her hand which she held out to show him.

'I made breakfast,' she said.

'Well done you.' He shrugged off his jacket and followed her into the kitchen. Cereal was spread over the counter, and on the floor. There was no sign of Gail.

Charlie moved through into the sitting room. It was the news. Annie must have come in and switched it on herself. She couldn't change channels and this is what he had been watching last night. He changed it quickly to CBBC and turned down the volume.

'Where's Mummy?'

'Mummy's sleepy,' said Annie, clambering on to the sofa, her attention caught by *Dora the Explorer*.

He took the stairs two at a time. The bedroom was dark and stuffy and the bed was empty. He heard a tap running in the en-suite. Jack was in his cot and asleep, but his face was red and blotchy as if he had been crying. He was out of his sleeping bag and Charlie could smell the wet nappy. He put a tentative hand down. Jack was soaking.

'Gail.' Charlie rapped his knuckles on the bathroom door.

'What?' Her voice sounded hoarse.

'Are you all right?' He returned to the bed and picked up Jack. He awoke with a start and Charlie pulled the changing mat out from beside the chest of drawers and dropped it on to the floor as Gail emerged from the loo.

'What?' She looked at him blearily. Jack had started to bawl and Charlie ripped apart the poppers from the baby's sleepsuit and vest and lifted the sodden nappy away.

'What's going on?' He sat back on his heels and stared at her. 'Annie's emptied half the cupboard out down there, and she was watching Sky News.

480

And look at this—he's soaking.'

'I was just going to do it,' said Gail unconvincingly. She walked past him and climbed back into the bed and sat upright, watching him with big empty eyes.

'Gail, what's happening? I've only been away—what, two and a half hours tops.'

'Well, don't go away,' said Gail. She lay down, facing away from him.

He wanted to swear, but he stopped himself. He leaned over and pulled the bag of wipes and a clean nappy from the floor by the bedside table. Jack was in full wail, fists rigid by his sides, legs kicking rythmically, like a furious little Irish dancer. Charlie fixed on the clean nappy, stripped off Jack's suit and vest with their large damp patches and wrapped him in a blanket while he went through to the washbasket of clean clothes that Gail's mum had left on the landing. He dressed Jack, still protesting, in a clean vest and romper and lifted him over to the bed, laying him down against Gail.

'He needs fed,' he said. 'And that's the one thing I can't do, so you're going to have to. Okay?' He switched on the top light as he left and shut the door.

*   *   *

Jamie laid the duck in the middle of his sweatshirt and wrapped the material around it until you couldn't tell what it was, just a hard lumpy shape. The X-ray men at the airport would see it, though, clear through the backpack. Maybe it would give them something to smile about when all they had

481

to look at was toilet bags and books and the other ordinary boring stuff people carried. He wouldn't even mind if they asked him to take it out so they could have a look. He would quite like that.

He had asked his mum if he could have it and for once she hadn't asked why, just said she would speak to his gran, which she did. Caroline said it was perfectly okay and he should help himself to anything else, like some of the books, if he wanted. He didn't want the books. All he wanted was the duck.

He pushed it carefully into his rucksack. He didn't need to think about his phone because his mum still had it, and everything else was packed. He stood up, swung the backpack on to his back and took a last look round the dead boy's room. Fiona had already taken off the duvet cover and sheets ready for Caroline to wash. The windows were open and he could hear voices down by the cars. It sounded like everyone else was outside. They would be calling for him soon.

He left the door open because it didn't seem right to shut it. Then it would have felt like he was closing a tomb or something, like Euan would be shut in there until someone else came to visit. He hoped Euan wouldn't mind that he had taken the duck. It didn't feel like stealing. He might even have quite liked him to have it.

He stood at the door for a second. 'Bye,' he said quietly, and didn't feel at all silly that he had.

Downstairs, his mum was rushing about like a crazy woman because Daisy had put her new phone somewhere and couldn't remember where. David was standing with his car keys because he was going to follow them in and give them a hand with the bags.

'We've got plenty of time,' he said, as Fiona surged past him in the hall, trailed by a disconsolate Daisy. David put his hand on Jamie's head, which was the first time he had done that all holiday. Caroline gave him a big hug, and Vonnie a bigger one.

'Take care of yourself, kiddo,' she said. 'Lovely to see you.'

There was no sign of Min, which was a shame because he wanted to say goodbye to her too. When people were that old, you didn't know if you would ever see them again. It might be more than a year before he was up in Scotland next time and she might not recognise him by then. Or she might be dead.

Fiona and Daisy reappeared from the drawing room and headed upstairs and Caroline went to help. Vonnie said she would go and look in the kitchen and David said he would too.

Jamie took his backpack out to the car. Riley was in one of the flowerbeds, sniffing about. Jamie tried to call him over, but he just paused and looked at him with one paw raised as if to say 'Who do you think you are?' which is the way he looked at everybody except Min. Jamie left the car and went round the corner towards Min's annexe. The door was propped open. It led straight into her sitting room, with just a mat on the floor for muddy feet. Although it didn't look like that worked very well, because the carpet was grubby for quite a way beyond it.

'Hello!' He didn't want to go in without being invited, so he stood on the front step and called out.

'Hello!' he shouted again.

He was just about to leave when she appeared from the doorway at the back. She was still in her dressing gown, a thick quilted one in a kind of yellowy colour. He hoped he hadn't woken her up.

'Yes.' She eyed him beadily as if he were a salesman or something.

'I'm just away,' he said.

'Away where?'

'Home,' said Jamie. 'Back to London. With Daisy and Ben.'

'Yes,' said Min.

He felt suddenly embarrassed. 'I'll practise my poker.' He gave a forced little laugh.

'Poker.' Her voice was very flat.

'Yes?'

'Bridge,' she said. 'Bridge is my thing.'

He felt his toes tense in his shoes. She didn't remember.

'Well, bye then. I just wanted to say "bye."' He turned away from the door and she followed him out. She had slippers on, dark felt ones with sheepskin inside. They looked a little bit too big, or maybe her feet had shrunk. 'Bye,' he said again, hoping she would stop and just wave.

But she suddenly gave an odd little smile and held out her arms and he bent in dutifully to give her a quick hug. She smelled of digestive biscuits and a strange kind of perfume and she held on to him very tight and patted his back as if he had been upset. 'David,' she said.

He pulled himself gently out of her grasp. Her eyes were watery but he didn't know if it was from tears or just because they sometimes were.

'Well, see you,' he said. He started to walk

484

backwards, wanting to run, but knowing it would be rude. She wasn't looking at him any more. She didn't seem to be looking at anything.

Daisy was already in the car and Fiona was fastening Ben into his seat. The phone had been found, near the biscuit tin in the kitchen, his mum said. Jamie clambered into the front. David had started the engine in his car and was sitting waiting. Caroline and Vonnie were by the door, ready to wave.

Fiona got into the driver's seat and fastened her belt, but not before she had run back to the door and given Caroline an extra hug.

'Right.' She looked harassed. 'Everybody in? We'd better get a move on.'

She started the engine, twisted to reverse the car round and out of the back yard. Caroline and Vonnie were waving. As they pulled out to head down the drive, with David leading the way, Jamie looked back. Min was where he had left her, standing perfectly still and looking entirely the other way.

It was all a bit of a rush at the airport. Someone had broken down on the approach road and they sat in the car with planes thundering in low overhead and his mum muttering, 'Come on, come on, COME ON!' in time to her frantic tapping on the wheel. By the time they had taken the car back and got to the terminal, the woman behind the check-in had pursed her lips at them and looked pointedly at her watch. Fiona had hung so many carry-on bags on Ben's buggy that when she let go of the handles to take the boarding passes from the woman, it toppled backwards. Ben didn't cry, just lay there looking surprised, and at the ceiling. It was David who stepped forward to pick him up. He'd gone straight to the car park and had met them in the terminal, but there wasn't much for him to do to help, other than wheel the cases on the trolley like a porter. Fiona only had time to give him a quick kiss before she was herding them all into the lift. He stood and waved at them. 'You take care of yourself,' Fiona shouted as the doors sliced shut. 'Let me know if—'

Jamie had looked out of the window as the plane had risen into the sky and watched the city grow small, until they bumped up into the clouds and everything was obscured from view. Daisy was singing quietly next to him. He laid his head back against the seat and felt a hand come over from behind. It ruffled his hair for a second and then was lifted away.

*   *   *

'This is a lovely surprise.' Frances stood back and let David into the hall. She looked a little dishevelled, her hair curling as if she had been caught in the rain, a spot of sauce on her top, just over her left breast. He could smell spices. Indian. He'd only called her fifteen minutes ago, just after he had convinced himself that she ought to know and now was as good a time as any to tell her. He had parked a little way away from her flat and had used the short walk to try to figure out what he was going to say. He still wasn't sure how to couch it when he reached the short run of steps with the two neat potted conifers positioned on either side of the door like stout little sentries. He had never liked the trees. They didn't look real.

486

'Have you eaten?' She led him towards the kitchen. 'I've got a chicken balti I'm trying out. You could be my guinea pig.'

'I should really . . .' he said, knowing he wouldn't have to finish the sentence.

'Of course.'

She made him coffee instead and shooed him through to the lounge, insisting the kitchen was too terrible a mess for them to sit there. He wouldn't have minded. It was warm and filled with rich odours and he could have watched her work, which he liked to do. She furrowed her brow when she cooked. And sometimes when she was lost in what she was doing she bit her bottom lip and dragged it inwards, like a doubting child.

She switched on the living-flame gas fire and came to sit close beside him on the bigger of her two sofas.

'Is that all the girls away?'

David shook his head. 'Vonnie's still here.'

'You look tired.' She put a hand to the side of his head and he turned and kissed it and could taste the garlic as he did so.

He realised then that he was exhausted. He wanted to lay his head back and close his eyes and just listen to her talk, nothing of any import, her latest commission, some gossip from the trade. She felt like the one constant in his life. He turned to look at her.

'You know Caroline is going to France for a few weeks, at the end of the month,' he said suddenly.

'Yes.'

He reached down and put his hand on her knee, whether to steady her or himself, he didn't know. 'When she comes back, she's going to be moving out.' He saw the confusion cloud her eyes. 'We're separating. She wants a separation.'

She sat forward as if her seat had just retracted, and a little of her coffee spilled on to her trouser leg. It must have been hot but she made no sound. Just set the cup down and brushed at the spot, her eyes never leaving his face. 'David.'

'It's all still a bit up in the air, but . . . well, there you have it.' He put his own coffee down.

'Oh my God. Was it . . . Did she—'

'She knows.'

A hand went up to her mouth and he saw panic in her widened eyes, almost as if she expected Caroline to walk in behind him at that exact moment. 'Oh, God.'

'It was at the party.'

'Oh, God.' She sat back slowly until she was pressed into the cushion of the sofa, her head shaking. She had gone very white. 'How is she?' It didn't strike him as odd that she would ask that.

'She's okay,' he said. 'Not really angry.'

She sat for a while as if she were taking it all in and then she said, 'Do the girls know?'

'Yes. They're pretty cut up. Well, Vonnie is. The other two are . . . actually, I don't think they're that surprised.'

'Oh, David, I'm so sorry.' She took his hand in hers. Her polish was clear with a slight hint of pink. He was suddenly very aware of his wedding ring, which she seemed to be avoiding as she held his fingers.

'It's not just that,' he said, not wanting her to misunderstand. 'Not just you and me. Other stuff too. That's what she said.'

'Are you okay?'

He glanced up. She was watching him closely and while she looked concerned, there was more in her face. Shock, certainly, and regret, but something else besides. They had never talked about what-ifs, about anything more to come. He had never imagined that they would have to. He looked at her eyes, dark and fixed on his. There was something there. Maybe hope; maybe that was what it was.

It struck him later, as he drove back in the failing light, that it would have been the one time they could have slept together and not felt guilt. Yet they had not. It had not felt right at all. So instead he had been the guinea pig for her balti and he could still taste the spices on his tongue: cardamom and coriander and mint. It was a helpful distraction, the fragrant stew in the clay pot, something to take their minds off each other and all the unasked questions that hung between them.

*   *   *

'Are there any testimonials?'

'I think so.' Elsa clicked back to the home page and searched the toolbar at the top. 'Yeah, this looks like it.' She double-clicked the mouse and stood back.

Deborah waited for the page to load. Their broadband wasn't always the 'superhighway' the phone company had led them to expect; sometimes it could take an age. Elsa stood beside her. She was tense, Deborah could tell; desperate for her to be reassured, impressed even. The page loaded. Deborah could see smiling faces and lots of exclamation marks. 'The Best Thing I Ever Did!!!'

'Amazing!!!' 'A Life-Altering Experience!!'

Perhaps Elsa was embarrassed at the ridiculous level of enthusiasm because she said, 'I'll leave you to it,' and slipped away. She had called the university first thing and had made an appointment to see her course adviser, who wouldn't, unfortunately, be back until the following week. Deborah and Doug had persuaded her to find out about a deferment before she even thought about changing course, and to ask the bursar's office about the possible financial implications. Deborah picked up her tea and sat back. She had lain in bed that morning watching Doug get dressed for work, all his little rituals. His tie knotted high and tight, shirt tucked in. Socks on last. And then in the kitchen, the mechanical movements she made without having to think. Kettle, cereal, milk, the opening of the cutlery drawer. As if everything were exactly as it had been. As if Christmas had never come and nothing had changed.

She looked at the screen. Caz from Dorset had been to Chile. Her picture showed a bright-eyed girl, a little on the hefty side, with a blinding smile. She was wearing an elaborate scarf around her neck and a wristful of bracelets. Caz had 'had a ball', apparently. Well, good for Caz, thought Deborah. She closed the page, suddenly weary.

She had cried for a long time when they had got home. She had waited until Katie was in bed and Elsa out with Matt. Doug had held her for ages until he needed to go to the loo and she had to sit up and get a grip and blow her nose on a piece of kitchen roll because they didn't have any tissues.

Except she didn't feel able to get a grip. She knew she was supposed to be adult and

490

understanding, the way Doug had been, but she wanted to scream at her parents and say, 'You can't. You just can't. You need to be here. Both of you. In case I need to come home.' Because always at the back of your mind was the knowledge that you had another home. One you could go to if everything went bad. And that home was the two of them. Mum and Dad. Your touchstone, which you might never need, but felt safe in knowing was there.

'What do you think?' Elsa was back, hovering and hopeful.

'Caz from Dorset went to Chile,' said Deborah, because it was all she could remember.

Elsa draped her arms over Deborah's shoulders. 'And Elsa from Edinburgh went to Ecuador?'

Deborah felt a small laugh bubble up in her throat. 'Elsa from Edinburgh went to Ecuador only after her mother had satisfied herself that it was safe, well-organised, properly funded and thought through, and there was a game plan for her return that didn't involve dropping out of uni altogether.'

Elsa bent lower and kissed her noisily on the cheek. 'That's not as catchy,' she said.

CHAPTER TWENTY-FIVE

TUESDAY, 5TH JANUARY

Caroline pulled the washing from the dryer and found a small pink trainer sock flattened and stuck to one of the fitted sheets. It gave a little spit of static as she pulled it off and laid it on the top of the machine. She guessed it was Daisy's. She could pop it in an envelope and send it down. She bundled the bedding into a plastic basket and reached across to pull the next load from the washing machine. It had just finished and was almost too hot to touch.

Apart from the sock, there was little to show that the house had been full of people. Hanna was down and had helped her gather the sheets and towels and straighten the rooms, and stow away the put-up that Elsa had slept in back in the loft, dust and hoover the drawing room and shut the door, leaving it still and untouched 'until the next big party.'

It was then that Caroline had sat her down and told her there would be no more big parties, and why. She didn't mention Frances, and Hanna did not ask. But she did reach over and pull Caroline in for a hug. It was warm and instinctive and Caroline realised, as she lay against the young woman, that none of her own girls had thought to do the same in the moments after they had been told.

Hanna was lovely. She said she was deeply sorry for both of them, and hoped that they would 'sort something out'. She didn't ask about her job and what it might mean, although Caroline tried to reassure her that nothing would happen for a while. And she said if Caroline ever wanted to talk, she would be happy to listen.

Caroline almost cried at that point and made Hanna promise to stay in touch whatever, and that she would bring Marek to see her.

She sat back on her heels, breathing in the hot damp air. Several times over the past few days the

492

enormity of what she had done, what she had initiated, had hit her. Thoughts that she tried to push from her mind. Min. The girls. The house. Frances and David. And then there were the selfish worries, the flashes of panic about growing older on her own. What if she became ill? What if there wasn't enough money? On more than one occasion she had wondered if she could take it back, apologise and call it an aberration, accept a life she had thought she could no longer stand, because it would be secure and familiar, and no one besides her would have to suffer. She knew, though, that it was too late for that. She could have lasted maybe a year with just her and David at home, formulating little routines that would keep them apart. Min fading further from them, and the sick, empty feeling inside her every time she woke.

She wanted to feel like she had purpose, to feel excitement and even fear. To feel the way she had felt just after they had discovered that Euan was coming and life, as they knew it, would change for good. She had swallowed the shock of it, the changes and strictures it would mean and had decided that she would not only have the baby but relish her new role, embark on a life with David and their child. And when the baby was grown she swore she would never tell him that he had been a mistake, because he wasn't. He was the richest blessing she could ever have imagined.

She heard the hoover start up in the hall. Hanna must be finishing. It was always the last space that she did. A hoover, a polish and she laid out letters or anything else that had been left on the bureau as neatly as if it were a five-star hotel. It was lovely to have her about because Vonnie still wasn't speaking to her, and Min wasn't speaking to anyone. Not in any coherent sense.

The washing had cooled enough to be transferred over. When the machine was emptied Caroline bundled in the last load of towels and pillowcases and got to her feet.

Min was in the drawing room in her favourite chair, with Riley prone on the floor a few yards from her feet. She was neatly dressed in slacks and a sweater but had made no effort to pin up her hair, which hung around her neck in lank strands. She had the paper on her knee but it was still folded and her pen lay unused on the table. She was looking out of the window, but there was no Boyd in the garden today to rouse her ire with his unfortunate cleavage.

'Would you like some tea? I'm just going to make a pot.'

'Thank you.' It was an automatic response and Min's head barely turned to nod her assent.

'Normal or Rooibos?' asked Caroline.

'Black,' replied Min, which was how she always took it.

Caroline moved to stand in front of her. 'How are you today?'

'Perfectly well, thank you.' It was what she had told the doctor the last time he was in. She was saying the right things, but Caroline could sense a disengagement. She hoped it hadn't been the revelation about her and David. Min had been so spry the last few days, but the doctor had said that stress would be unsettling.

She looked so tiny suddenly, tucked into the chair as if she had been carried in and just put there. Caroline suddenly saw her in a home, positioned exactly as she was now, but surrounded by strangers, without her beloved dog, without any of them. Just the terrors of her own closing mind. She dropped to her knees and took Min's hands. 'I am so sorry, Min. I'm so sorry.'

Min glanced down at her as if she had just noticed Caroline was there. 'About what, lovely?' she said and smiled so kindly that Caroline wanted to cry.

'Everything,' said Caroline.

'Such nonsense,' said Min, and pulled a soft papery hand away to lay it on Caroline's head. She turned her gaze again to the garden and gave a little sigh. 'Such nonsense.'

*　　　*　　　*

There was a certain odour in soft play centres, of feet and deep-fried food. Hanna and Boyd sat, each with a cup of bad coffee, and watched Marek tumble through the plastic chutes and alleys, pausing occasionally to wave at them through the safety mesh. He had latched on to a little group, two boys and a girl, with such distinctive red curls that they must have been siblings. They had accepted his presence in the easy way that children do and he was revelling in it.

It had been Hanna's idea to come to the Bear's Den. Marek loved it and she felt he had been stuck in the flat too much recently, and it was the only place she could think of where she and Boyd could chat without the constant interruptions of a bored four-year-old.

She had forgotten to tell Boyd about the bear, however, or rather the man dressed as a bear in a thin nylon suit with a grotesquely oversized head. He would appear periodically and shout, 'Are youse havin' fuuuun!' and the children would run around screaming, but not always in a good way.

'Fuck's sake!' said Boyd under his breath the first time the bear made an appearance, and then clapped his hand over his mouth. Hanna had a fit of the giggles. Marek, who had not heard the swearing, asked her why she was laughing, and she said because Boyd appeared to be scared of bears. Marek, who had always been a bit freaked by the man-bear, had looked at him and said, 'Are you really?' And Boyd said, 'Yes,' and Marek said 'Really, really?' And Boyd said, 'Yes,' again, 'but only bears that talk with a Glaswegian accent.'

When Marek finished his juice and headed back into the padded play zone, they had had a proper conversation. She said nothing, however, about what Caroline had told her. That had been such a shock. She wondered how the daughters had reacted, and the old lady. It didn't seem to make sense to reach that stage in your life and have to face starting again. They must have been married for forty years or more. Hanna suspected it would mean an end to her job there, no matter the assurances that Caroline had given. She was sorry for that. She liked the Haldanes. They were good people; warm and kind. Although there was always the chance they would reconcile, maybe realise now it was just the two of them and Min in the house, that they had built too much together to sweep it all away. You never knew. There was always the chance.

Boyd certainly did not seem to know about the Haldanes' break-up though, and there was no reason that he ought to. Hanna kept their chat on safer ground. She told him about wanting to move home and how difficult it was to find something decent and he said he would keep his eyes open.

She liked the way he looked at her; the eagerness in his eyes. They were interrupted when Marek shouted to them from the top. He wanted someone to catch him at the bottom of the slide. That meant going into the play area and negotiating a ball pool and a roller. Boyd stood up. 'I'll go,' he said. He looked at Marek and asked, 'Will I come?' and Marek nodded.

He was a big guy and it couldn't have been easy. She watched him get down on all fours and crawl through the garishly painted vinyl curtains, noticed the pads of fat just above his trouser waist as his T-shirt rode up. Love handles, she thought, and remembered the weight of him above her on the unwashed sheets. When he came back out he was sweating a little. 'Your shot next time,' he said, reclaiming his seat. She reached over and gave his hand a squeeze and he kept it, caught in his but under the table. It was Hanna who moved their hands into view, not minding now if Marek saw.

'Are youse havin' fuuuun!' This time even Hanna gave a little jump.

'Jesus Christ,' said Boyd, his face splitting into a grin. 'Not again.'

The bear must have just been outside for a fag because they could smell the cigarette smoke as he passed behind them. He went to stand by the play area and raised his plush paws to the roof. The children clustered to the edges to watch him.

'Are youse havin' a goood time!' The children screamed their assent, and Boyd bent close to her.

'Well, are youse?' he mimicked and Hanna found herself laughing. At the bear, and Boyd and the absurdity of her situation; her soft play date. And because she was having fun; a lovely time with a man she was beginning to think she could like a lot.

*   *   *

'Mum, come and see; she's twice the size!' Jamie rushed into the bedroom. 'And you can see her old skin on the bottom. She's not eaten it all yet.'

'Lovely,' said Fiona, but she smiled at him. Birgit, thankfully, had not managed to kill the Stig and had remembered to provide it with enough fresh privet to fatten it up. She had obviously provided herself with enough of something else to do the same. She was noticeably bigger, and she had been a big girl to start with. Fiona suspected she had spent the two weeks either on the sofa or in the kitchen. Although most of the house was neat and clean, no small feat when Allan was in residence.

She shoved her case over against the wall. The bed was completely dishevelled. Allan must have been rolling over on to her side while she was away. There was a head mark on her pillow, and a pair of boxers lay on the floor by her side, as if he had just stepped out of them. She poked them with her toe until they were scrunched against the chest of drawers and felt the little buzz of irritation.

'Mum!'

'Coming.'

Jamie was on his knees before the tank, with Daisy beside him.

'Look.'

'I can never see where the damn thing is.' Fiona bent and studied the mass of leaves and twigs.

'There,' said Jamie. 'On the big bit, beside the rock. It's kind of diagonal.'

Sure enough, the stick insect looked bigger, considerably so. She was wedged along the side of a thick twig, and the only thing to differentiate her from the wood was her long, spindly legs trailing out behind her.

'Wow,' said Fiona.

'And there's the skin,' said Jamie.

'I don't need to look at the skin,' said Fiona.

'What are these little brown bits?' asked Daisy. She pointed a finger at some specks on the kitchen roll laid on the base of the tank. 'Is that her poos?'

Jamie peered closer. 'No, her poos are smaller.' He put a hand up to the glass and Fiona heard his intake of breath. 'It's babies! She's had babies! Mum! She's had babies!' He turned to her and she felt her own breath catch, not at the miracle of stick insect procreation, but at her boy's face, alive with excitement and delight.

'How can she have babies?' asked Daisy. 'There's no daddy? Did Birgit bring her a daddy? Did she have a date?'

'No, she doesn't need a daddy, a male one. She does it on her own,' said Jamie.

'She's a clever girl, Stig,' said Fiona.

Jamie was counting. ' . . . twelve, thirteen, fourteen, fifteen, there're fifteen.'

'Can I have one?' Daisy wriggled excitedly.

'You can have more than one,' said Jamie, and Daisy clapped her hands.

The phone was ringing. Fiona heard Birgit

499

answer it, heard her voice change and knew who it was before she shouted up the stairs.

'Phone! Allan!' She pronounced it 'Alain', like Alain Delon.

Fiona took it into the kitchen and sent Birgit upstairs with Ben to see clever Stig and her many offspring. She perched herself on one of the stools.

'Get back okay?' said Allan. He must have been in his office because the sounds of the restaurant were faint and muffled.

'Fine,' said Fiona. 'Tired.'

'I won't be late after all,' said Allan. 'We've pushed the staff meeting out until tomorrow.'

'The kids will be pleased,' said Fiona. 'We've got lots to tell you.'

'More Jamie?' said Allan.

'No, no,' said Fiona. 'The stick insect's given birth. Fifteen babies, apparently. And they lost one of the suitcases in T5. It should be here later. They'll taxi it in. Oh, and one more thing. Mum and Dad are splitting up.'

'Pardon?' said Allan.

*   *   *

Gail switched her mug to her right hand and settled herself on to the sofa as far from Charlie as she could manage without actually being on the arm. She made a noise as she sat down, a soft exhalation. He'd read somewhere that that was a sign of middle age—if every time you sit, you make a noise, a kind of Bisto 'aaaah'. He thought better than to tell her. She still wasn't talking to him, even though he had apologised and made lunch and tea and played with Annie until she was so tired that she actually asked to go to bed.

Now Gail had just had a shower and her wet hair had left a stain like sweat on the back of her grey T-shirt. She was wearing the same velour joggers that she had had on since she came home, and he noticed that her toenails needed to be cut.

'Hey.'

'What?'

'How's my girl?'

'Fat,' she said.

'No, you're not.' He put down the pad of graph paper he had been doodling on and scooted along the sofa until he was next to her. She didn't pull away but then there was nowhere for her to go. She had her eyes on the television. He was looking at her breasts, heavy and engorged under the smooth grey cotton of her top. He put a hand on her still rounded belly and slid it upwards and felt her own hand come down and hold his still.

'No.'

'No?'

'No.' She turned to look at him.

'Not yet?'

'Not ever,' she said.

There was no smile playing around her lips, no playfulness at all in her voice. He pulled his hand out and put it in his lap, and adjusted himself to relieve the discomfort in his groin.

'Is it tomorrow you're working?' She was looking back at the television.

'Yes.'

'All day?'

'Pretty much,' he said. 'Is that okay?'

She gave a little shrug. 'It'll have to be.'

It was sitting by his place on the breakfast bar, still in its box, like Daisy's had been at Christmas. Fiona was putting coffee in the espresso machine, but stopped and came to stand beside him. She had some coffee grounds on her fingers, dark brown, like a smear of mud.

'If you don't like the style we can change it,' she said.

'No, it's fine.' It was better than fine. It was the absolute latest, shiny blue with a dark face.

'It's got a different number, obviously. You only give it to family and friends. Close friends. People you trust, okay, and only a few. Until we get this sorted out.'

He nodded, pulled the phone from the box and studied it. It felt pleasurably heavy in his hands.

'Thank you.'

'What's that?' Daisy appeared behind them and clambered up on to her stool. She was in her pinafore and her hair was in two plaits at the side of her head pulled so tight by Birgit that she looked like she'd had a face lift.

'Jamie's got a new phone,' said Fiona.

'Why?'

'He lost his old one.'

'Did you? Where?'

'I can't remember,' said Jamie.

'Maybe you left it at Granny's like I nearly did with mine.'

'Maybe.'

He sat down, still fingering the phone. He appreciated the gesture, he really did, but he felt sick all the same. Fiona must have sensed

502

something because she sent Daisy off to brush her teeth, and when Daisy said she'd already done it, told her to do it again for luck.

Jamie stuck his spoon into his Cheerios.

'You okay?'

'Do you have to?' He looked up at her pleadingly.

'Jamie, we've been over this. If we leave it, nothing's going to change. Nothing at all. And I'm sorry, but I just won't stand by and watch this happen. I've promised I'm not going to let it get out of hand, and I'm not. You have to trust me.'

'But they're not going to stop.' The fears that had kept him awake half of the night swamped him again.

'They are *absolutely* going to stop,' said Fiona, 'because they will be made to stop.' She made a funny movement with her hand, a kind of chopping motion. Maybe she used it in court, to convince the judge, or the jury, if she dealt with juries; which he wasn't sure that she did. She looked so determined, but she didn't understand. Things worked differently at school. He'd seen it before. If you made a fuss it simply made it worse. Best to keep quiet and just hope it would go away.

'I could just say something myself,' he lied.

'No,' said Fiona, but her voice went a bit softer. 'We've been over that, JJ.' She hadn't called him JJ for a long time. 'I'm coming in. I won't embarrass you. Promise. And we'll get it sorted. Honestly. We will.'

*   *   *

They dropped Daisy off first and she launched

503

herself into the playground with her plaits flying and her packed lunch in a bag with a Liquorice Allsorts pattern. It was the same primary school that Jamie had gone to and he wanted nothing more than to run in behind her and find his friends and have everything as it had been.

The high school wasn't too far away. He sat tensed in the front seat watching the children stream along the pavement in their black blazers, just like his. It felt like he couldn't breathe. Fiona must have noticed because she reached a hand across and put it on his arm, and said, 'Come on, it'll be fine,' and still sounded like she believed it. She pulled into the car park, which nobody was supposed to do, but she said she wasn't walking half a mile and if it meant that some teacher had to park somewhere else, then so be it. They could probably do with a bit of exercise.

She switched off the engine and the radio died with it. Fiona glanced at her watch. They were a little early. It would be fifteen minutes before the bell sounded. She looked out of the window.

'Do you see any of them?' she said suddenly.

He didn't reply. He had. One of them, not the worst, not the ringleader, but he had still felt sick when he caught sight of his face.

She turned to look at him, and laughed. 'Don't worry. I'm not going to go out there and wallop them!'

'Over there,' he said. 'By the steps. With the blondy bit in his hair.'

'Him?' Fiona nodded towards the boy. 'The fat one?'

'Yes.'

'Ugly little shit, isn't he?' said Fiona.

He knew she was just trying to make him feel better and he managed a small smile for her benefit.

'Right,' said Fiona. 'Well, I think we should head in. You ready?'

He wasn't. She gripped his hand, but low, so no one would see. 'I can't tell you what will happen, love. But I can tell you I'll do everything in my power to make it okay. All right?'

He nodded and they got out of the car.

'Off you go,' said Fiona. They had already agreed that he would go and tell his form teacher that he would be seeing the headmaster, and then he would meet Fiona there. Better that than being called out of class.

'You don't have to say I'm your mum,' she said, as they moved towards the building and the black-blazered swarm of pupils gathering around it. 'If anyone asks'—she gave him a dazzling smile and a wink—'tell them I'm your lawyer.'

*   *   *

It was the first time that Vonnie had seen Riley looking tired. He slumped by the back door, his tongue lolling from his mouth. She hoped she hadn't overdone it. If he keeled over now like Hector, Min would never forgive her. She bent down and unclipped his lead and he staggered to his feet and made off in the direction of Min's and his water dish. Vonnie followed him, steam rising from her body, her breathing still harsh. She hadn't run quite as fast as she would have liked because Riley was with her, but for a small dog he had gone a long way.

Min was in her sitting room when Vonnie poked her head around the door. 'I said a quick run,' said Min, staring at her over the top of her glasses. 'Not the bloody Grand National.' But there was humour in her eyes. She looked across at Riley who had thrown himself on to the rug. 'Not had a walk like that for a while, have you, beastie?'

Vonnie was still by the door and Min motioned her in.

'I'm all sweaty,' said Vonnie.

'Sit,' said Min, who was already seated side-on to the fire with a book on her lap.

Vonnie moved over to one of the two other upright chairs and balanced herself on the edge of it. She felt rather guilty that she had spent so little time alone with Min this holiday, just the odd snatched conversation. And in the last few days, when she had had every opportunity, she had not felt like talking to anyone.

'I've got some biscuits about.' Min looked around her. 'Would you like a biscuit?'

'No, I'm good.' Vonnie smiled. It was what Min had done when they were small and upset. Biscuits. To make them forget a row, a fight, a mislaid toy. She was very different from other grannies: prickly and unpredictable, not one for cuddles or stories, or turning up at school plays. But she had her own ways of making them feel valued and loved.

'When are you heading off?' Min settled herself back in her chair.

'Tomorrow.'

'It's going to be rather quiet here,' responded Min.

'I should say.' Vonnie used her forearm to wipe the sweat from her eyes. When she looked back up,

506

Min had taken off her glasses and was staring directly at her.

'It's been quite a time,' she said.

'Yeah.' Vonnie nodded. 'Quite a time.'

'And getting married.'

'Probably.' Vonnie gave a little forced laugh.

'It generally does follow an engagement,' said Min.

Vonnie raised another smile.

'Well, what do I know?' said Min. 'You all do it your own way these days, don't you?' Her voice suddenly went uncharacteristically gentle. 'You're upset about your mum and dad.'

She was so good that way, thought Vonnie. No dancing around. No pretending.

Vonnie picked absently at the edge of the armchair. She had sat with David last night, just the two of them in the sitting room. Min was watching *24* through in the drawing room, and Caroline was having a bath. They had been quiet in each other's company until Vonnie had turned suddenly from being curled up with her thoughts, and said, 'What are you going to do? You know, once Mum . . .' And he had looked at her and said nothing because he had no answers to give.

'It doesn't make any sense,' she said to Min.

'Not really,' replied Min, 'but such things rarely do.'

'Have you talked to them?' Vonnie felt guilty for asking, but if anyone could make them see how ridiculous they were being it was Min.

'A little,' said Min. 'But it's not for me to offer advice.'

'Dad's so hurt.'

'I know. So is your mum though. And I'm here.

507

For both of them. You mustn't fret. It's quite raw just now but it will get better. It always does. And we'll all be fine.'

Vonnie looked at the old lady across from her. She was on good form today, but not always so any more; her mind flickering on and off, the connections weakening. She shouldn't have to be facing this; she shouldn't have to be strong for anyone.

Maybe Min sensed Vonnie's train of thought because she adjusted her position in the chair and her tone brightened. 'Anyway. Let's not dwell. Being maudlin never helped anyone. Caroline said you might be moving back. Is that so?'

'To London. Maybe,' said Vonnie.

Min threw her hands in the air. 'God in heaven, child, you're a hard one to pin down! *Might* get married. *Might* move back. Does this man of yours know you're indecisive?'

'Yes.' Vonnie laughed in spite of herself. 'Yes, he does.'

'Martin,' said Min.

'Michael. Mike.'

'Michael. Of course. I seem to remember a moustache.'

'Goatee,' said Vonnie, 'but not any more.'

'Clean-shaven, eh? I do like a clean-shaven man.' Min gave a little smack of her lips when she spoke and Vonnie laughed.

'Scrubbed and brought to your room, eh, Min?'

There was a flash of mirth in Min's cloudless blue eyes. Not many people could speak to their grandmother this way. 'My dear girl, if you could find me one that wouldn't need to be brought here under duress, then you're a better woman than

508

me.'

When she left the small annexe, Vonnie stopped in the kitchen for a glass of water and then made her way upstairs and ran herself a bath. She lay in it for the longest time, feeling the warmth seep back into her. Her spirits had lifted a little. The run had helped. But not as much as Min.

*   *   *

It had been six months since Fiona had rearranged her office according to the principles of feng shui. She had watched a documentary on BBC4 and it seemed to make such good aesthetic sense that she had decided to give it a try. So her desk had been moved from the wall with the window to the far left-hand corner of the room, which was meant to be the area of wealth; and her couch to the near right for study, knowledge and meditation. She liked having a couch. Most of her colleagues had single chairs which they pulled away from the wall as needed, but Fiona had found that people expressed themselves better when they had a bit of space to move.

The woman across from her, however, was hardly moving at all, words coming out through her barely parted lips, like steam from a lidded pot.

She was an attractive woman, a little on the thin side, but well-maintained, her hair stylishly cut and coloured, her nails beautifully manicured. But one button on her jacket was hanging loose and she had a long scratch on her left hand. The new kitten, she had said, a present from her husband to their two children. He hadn't even asked her, just turned up on Christmas Eve with the damn thing

509

in a cardboard box. 'Daddy Fucking Bountiful'. She was allergic to cats and he knew that. Her mouth was still moving. The cat was the least of it. Money spent like there was no tomorrow; every Saturday given over to his bloody squash; his drinking, don't get her started on his drinking.

Fiona watched her. She wanted to hold up her hand and say, 'Hang on a sec, you think you have problems? I hate sex, can't stand it when he touches me; and he looks at other women, all the time. Not just looks. Fantasises too. Even my niece. And touches himself while he does. Oh, and my mum and dad are separating, just like that, after forty-old years. And my son is being bullied, really badly bullied and it looks like the school is going to do bugger all.'

That's what she wanted to say, but she didn't. Instead she said, 'Mmm,' and 'I see,' and made notes on her fancy pad and nodded her sage, lawyerly smile.

The head teacher had been even more feeble than she had feared. A self-important jobsworth with a slack handshake and a polyester tie. She sat opposite him in the office that didn't smell clean, with Jamie in the seat beside her, a study in rigidity.

The head had leaned forward on the desk and touched the tips of his fingers together once she had said her piece, and Jamie had named the bullies, and they had shown him the messages. 'I appreciate how strongly you feel,' he had said, 'but I would want to get the whole story before I take any action.'

Fiona had laid the phone back in front of him and said, 'This *is* the whole story.'

He had then turned to Jamie and said, 'Why didn't you come to us?'

Jamie had shrugged and Fiona felt her fury turning on him. Sit up. Speak to the man. Don't leave it all to me.

'I understand that you have a zero-tolerance approach to bullying,' Fiona had said, when Jamie would say nothing. 'In fact the council launched a new anti-bullying strategy just last year, isn't that right?'

'We do and they did.'

'Well, *this* is bullying,' she had said.

'It would appear to be, but, as I said, I would want to get the whole story.'

She had grown so frustrated with him that she had done what she had promised not to do, and had mentioned her job, prefacing one observation with: 'I find in my line of work . . .'

'And what is your line of work?' he said and she replied, 'Family law,' and saw his lip curl, but whether it was panic or contempt she couldn't say.

They were out after twenty minutes with a promise that he would carry out 'further investigations' and then contact Fiona to let her know how they would proceed.

The floor of the long, deserted corridor was glassy with polish.

'Well, I think that went quite well,' she had said for Jamie's benefit, but he had looked at her with such doubt in his eyes that she had had to look away and down at her watch.

'I'll have to head off,' she said. 'But I'll see you at home tonight, okay?' Then she had given him a thumbs up, a really dorky thing to do, but also deeply disingenuous, because as she turned away from him she realised she might not have helped much at all. She turned at the end of the corridor and saw him disappear slowly around the corner at the far end, such a small figure. And she stood for a moment and made another promise to the empty air that she would make it right for him no matter what she had to do; no matter what it took.

CHAPTER TWENTY-SIX

'What time's your mum coming in?'

Gail looked up from her bowl of cereal. 'Ten-ish,' she said. 'She's got her club this afternoon so she has to leave at lunchtime.'

'I shouldn't be much beyond three,' said Charlie.

'Uh-huh.' Gail's head went back down.

'Give me a shout, though, if you need anything.'

'Uh-huh.'

He bent and kissed the top of her head. Her hair smelled of bedsheets and baby sick. 'Bye, babe,' he said.

'Bye.'

Annie came with him to the door. 'You be good and look after Mummy.' He used to say that all the time and mean nothing by it.

Annie nodded and threw herself into his hug, then stood on the step and watched him leave, waving as if he were off to sea. She had her favourite pyjamas on, the palest pink with a giant butterfly on the top. She must have needed the loo because she started to jump up and down, little running steps.

He blew her a kiss and pointed her back into the house. 'Shoo. Monster.'

'Byeee!' The sweetness of her voice followed him into the van.

It was past ten when they reached Fortune. A lorry had jack-knifed just outside Haddington, and he and Boyd had sat in the long queue of nudging traffic for almost forty minutes. David must have been waiting for them because he appeared as Charlie was pulling on the handbrake. Charlie had been hoping to start straight away, but David insisted they have a coffee. He had a pot on, he said. They sat in the kitchen in the quiet house and talked about the vote. Charlie liked to hear David's views on it, liked to have him challenge his nationalist leanings. There had been an intervention by a cabinet minister at the weekend who had accused Scots of 'sleepwalking into oblivion'. A terrible cliché, said David, but apt.

Charlie asked why.

'It's just not necessary,' said David. 'Devolution means we have the best of both worlds.'

Charlie said there was no such thing and you had to have the courage to choose one option and make the best fist of it that you could. And David said, 'Maybe so.' Vonnie, the youngest Haldane girl, had appeared then, looking like she had just got up, and Charlie was grateful to her because it allowed him to stand up and say they must get on.

There was more to do than he had remembered. They cut back the last of the rhododendron bushes in the hide and placed the sleepers in a rough rectangle in the inside of the structure, as David had asked them to do, to shore it up. There was no need, really. The rhodies had formed into a natural shell and needed nothing to support them. They were rapacious plants, obliterating anything that tried to grow near them, hooking their roots so firmly into the ground that it could take two men to wrench out even the smallest of their kind.

They saw Vonnie heading out for a run, and Mrs Haldane return from somewhere. She gave them a distant wave, but didn't come over.

David reappeared a short while later with more coffee and asked Charlie if he had a moment. 'I was thinking of putting some terracing at the far end,' he said. 'It's just wasted space at the moment. Pretty steep. Could you take a look?'

Charlie walked with him to the garden's furthest edge. The slope was thick with privet and bramble, a bugger to pull out. But it was south-facing and the soil was good, so it made sense to cultivate it.

'What do you think?'

'Yeah,' said Charlie. 'It's doable. What would you put in?'

'I thought about a herb garden and a couple of raised beds, maybe some peas. You know, cultivate it for when we sell . . . if we ever sell.'

'Good spot for it,' said Charlie.

'So you can take it on?'

'I'd like to,' said Charlie. 'Might not be for a week or two, but I can get you a quote.'

'If you wouldn't mind,' said David.

They stood for a moment looking beyond the slope to the fields and the low hang of fog near the sea's unseen edge.

'Chilly today.' Charlie took a sip of his coffee. It was good coffee, lukewarm but strong.

'Mmm.'

'Lucky it wasn't last week,' said Charlie. 'You'd

have had to abandon the marquee.'

David turned to look at him. 'How're Gail and the wee one? I didn't ask.'

'Yeah, okay,' Charlie said.

'It's a handful, having two,' said David. 'Big change.'

'Big change,' echoed Charlie. There must have been something in his voice because David turned to look at him. 'I think she's got a touch of the baby blues, actually. Gail.' Charlie cleared his throat. He hadn't meant to say anything, but it didn't feel strange telling David.

'Really?'

'I think so. She's pretty down. Doesn't want to leave the house or anything.'

'You have to watch that.' David sounded concerned. 'Our Fiona had that with her last. It's more common than you think.'

'I'm thinking I might need to cut back a bit. It's tough when she's got Annie to deal with as well. Her mum's helping out, but, y'know, it's not the same.'

'Absolutely,' said David. 'Well, I'm sorry to hear that. I hope you can get it sorted out. Have you spoken to your doctor?'

'Not yet.' Charlie shook his head. 'I'm not convinced it's at that stage. Might just be exhaustion. He's not sleeping much, the wee one. But we'll get there. For better and for worse, eh? You just crack on and deal with it, don't you, when it's your wife and your kids. Your family.' His voice softened. 'Well, you know that.' Of all people, he thought, David must know that.

David was nodding. He had turned back to face the fields. 'Keep talking,' he said, and his voice grew quieter, 'keep talking. That's the key.'

'Wise words,' said Charlie. He appreciated David talking to him this way, and it felt good to voice what had been on his mind.

'Although often too easy to say.' David turned again and smiled at him. 'It'll work out. The two of you will get through it.'

'Thank you,' said Charlie, and meant it. 'Well, look, I'll put together a quote,' he said. 'I won't be able to give you a date, though. For starting.'

'I'd appreciate that,' said David. 'Thank you. And that's fine. Just whenever you can.'

He walked Charlie back over to Boyd and did as he always did before he took his leave; shook both their hands and thanked them again for all their efforts.

*   *   *

The next job, digging out and replacing some crazy paving for a young couple in Gullane, was straightforward and finished by 3.30 p.m. Boyd knew better than to suggest a pint and Charlie was pulling up outside the house at 4 p.m. The lights were on, a good sign. Maybe Gail would meet him in the hallway; dishevelled and tired but with a glint in her eye, cross, even, that he was an hour late. He could smell food as he opened the door, and noticed the neat piles of washing on the edge of the stair. Gail's mum had been busy and he was grateful for it.

Annie barrelled around the corner. 'Dadddyyy!'

He scooped her up and gave her a noisy kiss. 'Hey, baby, where're Mummy and Jack?'

'Shhh!' Annie pressed a small finger to her lips.

516

'No shoutin'!'

'I wasn't,' said Charlie. He carried her through to the lounge. Jack was in his swing seat, rocking back and forward. He was awake and looking rather taken aback. The seat squeaked a little at every backswing. Charlie wondered how long he'd been in there. Gail was on the sofa, her legs slightly apart, the way old ladies sometimes sit. She was still in her pyjamas. She didn't look round at him but he could tell she had been crying at some point because her eyes were puffy and small. Charlie put Annie down and she trotted over to the chair closest to the TV and clambered on to it. It looked like a talk show, but the volume was turned right down.

He sat down on the arm of the chair next to Gail and put his arm around her. She leaned into him. He must have smelled a bit: bark and mud and sweat and the like, but she said nothing. He put his hands in her hair and pulled it clear of her face. Her ears were bare.

'Hey,' he said quietly and with a heavy heart.

*   *   *

Boyd was great when Charlie called him; said he'd handle the job tomorrow, get one of the lads in and Charlie wasn't to worry. Even next week, they could cope if need be. Charlie phoned the surgery after and left a message for the health visitor. He knew when something was beyond him.

It was almost time for tea, so he went into the kitchen and filled the kettle and stood to wait for it. Gail's mum had made a chicken curry which she had left on the counter in a foil-covered dish. All he needed to do was boil up some rice. It was dark outside and the wind had picked up and the leafless branches of a small apple tree were waving frantically from the garden's furthest edge. He heard his mobile go and left it. Maybe when everyone was asleep, he could do a little work then. The kettle clicked off and he turned his attention to the tea.

*   *   *

If it had been a normal night, Deborah would have worn one of her functional nighties, one of the cotton jersey ones, stretchy enough to let her move when she got an attack of the kicky legs. But it wasn't a normal night and she had brought her nicest one through from the bedroom. It was silky, without being the real thing, and had tiny spaghetti straps and a lace trim at the sculpted neck. The problem with it was that it was bias cut and full length and on the few occasions that she wore it, she would wake so tangled at the legs that it felt as if she had been mummified. But tonight, nothing less would do.

Doug was already in bed and had chosen not to read. He whistled when she emerged from the en-suite and she gave him a twirl.

'To what do I owe?' he said, and she laughed and got in beside him and left the small light on. She put her hand on his chest and in through the fastened buttons. He had a smattering of hair but not enough to call it a hairy chest. She stretched up to kiss him and her lips found his chin. He kissed her back and landed on her forehead. He didn't seem to be taking the hint, so she got hold of his

518

hand and placed it on her breast. He gave it an affectionate squeeze. 'Don't think I can,' he whispered into her hair.

'Really?' She looked up at him.

'I'm sorry.'

'You don't need to be sorry.' She was secretly relieved. She had wanted to make the effort on the night before he went into hospital, but she was scared and anxious and a cuddle would have suited her better.

'I will be able to,' he added. 'Afterwards.'

'I know.'

'Just not immediately.'

'Of course.' Deborah pulled her hand out from inside his pyjama top and laid her head on his chest. She hadn't actually thought how she would react after the operation, when she saw what they had done for the first time. She hoped it didn't look too awful, hoped that her face wouldn't give her away. She leaned across and switched off the light, then slipped back over towards him.

'What's that?' asked Doug, at the smallest flash of blue.

'My nightie,' she said. 'The static.'

He managed a laugh. 'We're making sparks.'

'We are,' she said.

He turned to his side and she spooned into him and curved her free arm round to his chest. He caught her hand and pulled it up to his mouth, then pinned it over his heart. They lay like that a long time, until she felt his grip loosen; his body give the little flicks and twitches that meant he was drifting off. She lay awake a while longer until she heard a car and then the door and knew that Elsa was safely home. And a little of the fear went out of her heart. She turned her head into the pillow and by the time the light she had left on in the hall went out, she was asleep.

*   *   *

The light was wrong, too starkly yellow. No late night café would be that bright. Caroline studied the Van Gogh painting on the front of the brochure. If you could look past that one aberration, he had captured a sense of the place. The lingering warmth of late sun on old stone, even though the light was gone, people moving into shadow, a table with three chairs straight and one misaligned. She wasn't surprised the company had used it in their advertising because one of the excursions was to Arles and the café itself, cheesily renamed Café Van Gogh. Caroline thought she might not go, or if she did she would slip away and find the cypress trees that he had painted, capturing the bark so beautifully that you expected to find it rough when you placed your hand on the paper of the print.

He would have known how to paint the pines by the beach, would have caught their sinuous motion in a few bold sweeps. She placed the brochure back on the pile of literature on her chest of drawers. It had been downstairs in the small sitting room, but she had moved it up, conscious that it advertised her leaving.

Deborah had phoned last night and had grown tearful as they talked, looking for reassurances that Caroline couldn't give her. Deborah had asked them to try to stay together, to make her promise that they would. Caroline wondered what she *would* do if David did ask her not to go; if he fought for the marriage. She wasn't completely sure. But he wouldn't, so there was no point in wondering. He had surrendered it with just one quiet asking. And he had returned late from seeing Fiona and the kids off at the airport the other day. She knew where he was and imagined it was a celebration of sorts. He must have told Frances by now. She wondered if they were making plans, if David's subdued demeanour these past few days hid the thrill of a new start with someone who excited him. It pained her to think that way but she had felt the oddest little flash of regret when she realised she would have no contact with Frances from now on.

She picked up the book she had come into the bedroom to find. It was a biography of Elsie Inglis, the doctor from Edinburgh, who trained female medics for the killing fields of the First World War. The cover showed a stern-looking woman with fierce eyebrows, and a steady, almost arrogant gaze. She had been captured in Serbia by the Russians and Caroline expected she had given them short shrift. She had thought that she would give it to Vonnie for the flight home, what with them both being scientists. Of course Vonnie would see it as a feeble peace offering and would probably leave it here, if not reject it outright.

Vonnie was in the drawing room watching daytime TV with Min. She was sideways in a chair, her legs hooked over one arm, a coffee cup cradled in her hands. Caroline watched her from the doorway. She had always been such a purposeful, independent child. Of all of her girls, she had expected Vonnie to do something spectacular. And now she seemed so adrift.

Vonnie looked up as Caroline entered and her expression changed to the cold distaste that had settled on her since she had found out what was happening.

'I thought you might like this.' Caroline handed her the book. Min turned briefly, brows furrowing at the interruption to her viewing and then returned to the screen. It was one of those confessional shows, from what Caroline could see. Someone slack-jawed, another spitting mad, the tanned host swivelling delightedly between them.

Vonnie took the hardback and turned it over to glance at the fly-leaf. 'Thanks.' She looked away and back at the television.

'I'm just going to make some lunch,' said Caroline. 'What would you like?'

'Don't mind,' said Vonnie, without looking round.

'Cheese,' said Min from the depths of the high-backed chair. She was more like herself again, but the change this time had not been so sudden, a slower emerging, as if she were fighting her way out of sleep. Caroline didn't know if that was a good thing or a bad.

'You can't have cheese,' she said. 'It upsets your gut.'

'Buggers,' said Min.

'How about ham? I've got some nice ham.'

Min made a snorting noise, which Caroline took for assent. She left them to their viewing and went to the kitchen, and had cut and buttered almost half a loaf when Vonnie came in. She moved across to the sink and put down her mug. David was in the garden, stacking logs by the edge of the summerhouse. Vonnie stood with her back to Caroline, watching her dad through the glass, and then all of a sudden she said, 'Don't leave him.'

Vonnie turned. Caroline put down the butter knife.

'Don't, Mum. Please.'

Caroline felt the sting of tears. It would be so easy to hold out her arms, to soothe and promise and make it all right. But for some reason she couldn't, so she said, 'Vonnie,' and watched her sad and angry girl stalk past her and through the door.

CHAPTER TWENTY-SEVEN

David waited until mid-morning to call the *New Statesman*. When they had first approached him some months previously, they had talked about a piece 'early in the New Year'. It was a little soon to be getting in touch, but if he knew his deadline he could be gathering his thoughts. It would have to be a considered piece, something with real heft, if it was to lead on to anything regular.

He dialled the main number and was put through to an editorial assistant who was terribly nice, but clearly had no idea who he was or why he might be calling.

'David who?'

'Haldane,' he said patiently, then spelled it out for the woman's benefit.

'And will he know what it's about?' she said when David asked to be put through to the political editor.

'I hope so,' said David. He waited. It seemed to

take an age. If she came back and said he was busy then that would be that. All bets off.

'David.'

He felt a ridiculous surge of relief, but it was to be short-lived. They had not forgotten, but neither had they figured him into their immediate plans. If anything, David thought, they appeared to be tiring of the whole thing. It happened, sometimes, when a campaign seemed to have been going on for ever. The excitement would grow again, nearer to the poll.

'Maybe February/March,' said the editor. 'We'll give you a call round about then.'

'Of course,' said David.

'So, I expect your handicap is shrinking. Gullane links taking a bit of a battering, is it?'

David gave the laugh the man was expecting. They spent a few more minutes on small talk before the editor brought the conversation to a close. Much to do, he said.

David sat at the desk afterwards. It wasn't the money. Anything he made now would be incidental. It was the sense of purpose. He had always worked. At school, he had a paper round, at university he spent the holidays as a janitor for one of the language schools in the New Town, then straight into newspapers after graduation. He looked at the drawer that held the notes for his book and knew that he would leave it shut. Behind him, through the partially opened window, he heard the call of an oystercatcher and turned in time to see it disappear over the garden, wings curved low for landing. It was such a distinctive call, sharp and mocking. He could go and watch it from the hide. It would be in the field, swaggering through the stubble like a boy spoiling for a fight. He could find Vonnie and take her with him. She was packing upstairs, in the room that had once been hers, and might like a break.

He stood up. His new diary was on the desk in front of him, opened and empty, in readiness for the call he had just made. He closed it, and noticed, as he did so, how the thin, gold-edged pages pressed together as if it had never been opened at all.

*   *   *

The main concourse of the departures hall was heaving with people. Vonnie liked to watch them all, try to guess where they were headed. She liked that she was one of them; wondered if someone was looking at her, trying to figure out her destination. She found a seat beside an older couple who could be nothing other than American, so blindingly white were their trainers and matching bomber jackets. They smiled at her as she sat down and she smiled back. It was a relief not to be carrying her bag, which was stuffed with magazines that she had bought for the flight and the book that Caroline had insisted she take. She had avoided most of the shops, knowing she would be seduced by sunglasses or perfume. She pulled out her bottle of water and looked around. Beside her, the elderly woman was fussing about their flight, wondering why it had not been called. Her husband reached across and patted her hand and left his own there, laid over hers. His fingers were lined and waxy with age, but his wedding ring gleamed as if it had been bought and polished that very day. Vonnie watched them, envious of their easy intimacy. They must have been in their late seventies, and so attuned to each other that words were unnecessary. They were called to the gate before she was and she watched them until they had almost disappeared down the tunnel, two figures merging into one.

It had been an awkward farewell at Fortune. It was David who took her to the station because Min could not be left. She had said goodbye to Caroline by the car; the quickest of hugs and a dutiful kiss on the cheek. Caroline couldn't say too much with David standing there, so she had just touched Vonnie's cheek and said, 'Love you and look after yourself. Phone us when you get in.'

Vonnie had a little cry with her dad, however, and had clung on in the concourse of Waverley until he pulled himself free and said kindly, 'Enough with the waterworks. It'll be fine.' But his eyes were wet too. She tried to catch a glimpse of him from the window of the train, but her seat was too far down. She had hoped to see him smiling.

She looked up at the screens. 'Flight CO157 to Vancouver. Please go to Gate 8.' She stood up and swung her bag on to her shoulder and joined the mass of people moving as one, like starlings in a darkening sky.

*   *   *

She had told Mike not to bother coming to meet her, but had suspected that he would. He wasn't in the first throng of waiting friends and relatives, but a little way back, leaning against a pillar. She let go of her trolley and threw herself into his embrace.

'Whoa!' he said, but she could tell that he was pleased. He kissed her on the lips, a good kiss, and put his hands into her hair. He had gone climbing with some friends at the weekend and the snow and sun had burnished his skin, leaving faint goggle marks around his eyes. He looked good.

'Babe,' she said.

They stayed wrapped in each other as they pushed the trolley—awkwardly—out to the car. It was even colder than Scotland, and Mike turned the heating up full and kept one hand on Vonnie's until she had stopped shivering. They didn't talk much on the way in. Vonnie laid her head back against the seat as the car grew warm, and watched the skyline grow nearer, sketched in bright lights. She wanted to open the window and breathe in the city. She wanted Mike to say that nothing had changed, when everything had.

Lil was in the hallway and coiled herself carefully around Vonnie's legs. 'I missed you too,' said Vonnie and bent to feel the softness of her ears.

'You've got a bunch of mail.' Mike nodded his head towards the kitchen counter, and Vonnie glanced over, her heart sinking. The envelopes were all white and slim. Bills and reminders. The money David had given her before she left would help, but she doubted it would cover them all.

She didn't take off her coat but went through to the lounge and slid open the balcony door. The apartment seemed very small after Fortune House, and shabbily familiar. Lil followed her and sat in her usual spot by the railings. The view was partially obscured by the apartment block on the opposite side of the road, but in the daytime you could see the sharp lines of the Coast Mountains and a glimpse of sea.

'I'm sorry about your mum and dad.' Mike was at her back.

'I know.'

'Happens, though,' said Mike gently.

Vonnie didn't reply, just leaned back against him.

'And I'm glad you said "yes",' he whispered, and she nodded. She was glad too, and scared, although she could not tell him that.

'I'm going to jump in the shower.' His hands slid round her waist. 'Join me?'

'In a minute,' she said. She waited until he had gone back inside then dug her phone from her pocket.

She had thought a lot on the plane of everything that had happened and what might be to come. And she had remembered, too, the worst day of all their lives, and how it had been her sisters who had done their best to reassure her, to help her through. Deborah's hand on her knee, Fiona's voice as calm as she could make it, saying, 'It's okay. It'll be okay.'

It would be ridiculously early in the UK, but she needed to call, needed to let Deborah and Fiona know that she was here and safe.

She was not on the phone for long, but was smiling when she switched it off. Fiona was cross at being wakened. Deborah was worried something had happened. 'When the phone rings this early you always think the worst,' she had said. Vonnie had laughed at her, but gently, and had asked how Doug was. He was home, and sore, but it was done, and Vonnie could tell Deborah was relieved.

'It'll be fine,' Vonnie told her, the same as she had said to Fiona after she had asked about Jamie. She didn't know it would be fine, of course, but she hoped that it would and she wanted to be the one offering reassurance for a change. 'Let me know how you are,' she told them both, and made them promise that they would.

She slid her phone back into her pocket and shivered. Lil had given up and retreated back into the lounge and Vonnie did likewise. She shut the door on the city and made her way down the narrow hall towards the sound of running water and the man who was waiting for her.

*   *   *

Deborah carried the two mugs of tea carefully up the stairs. Doug had fallen asleep again after being woken by the phone and she placed his on his bedside table. He needed his rest. He had two days off and then it was the weekend and she wasn't going to let him lift a finger.

The procedure—they didn't even call it an operation—had been surprisingly quick, although Doug had to stay in recovery for several hours afterwards until the epidural had worn off. The girls still did not know, and it would stay that way until the hospital confirmed whether or not there had been any spread. It had been easy to do it all without their knowledge. Elsa was staying at Matt's, and Deborah had arranged a schoolnight sleepover for Katie, which was such an unexpected treat she had not tempted fate by asking why. If they wondered, once they were both home, why their dad was moving gingerly, he would say he had

529

slipped a disc or something.

She set her own mug near her pile of unread books and climbed back under the covers. It was still dark outside, but she could sense that the city was waking. Lights on, showers running, kettles boiling, engines starting.

Doug shifted a little and she reached out and patted the covers above him. She had not looked yet, not even at the dressing, and got a strange sensation in her stomach when she thought of doing so.

It would be fine, though; she would manage when the time came. She reached for her tea and took a little sip. She was glad Vonnie had called, glad she had told her, and glad she was thinking of them. Deborah laid her head back against the propped-up pillow and closed her hands around the warmth of the cup. Vonnie had said everything would be okay. She had no way of knowing, of course, but it had been good to hear her say it nonetheless.

*   *   *

Fiona sat down on one of the high stools by the breakfast bar and placed the phone on the cold black granite. There was no point in going back to bed. She wouldn't fall asleep anyway and the alarm was due to go off in less than an hour. Trust Vonnie to pick the crack of dawn for a sisterly chat. Fiona hoped she wouldn't make a habit of it, although it would be nice if she did call more.

Allan had barely stirred when the phone rang. He had come in late, well past 1 a.m., and had made no move to touch her.

'How's Jamie?' Vonnie had asked, and all that Fiona could think of to say was, 'Okay.'

'Just okay?' said Vonnie, and Fiona had whispered it back to her as she carried the phone from the bedroom. 'Just okay.'

She had glanced into Jamie's room as she passed. His door was a little ajar and she could make out his bundled form in the bed, asleep and hopefully at peace.

It was warm in the kitchen. She had not put on the top light, which would have been painfully bright, but just the small downlighters under the cabinets. She stifled a yawn. If she went for a shower now Allan might waken properly and think he could join her. She had a court hearing today— nothing too complex, but there was no harm in going over some of her notes. She retrieved them from her bag and returned to the stool.

She read until she heard the soft dunt of feet in the upstairs hall. Fiona hoped that it was Jamie, because they could spend a few precious minutes together, just the two of them. She put her notes back into her folder and waited, her face breaking into a smile when she saw that she had been right.

'Hello, my darling,' she said, as her boy, crumpled and sleepy, slipped into the room.

CHAPTER TWENTY-EIGHT

Caroline lifted the secateurs and snipped off the end of the last sprig of holly. She had cut much more than she needed, but she wanted something big to fill the empty space in the hall.

Up until a few days ago, the table had been covered in discarded mitts, and small hats, and newspapers and clutches of car keys. Now it was bare save for the crystal vase overstuffed with winter greens. Hanna had polished the teak surface until it shone, removing all the finger smudges and sticky marks that the children had left. On the small bureau by the front door was an assortment of objects. A small soft-toy rabbit, Vonnie's lightweight running jacket, a bottle of expensive cologne that Caroline had assumed belonged to Allan, and a pair of Fiona's sunglasses. Caroline had gathered them all as she worked her way through the rooms and had brought them downstairs to be sent on.

The house was too quiet. She had left the radio on in the kitchen and had even turned up the volume and left the door ajar so she could hear the steady chatter. Min was in her annexe. Some of the spark had gone out of her since everyone had left. Last night, she had not wanted anything to eat, and Caroline and David had shared an awkward supper in the den with the television as chaperone.

The mail had arrived that morning with Caroline's tickets for France, in a large brown envelope stamped with the tour company's name. David had handed it to her without comment. She had not opened it and had laid it on the stairs to be taken up to her room.

She stood back. The display would win no prizes for flower arranging, but it made the hall look less desolate. Min had been right all those many years ago, when she said the house deserved a family to fill it.

She gathered up the holly stalks and the

secateurs and scrunched up the newspaper she had laid down to protect the wood. David was by the back door, and about to slip off his boots. His cheeks were red with cold, and his lips looked dry.

'Is that for recycling?' He glanced down at the paper and plant clippings in her hands.

Caroline nodded.

'I'll take it out,' he said.

'Thanks.' She handed the bundle to him and headed for the kitchen. She was in the larder when she heard him come in.

'Caroline.'

She poked her head out of the door.

'Oh, there you are.' His cheeks were still flushed. 'Look, I was just wondering. Would you like to go out for lunch?' He spoke hesitantly, as if he were unsure of her response.

'Oh, em . . . I was just looking to see what we had, but if you'd prefer . . .'

'I thought. With everyone away, and . . .'

'Of course. Yes, that would be nice.' She found herself nodding, hating the formality between them, her inability to know what was on his mind. 'What about Min?' she added.

'She seems good today. And we would only be gone an hour or so,' said David. 'Just a quick bite somewhere.'

'I suppose.'

'We could go now, if you're ready.'

'Em, yes. Yes, why not. Just a sec. I'll get my coat.' She put on her coat, and the new scarf that Fiona had bought her for Christmas, a lustrous cinnamon-coloured affair, edged with tiny glass beads, and took a minute to pull a comb through her hair before the hall mirror.

David was walking back from the direction of Min's when she stepped outside.

'She's fine with that,' he said. 'I just need to get my wallet.'

Caroline settled herself into the passenger seat of his car and sat like a nervous schoolgirl. She wondered if Frances had sat here. It was just lunch; a chance to chat. Her hands were cold and she had forgotten her gloves.

The first restaurant they tried, a little bistro in Gullane, was full. They had the option of waiting half an hour or so for a table but chose to drive on to Aberlady where they found a table at a new restaurant in one of the hotels. It was a little fancier than Caroline had been expecting for a spur-of-the-moment lunch, but lovely all the same. She ordered smoked salmon in a caper dressing and a glass of house white when David said he would drive back.

They managed to talk about everything except each other, a skill they had honed to perfection in recent years. They wondered how Jamie was doing. Fiona had another meeting with the school the following week. Such bullying was not something any of their own had experienced and they had been at a loss to advise her on the best course of action. They talked, too, about Min, and agreed that another appointment should be made with the doctor, just to get his assessment. And they wondered if Vonnie would actually get married and move back to the UK with Mike, and agreed it would be nice to have her closer.

Anyone listening in, thought Caroline, would hear nothing other than an old married couple musing on family life.

They had coffee and then paid up and made their way out to the car. It was only 2.30 p.m., but the light had started to change. The hotel was just across the road from the sea, and the wind was blowing stiffly onshore. Much of the bay in front of them was a bird sanctuary and Caroline saw David's eyes track a wader, pottering along the tideline. He used to spend a lot of time down here with Euan, watching redshank and eider ducks in the shallows, and long skeins of geese in the sky overhead. She saw in her mind her small boy, his father crouched close beside him, and felt a sudden rush of affection. He was a good father; a loving dad.

'Looks like snow.' David had stopped at the driver's door and leaned for a moment on the roof of the car, his eyes on the sea and the far coast of Fife, a dark outline under the lowering sky.

'Could be,' said Caroline. 'It's cold enough.' She followed his gaze and watched the white-tipped waves scurrying towards the shore. After a moment, she realised he was no longer looking out to sea, but at her.

'What?' She turned her face to him.

'Can we fix this?'

There was no pleading in his voice, but the question was heartfelt, that she could tell.

'I don't know.' It was the only thing she could think of to say, and it was the truth.

He nodded, and she heard the lock click open on the car door. She slipped into her seat and pulled on her seat-belt as he started the engine. Her head felt light. Such a small step, really, and one that she was not even sure she wanted to take. But it had gladdened her heart just a little that

535

now, after everything, he wanted to try.

*   *   *

On the steps of the house, Min pulled her cardigan tighter around her and cursed the weather forecaster. She had said nothing about it being this cold. Temperatures average for the time of year, she had said, but not Baltic. Riley was oblivious to her discomfort. He had skipped over the small privet hedge and was snuffling around in the vegetable patch. If he did his business in there she would have to tell when David and Caroline got back.

They had been gone for almost two hours. She knew that because she had looked at the clock when David had come to tell her they were off. She hoped that was a good sign; that they were taking their time.

In the middle of the vegetable patch, Riley bent into a squat. Maybe tomorrow, if the weather was still clear they could go to the beach and the dog could get a decent run. Min was feeling well; she could walk a little way.

She had turned to go in when she felt the first one on her face, such a faint touch like a reluctant kiss. She looked up. There wasn't enough to see yet. Not properly. She remembered suddenly. A girl in bitter winters, face upturned to the falling snow in happy expectation. Catch it on your tongue. Riley was at her feet, oblivious to what was happening. Min held out a hand and another settled on her palm, a small and fragile shape. She felt the icy sting and then the warmth of her destroyed it. It dissolved and was gone.

536